A LITTLE MURDER

London, early 1950s, Marcia Beasley of St John's Wood is discovered dead in her home, naked and wearing a coal scuttle on her head. Detective Sergeant Greenleaf is tasked with solving the crime and bringing meaning to her gruesome death. It is a discomfiting matter, not only for the victim's niece Rosy Gilchrist – eager to distance herself from her aunt's fate and raffish reputation – but to all members of the deceased's social circle. The floral Felix and the acidic Cedric, awful Vera, self-enamoured artist Clovis Thistlehyde, the amiably inane Fawcett family – all, it seems have secrets to hide and grudges to bear.

A LITTLE MURDER

by

Suzette A. Hill

Magna Large Print Books
Long Preston, North Yorkshire,
BD23 4ND, England.

British Library Cataloguing in Publication Data.

Hill, Suzette A.
    A little murder.

    A catalogue record of this book is
    available from the British Library

    ISBN   978-0-7505-3856-5

First published in Great Britain by Allison & Busby in 2013

Cover illustration by arrangement with Allison & Busby

Published in Large Print 2014 by arrangement with
Allison & Busby Limited

Magna Large Print is an imprint of Library Magna Books Ltd.

Printed and bound in Great Britain by
T.J. (International) Ltd., Cornwall, PL28 8RW

To the happy memory of Peregrine Blomefield

CHAPTER ONE

When Marcia Beasley was found dead, naked, and wearing a coal scuttle on her head eyebrows were raised and questions asked. Both were further raised when removal of the coal scuttle revealed a neat bullet wound in her left temple. Other than that defect all was seemly: toenails freshly painted, lipstick applied, and hair (except that disturbed by the ingress of the bullet) neatly permed.

When interviewed, her associates – friends would be an exaggeration – expressed surprise at the choice of headgear. 'You see,' said Amy Fawcett earnestly, 'Marcia had an aversion to coal fires. There wasn't a grate or fender in the house – all central heating, fearfully extravagant!'

'But, my dear,' said her mother, 'she could afford it. The errant husband left her more than well endowed – although I have to say that was not always apparent!' She spoke with some rancour, having once been invited to lunch by Marcia at Fortnum's and then left to foot the bill while the other rushed off to ogle Frank Sedgman at Wimbledon. The wound had gone deep.

'Well one thing is certain,' opined her nephew, 'the headdress would hardly have passed muster in the Royal Enclosure.'

His aunt regarded him coldly. 'Can you think of nothing but horses, Edward? It wouldn't be so bad if you won occasionally.'

9

Amy giggled. 'I am not so sure about the hat – it's amazing what they accept these days. Can't tell you what an abomination Lily Smithers was wearing the other day – it was a sort of sick yellow and covered in masses of–' The detective sergeant cleared his throat uneasily. The interviewing process was not going quite as he had envisaged. Clearly strong-arm tactics were required. 'We don't need to know those things,' he said severely. 'What I do need to know is when you last saw the deceased.' His eyes swept Lady Fawcett's drawing room and rested on a small man ensconced in a large chair. 'For example, sir, when did you last see Mrs Beasley?'

'Well that rather depends on what you mean,' answered the metallic voice of Professor Cedric Dillworthy.

'What I have just asked,' replied his questioner evenly.

'If you mean when did I last have contact with the lady, it was Tuesday evening via the telephone. Alternatively, if you mean when did I last physically see her ... on the whole I try not to.' He gave a thin smile. 'Although as a matter of fact it was probably about three months ago. Not one of life's more enlivening experiences.'

'And why was that?'

'Tight as an owl. In one of my lectures too! It was on board the *Queen Mary* where I was one of the guest speakers. I was ten minutes into my topic – rock formations in upper Cappadocia – when there was a series of protracted yawns from the second row followed by a loud crash. She had keeled over into the aisle and had to be carried out – soused in gin and mouthing obscenities.'

'I see. Lecture not to her taste?'

'Evidently not,' replied the professor frostily.

'So what was the phone call about?'

'Delphiniums. I exhibit regularly at the Chelsea Flower Show. She wanted some seeds.'

'Just typical!' broke in Lady Fawcett. 'Always cadging. And what's more she would have upstaged you next year. I hope you didn't offer her any, Cedric!'

'Certainly not,' was the indignant response.

'I see,' said the sergeant heavily. 'And did anyone else see or *speak* to her recently?'

There was a pause, and then Amy said brightly, 'Actually, yes. I had coffee with her at the Duke of York's last week. It was a matinee, a revival of Emlyn Williams' *Night Must Fall* – awfully good! I was supposed to be meeting a friend but she didn't turn up; and I was hanging about in the foyer feeling a bit of a fool when I suddenly saw Marcia coming through the swing doors. She was on her own – although I did just glimpse some man with her on the pavement outside. Anyway, she came in, collected her ticket at the box office and then saw me. And as there was ten minutes to go before curtain-up we decided to have a coffee.'

'You never told me this!' her mother said.

'Well no, Mummy. There are lots of things I don't tell you. Besides it wasn't an event that ranked very highly among the dramas of my life.' Amy smiled sweetly.

'So this person you saw her with outside the theatre, did you recognise him?' asked the sergeant.

'Not at all. But I can tell you one thing: it certainly wasn't the errant husband. This chap had a wooden leg ... a war casualty, I suppose.'

'What on earth was Marcia Beasley doing with someone with a wooden leg?' exclaimed Lady Fawcett. 'Mingling with the afflicted was hardly her forte.'

'You are right there,' the professor agreed, 'her preferences were distinctly for the hale and loaded. Although,' he added reflectively, 'I don't suppose that lifeguard on Bondi Beach was financially laden – but he was certainly extremely *hale!*' He gave a quiet snigger.

There was a guffaw from Edward. 'So was old Taps Trotter but she did for him all right – snuffed out with a heart attack *in medias res,* or so they say.'

'Be quiet, Edward!' Amy's mother said. 'You will embarrass our guest.' And she smiled apologetically at the sergeant. The latter looked grim, and enquired of her daughter whether she had noticed anything distinctive about the victim when last seen having coffee in the theatre.

'Well she hadn't been drinking,' Amy volunteered. 'And I did spy an enormous ladder in her stocking. It was her own fault; she was such a snob, always had to order them from Paris. The French ones are so much flimsier than ours. Swan and Edgar's are far tougher.'

The sergeant sighed and explained he meant had she observed anything unusual in the lady's manner or had anything been said to suggest that all was not well.

'He means,' interjected Edward helpfully, 'did she give the impression of expecting to be found

12

dead in her birthday suit with a coal scuttle on her head?'

'Well no, not really,' said Amy Fawcett.

As interviews went it was not among the detective sergeant's better ones. In fact, he grumbled to himself, it had been God-awful useless. Tiresome women, some cretinous ass, and a snide little pansy! He hadn't much liked the sound of the victim either – clearly one of those toffee-nosed predators and a lush to boot. Not his cup of tea at all! Still, that was the job and he must get on with it, especially if there was a chance of promotion to be had at the end of it all. He consulted his notebook. There was only one entry: *Pursue the wooden leg.* Yes, well, he would do that, of course, but not before he had gone home for a nice bit of steak and onions and a game of darts.

He turned up his collar against the evening drizzle, and seeing a number 14 bus trundling past jumped deftly on to its platform. As he took his seat the naked image of Marcia Beasley came to mind, and he made a mental note to refill the coal bucket before going out for darts... That way the wife would have no excuse not to have the fire properly stoked for when he got home.

At least his scores had been good, Greenleaf thought that night as he lay in bed listening to his wife's snoring and the rain pounding on the tool shed roof. Yes, he had a skill with the old arrows, no doubt about it; the team was lucky to have him. If only police work were as simple as hitting trebles he would be a chief constable by now,

13

head of Scotland Yard even! As it was...

He frowned at the patch of dawn pushing its way under the curtains, covered his eardrums with the eiderdown and brooded on the fate of the Beasley woman. Why naked? Why downstairs undressed like that in the posh drawing room? And why, for God's sake, sitting with her head in that bloody bucket? 'A fascinating conundrum' his boss had called it. Fascinating? Plain daft more like.

The rain stopped abruptly as did the snoring. Cautiously Greenleaf surfaced from the eiderdown, and turning on his side began to reflect upon the scuttle. It had obviously been imported specially for the job, for as the Fawcett people had observed, the grates had been bricked up and the house run on central heating. And apart from the smeared patches of blood and such it had also looked brightly untarnished, brand new in fact – what you might call a 'special purchase'. Needless to say there had been no fingerprints, nothing discernible at any rate. The perpetrator must have worn gloves or made good use of a duster or handkerchief... But then why bother with the thing in the first place? If you were going to shoot someone and scarper quickly with minimum palaver, why complicate matters by messing about with extraneous household articles?

The rain started again but the snoring held off, and in the comparative peace Greenleaf's mind moved from matters of circumstance to those of motive. The bucket feature would seem to preclude casual burglary, and besides, there was no sign of disturbance; and despite the nudity neither was there evidence of sexual 'interference'

14

as the newspapers would so coyly put it. Nor had there been a violent attack or even a struggle. Indeed, apart from the ramming on of the helmet the dispatch had been executed with apparent ease, an almost modest decorum – something which suggested a person known to the victim and whose presence would not cause alarm.

He shut his eyes and cogitated. Such an acquaintance was unlikely to be the milkman (well, presumably not), and in all probability came from among her own ilk – though not of the sample recently encountered – far too dippy. On the other hand he hadn't much liked the look of that professor bloke; the others had gabbled on garrulously while he had sat silent and lynx-eyed, and from what little information he did yield it was clear he held no torch for the deceased. Greenleaf made a mental note: A POSSIBILITY.

And then he thought about the girl Amy and her tale of the man with the wooden leg. Had she really seen such a one? If so he shouldn't be too difficult to trace – assuming she was telling the truth. But you never knew with these types, didn't always take things seriously. He sighed. Yes, he would have to go back and quiz her a bit more. He could fit it in before the niece was questioned in the afternoon. With a bit of luck they might ferret out quite a few things from that quarter – assuming of course she was compos mentis!

With that in mind and suddenly lulled by the rain he lapsed into twenty minutes of blessed sleep before the clarion of the alarm clock.

'This leg, then,' he persisted some hours later, 'are you sure it was wood? Metal is the more usual material these days.'

Amy reflected. 'You are probably right, Officer. On the whole I would say it was a tin leg.'

'*On the whole*, Miss Fawcett?' queried Greenleaf. 'Are you by chance suggesting it was two-thirds metal and one part wood?'

'No, of course not,' replied Amy with a giggle, 'the whole thing was tin ... at least I assume so. I only saw the ankle part. He *was* wearing trousers, you know.'

'And what else was he wearing?'

'The usual sort of things ... darkish overcoat and hat. I really can't remember – oh yes, he did have a stick. Something to do with the leg presumably...' Her voice trailed off, as gazing past the sergeant she made nonsensical eyes at a Sealyham sprawled stoutly on her mother's sofa. 'I don't think you've met Mr Bones, have you? I know he looks terribly grumpy but he's really very sweet!'

Bugger Mr bloody Bones, thought Greenleaf angrily. Was the girl really dim or just taking a perverse delight in obstructing police enquiries? Either way that was certainly the effect. He tried again. 'Look, Miss Fawcett,' he said patiently, 'I don't want to take up your time more than necessary, but do you think you could manage to recall what Mrs Beasley was talking about when you had coffee with her? You see it is quite important. As you know, the lady was found shot only forty-eight hours later. For example, did she say she was expecting a visitor in the next couple of days?'

'Oh no,' replied Amy firmly, 'we talked exclusively about the coronation and how lovely it had been. As a matter of fact she was rather excited because somehow or other she had wangled an invitation to a royal garden party later in the season. I think she thought I would be impressed. But when I said I gathered that only mayors and headmistresses went to that sort of thing she seemed a bit put out... Oh well, doesn't even have that dubious pleasure now, does she?' For a brief moment a look verging on sympathy crossed her face, but it was replaced by a cheery smile. 'I tell you what, though, he wore glasses – tortoiseshell.'

'What?'

'The chap with the wooden leg – he had spectacles. Wasn't very tall either – though I don't mean a dwarf, of course.'

Greenleaf nodded, and into his notebook under the heading of *Wooden Leg* added *glasses and not a dwarf*. And then feeling that nothing further could be gleaned from the Fawcett household he took his leave, and turning into South Audley Street retreated to the darkened sanctuary of The Volunteer. Here he meditated over a pint and a pork pie, assessed the case and came to no conclusion.

CHAPTER TWO

Rosy Gilchrist had never really liked her aunt, but news of her death – particularly in such distasteful circumstances – had aroused a level of sympathy she had not previously felt. It aroused other things too: shock, irritation and cringing embarrassment. Only Marcia would have sported a coal scuttle in which to meet her Maker, and only Marcia would have ensured that the fact was blazoned across every newspaper in the land. And it was typical that Marcia should have enacted the ultimate drama of getting herself murdered ... with or without coal scuttle. Alive, her delight in attention had sometimes been amusing but more often than not tiresome; and now and again spectacularly awful. (Rosy shuddered, recalling the incident of the dead hedgehog and the French ambassador – not to mention the ambassador's wife.) Nevertheless, being murdered seemed a high price to pay for notoriety... What the *hell* had been going on?

She poured a glass of sherry and stared in the mirror, seeing not her own reflection but her aunt's: grey-blonde hair, scarlet mouth and pale, lazily defiant eyes. And just for a moment she caught the sound of the drawling voice and high grating laugh. Well, she would never hear either of those again, that was for sure... Would it matter? Probably not. But you got *used* to people – even if you didn't know them terribly well or like them much. Besides, she thought soberly, there was no one else left now, not of her own at any rate (unless you counted those distant and eccentric Oughterard cousins down on Romney Marsh or some such littoral place. Pevensey, was it?) Her sister and parents were dead – caught by a bomb in the Blitz – as was the man she thought she might have married, Johnnie Steptoe, shot down over Dresden just before the end. It had been her twenty-first birthday and she had wanted to die. But she didn't, and like thousands of others survived the remaining months of the war and coped as best she could with the peace.

Actually, she thought (the image in the mirror reverting to her own dark hair and eyes), she hadn't coped badly. Coming out of the ATS she had battled her way up to Cambridge – difficult with so much competition from the returning men – and getting into Newnham had somehow wrested from that college a good-class degree in history. With that under her belt she had taken a part-time job as academic factotum to the irascible but distinguished Dr Stanley at the British Museum, and with her parents' legacy bought the lease of a flat just off Baker's Street. So far so good: she had friends, moderate money and an interesting job... But *now* her mother's sister, her nearest though hardly dearest relation, was dead, and dead in appalling circumstances. It felt distinctly peculiar.

It had also felt peculiar being questioned by the police. As with most people, this was not a familiar experience; and apart from its dubious novelty she felt somehow that she had been tested and found wanting. They seemed to assume that she must have had an intimate knowledge of her aunt's life and would provide their enquiry with some dazzling insight. But unless you counted the acrimonious divorce from Donald, titbits of social gossip, the occasional newspaper item recounting drunken rows with taxi drivers or some ghastly brouhaha such as the embassy gaffe, Rosy knew little about her aunt – indeed had preferred to remain largely in ignorance. Had she *known* the woman was going to be murdered she might have shown greater curiosity, or indeed concern... Guilt moved stealthily within her as she recalled the dismissive impatience with which she had heard reports of Marcia's tedious and occasionally outlandish behaviour. Yes, she had kept a wary distance. Should she have closed the gap and made kindly overtures? Tried to maintain closer links?

She sipped her sherry comforted by the thought that the older woman had never shown much interest in her niece. Their rare encounters had been cordial but essentially indifferent, their conversations limited to the trivial and humdrum. No, clearly Marcia had not found Rosy worth cultivating. She had had her own rather specialised coterie and her niece was not of it.

This lack of familial warmth had clearly been a source of puzzlement to the two investigating police officers. One of them, a Detective Sergeant Greenleaf, was keen to follow the financial angle, and Rosy had felt vaguely apologetic about the answer she had given to his question regarding Marcia's legatees: 'Oh no,' she had said, 'I wouldn't have expected anything. Besides, my parents left me pretty well catered for and I'm sure she knew that.'

'So where did it all go?'

'To a donkey sanctuary,' she had replied.

He had thought she was joking and frowned at what he took to be her flippancy. But when she had supplied the name and address of the sanctuary, a place in Ireland, and reminded him of the painting of a Jack and a Jill hanging prominently in the hall of her aunt's house in St John's Wood, he had nodded and ticked something off in his note-book, making a brief entry. She had almost giggled, envisaging the words: *Legal beneficiaries? Donkeys.*

Yes, she reflected wryly, possibly it was her own failure to share her aunt's partiality to the creatures which had opened the gulf between them. She remembered as a small child being given the treat of a donkey ride on Cromer sands. The animal had stumbled. She had fallen off, and bawling like a wounded bear had refused furiously to be put back on. Her mother had been sympathetic; but not Aunt Marcia, who had expressed withering scorn, seeming to ascribe the fall to the rider's lack of empathy with its steed.

Yes, grossly unfair... But then so was murder. And given the personal connection, distinctly frightening. However, more insistent than fear was the now overmastering curiosity. She asked herself again, '*What the hell had been going on?*'

CHAPTER THREE

The announcement in *The Times* obituary column was brief and non-committal:

BEASLEY – Marcia (née Winter). Died sud-denly on 30th September. Funeral 12 noon 9th October at St Anselm's Church Brierly St London W1. Enquiries to Messrs Box & Simpson. Tel: KNI 6858.

It had obviously been inserted by the executive solicitors, but possibly in conjunction with Mr and Mrs Harold Gill, Marcia's long-suffering neighbours, a quiet couple of the sort that 'keep themselves to themselves'. Rosy had met them only twice, but both times had been impressed by their stoicism in the face of adversity, i.e. a persistently wailing gramophone, inebriate revels, lost latchkeys at midnight and the periodic attentions of the fourth estate. Life next door to Marcia cannot have been easy, but their forbearance was repaid (or explained) by the fact that she was punctilious in feeding their cat when they were away – which was often. Presumably their role in the funeral initiative was a kind of thanksgiving for a service rendered and peace restored.

It seemed strange seeing her aunt's name staring at her from such a context, and the starkly rendered facts conferred a cold reality to the whole shocking event. Yet the more Rosy studied the words the more remote the death became ... the more remote Marcia herself became. She was of the past now, far away – over and done with. Irrevocably. *Died suddenly on 30th September.* Nothing could be clearer or more absolute.

Rosy pondered. Eight years previously, with the loss of parents and sister, and then of airman Johnnie, she had been torn apart with grief, excoriated; breathless with incredulity, anguish – anger. But this bore no resemblance to any of that. What she felt now was a discomfort, a vague regret: listless nostalgia for something or someone that willy-nilly had once been part of her and no longer was. It didn't hurt but it was *unsettling* and she felt strangely adrift.

Well at least she could muster a floral tribute. The notice hadn't stipulated 'No flowers', and in any case, being the niece surely she had a prerogative in such matters. Yes, a large sheaf of colourful dahlias and late-flowering clematis might be appropriate, something sufficiently lavish to fit the identity of the deceased. Marcia, she was sure, would have been unimpressed by a discreet sheaf of pale lilies. She telephoned Selfridges and made enquiries.

On the day of the funeral Rosy approached the church (Victorian Gothic with truncated spire) with some curiosity. It was tucked away in a secluded cul-de-sac and seemed a strange choice for Marcia whose preference one might have assumed to be something more fashionable and conspicuous. In any case, as far as she was aware, her aunt had never shown any particular religious leanings. Not that that meant anything really; it was probably the decision of the decorous Gills. And besides, given the choice, wouldn't one prefer one's last appearance on earth to be spent amidst the moderate aesthetics of psalm and incense than the glum austerities of a civic crematorium?

As it happened, apart from copious incense, the alternative was not so different. The service at St Anselm's was tepid and perfunctory: a hymn was played which clearly nobody recognised, the great sonorities of the Prayer Book gabbled and a clerical address given whose flat monotone did little to convey the *joie de vivre* of which the

23

deceased seemed to be mildly accused. The church was dim and Rosy took scant account of the congregation, being too preoccupied with trying to revive hazy memories of her aunt in the prewar years and censoring images of the gruesome end. One or two people she recognised, but for the most part the assembled remained faceless and shadowy.

An announcement from the pulpit invited mourners (attendees?) to a small reception being held afterwards in the adjoining hall. She decided to give this a miss, hoping to slip away unremarked – but was caught by Mrs Gill who, leaning over from the pew behind, had whispered: 'Do hope you'll come, my dear, not seen you for ages.' (No, Rosy thought, you haven't. She had made it her business not to go near Aunt Marcia or St John's Wood ever since the ambassadorial crisis of three years earlier.) Thus caught on the hop yet wedged in the pew, there was nothing she could do except smile and nod compliance.

The ritual over it was with some relief that she filed outside with the Gills and a handful of others to the cramped burial ground, and watched the coffin as it was lowered into the allotted space. There was in fact a good number of floral tributes and she noted that hers was prominently placed. But the observation gave little satisfaction for she knew that the flowers were no substitute for warmth, let alone real love...

After the final benediction and the sprinkling of earth she lingered diffidently by the graveside – partly through awkward respect, partly through reluctance to join the melee in the church hall. Then with the first gust of rain, and with a mixture of guilt and defiance, she turned abruptly and walked towards its door.

Surveying the room and its occupants Rosy wasn't entirely enamoured of what she saw – an ill-assorted crowd who, collectively at least, held little promise of appeal or interest: a few elderly indeterminates downing minuscule glasses of British Sherry as if their lives depended on it (which they probably did); a small coterie of what she took to be members of Marcia's 'so talented, my dear' art group (distinguished by their studiedly 'bohemian' attire, i.e. florid colours and cultivated beards); a trio of heavily cassocked priests all wearing the same expression of benevolent indifference; a fair number of the louche and raddled, and a sprinkling of Haslemere types looking out of place and out of sorts. Slightly to her surprise, Donald the ex-husband was not in evidence, and neither were the Oughterard cousins (too busy wrangling among themselves on Romney Marsh, she supposed).

But the cranky Fawcetts were there all right – asinine Edward, Amy of whose mentality she had never been quite certain, and of course the genial but astonishingly tactless mother. (Once known to enquire of the young Princess Margaret if she didn't occasionally tire of playing second fiddle to her sister. The fact that the princess most certainly did seemed of little help in defusing the ensuing furore.) Gobbling a cucumber sandwich, Lady Fawcett was also talking intently to the ubiquitous

25

Professor Dillworthy, looking superior as usual and casting sidelong glances at his companion Felix Smythe, 'the wittiest florist in Knightsbridge'. Felix, however, was busy scanning the other guests, and catching Rosy's eye blew a kiss. 'Huh,' she bridled to herself, 'we've hardly ever met and the last time was when he was ginned up to the eyebrows with Aunt Marcia outside the Ritz. I'm surprised he remembers me.'

But he evidently did, for detaching himself from the group he slithered over to Rosy and in unctuous tone murmured a blend of compliment and condolence. She thanked him politely, whereupon, lowering his voice and with a glint of relish, he said, 'But, oh my goodness, it must have been *excruciating* for you to learn the precise circumstances! Very odd. Poor girl, I hope she didn't suffer much.'

Rosy inwardly agreed with both observations but was disinclined to pursue the matter with Felix, and instead enquired brightly after his horticultural pursuits, wondering vaguely whether she should have placed her recent order with his own firm Bountiful Blooms instead of Selfridges. (In fact, she learnt later that Felix never catered for funerals, these apparently being too stifling of the spirit.)

'Well, my dear,' he confided eagerly, '*trade*, as they say, is booming! The *Tatler*, of course, is always begging me to write articles for their house and garden section, but just recently the dear Queen Mother has rather honed in on things. She gave a cocktail party last week and wanted nothing but sweet peas... Just a titchy bit vulgar I thought.

26

But then who am I to question a royal diktat?' He paused and with a light laugh added, 'Although as a matter of fact that is exactly what I did: "Oh Ma'am," I said, "do you really want *every* bloom a sweet pea?"'

'And did she?' asked Rosy.

He nodded. '"Indeed I do, Mr Smythe," she said, "I like the smell and so do the corgis."'

Rosy giggled. 'Well that put you in your place, didn't it!'

Felix shrugged, and taking her by the elbow steered her towards a small group which included Professor Dillworthy and the Fawcetts.

They welcomed her with interest and suitably sympathetic faces. 'Weren't you terribly surprised?' asked Lady Fawcett. 'I mean it's not the sort of thing one expects of an aunt, is it?'

Of course I was bloody surprised, thought Rosy irritably, what does she imagine? But she agreed politely that yes she had certainly been surprised, and it was all very mysterious.

'Ah,' said Edward darkly, nodding in the direction of his own aunt, 'but you never can tell. Sometimes they step out of character.'

Lady Fawcett regarded him coldly. 'I don't know what sort of character you have in mind, Edward, but another absurdity like that and I shall indeed step out of it and box your ears!' She took a sharp bite from her sandwich.

'Dear Marcia,' exclaimed Cedric Dillworthy, 'she leaves such a gap in our lives.' Rosy rather doubted this but nodded in dutiful agreement.

'Absolutely!' cried Felix Smythe. 'I mean she was so – so, well...' He wafted a limp hand in the

27

air, indicating God knows what.

'*Game?*' suggested a deep voice at Rosy's shoulder.

Rosy turned and was confronted by a middle-aged woman clad in tweeds, lisle stockings, and wearing a rather battered pork-pie hat with a small scraggy feather. Felix raised his eyes to the ceiling and murmured sotto voce, 'Well not for you, dear, that's for sure!' And then in a louder voice and addressing Lady Fawcett, he introduced the newcomer as 'Vera Collinger – *such* a stalwart and an old pal of Marcia's.'

'But you've just implied...' interrupted Edward clumsily.

'Just one of Felix's feeble little witticisms,' said the newcomer. 'You see,' she added, thrusting out her jaw and lighting a small cheroot, '*I* am of the Sapphic persuasion.' The announcement elicited a brief silence and blank expressions.

'How nice...' said Lady Fawcett, '...and er ... what does that entail?'

'Oh, Mummy,' protested Amy, 'surely you know about that! She doesn't like men.'

'Few of us do, dear, but one must be charitable... I mean, I know that they are not awfully good at fixing things, but they *are* quite smart at playing footsie under the luncheon table... Wouldn't you agree, Miss Bollinger?'

'*Collinger,*' muttered the other, scowling and emitting a cloud of acrid smoke.

There was a stifled snigger from Cedric Dillworthy, who, projecting his voice and addressing the room in general, said 'It's *such* a fascinating island, you know. In fact in my opinion by far the best of all the Aegean ones, and of course there is that extraordinary petrified forest. I remember once–'

'What *are* you talking about?' asked Edward.

'Why Lesbos, of course. Didn't you come to my course of lectures, "Denizens of Lesbos", at the National Gallery?'

'No,' Edward replied.

'Ah well, missed a treat,' sighed the professor. 'But I expect Miss Collinger may have.' He turned to her and added slyly, 'Rather up your street, I imagine, dear lady.'

'Hardly,' the lady answered. 'I avoid abroad, and I also make a particular point of avoiding the National Gallery – it attracts so many charlatans.'

Cedric pursed his lips in displeasure, while Rosy thought, *Perhaps not abroad, but she does go to the National Gallery. I saw her there last week talking to a man with a gammy leg under the Titian in the third room – and wearing this same pork-pie hat with mangy feather...*

'It was quite awful!' she later confided to Leo, the young research assistant in Dr Stanley's archives department. 'The most dreary service, a vacuous address by some priest with adenoids, and nobody there who seemed remotely concerned about Marcia's death – except for the actual circumstances, of course. The food was stale too,' she added as an afterthought.

They were huddled at a small table in the pub opposite the British Museum, consuming pickled eggs and Guinness to offset the autumnal damp and their employer's exacting demands. It had been a more than busy afternoon in the office, and the rigours of the earlier obsequies had not exactly fortified Rosy for dealing with fractious scholars and the earnest, frequently meandering telephone enquiries from the public. Along with arranging conferences and keeping her boss insulated against the more deranged of his fellow academics, such matters were all in a day's work, and normally she coped with cheery efficiency (sometimes, indeed, with mild fervour). But today was different. She felt tired, flat – oddly dispirited. Ennui induced by Marcia, she thought wryly...

'But then you're not specially concerned either, are you?' asked Leo, biting into one of the rubbery eggs. 'I thought you said you had nothing in common and hardly ever saw her.'

'Hmm,' agreed Rosy soberly, 'but that was *before*...'

'Before the coal scuttle?'

'Yes, I suppose so. I feel guilty somehow.'

'Can't think why. I mean it wasn't you who shoved it on her head, was it?'

She smiled. 'No, of course not. Nor did I shoot her. But maybe if I had been more aware, more *involved*, made more of an effort to get to know her, things might have been different.'

'I shouldn't think so. From what you say she clearly wasn't very interested in your life. Didn't even send condolences when your chap was killed – too busy pursuing her own ends, whatever they may have been.'

Rosy lit a cigarette, considering his words. 'Well, yes, that's it, isn't it: what *were* her own ends? From what I could make out she seemed to spend her days wrapped in a veil of alcohol pursuing what the moralists would call folly and trivia.'

Leo laughed. 'Sounds pretty good to me – assuming you manage not to get bumped off in the process.'

'Exactly. People don't get murdered for being silly (well, not usually). There must have been something else, something going on beneath the surface.'

Her companion cleared his throat and in a mild tone said, 'If you don't mind my saying, that is a remark of the most fatuous triteness.'

'Well really!'

'*Of course* something was going on under the surface. And what's more I think you should make it your business to find out. I'll give you a hand if you like.' He stood up abruptly, unwound the muffler from around his neck, shrugged off his raincoat and shapeless cardigan, and before she had a chance to speak, pushed his way to the bar to order more Guinness.

When he returned she gestured to the heap of garments. 'I thought you were cold. Do you propose taking anything else off?'

He looked rueful. 'Not for some time I shouldn't think. She's chucked me again.'

'Who? Polly?'

'No, the one before – Miranda. It was just coming right again, and then all of a sudden, pouf! Off she goes with some creeping Jesus from the gas board who is going to convert her to piety and six children, the sod.'

'Does she want either?'

'Seems so. Anyway she certainly doesn't want

31

me – which is why to allay my spleen and melancholy I propose helping you pursue the mystery of the murdered lady.'

'The murdered lady happens to have been my aunt; I am not sure I take kindly to your using her as a sort of palliative to hurt pride.'

'Far more than hurt pride,' he retorted plaintively, 'a broken heart no less.'

'Broken heart, my arse. That'll be the day!'

He looked at her in mock surprise over the rims of his reading glasses (for some reason invariably donned when sipping stout). 'I am not used to hearing such language from females of a certain age, it shatters my illusions.'

'Of a certain age!' she yelped. 'I'll have you know I'm not yet thirty. *And* I know how to use a searchlight and strip an ack-ack gun. I bet they didn't teach you that in the Boy Scouts!'

'Yes, sorry. I forgot you were a war *veteran* – explains the verbal bluntness, no doubt.' He grinned and added, 'I say, could I cadge a fag? Dr Stanley took my last one when he was squaring up to Mrs Burkiss over the missing gin bottle. She refuses to give him the key to her broom cupboard. He's convinced the gin is in there but she won't budge an inch.'

'Ah, well, that's a lost cause then... But, Leo, are you really serious about wanting to fish up something about Marcia? Surely the police are doing all that. And besides, you haven't the time. I mean, quite apart from your work for Stanley, what about your own researches – something to do with Gladstone and the Bulgarians, aren't they? I'd hate to think of Aunt Marcia standing in

32

the way of you and your doctorate, or indeed of the Grand Old Man!'

'Your Aunt Marcia may have stood in the way of a lot of things – or people – hence her death. But don't worry, she won't prevent me scaling the heights of academia, and I am sure that the venerable GOM will shut an eagle eye if I "absent" myself "from felicity awhile".'

'He never said that!'

'No, it was another mighty craftsman. But let's get back to the subject in hand: who was the assassin and why did he favour that particular brand of millinery?'

'Or why did they?' murmured Rosy.

CHAPTER FOUR

Leaving Leo to return to his lodgings in Blooms-bury, Rosy caught a bus to Marble Arch, but ignoring drizzle and rush-hour crowds decided to get off at Marshall & Snelgrove and walk the rest of the way. Normally exercise for its own sake held little appeal, but after the funeral and the Fawcetts et al she felt the need to stretch her legs as well as her mind. The warmth of her flat beckoned; but just for a little longer she sought the harsher stimulus of the London streets.

Skirting round the back of Marshall's and walk-ing briskly along Wigmore Street, she brooded on Leo's words: *Of course there was something going on under the surface ... and I think you should make it your business to find out.* Well yes, obviously quite a lot must have been going on (unless the thing had just been a random attack by some crazed intruder – though that seemed improbable). Still, surely there was no need for a personal pursuit. Wasn't that the job of the police? Certainly the whole business was horribly bizarre and her natural curiosity looked for an explanation... But Leo had urged her to take some sort of initiative herself: to 'root things out like a truffle hound' he had said.

All very well for Leo, she thought, it wasn't his aunt who was the victim. Did she really want to root around in Marcia's life (least of all like some slavering canine!)? Wouldn't it be better to leave well alone, draw a veil and get on with her own life while others did the digging? Yes, by far the most sensible course... And in any case, it occurred to her with a jolt, certainly the *safer!* After all, it wasn't as if the matter were simply some abstruse conundrum, a cerebral challenge to be solved and discarded. A raw brutish thing had happened, perpetrated by someone with malicious intent: someone with an agenda which may or may not have been satisfied, and who might conceivably take things further. And whatever the motive, and whether satisfied or not, the assassin was still out there somewhere: an individual going about his (or her) daily business, to be encountered perhaps at a Tube station, on the top of a bus, in a Lyons Corner House or the little greengrocer's off the Edgeware Road ... perhaps the very next person she passed here in Wigmore Street! Rosy flinched, and then smartly sidestepped a large woman bearing down on her

34

shoving a perambulator of tank-like girth. She gave a perfunctory smile to its twin and bawling occupants. Presumably no murderer there.

And then with Leo's metaphor still in mind, she slipped into the Greek café to buy a quarter of rather ersatz chocolate truffles. Having firmly decided to decline the role of truffle hound she might at least safely pursue the sugary imitations.

Back at the flat she was busy sampling the third of these when the telephone rang. 'I have a long-distance call for you from New York,' announced the operator's clipped tones.

New York? She didn't know anyone there. Obviously wrong number. She waited, and mechanically stretched for a fourth truffle while priming her ear to catch an American accent.

'I say, is that Rosy?' asked a distinctly English voice.

'Er, yes,' she replied hesitantly, replacing the chocolate.

'Good. Hoped to catch you, thought you might still be at work or something.'

Despite the crackling line the voice sounded familiar but she couldn't quite place it. 'Uhm – sorry, you are?'

'Donald. Donald Beasley. Once married to your aunt. Remember?'

'Oh yes, of course! I am so sorry – it's been a long time and–'

'Look, I've just heard the awful news. There was a small item in the *Tribune*, colourful to say the least, but in its way oddly flattering. Describes her as the "fashionable high-spirited English belle". I

35

suppose that's because she was once seen on the arm of old Joe Kennedy at the Waldorf. "High-spirited" is a bit of a euphemism if you ask me... Still, that's beside the point. I just wanted to give you my sympathy, and to say that I'm coming over to London next week to negotiate a publishing deal for my firm. Perhaps we could meet for a drink – there are one or two things I need to discuss.' He paused, and then clearing his throat, added, 'As you know, she and I didn't get on – not latterly at any rate – but it's a bit of a shock all the same, particularly in those appalling circumstances. It's grotesque, and I'd just like to...'

'Yes, yes of course,' Rosy said hastily. 'I only work part-time so I can be fairly flexible: a Wednesday or Thursday afternoon, perhaps. Or an evening if you prefer.'

He settled for the Friday evening at his hotel, saying he would call to confirm after arrival. Then muttering something about it being a ghastly business, he rang off.

Exchanging truffle for a small whisky, Rosy went into the narrow kitchen, switched on the wireless and started to chop cabbage and remnants of boiled potato for a bubble and squeak. She felt quite hungry, and levered open a tin of corned beef to add to the mixture in the pan. Later, sitting at the kitchen table, half listening to the absurdities of *Much Binding in the Marsh*, she reflected upon Donald and his imminent visit.

She could not quite remember when Marcia had introduced him as her husband – 1944, early 1945?... No, of course it had been '44 – not long

36

after the D-Day Landings. Rosy had been on leave staying (rather strainfully) with the Oughterard cousins in Sussex, and Marcia had appeared from out of the blue dragging Donald on her arm. Their arrival had caused a minor upheaval, i.e. requiring Mrs Oughterard to curtail her afternoon rest, and her husband to forego his daily session with their soldier son's abandoned train set. However, things had settled down and the next few hours had passed pleasantly enough. The newly-weds were clearly pleased with each other and generated an air of mild jollity in a household not noted for its exuberance.

At first Donald had struck Rosy as rather stolid and, certainly from her standpoint, distinctly aged. (He had been a little older than Marcia, about forty-seven perhaps, and previously married.) However, under the staccato barrage of Charles Oughterard's interrogation he had responded with wit and patient good humour. (Charles himself had been later heard to mutter that a chap so knowledgeable about the manufacture of parts for Hornby rolling stock must be all right, and it just went to show that 'these Air Ministry bods know a thing or two!')

Subsequently there had been the occasional brief encounter with both of them in London ... though one rather embarrassing occasion when she had bumped into Donald in a nightclub, distinctly the worse for wear and with another woman on his arm. Gradually there had emerged rumours of Marcia's own infidelities, public skirmishes between the two of them and finally the divorce. After which he had faded from the scene. Until now. Yes, he had been an unremarkable presence in Rosy's life. But one thing she recalled clearly: his words of shy concern when she had once let slip a reference to Johnnie's death. It was a concern which she could not recall Aunt Marcia ever showing.

Rosy frowned, considering sartorial possibilities for their meeting. What would be the most suitable? Turquoise satin with paste diamonds and snazzy bolero? He might think that frivolous – especially given the subject of their meeting. Perhaps something more svelte was required: the grey silk with pearl choker, navy wrap and matching handbag. Yes, probably better. Her new stockings had fashionable black seams but reluctantly she discounted these in favour of conventional ones, hearing her mother's now distant voice murmuring: 'Just a trifle fast, dear, don't you think?' She smiled sadly, remembering the battles over the blue eyeshadow.

And then she thought of Donald himself: would she recognise him? Had he altered – put on weight, gone white-haired or bald, lost his teeth? Might he turn up in crêpe soles, sporting a loud American jacket? Like Marcia he had used to drink quite heavily. Supposing he had gone teetotal, joined a temperance society and appeared with a badge on his lapel proclaiming the fact! Unlikely: after all, he was with a firm of publishers now. Still, it was amazing how people changed. She recalled a chance encounter in Piccadilly a couple of years previously with a girl she had once known in the ATS – a wild pretty kid they had dubbed Molly the Minx. Six years after the war's end she had suddenly reappeared outside Fortnum & Mason, draped in a nun's habit and carrying a cat. It was the cat that had been the greatest shock: the girl could never abide them.

CHAPTER FIVE

'So why have you come forward only now?' asked Detective Sergeant Greenleaf sternly. 'Mrs Beasley was found dead a good two weeks ago, it was all over the papers. If you've got what you believe to be vital information you should have reported it immediately.'

Clovis Thistlehyde cleared his throat and explained rather impatiently that he had been *abroad* when the news broke– 'Venice, actually. I like to browse the Accademia periodically; it stimulates the Muse, you know.'

Greenleaf didn't know and he wasn't too sure about the Accademia either; but nodding briefly, said, 'So what have you to tell me?'

'I should like to *tell* whoever is in charge of the case,' replied Clovis tartly, 'is that you?'

'I am one of those immediately responsible for its handling,' Greenleaf informed him stiffly. 'Anything relevant to our enquiries will be given all due attention, you can be sure of that, sir.' He didn't think he liked this man very much. He certainly didn't like his tie which was scarlet (obviously a Bolshie) and his hair could do with a good chop too.

'In that case,' said Clovis, settling back in his chair and crossing a green corduroyed leg, 'I have reason to believe that apart from the murderer I was quite probably the last person to see Marcia Beasley alive.' He gave a deprecating smile, clearly expecting his questioner to express grateful amazement.

'And what makes you think that?' asked Greenleaf woodenly.

'Because I just happened to be *there* that afternoon, not long before the poor woman was found. Just before I set off for abroad.'

'Oh yes? Why?'

'She was my model.'

'What?'

'My model. I happen to be an artist – portraits mainly. She was a keen patron of our group. I realise that this sort of thing may not be your line of country, so you might not have heard of me, but I have a modest claim to fame – quite a following in fact, especially from abr–'

'Abroad?'

'Precisely.'

'I see. So you went to paint her at her house?' Clovis nodded.

'In the nude?'

'Oh yes. One has to admit that for a woman of her years she was in pretty good shape – only moderate sagging at the thighs and tum; lines on the neck, naturally – but, between you and me, still remarkable breasts. *Very* paintable one might say! Indeed I had every intention of doing a couple of studies for my next exhibition at the Islington Attic – rather a modish little joint.

40

Perhaps you know it?'

Greenleaf shook his head and confessed he didn't. 'So while this painting was going on, was the deceased with or without the coal scuttle?'

'Without... *What?* Well of course she was without! You don't imagine I would select a sitter wearing a coal bucket do you? For God's sake, man!' Clovis scowled and tugged at the scarlet tie.

'We have to check these details,' Greenleaf explained patiently, 'it's a question of getting things just right, building up a *picture*, as you might say.' He smiled and added, 'But mind you, these days you artist gentlemen seem to put anything into your pictures. Take that Picasso bloke, for example – some very rum ideas he seems to have. All a bit bizarre to a layman's eye if you ask me... But then, of course, you're not a layman are you, Mr Thistledown?'

'I am not,' snapped Clovis. 'And the name is Thistlehyde.'

He supplied further details, and Greenleaf made notes to the effect that the witness had arrived at the victim's house at about one-thirty in the afternoon, stayed for a couple of hours, and then left a little earlier than usual to prepare for his trip to Venice, picking up a taxi at the nearby rank.

'And during this time,' Greenleaf continued, 'would you say Mrs Beasley was acting in her normal way?'

'Entirely. Throwing down gin and cursing the government.'

'Cursing the government?'

'The previous one, Attlee's. A hobby horse.

Couldn't stand the man and she generally started on him sooner or later, especially if she was bored with other topics or had had a few. Naturally one agreed but it could get a bit repetitive all the same.'

Greenleaf was about to observe that he had always thought Mr Attlee a rather sane fellow, when Thistlehyde suddenly leant forward and said, 'Tell you what, though, she did get a bit queer towards the end.'

'Queer? In what way?'

'Well, she said that she was getting tired from holding the position and wanted to stretch her legs and have a fag. As said, I was rather pressed for time, but agreed anyway and we took a break. I nipped off to the lavatory, and when I came back she was pulling the brown paper off a package which must have arrived earlier. From what I saw it seemed to be a black box, gift-wrapped with a pink bow. She began to open the lid and then suddenly shut it and cried, "Oh Christ Almighty, not another effing one!" When I asked, "Another effing what?" she sort of shrugged and simply said, "Oh nothing really – all just so boring," and chucked it into the waste-paper basket. Then she stubbed out her cigarette, resumed her pose and I picked up my brushes... But I can tell you, it was no good. Her face was white, eyes blank, and she had gone what you might call all saggy. No good for Clovis Thistlehyde! So I packed up my things and said I would see her when I got back from Venice.'

'Hmm... So you left, and didn't see anyone on your way out or in the street?'

42

Clovis shook his head. *'Personne,* as our Gallic friends would say.'

Greenleaf didn't have any Gallic friends but assumed the answer was intended as a negative. 'Tell me, Mr Thistlehyde,' he asked, 'did you often visit the lady in her home?'

'Visit the lady? Only to paint her, if that's what you mean.' He looked slightly put out.

'But I thought you artists had studios for that sort of thing, with easels and canvases and such ... and ... er, skylights,' Greenleaf added vaguely. 'But I daresay they're a bit pricey; don't suppose everyone can afford one, especially these days – not after the war and Mr Attlee's austerity drive. Mind you, I don't think Mr Churchill is going to–'

'Of course I can bloody well afford one!' retorted Clovis angrily, 'I'm not some jobbing little tyro, you know! Not far off an RA – an FAG actually.'

Greenleaf was intrigued. 'What's that?'

'Fellow of the Artists' Guild, naturally.'

'Ah yes, stupid of me... So why didn't she come to your studio, then?'

The latter paused, frowning slightly. 'Well, as I've told you, I have a place, of course – but it's near Paddington station, not exactly the most enticing area. Absolutely nothing to do with cost, you understand,' he added firmly, 'but it's a question of the right light. Such things are difficult to come by and you have to grab them when you can. Anyway, Marcia – God that woman was such a thumping snob – declared she had no intention of being seen lurking around the back-streets of Paddington and visiting some rabbit hutch three floors up. When I said that there was no need to lurk and that by some standards my atelier was no hutch but a unit of penthouse proportion, she replied that anyone seen on foot in that area was bound to be thought lurking, and that the concept of size was entirely relative, thus it would be far more convenient if I visited her in St John's Wood. Which I did.' He folded his arms.

'Often, was it?'

'Often enough – *and* it cost her!' Clovis grinned. 'Yes, one has to admit Marcia was pretty generous with the old expenses, not bad at all! In fact, come to think of it, she owes me the taxi fare for the last session. I'd better get on to the executors pronto...'

'I see. So she took her clothes off, you took out your paintbox and she paid you big compensation for the inconvenience?' Greenleaf gave a kindly smile which was not returned.

'I must say,' Clovis said testily, 'the police do have a raw way of putting things. But I suppose that's all part of their training – cut the cackle and nail the poor buggers!' He gave another wrench to the red tie and stared defiantly at Greenleaf. And then with a sudden smirk, ran a hand through the trailing hair and, adjusting his voice to a confidential murmur, said, 'As a matter of fact it wasn't just Marcia's snobbery that persuaded me to visit her, least of all what you clearly like to see as my mercenary intent. It's my current mistress: she is *insanely* jealous and has a wild imagination. I fear that visits from Marcia would have been grist to her suspicious mill. She harbours visions of wild orgiastic frolics being enacted in my modest garret.'

'And are they?' Greenleaf asked with interest.

'Ah well, that would be telling,' was the roguish reply, and he gave what was evidently meant to be a man-of-the-world laugh. Greenleaf took his pencil and scribbled something on the blotting pad: 'Berk'.

'I say,' exclaimed Clovis in apparent alarm, 'you haven't recorded that, have you? I shouldn't like anything of that sort to reach the ears of my public!'

Oh yes you would, thought Greenleaf. Have 'em flocking to your next exhibition. Double the price of the pictures! However, he assured the artist he need have no fears, and feeling the pangs of hunger starting to assert themselves, thanked him warmly for his cooperation and said he had been most useful in clarifying one or two aspects of the case. They would contact him again if necessary.

'Always happy to be of service,' replied Thistle-hyde smoothly. 'Naturally I know all of this is in the strictest confidence, but if by any chance your superiors felt it *useful* to the investigation to inform the press that I had volunteered some help, then of course you have my fullest permission. Personal publicity can be desperately tiresome but sometimes one just has to bite on the bullet!' He gave a rueful smile, uncrossed his legs, and with a brief nod strolled from the office.

'Huh!' thought Greenleaf irritably, 'I suppose he hopes for banner headlines. *MURDER VICTIM'S LAST HOURS WITH FASHIONABLE PORTRAIT PAINTER:* "*She was such a*

45

dear friend," confides Clovis Thistlehyde... Well he ain't getting 'em!'

Later, in the canteen over mince and custard sponge, he reflected on the tale of the package containing the small black box. The artist chap had said it had been tied with a bow as if it was some sort of gift, though judging from the woman's alleged reaction it was not one she had found especially welcome. In fact it sounded as if she had been thoroughly unsettled by it. Any significance? Probably not. And Thistlewaite or whatever his name was had said she had chucked it in the waste-paper basket, so it couldn't have been that important... Yet no such thing had been found by the investigating officers when they had been called only a few hours later. The room had been thoroughly combed and the basket reported as empty. Either the chap was lying, probably to enhance his own importance, or for some reason the assailant(s) had taken it; or – perhaps most likely – the woman herself had retrieved it and put it elsewhere before being 'overtaken by events'. In the dustbin? Some place in the house?

On the other hand, he brooded, it was the char who had had the bad luck to find the body when she had arrived for her early evening stint. Just conceivably she might have snaffled the thing and not bothered or cared to mention the fact when interviewed. He sighed. The poor old girl would have to have another grilling. Best to get young Harris to do it, he was good with old ladies.

At that moment Greenleaf's superior joined him at the table, and the detective sergeant told

46

him all about the morning's interview with the 'pinko' painter. 'And do you know,' he confided, 'the geezer has an atelier which he reckons is of penthouse proportion.'

'You don't say!' grinned the inspector. 'I better not tell that to the missus, she might complain!'

CHAPTER SIX

Stanley had been impossible – demanding this, that and the other; cowing his students and even reducing Mrs Burkiss to baleful silence. (She still hadn't yielded up the key to her broom cupboard, and given the latest display was unlikely to do so.)

'The flak's flying today,' Leo had announced cheerfully. 'I rather suspect someone has questioned his judgement over a footnote in *The Museum Quarterly*. Smithers probably – he bides his time, you know, and then pounces.'

Rosy did know. The academic rivalry of the two colleagues would occasionally rise to cabaret heights, but most of the time it was merely irritating and today was no exception. She was tired and not in the mood for Stanley's tantrums or Smithers' pettish complaints. There was plenty of work to do as it was, and she was impatient to get home, have a bath and brace herself for the rendezvous with Donald. Brace? Well perhaps not that exactly, but to focus her mind on meeting this man whom she hadn't seen for several years and of whom she had only a vague memory. As promised he had telephoned earlier in the week to say he was staying at the Shadwell and hoped she would join him for dinner at seven-thirty on the Friday. She was both nervous and curious. Apart from the topic of Marcia, would they actually have anything to say to each other?

Eventually escaping Dr Stanley and the museum's portals, she hurried home, and between sips of vermouth started to put her hair in rollers and run the bath. It all seemed to take a long time, particularly as in her haste she had smudged the mascara and had to redo the ritual of spitting on the brush and carefully flicking the tips of her lashes. But at last, smoothing down the silk dress and grabbing coat and handbag, she was ready. She looked out of the window. What had she expected – moonlight and stars? Bloody raining of course!

He was in the foyer when she arrived, and contrary to earlier fears she recognised him immediately. His hair had receded and there were slight pouches under his eyes, but otherwise he was much as she remembered: tallish, ungainly and mercifully sober-suited.

He greeted her affably and said she was looking well (by which she assumed she must be looking quite nice. It was something men said, she had noticed, when they were too diffident to pay a compliment.) She deposited her coat in the cloakroom and joined him in the cocktail lounge. The hotel had received a direct hit in the war and had since been resurrected into a palace of aggressive modernity. The bar, however, still

48

retained an air of amiable chic, and the shaded lights and discreetly upholstered sofas looked inviting. To her surprise she saw he had ordered Manhattans. In the old days she had chosen them fairly often, but not recently.

'Still happy with these?' he asked.

She said she certainly was, flattered that he should remember.

'Good, good!' he replied vaguely, smiling but looking awkward. He flicked open a cigarette case and offered her one. 'So, uhm, how's life treating you these days – things going all right, are they?'

She said that they were, and told him a little of her job at the museum and Dr Stanley's vagaries, and he in turn told her of his new publishing venture in New York. The cocktails helped, as did the piano tinkling softly in a corner, but the first ten minutes were sticky and it was with mutual relief that they fell to the subject of Marcia.

'You see,' he explained, 'she telephoned out of the blue about a month ago and said she had something she wanted to send me – some document, apparently – and would I mind keeping it for her. I was pretty surprised because we had virtually lost contact and weren't exactly on hobnobbing terms. When I asked why she couldn't keep it herself, she said, "Like hell, it's dynamite." I was rather busy at the time and didn't see why I should get involved in Marcia's business affairs – I'd had enough of that when we were married. So I suggested that if it was really that important she should deposit it with her bank; to which she replied she had no intention of giving fawning Foxley (presumably the bank manager)

49

the excuse to get his hands on any more of her funds, and in any case she would prefer it to be out of the country.'

'Out of the country? So whatever was it?' asked Rosy.

Donald shrugged. 'I've no idea, she never said. And as it turned out I never got it. Changed her mind, I suppose. As you know, she was full of whims.' He paused and lit another cigarette. 'But... well *now*, I rather wonder if perhaps...'

'You mean it may have some connection with her murder?'

He shrugged again. 'Your guess is as good as mine. But it seems a bit of a coincidence: to suddenly ring up saying she has something vital she wants to get rid of – too hot to handle as it were – and then only weeks later she's found battered to death.'

'She wasn't battered,' Rosy reminded him quietly, 'she was shot wearing a coal scuttle.'

'Yes,' he said reflectively, 'funny that.'

'Hilarious,' replied Rosy dryly.

He said nothing, staring at the revolving door; and then, as if shaking himself from a reverie, signalled the waiter to bring two more Manhattans.

Rosy sipped hers with pleasure. It was not often she basked in a plush hotel drinking cocktails at another's expense. Whisky in Soho's French pub was a more familiar experience, and while she enjoyed its raffish camaraderie a little elegance now and again made a welcome change... Then with a pang of guilt she reminded herself of why she was there at all – to discuss the circumstances of her aunt's murder with her erstwhile uncle, not to have a gay night out! She glanced at Donald scanning the restaurant menu with indifferent eye. He was tapping his forefinger on the ashtray, and she wondered uneasily if he was perhaps bored with her company. But the next moment he cleared his throat, and bending towards her said abruptly, 'Do you know what Marcia was doing during the war?'

'In the war? Well ... some sort of admin I think. Organising refugees – or was it evacuees? Something like that...' She stopped, guilty again at her own vagueness. Why hadn't she known exactly what her aunt had been doing or indeed bothered to ask? Too busy with her own life, that's what! She was about to mutter a defensive excuse but he pre-empted her.

'Oh yes, those things of course – but there was something else too, something quite important.' He paused, and then said, 'As it happens, Marcia was in SOE.'

Rosy gaped. 'Aunt Marcia was in Special Ops! Surely not! You're pulling my leg.'

'Yes, seems unlikely doesn't it? But it's true enough: she was what you might call a spare-time agent. And much of that spare time was spent flat on her back wheedling information out of fifth columnists. An activity at which, I gather, she was extremely adept.' He gave a sardonic smile.

Rosy absorbed the news with wonder: wonder at why anyone should have judged Marcia sufficiently reliable to be recruited by such an elite group, and additional wonder as to how she had remained discreet about her involvement.

Reticence was not part of Marcia's reputation. As to the exact nature of her fact-finding contribution, that was perhaps less surprising.

'But it's better if you don't mention it to anybody,' he continued, 'they tend to be sensitive about this sort of thing, it's still pretty hush-hush. Keep it under your hat, there's a good girl.'

The good girl nodded. 'Yes, of course ... but if it's so hush-hush, why are you telling me? Against the rules, presumably.'

'Yes, well, you are an intelligent woman – or so it always struck me – and according to the grapevine did a pretty good job with the Anti-Aircraft Command down at Dover. A person needs discipline for that, control. So I guess you will be discreet... And now that this fearful thing has happened it seems only fair to redress the balance a bit, i.e. acknowledge her strengths. Admittedly she drove me mad, and I wasn't the only one: she had what might be called a knack for havoc. Fun all right but increasingly impossible – what my mother once called "a loose woman and a loose cannon". A description not entirely unfair, you might agree. To put it politely she could be bloody awful! But the thing *is* she had grit, independence and a sort of dogged indifference to danger; and underneath all the absurdity and exhibitionism there was a shrewd intelligence. Used to be at any rate; and that's obviously what the SOE scouts recognised in 1940... Just thought you ought to know, that's all.' He fell silent and fiddled awkwardly with the stem of his glass.

'Thanks,' murmured Rosy, also feeling awkward. She wasn't sure what to say – or indeed think. Her own impressions of Marcia had never been particularly favourable – aloof, self-orientated and certainly not one to amuse or endear a young niece. But evidently there had been more than met the eye – and more which on the face of it had been valuable. She said diffidently, 'Do you think we should raise her a glass?'

Donald gave a lopsided smile. 'I expect we could manage that but we'll do it in the restaurant over dinner.' He passed her the menu. 'I hope you can find something here, it's no great shakes. The dining room vaunts itself as rivalling the Savoy Grill. I can assure you it doesn't.' They settled for the consommé and turbot, and her host ordered a bottle of Meursault.

As predicted the food was moderate, but the wine was good and Rosy sipped it with pleasure. In his rather clumsy way Donald made a companionable escort – better than she remembered – and with the strains of 'How High the Moon' wafting in from the bar, and despite the reason for their meeting, she began to enjoy herself. And even when the pianist switched to 'Stardust' with its melancholy beauty and languid sweetness (Johnnie's favourite and thus her own), she could almost listen without the usual pangs of loss.

But over coffee and cigarettes things grew serious again. 'Listen,' he said, dropping his voice, 'this coal bucket business, I have been giving it a lot of thought–'

'Not surprised,' said Rosy. 'Who wouldn't? It's ghastly!'

'Yes, of course. But you see it rather strikes a note.'

'Really? What sort of note?'

'It may be of no significance at all, just one of those odd coincidences ... but when we were together and sharing the marital bed things didn't go too well.'

Oh Christ, thought Rosy, what's that got to do with it? Do I really need to hear about these matters? Perhaps I can make an excuse and go to powder my nose...

'Yes, rather disturbed nights which made us both crotchety. In fact, in the end we used separate rooms.'

'Oh yes?' she said vaguely, wondering if she had brought her flapjack and if there would be a good light in the Ladies.

'You see, I snored and she shouted.'

Why on earth was the man telling her this? 'You mean she shouted at you for snoring? Well I suppose people do get a bit ratty...'

'No. I mean she sometimes talked, shouted, in her sleep. It was really very trying. Anyway, one night we had been drinking heavily and had had a row, and that seemed to set her off. She was tossing and turning and mumbling into the pillow, when she suddenly sat bolt upright and yelled, 'Oh, fuck the bloody coal bucket!'

Fuck the–?' Rosy cried. She clapped her hand to her mouth and glanced around, fearful that her voice had carried to neighbouring tables. But the only diners within earshot were a group of elderlies bellowing their heads off with (presumably) defective deaf aids. 'Are you sure?' she whispered.

'Oh yes, her voice was clear as a bell – as is yours.' He grinned.

'So did you ask her about it in the morning?'

'No. Typically we got sidetracked by another spat and I never thought of it again.'

'Until recently.'

He nodded. 'Until recently.'

There was a silence. And then Rosy said, 'It's a pretty strange coincidence if you ask me – unless she was psychic or something. Perhaps she had a premonition, a sort of mystic intimation.'

'Nothing mystic about Marcia,' he replied dryly.

'No ... no, I don't suppose there was. In which case it would rather suggest a connection, though I can't think what.'

'Well, presumably she had been thinking about the coal thing so much that it figured in her subconscious – hence the nocturnal drama.'

'But whoever bothers to think about coal scuttles? I certainly don't!'

He frowned and poured her the last dregs from the coffee pot. 'It must have had a significance which we obviously don't grasp but which the assailant did.'

'So something from the past, you think. The past catching up with the present?'

'Could be ... but to be frank I don't really want to know. Whatever it was happened a long time ago; it's like another age. I am no longer her husband, not even technically her widower, and I've got a completely fresh life in New York... Besides, it would embarrass Priscilla.' He flushed slightly and bent to pick up his fallen napkin.

'Who is Priscilla? Your wife?'

'No, but with luck and patience she may be. Things are at a delicate stage and I don't want

55

anything to rock the boat. Her family are Boston Brahmin – they wouldn't take kindly to a Limey in-law whose ex-wife was found murdered in bizarre circumstances. It wouldn't look good.'

'So you don't think we should mention this to the police?'

'Absolutely not! I just wanted to set the record straight, as the Americans say, not to start opening things up. Get on with your own life, Rosy. Look forward not back. It's the only way. I can assure you – life's too short!' He lit another cigarette, forgot to offer her one and cleared his throat.

She regarded him soberly, noting the greying hair, coarsening cheeks and heavy lids. Must be pushing sixty... He was right: it didn't last long, not the best part anyway. And she wondered briefly what she herself would be like at sixty ... assuming she reached that far and wasn't snuffed out prematurely like Marcia! 'No, I agree,' she said, 'best not. Let them make their own conjectures.'

He looked relieved. 'Sensible... Now tell me, have the executors got in touch with you?'

'Only to say that currently everything is under probate and that in any case the whole estate is destined for a donkey sanctuary.'

'Yes, the donkeys get the bulk – cash, house and major furniture – but apparently she inserted a clause about the minor things: ornaments and stuff. They were to be sold too, but if you or I wanted first pick we were welcome to select a couple of items prior to the auction. Personally I have no desire. I don't fancy traipsing around in that ghost of a house, and besides I've got quite

56

enough of my own paraphernalia. And I doubt whether Priscilla's taste would be the same as Marcia's – assuming of course we get that far.' He grimaced. 'Still, I suppose there may be something there that appeals to you.'

Rosy was surprised. She did not recall the solicitors saying anything about the minor assets, nor indeed that Marcia had made any reference to herself in the will, however cursory. One should be grateful! In fact she couldn't think of anything she wanted particularly – although there had been those nice photographs of her parents on a side table. Yes, they would be welcome. Perhaps she should call the solicitors to check.

They said goodbye and he put her into a taxi; but before doing so he pulled a small package from his jacket pocket and rather awkwardly thrust it into her hand.

'Some scent. Don't worry, it's not one of Marcia's. Rather nicer, really – a Jacques Fath. Hope it suits.' He gave her a quick peck on the cheek, and saying something about seeing her in the States sometime turned and ambled back into the hotel.

In the taxi going home she wondered why he had waited till the end of the evening to present her with the scent. Perhaps he had wanted to see what she was like these days. If so she had presumably passed muster. She smiled... It was nice of him anyway. She hoped the Boston Brahmins would not be too pernickety.

CHAPTER SEVEN

It was one of those days, Greenleaf grumbled to himself, i.e. God-awful. First Mrs Greenleaf had engaged in a spectacular turn at breakfast because he hadn't taken her to the pictures the night before, then the bus broke down halfway to work making him slog the rest of the way in the pouring rain; the superintendent was fractious and the canteen tea tasted even more dire than usual. And then just as he was easing himself quietly into his desk and taking a quick shufti at the crossword, young Harris had phoned in reporting sick: languishing in bed it seemed, valiantly parrying death and pneumonia plus any other ague you cared to mention. This meant that apart from himself there was no one to reinterview the char about the waste-paper basket in the Beasley case. All left to Muggins, Greenleaf thought grimly.

The old girl would be due shortly, and he reminded himself to be gentle as she was bound to be nervous. Meanwhile there was just time for a quick Woodbine and to check the afternoon runners at Kempton Park. He reached for his cigarettes and the sports page but was thwarted in both by the lady arriving early. And far from being intimidated by a visit to a police station, Mrs Perkins exuded an unsettling confidence.

'So what's all this, then?' she began belliger- ently. 'I told you geezers everything I knew when

58

I found the body. I don't like to boil my cabbages twice you know! Besides, I'm a busy woman, I got things to do.' Her gaze swept around Greenleaf's office and alighted on the street map pinned to the wall. 'Hmm, I suppose that's where you record all them suicides and stabbings and such. "X marks the spot". I know all about that, seen it on the films. That's what they always say: *X marks the spot*. And then they goes and shoves in a drawing pin at the place where it happened.'

Greenleaf cleared his throat. 'I, er–'

'Mind you, I don't see no photographs.'

'Photographs?'

'Yes. You know – the Rogues' Gallery. That's what they call it. All them mugshots of the villains. Haven't you got any of those?' She sounded disappointed.

'Well, no – I mean, at least not here. That's in a different section...' He felt oddly disadvantaged and asked tentatively if she would like a cup of tea.

She declined the offer but demanded cocoa with plenty of milk and three sugars. 'A couple of biscuits wouldn't come amiss, neither. I like those H & P Ginger Nuts best, they're ever so good.'

Greenleaf nodded dutifully and got up to catch one of the constables in the corridor. When he returned to the room he saw that the witness had taken his cushion from the desk chair and put it on her own. She had also taken out her knitting: four needles and a sock.

'Now, dear, what was it you wanted to ask?' she enquired graciously. 'I'm all ready for the third degree. Elsie Perkins can stand anything!' She leered toothily.

59

'I'm sure she can,' he murmured. 'So would you mind telling me what you found in the waste-paper basket?'

'In the...? Well, blow me!' she exclaimed. 'You don't think I've been snooping around while you was out of the room do you? That's just typical of your sort. You don't trust no one! And here was me thinking we was going to have a nice cosy chat about that poor murdered Mrs Beasley, while all the time you was suspecting me of having a good old rummage in things what aren't my concern. I don't know what types you're used to having in here, my lad, but whatever they are I ain't one of them!' She gave a withering glare and needled the sock with vicious dexterity.

It was a long time since Greenleaf had been addressed as 'my lad' (not since his old granny, in fact) and he felt a fool, and cursed the ailing Harris huddled safely in his deathbed. However, the confusion was rectified and the injured one assured that her probity was never in doubt. The timely arrival of the cocoa aided the healing process.

'So, the wastepaper basket in the deceased's drawing room,' he continued, 'did you by any chance see whether it contained anything?'

'Waste-paper baskets are not the sort of things you think about at times like that,' was the tart response. 'Not when there's a corpse in front of you wearing a coal scuttle on its head – especially when she's as naked as the day she was born. Disgraceful it was!'

Greenleaf agreed that it was indeed disgraceful but persisted with his question. 'But as far as you

60

were aware there was nothing in the basket? Or were you too shocked to notice?'

There was a long pause while Mrs Perkins appraised the sock and appeared to meditate. And then with a sudden toss of her head, she said, 'Well, nobody bothered to say anything about it at the time, did they? No one mentioned no bleeding basket. Not to me they didn't. How was I to know it was supposed to be important?' Thrusting the sock aside she stared at him defiantly.

Greenleaf gave a sympathetic smile and pushed the biscuits towards her. 'Of course not, you were far too shocked. Must have been dreadful ... but you noticed something, did you?'

She shrugged. 'Well since you mention it, yes. But it wasn't anything at all – leastways nothing what mattered.'

'Perhaps not. But all the same you must have taken it out because my men reported that the basket was empty.'

'All right, all right! Yes I did as it happens. There was no point leaving it there. After all, *madam* had got no more use for it.' She gave a mirthless laugh. 'Anyway, she'd chucked it away, hadn't she.'

'Was it a little parcel?'

'Yes. A box in black shiny paper and tied with a pink ribbon, though that had mostly slipped off like it had been half opened, and some of the wrapping was torn. Still, it looked quite posh to me and I thought I might as well have it as not. And why shouldn't I? It's not as if we all get whopping wages!' She eyed him with sharp truculence.

'No of course not,' he agreed hastily. 'And what

61

did you do with it? What was in it?'

'Well I took it home, of course. Didn't have time to open it properly, did I? Not with your lot hanging around and shouting the odds. And then ... well I threw it away. It was just *silly*, disappointing.'

'So what was it?'

Mrs Perkins gave an impatient sigh and raised her eyes to the ceiling. 'A lump of anthracite – a filthy bit of coke, if you please. I ask you, what sort of stupid present is that?'

'So what sort of stupid present is that?' Greenleaf echoed to himself after she had gone. Then recalling the dead woman's reported response of 'Not another effing one!' he lit the delayed Woodbine and answered his own question: 'Another piece of coke to put in the coal scuttle, that's what.'

CHAPTER EIGHT

Rosy had spent one of those uneventful 'domestic' weekends; one when delayed chores were attended to, letters written, newspapers fully perused and a chance taken to enjoy a leisurely stroll in nearby Regent's Park. It had also enabled her to mull over the events of Friday night's dinner with Donald and his curious revelations about Marcia and the part she had played in Special Ops.

It was the last thing she had expected of her aunt, and surely went to show how little one knew of other people's lives and capabilities. But even more curious was the sleep-talking outburst re the coal scuttle! It was intriguing but also unnerving. Could there really be a connection between that cry in the night and Marcia's dreadful fate eight years later? Or was it simply one of those extraordinary coincidences that occasionally occur against umpteen odds? Uneasily she thought that unlikely, but shelved the matter to ponder her apparent mention in Marcia's will.

Did she really want to forage for mementos? Not specially. And besides, from what she remembered of her rare visits to the house, except for the snapshots of her parents there was nothing there of particular interest. Still, it would be nice to have the photos, and if Donald was right and Marcia really had remembered her surely it would seem churlish not to take up the offer.

Thus on Monday morning, and temporarily dodging Dr Stanley's hectoring requirements, Rosy made a hasty phone call to the executors.

Oh yes, the girl assured her, Miss Gilchrist had indeed featured in Marcia Beasley's will; she and Mr Beasley had both been mentioned in a codicil. Hadn't she received a copy?

'Of the will, yes. Not of the codicil,' Rosy said dryly. 'I have only just learnt about it from her former husband, Mr Donald Beasley.'

There was a pause while the girl inspected her files – or formulated some excuse. Eventually she said, 'Well, your name *is* ticked off, but there may have been some slight misunderstanding. I'll send it immediately if you–'

'No, that won't be necessary. I gather my aunt

simply says I may select a couple of items, mementos as it were. Perhaps you would just confirm that and give me a date when I could have access to the house.'

The girl replied that they were currently short-staffed, that she was *ever* so sorry about the oversight but if Miss Gilchrist cared to come to the office in a week's time she was sure somebody would be available to accompany her around the property. (Huh! Rosy thought, terrified I might nick something prior to probate – take a picture off the wall and replace it with another, I suppose!) A time was fixed. And she started to hasten back to the dramas of Stanley's heated domain but was waylaid by Leo clearly eager for a chat.

'I shouldn't go in there,' he warned, 'not just yet at any rate. He and Smithers have had a set-to and the old boy's having the vapours. Talk to me instead.' He beamed ingratiatingly.

'Why?'

'Thought you might have something to report about "things".'

Rosy hesitated, and then briefly gave him an account of her meeting with Donald and what the latter had revealed about Marcia's startling allusion to the coal scuttle. She was on the point of mentioning the SOE connection, but discretion prevailed and she merely said, 'It was obviously a reference to something worrying her *then* and which presumably has some special significance now. It's all pretty odd.'

'The husband sounds a bit odd too,' said Leo darkly. 'Are you sure he was in America when it happened?'

'Whatever do you mean?' Rosy exclaimed.

'What I say. It's nearly always somebody known to the victim, i.e. husband or boyfriend. If he is so keen to marry this smart American bird the existence of a flamboyant ex-wife popular on the casino circuit might be a bit of a liability. For all their sophistication, Americans can be pretty strait-laced about these things, especially "old money" Bostonians. And although Marcia's reputation might have been a bit wild – from what you've suggested – I doubt if *his* past was exactly like driven snow. Who knows what jolly tales your aunt might have had up her sleeve! I bet she could have scuttled his Priscilla chances if she had wanted. Definitely a potential hazard I should say, and getting rid of her could smooth his matrimonial prospects no end... Mark my words!' He grinned smugly.

'What nonsense you talk,' Rosy replied irritably. 'Total fantasy. I hope you don't treat your poor Mr Gladstone to such lurid speculation. Entertainment for the examiners, no doubt, but hardly likely to secure that doctorate.'

He saluted her in mock deference. 'Yes, ma'am! I stand corrected. Just trying to be helpful, that's all.'

'Well go to someone else's aid. I've got work to do,' she retorted, and continued in the direction of Stanley's lair.

She opened the door to be greeted by a barrage of protest: 'Have you *any* idea what I have been subjected to?' stormed her boss. 'He actually had the gall to suggest I omit the third footnote in my appendix as it was redundant to all but the culturally blinkered! And then when I naturally started to put him right on that particular point, do you know what he said? Can you *imagine?*'

Rosy shook her head knowing speech to be pointless.

'He *said:* "In fact I rather question the point of the appendix at all – it's not as if anyone is likely to read it." I can assure you, Rosy, the fellow is totally off his head! There's nothing for it, he will have to go. Can't you arrange it?'

She sighed. 'Probably not. But I *could* arrange a nice gin and tonic. It's nearly twelve o'clock. Would that do?'

He fixed her with a pitying glare. 'No it will *not* do. The tonic is flat and Mrs Burkiss still refuses to yield her keys to the broom cupboard. Thus, until we can obtain said articles all drink is out of the question.'

'Then in that case she will have to go as well,' Rosy replied briskly.

Later that afternoon she just had time to get to the Royal Academy for the closing hours of its Lautrec exhibition. The paintings had been ravishing, the crowds less so; and emerging into the sunlight she decided to amble in Green Park before catching her bus home. Entering at the gate by the Ritz end she started to walk slowly in the direction of Hyde Park Corner watching the squirrels and scenting the first whiff of autumn. But the sun was still warm and it was pleasant to stroll with only an occasional passer-by or scurrying dog for distraction. With Lautrec's scenes still in her mind she found herself conjuring up absurdly romantic images of *fin de siècle* Paris with its glowing gas lamps, gay elegance and raffish brasseries...

But the reverie was broken by a sudden clatter of heels on the path and the sound of her name being called. 'I say,' cried Amy Fawcett breathlessly, 'I thought it was you – just the person I've been wanting to see. What luck!'

'Oh ... yes,' Rosy replied guardedly, not over-eager to become embroiled in the girl's effusions. 'Er, how are you?' she enquired dutifully.

'Oh, pretty chipper,' Amy replied with enthusiasm, 'and all the more for seeing you!'

Why? thought Rosy with some unease, it's not as if we're bosom pals.

Aloud she said, 'I'm flattered, Amy. Any particular reason?'

'Well, it's the *fur coat*, you see.'

'Fur coat? I'm sorry, I don't quite understand–'

'Marcia's, your aunt's.'

Rosy stared nonplussed. What on earth was the girl talking about?

'Yes,' Amy continued still breathless, 'the one she said I could have. I quite forgot to ask you about it at the service the other day.'

Rosy was none the wiser but thought it fairly typical of Amy Fawcett to have considered mentioning such matters in the church hall with the said donor only recently delivered to her grave.

'I am afraid I don't know anything about my aunt's things,' she said politely. 'Have you asked the solicitors?'

'Well that's just it, you see,' replied Amy

earnestly. 'I am sure it didn't feature in her will because it was only just before her death that she said I could have it. I bumped into her at the theatre and she told me all about it.'

'The coat?'

'Yes – about the fact that she didn't want it any more as she had just ordered a fabulous new sable one from Calman Links which made her old mink look positively *ordinaire*.' She giggled and added, 'Frankly, I don't mind prancing about in a mink coat – *ordinaire* or otherwise – and Mummy said never to look a furry gift horse in the mouth!' The giggles expanded to gales of hiccupping mirth. 'Anyway, Marcia told me – in strictest confidence of course – that she had received an unexpected windfall (rather a big one, I gather), which was why she was going to chuck the mink and flaunt the sable... As a matter of fact she did say she had been thinking of giving it to *you* but had remembered you were only five foot three and would probably look like an Eskimo.' Amy gave a further splutter of mirth, adding, 'You have to admit, she was probably right.'

Rosy did not admit but inwardly agreed all the same. She had no desire for Aunt Marcia's cast-offs (furry or otherwise) but irrationally could not help resenting the fact that idiot Amy had been chosen over herself. However, she reflected, being a good decade older than Amy it was only fitting to be aloofly magnanimous. Thus piqued but poised she replied, 'Well that's absolutely lovely, Amy, but I really don't see how I can be of any help...'

'Oh, but you can,' exclaimed the other eagerly.

'I mean to say, I assume you've got access to your aunt's house. So next time you are there – making inventories or whatever it is people do at these times – couldn't you just sneak up to her bedroom, pick up the thing and come out with it casually over your arm as if it were your own?' (As opposed to yours, thought Rosy grimly.) 'Nobody would know,' the girl continued, 'least of all the solicitors and I would *so* love it!'

She gazed at the older girl, wide-eyed and hopeful; and Rosy, despite her irritation, thought, 'Oh well, anything for a quiet life. If it's that important to her I daresay I can get it when I go to pick up the photographs.'

Thus promising to do her best, and with Amy's shrieks of gratitude ringing in her ears, she hurried on towards Park Lane and the bus for Baker Street.

CHAPTER NINE

'That bitch never mentioned me in her will you know,' grumbled Clovis Thistlehyde, 'and she hinted she would on at least two occasions.' He flicked a small pebble in the direction of a basking duck.

'How quaint,' Felix remarked, eying the duck's discomfort and wondering whatever had prompted him to select this particular bench. Had he kept to his usual one under the trees the encounter might have been avoided. 'But why should you feature?' he asked. 'I didn't realise you were that close. Besides, why was she talking about wills – a bit premature, wasn't it?'

'Obviously not as premature as all that! And as to being close, well it depends what you mean. She did owe me a few favours I have to say.'

'Really?'

'I was what might be termed a reliable escort – always willing to supply a supportive arm, order cocktails and taxis, tip the maître d' – that sort of thing.'

'And pick up the tab?'

'Certainly not.' Clovis looked mildly shocked. 'I'm no mug! But quite apart from my social usefulness there was the question of the painting.'

'What painting?'

'You may recall that it was yours truly who was responsible for getting Marcia's head and shoulders on the front of Sotheby's catalogue, and–'

'But that was *years* ago,' Felix said, 'and from what I remember it was a very slim catalogue and a very slim exhibition – not exactly one of their major shows. And,' he added slyly, 'I also seem to remember that in the ensuing auction the portrait never reached its reserve. The public are fickle creatures, they lose interest so quickly. Where is it now – in some attic?' He smiled benignly. Clovis did not.

'It is not in some bloody attic! If you must know, she gave it to her sister who perished in the bombing along with the picture. The house was destroyed. Which is why she recently decided to commission another... Saw herself as a sort of phoenix, I suppose. It was to be a tasteful nude

70

and entitled *Marcia at Forty.*'

'She was fifty if a day,' murmured Felix.

'Immaterial,' snapped Clovis. 'The point is I had given her a few sittings and it was beginning to shape up quite nicely. In fact I had already contacted that new journal *Life Lyrical*. They are bringing out a special edition devoted exclusively to "Changing times: artists and their sitters in maturity". Marcia's new portrait plus photographs of the earlier one was scheduled as one of the major items. I can tell you, a brisk boost to sales that would have been! As it is...' He broke off, looking rueful.

'Well,' said Felix helpfully, 'perhaps if you just submit the preliminary sketches you could call it "Marcia Unfinished".'

Clovis gave a snort of mirth: 'Unfinished? She was finished all right, and how!'

Felix tittered but inwardly thought: What a boor he is. One of Marcia's better moves – to exclude him from her will. I am so glad.

'Mind you,' continued his companion, 'in terms of marketing, i.e. keeping one's name in the van of things, my having been the last person to see her may be of no small benefit. It never hurts to intrigue the punters. Little things like that can do wonders for the old reputation!'

'It's little things like that,' echoed Felix snidely, 'that can bring one to the scaffold.'

'My dear man,' laughed Clovis, 'no danger of that. I was off on my annual Venetian spree. Caught the boat train that very afternoon, and the cab driver can verify picking me up well before the ghastly event, as I made clear to that rather dreary

71

copper Greenleaf or some such. Oh no, I was en route to the seductive arms of La Serenissima. Didn't know a thing about it till I got back. Frightful shock!'

'Hmm ... of course. So I take it you didn't see anything?' enquired Felix.

'Such as Chummy brandishing a coal scuttle? No such luck – now *that* would have been something for the newspapers: *Artist provides vital clue to Marcia Beasley's killer. "You couldn't mistake a type like that," declared distinguished portrait painter Clovis Thistlehyde.*'

Felix smiled wanly, wondering if he could risk savouring the lush choux bun he had bought specially for his luncheon snack from the new French patisserie on Sloane Street. (Such a delight after the rigours of rationing!) The young man had been most civil. Indeed now he came to think of it, *most*. He smiled again, warmly not wanly. At the same time he decided to delay the confectionary treat: it would go nicely with a cup of Earl Grey at four o'clock. Thistlehyde was such a cadge and was bound to demand a piece. Yes, a much better idea: tea and a treat consumed *alone*. 'Divulge nothing': Cedric's warning echoed in his head. Well, presumably such advice could apply equally to a cream bun as to matters of a more complex kind. And regarding the latter, judging from what he had just gleaned, at least Thistlehyde would pose no threat. One mercy at any rate!

'Yes, that would have made a handy little headline,' Clovis prosed on, 'and what's more–'

'Actually,' Felix said hastily, 'if you don't mind

72

I simply must fly. I have a client at two o'clock and there's a delivery of orchids from Covent Garden. The new van man is utterly clueless and if I'm not there to supervise he'll leave the whole lot in next door's dustbin.' He rose and by way of apology added vaguely, 'See you at the Fawcetts' party, I expect...' Clutching the boxed bun and deftly sidestepping the ducks, he trotted briskly in the direction of Knightsbridge.

'Prissy little bugger,' thought Clovis.

In fact it was not a client that Felix was expecting at two o'clock but Cedric Dillworthy. Recent events had given the pair much to discuss, and as Felix hurried towards his premises he wondered anxiously what fresh insights his friend might bring to 'the problem', and indeed whether such insights might be advantageous. After all, it was no use having an insight unless it had some material application. And fond though he was of Cedric (well, on and off) the latter's observations did tend to favour the academic rather than the practical... And oh God, didn't one just need something practical now!

He checked his watch. Just time to change the flowers and titivate the drawing room. Not that Cedric would care. The pristine austerity of the professor's ménage was far removed from Felix's own rococo tastes. But it was all a matter of *principle:* abrasive topics needed emollient settings. And given the current situation, emollience was exactly what Felix craved.

'And are you *quite* sure he didn't notice anything?' Cedric asked an hour later.

'Evidently not. Attention obscured by his own ego, I imagine.'

'Let us hope so. The last thing one wants is that yahoo Thistlehyde shoving his hoof in matters. And unfortunately one can never be sure. Memory is a capricious thing – it suppresses and resurrects on a whim. Who knows what telling detail may have lodged in his subconscious. I remember an extraordinary case when I was doing a debriefing at the ministry just after Arnhem; quite Proustian really, and so–'

'Look,' said Felix testily, 'I do not need to be reminded of the quirks of memory. If Thistlehyde produces any "telling detail" then we are in the soup. The consequences could be dire.'

His visitor gave a discreet cough and observed that actually the consequences might affect Felix rather more than himself, but naturally should things prove difficult he would do his best to lend support – assuming that were possible.

Felix felt himself going pink with indignation and he glared accusingly at Cedric. Really, there were times when the man was utterly impossible! 'I take it that remark was intended as a joke,' he replied icily, and to steady his nerves stared hard at the porcelain Pierrot on the console.

'Of course, my dear fellow. Just testing!' Cedric smiled soothingly.

'Well don't fucking test!' Felix nearly yelled, but restrained himself with another glance at the Pierrot, and instead asked calmly whether the professor had formulated any further views on the matter since their last appraisal.

'As it happens I have,' replied his friend leaning forward intently. 'You see I've been considering that idea of yours – a crude tactic admittedly and a long shot, but if it works it could just be our saving grace... I'll see what I can do about it.'

Five days later Felix sat in Cedric's sitting room immersed in a game of solo patience. The hall door slammed and a few minutes later his friend appeared.

'Did you get it?' Felix asked, glancing up from the spread cards.

'Oh yes, no difficulty – except for the wretched salesgirl. I cannot imagine where they get them from these days. You would have thought that Gorringes might produce a better class,' replied Cedric.

'Really? What was wrong with her?'

'Most things. But principally lack of interest. She seemed less concerned with me than with her nails. When I explained I was looking for one with a square handle she said she had never seen that type and they were usually curved. And then when I pointed out that I knew for a fact the store kept them because a friend had bought such a one only recently, she shrugged and said she wouldn't know about that. To which naturally *I* said that perhaps she might gain enlightenment were she to investigate the stockroom.'

'And did she?'

'Gain enlightenment? I shouldn't think so for one minute ... but she did eventually produce the goods, as you can see.' Cedric gestured towards the large parcel he had deposited in the middle of the floor. 'It's the absolute replica of the original.'

'That's a relief, then – but I take it you didn't put it on your account this time?'

'No, of course not. Cash, naturally. You don't think I would make that mistake twice, do you?'

The other said nothing, contemplating the box. 'But you are sure it is exactly the same?'

'I've told you, the self-same model. Look.' Cedric cut the string and eased the object from its wrappings.

Felix inspected it carefully and then nodded in satisfaction. 'That should do the trick all right. We'll grubby it up a bit, put it by the grate, and Greenleaf and his heavies will never know the difference.'

'Let us trust things won't get that far. It seems rather excessive. Are you sure one isn't being a trifle fussy?'

'Were you ever in the Boy Scouts?'

'The Boy...? No, certainly not.' Cedric sounded slightly indignant. 'Why?'

'Because had you been so you would recall the injunction "Be prepared". You must admit it has a certain relevance.'

'Possibly. But I doubt if our predicament is quite what Baden-Powell had in mind.'

'It still holds good,' replied Felix grimly.

As indeed it did. For when later that week Sergeant Greenleaf called at the house asking to see the coal scuttle purchased from Gorringes four weeks previously, Cedric was able to flaunt the item with pride, even going so far as to point out the unusual design of its handle. 'What a thankless task,' he exclaimed, 'having to check all those grimy coal buckets, and how clever of you to have my name on your list. How on earth did you find it, officer?'

'Wasn't me,' replied the sergeant. 'That was young Harris's job. He likes doing that sort of thing – foot slogging with lists and ticking off names and such. Gives him a thrill. Can't think why... Anyway it wasn't too difficult. The thing was brand new and there are only two shops in the London area that stock that sort – Gamages and Gorringes. Eight scuttles were bought on an account and yours happened to be one of them. Funny coincidence really, you being a friend of the deceased. Of course, what Harris was *hoping* was that one of those buyers would not be able to produce the item – it having been left on the murdered woman's head. But as I told him, "Things don't happen like that, old son. It's a long shot too far!" And besides, I said, what about the three cash buyers? Odds on it was one of them... Still, he's as keen as mustard is Harris, doesn't do to damp his snout, all good practice.'

'Good gracious,' cried Cedric, 'but just think, he might have been right! I mean supposing I had not been able to show you the thing. Whatever then?'

'Ah well, then we would have had to take you in for questioning, wouldn't we, Professor?' Greenleaf gave a slow smile and wondered if he might wangle a cup of tea. He suspected not.

CHAPTER TEN

When Rosy arrived at the solicitors' office things seemed in a state of some disarray. Phones were ringing unheeded, an elderly female clerk was tutting and clucking, and a rather desiccated man was mopping his brow and muttering, 'Disgraceful, disgraceful!' It was unclear whom he was addressing and nobody seemed to care in any case. A young girl on the front desk smiled cheerfully at Rosy and said, 'It's all go, isn't it!'

'Er, yes, I suppose so,' Rosy agreed doubtfully. 'I have an appointment to visit my aunt's house, The Larches. She, uhm, died recently and...'

'Oh yes,' the girl said, 'I've got a note on that. Here's the key.' She fumbled under the counter and produced an envelope. 'That will get you in but it must be back by five o'clock. Mr Hughes is very particular.'

'But I thought somebody would be accompanying me—' Rosy began.

'Oh, not today they can't,' the girl replied, 'there's what you might call a *crisis*. As a matter of fact we get a lot of those and this time it's Barbara. She's had a turn and won't be in so we're short-staffed. You won't mind will you?'

'Er, no ... no, not at all,' said Rosy gratefully, grasping the envelope and preparing for rapid flight. 'Don't worry, I'll bring it back in good time!' The girl waved vaguely and picked up a nail file.

She walked into the shadowy hall where, just as she had remembered, the portrait of the two donkeys, Jack and Jill, gazed down benignly from their place above the staircase. Whatever one's view of donkeys, it had to be admitted that the picture was really a rather good likeness, and she wondered who the artist had been. Possibly one of the painting coterie Marcia had seemed so chummy with ... though presumably not the ghastly Clovis Thistlehyde, first encountered at a Royal Academy private view and to whom she had taken an instant dislike. It had been an event which Marcia had also been attending, along with a few cronies including the Clovis person. He had been holding forth loudly – patronising, consciously witty and employing a jargon clearly designed to confuse rather than enlighten. It had been a tiresome display and matters had not improved when detaching himself from Marcia's group he had made a beeline for Rosy and attempted to pick her up.

'What's a nice girl like you doing amongst us old codgers?' he had oozed, placing a confident arm around her shoulders and leering hopefully.

She had told him that even old codgers had their uses and would he kindly fetch her another glass of champagne. Alas, the requested champagne never materialised, for rather sourly he had wafted off to waylay a duchess in diamonds... No, she doubted whether Clovis Thistlehyde would ever sully his paintbrushes with anything as simple as donkeys.

She moved into the drawing room, its blinds half drawn, and which despite the once undoubted style was already wearing an air of embalmed indifference. Pausing diffidently in the centre of the Aubusson carpet, she scanned the stiff settees, console tables, tasselled standard lamp, and the art deco cocktail cabinet assertive in a corner. On its top stood a trio of half-finished bottles – gin, vermouth, Cointreau – a collection of dusty glasses and a tarnished cocktail shaker. These, plus a pile of *Tatlers* loosely stacked on a coffee stool, a tattered Edgar Wallace and a discarded cigarette box, were the only signs of the room having recently housed a human presence – unless one counted the photographs.

There were four of these, grouped together on one of the consoles: a snapshot of Marcia and Donald on a beach, looking more than fond and which must have been taken early in the marriage; one of a man she did not recognise (a lover?), and the two she had come for – the snapshot of her parents clasping herself and her sister as tiny tots, and a studio portrait of them on their own looking absurdly young (younger than herself now) giggling into the camera. She examined the photographs, studying the past with its faces frozen palely in time and already alien, and felt an unbearable spasm of loss... Yes, she would rescue those two all right. And taking the frames from the table she placed them carefully in the holdall; and then surveyed the room again.

Was there really nothing else she wanted? Ornaments, cushions, the art deco wall clock, the Japanese vase? No, not really: there was nothing there that couldn't be found at Heals, and certainly nothing of any sentimental value. But the photos were nice and would be nicer still enhanced by silver frames. She hesitated, wondering whether to add the one of Marcia and Donald. Left here it would presumably only be discarded, lobbed into a dustcart. She stared down at her aunt's bold features, the wide laughing mouth and heavy Veronica Lake hair – and caught unawares in a wave of inexplicable nostalgia, thrust it into the bag with the others.

Then, remembering her mission for the wretched fur coat, she was about to turn away, but stopped, gripped by the thought that it was presumably in this very room that the charlady had discovered the body. Where – by the window? Next to one of the sofas? Perhaps the spot where she was actually standing! She shifted uncomfortably, but with relief recalled the police sergeant saying it had been in the anteroom, the curtained alcove where Marcia kept her writing desk and the mammoth radiogram... No, she had no need or desire to investigate there. So retreating to the hall and the placid donkeys she started to mount the staircase.

On the landing she paused trying to get her bearings. She had only once before been upstairs – to comb her hair and use the lavatory – and now felt oppressed by the silence, the listless shafts of yellowing light from the small Pugin window, and the blankly closed doors. She opened one of these to find a bathroom familiar from her previous visit: a guest bathroom with green linoleum tiles, piles of faded monogrammed towels and an

81

elderly splay-footed bath harbouring a spider. The next door opened into a bedroom, but like the bathroom obviously a spare one intended for guests and of a bleakness Rosy had often encountered: north-facing, chilly and cheerless, with marble washstand, a bare mahogany chest of drawers and a couple of divans looking distinctly of the utility mode. The air held the faintest whiff of mothballs.

She wandered back to the landing and tried another door... Ah, much more like it. No mistaking this for a spare room! It was spacious, well padded and well mirrored, with modern chromium wall lights, thick cream carpet and an enormous bed draped in a coffee-coloured satin counterpane. Piled on a small chaise longue were a couple of hat boxes and three delivery cartons marked *Harrods* and *Debenham & Freebody*. Tissue paper and bits of string festooned the floor.

Rosy regarded these sombrely, curious as to her aunt's last purchases yet somehow disinclined to take a look. Besides, it was nothing to do with her: that was Mrs Gill's elected domain – it was her task, hers and that of the Red Cross people. She examined the dressing table with its plethora of pots, powder and scent bottles – Chanel, Schiaparelli, Molineux. She could take some if she chose, shove it in the bag with the photographs. Nobody would notice or care.

Surveying the choice Rosy felt guilty... Not because she was tempted but precisely because she was not. That was just it, she didn't want the damn stuff! The moment of sudden sentiment experienced in the drawing room did not revive itself here; and though surrounded by the intimacies of a life so recently extinguished, her sympathy was abstract rather than personal. Yes, she mentally saluted the wearer of the scent, the woman who had so eagerly unpacked the dress boxes; but she felt no real affinity. The link with Marcia was too fragile: her aunt had been like an actress seen from afar, notable but never known, never really *felt*...

Abruptly she turned from the dressing table to the wide mirrored wardrobe; and sliding back the panels started to flick through the racks of clothes. Jackets, skirts, two pairs of linen slacks, floral tea frocks, evening gowns, and finally coats: a couple of tweeds, a Burberry, and a grey seal-skin bolero. But next to them, encased in a plastic cover, was indeed the full-length mink. She removed it from its hanger, laid it on the bed and started to close the cupboard doors. But as she tried to slide the panels one of them jammed; something had got in the way – a shoe, a fallen coat hanger?

She peered beneath the trailing hems to the clutter of footwear below; a shoebox lay caught against the runner. Impatiently she pushed it aside, but as she did so the lid fell off to reveal not evening slippers or sandals ... but a large, black, glistening lump of coal – a piece of coal tied up in a jaunty tartan bow.

Rosy gazed down at it stunned by the raw incongruity. The adornment alone was strange enough, but what the hell was such an object doing among the silks and furs of her aunt's wardrobe? A scrap of paper was stuffed beneath the thing, and gingerly holding a corner of it between finger and thumb, she drew it out and studied the begrimed inscription: *To fuel the flames of memory,* the scrawled writing announced.

Absurd! Meaningless! The sort of vapid punning cliché one might find in a Christmas cracker... But perhaps that's what it was: some jocular souvenir, a piece of arcane festive ephemera. Come to think of it, she did remember Marcia babbling about a magnificent Hogmanay ball she had attended in Edinburgh just before the war. Didn't they do something with coal up there – first-footing or some such ritual? Yes, probably that was it – a rueful keepsake from gayer times. It was amazing the sentimental value people attached to bits of junk... And with a pang she recalled the squashed half-smoked cigarette found in Johnnie's wallet after his death, and which even now she kept lovingly wrapped in a box by her bedside. Again she felt a flash of empathy with the dead woman. But the flash was doused by the thought of the outlandish helmet gracing Marcia's demise, and for one risible instant it crossed Rosy's mind that her aunt might have been a carbon fetishist.

Dismissing such shameful frivolity, she glanced at her watch and firmly slid the door shut. Then lifting the coat off the bed she slung it over her arm, and without a backward glance left the bedroom and started to walk down the stairs.

'My God, but you gave me a fright!' a voice said. 'Thought the place was haunted!'

Rosy froze, her free hand clutching the

banister. She peered down into the hall and saw the crown of a brown pork-pie hat – and then the short neck and squared shoulders of the Collinger woman (or was it Bollinger?) whom she had met at Marcia's funeral and glimpsed earlier in the National Gallery.

'Oh, I'm sorry,' she called down nervously, 'I didn't realise there was anyone here!'

'No more did I,' replied Miss C or B accusingly. 'You're the niece, aren't you?'

By this time Rosy had reached the foot of the stairs and was able to confirm that she was indeed the niece.

'Hmm,' said the other, appraising her quizzically, 'I wondered if you would turn up again. Collecting some of her things, I suppose.' She gestured towards the coat on Rosy's arm.

'Oh, nothing really, just a couple of items – this coat is for someone else,' Rosy explained, and felt ridiculous for sounding so defensive. Why should she have to explain herself to this person? And then emboldened by her own annoyance, she said coolly, 'I am sorry, I know that we have met but I'm afraid I don't remember your name. You are...?'

'Vera Collinger,' the woman answered. 'My own memory being good, I know yours to be Rosy Gilchrist.' The latter observation was delivered rather as a magistrate might address a reluctant witness.

Rosy nodded, not sure what was expected, but inwardly asked herself what the hell the woman was doing in the house. 'You were obviously a friend of Aunt Marcia's,' she began tentatively.

'I knew her well,' responded Miss Collinger (a remark which, Rosy noticed, did not actually admit of friendship). 'We were together in the war and afterwards kept in touch on and off for old times' sake. As a matter of fact I lent her a number of books which I am rather keen to get back before the *scavengers* set in, hence my being here.' She indicated a bulky haversack by the hall table.

'Ah, good,' said Rosy politely (wondering uncomfortably whether the word 'scavenger' held a personal reference), 'glad you found what you wanted. But, er, how did you get...'

'Get in? Well I have a key of course, to the basement door. Had one for ages. I'm going to drop it off at the solicitors on my way back, they are on my route. No use for it now, not after what happened.' She paused, staring hard at Rosy as if challenging her to pursue the subject of the murder.

But other than murmuring something about how frightful it had all been, there was nothing that Rosy felt she wanted to say about the business, particularly to a comparative stranger and let alone one as abrasive as Miss Collinger. She shot a covert glance at the haversack. What books? Had Marcia been a keen reader? Apart from the Edgar Wallace in the drawing room she did not recall seeing any – crowded bookshelves being conspicuously absent. Her mother's voice came back to her saying laughingly: 'Despite my sister's brains she never reads a thing other than the columns of *Harper's Bazaar!*' An exaggeration no doubt; but all the same it seemed curious that Marcia should have been the recipient of so large a loan of Miss

86

Collinger's reading material...

'Anyway,' the latter said brusquely, 'I must be off. Things to do. Glad to have met you again.' (She didn't sound particularly glad.) And shouldering her literary swag she marched off in the direction of the basement kitchen, from where the distant slamming of the door announced her exit.

The house returned to its silence and Rosy was left standing irresolutely in the hall, clutching the fur coat and contemplating the now darkening donkeys.

As with the other intruder, she had retrieved what she had come for and there was nothing to delay her further. And yet she hesitated, curiously loath to detach herself for ever from surroundings which, after all, held no special meaning. So not quite knowing why, she found herself wandering back into the drawing room, its corners fading in the gathering dusk. But what still remained clear was the bright jacquard curtain dividing the rest of the room from the alcove housing her aunt's desk and radiogram. Earlier, knowing that this was where the victim had reportedly been found, Rosy had carefully avoided the area. But whether it was the startling encounter with Miss Collinger or simply an access of morbid curiosity, she now felt impelled to confront the space. She swished back the curtain and stared into its depths.

Just as she had remembered: the rather ugly walnut radiogram, its surface strewn with sleeved records, a two-seater sofa bearing the faint imprints of its last occupant (Marcia presumably), and of course the handsome Regency writing desk inherited from a maternal grandparent. A sort of moral duty, not desire, made Rosy briefly scan the carpet between it and the sofa where apparently the body must have lain.

To her relief there seemed nothing to betray any trace of the gruesome find – and she had no intention of going down on hands and knees to make a closer analysis. The forensics would have done that; the niece certainly wasn't going to! She recalled Leo's allusion to the truffle hound, and just as in the bedroom she had an unseemly urge to giggle. But the impulse was stifled by the sight of the desk's lower drawer half pulled out – or half pushed in. Either way, somebody (presumably the police) had been having a hasty rummage, for a jumble of rubber bands, paper clips and what looked like old postcards had spilt on to the carpet.

An instinct for order made Rosy automatically stoop to replace the things and close the drawer. But as she did so she saw something else on the floor: a curling mottled-green feather; such a feather, in fact, of the kind that Miss Collinger had sported in the crown of her hat at the two earlier encounters in the gallery and at the funeral. Rosy recalled the glimpse she had had of the woman's head and shoulders from the top of the stairs, and visualised the felt trilby with its characteristic raised rim. The image was clear in her mind, and this time there had been no feathery embellishment... Dislodged perhaps during its wearer's searches?

She stared at it in annoyance. The nosy old bat, she must have been in there. Looking for books in a shallow desk drawer? Doubtful. Most likely having a good old snoop. But snooping for what? Something specific? Or was the pursuit nothing more than the inquisitive intrusion of the living into the privacy of the dead, a prying rummage for unconsidered trifles? Either way the thought was distasteful. She glanced around for a waste-paper basket, and seeing none impatiently thrust the feather into her pocket.

Oddly unsettled and encumbered by coat and holdall, Rosy walked as quickly as she could to the turn in the road which would take her back to the solicitor's office. If she hurried she would just have time to return the key before the place closed and thus save herself a repeat journey the following morning.

When she arrived the premises were still well lit; but clearly the office girl was a zealous time-keeper, being already clad in hat and coat and busily yanking blinds and closing windows. Rosy slid the key across the counter murmuring mild apologies for being late, adding, 'Still, that's two keys from The Larches back in safe custody; this is the one for the front door.' She smiled.

'What?' said the girl absently.

'This is the front door key that your colleague lent me earlier this afternoon, but I gather a friend of my aunt was also intending to drop a Yale one back to you – for the kitchen door, I think.'

'Not as far as I know,' replied the girl indifferently. 'Maisie left at two o'clock and I've been here *ever* since. There's been no one in, except Mr Pensnip, and he's been stuck in his office at the back all afternoon... A good thing too,' she muttered under her breath, and stooped to adjust a stocking seam.

'Oh well,' said Rosy, 'I daresay the lady forgot and will slip it in tomorrow.'

'Probably,' replied the girl. Her tone carried little conviction or concern, and rather pointedly she snapped the clasp of her handbag shut with a loud click. Rosy took her cue and retreated to the street, where feeling justified by her impedimenta she hailed a taxi home.

CHAPTER ELEVEN

Twirling a monocle like a slingshot, Miss Collinger bellowed that one feather didn't make a summer, and that naturally what she *always* carried in her haversack were the Crown Jewels together with a King James Bible and copious pictures of donkeys. If Rosy Gilchrist had any other bright ideas she would be glad to hear them!

Bathed in a clammy sweat Rosy awoke and lay staring blearily at the first hints of light creeping through the gap in the curtains, and tried to recapture the shape of the dissolving dream. There had been more, definitely much more... But even as she willed the images to re-form, they slipped and melted into a muddled limbo, and she was left only with an aura of a hollow house, a hectoring voice, a slamming door, and in a distant bedroom the insidious stale aroma of a fading scent... Had the mink coat featured? She didn't think so. Nor, perhaps surprisingly, that peculiar lump of coal. What a ridiculous place to keep such an object – even if it was tied up in tartan ribbon!

Closing her eyes again, she stretched and turned on her side, her thoughts also turning back to the questionable Collinger woman. Questionable? Well, yes, she was rather – elliptical, not quite straight. *(Who of us is?* the question occurred; but the day was too raw for such reflections.) Still, perhaps after all, and like herself, the visitor had entered the house for a perfectly legitimate reason and there really had been books in that satchel thing... But if so, where did they come from? No bookshelves, no tables strewn with heaped-up volumes, no sign of any accumulation by Marcia's bedside ... and now she came to think of it, even the Wallace had been a library edition.

So if there weren't books in the bag, then what was? Had the woman simply been looting the house, picking up whatever took her fancy in the way of ornaments and porcelain? Possibly – but rash, surely. After all, there was the question of probate, and the solicitors would already have made an inventory of the most valuable items. She must have known that. Despite the gruff gaucherie Miss Collinger did not seem especially foolish, rather the reverse. (Rosy remembered how keenly she had regarded her in the hall, how quick she'd been to recall her name ... and how deftly she had dealt with – and glibly lied to –

91

Professor Dillworthy at Marcia's funeral.) Besides, what about the acid allusion to scavengers? A deliberate feint? Perhaps, but the note of disdain had seemed genuine enough. No, there must have been something *else* in the bag, neither books nor conventional valuables. What?

But the hour was too early for such probings. Why waste valuable snooze-time in pondering the contents of the Collinger rucksack? There would be plenty of time for that later – should she care. Perhaps the thing was of no account anyway, she mused sleepily as she began to drift into the final doze before dawn: probably just full of the old bat's groceries, nothing to do with Marcia...

The next moment she was wide awake, her mind suddenly focused. That was it! Of *course* the bag was an irrelevance: it had been full from the outset and had no link with the house at all. The tale of the books had been an impromptu pretext to conceal the fact that she was indeed after something specific, something likely to be in Marcia's desk, i.e. not artefacts but papers – letters, documents, even a diary perhaps. The woman would have arrived a good while after Rosy herself, and been on the premises for no more than ten minutes ... but long enough to get to the alcove and start raiding the desk. She must have been kneeling there when she heard movements in the room above, and hastily pocketing her find – or intending to continue the search later – scuttled out into the hall to confront whoever might be coming down the stairs; and the bulky haversack she had happened to bring with her, and which she had dumped by the table, suddenly became a useful prop in creating her excuse!

Impatient to confirm her suspicions, Rosy slipped out of bed and padded into the passage to the hallstand where she had slung her raincoat the night before. She scrabbled in the pockets and drew out the feather. Yes, it was definitely intended to grace a hat, its underside even bearing traces of adhesive. Surely her first instinct had been right: in size, style and colour the feather matched exactly the one she had seen stuck in Collinger's hatband at the funeral. She smiled grimly; the old trout had lost a feather, but ten to one was keeping the key for another try!

CHAPTER TWELVE

'Far be it from me to interrupt your investigations,' said Greenleaf's superior mildly, 'but are you quite sure that this artist chap is as clean as he sounds? I mean, it's all very well to assume that only a total innocent would be crass enough to boast he was the last to see the victim, but how do we know he isn't bluffing – using admission as a means of denial? It's been done before.'

'Not with a cast-iron alibi it hasn't,' retorted Greenleaf. 'We've checked his story about the taxi driver and catching the boat train at Victoria. He was on it.'

'But are you sure about the time of crime?' his boss persisted. 'I don't entirely trust that new pathologist, too cocky by half. After all, if he's miscalculated by just forty minutes we stand an even chance of pinning it on the painter.'

'Motive?'

'Oh, I expect something will emerge – sex probably, a lot of it about.'

'Not where I live,' replied Greenleaf gloomily.

'After all,' the other continued, 'didn't you say he likes blowing his own sexual trumpet?'

Greenleaf's imagination momentarily quailed, but he nodded.

'Well there you are, then – painter makes a pass, lady laughs like a drain, painter piqued and clocks her one. Simple!'

'She wasn't clocked, she was shot; and besides, what about the coal bucket?'

'Artistic licence. They get funny ideas, these creative types. Probably thought it would add a splash of colour or something. There's a chap called Dali, for instance, who's always–'

'Doesn't explain the pistol, he would have to have come prepared,' said Greenleaf woodenly, and wished his superior would go back to the canteen and stop wasting his time with damn fool comments.

'All right, so it wasn't a heat-of-the-moment thing. It was done with malice aforethought because she had been repulsing him for weeks ... or do I mean repelling?'

Greenleaf glared. 'Try rebuff, *sir.*'

'That's it, rebuffing him for weeks!' The inspector smiled happily; and then bending over Greenleaf's shoulder, murmured, 'Anyway, whatever the frigging word is, I'd like him brought in again, *pronto*. I'll be there myself this time, and we'll try breaking that "cast-iron" alibi. See to it, would you? Smartish!' Whistling under his breath, he shambled to the door, where he paused and said, 'As a matter of fact, I think "rejecting his advances" would be best. Don't you...?'

Sighing heavily Greenleaf reached for his notebook and started to scour the pages for the telephone number. As if he hadn't got enough on his plate without having to pursue the dead end of Clovis Whatsit! There were more pressing matters – as, for example, the bits of coal. The char's tale in itself had been curious, but only that morning young Harris had dug up another piece in the bottom of the woman's wardrobe – and just like the other, all tied up in ribbon, if you please! Greenleaf grinned: perhaps she had been having a liaison with the coalman – a possibility which would also conveniently account for the scuttle. Might that have been a final blackened offering from the injured lover? Death with a dusty flourish, a sort of *coup de charbon,* his ultimate homage! No, an appealing fantasy all right but hardly sustainable. Central heating: no coalman. But what about that note, 'To fuel the flames of memory'? What the hell was that supposed to mean? A fling with some arsonist or wartime firewatcher?

He pondered. Perhaps his boss was right and it might just be worth interviewing the witness again. At least he could be grilled over the woman's reaction when undoing the parcel. According to his earlier account it had given her quite a nasty turn. With a bit of luck she might have said something revealing, something the painter had omitted to mention... He stretched for the telephone.

'Ah, Mr Thistledown? Would you mind–'

There was a mild explosion from the other end.

CHAPTER THIRTEEN

Rosy left the museum, and turning right walked briskly through the quiet streets towards the hubbub of Tottenham Court Road. The day had gone well: agendas completed, questing scholars satisfied, and the affairs of the department's finance committee completed without let or hindrance. This last achievement was due largely to Dr Stanley who, through a mixture of stealth and grimly assumed charm, had finally persuaded Mrs Burkiss to relinquish the keys of the broom cupboard. The afternoon's meeting had thus been conducted in a spirit of gin and rare benignity. Indeed, so pacific had been the proceedings and so swiftly concluded, that Rosy found herself with little more to do, and Stanley, flushed with his recent triumph, had suggested she leave early. 'Go to the flicks, my dear. You have just time to catch the rerun of *The Seventh Veil* at the Odeon. Mason and Todd, what a combination!'

As it happened, Rosy had already seen the film, and while sharing Dr Stanley's enthusiasm had no particular urge to see it again so soon. But grateful for the gesture and not wishing to upset the fragile spate of bonhomie, she had smiled her thanks and left quickly.

Oxford Street before the evening rush hour was almost pleasant, and having no particular reason to hurry she amused herself with a bit of window shopping and wondered if when she reached Bourne & Hollingsworth she should try on the blue taffeta evening skirt she had noticed there the previous day. Reduced from seven guineas to three it seemed a bargain, and in any case might be just the thing for the Fawcetts' looming cocktail party.

This was an event she viewed with mixed feelings. The last time she had been invited to one of their jamborees had been nearly three years previously; indeed, it was there that Marcia had blotted her copybook with the French ambassador – or rather his wife. It had been the only occasion Rosy had seen Lady Fawcett at a loss, and it was an embarrassment she had no desire to be reminded of. There was also the risk of being subjected to further quizzical condolences about the 'ghastly Beasley case'. But in a masochistic way she quite liked the Fawcetts and they certainly gave good parties; perhaps after the sobriety of the last few weeks it would be good to re-engage with the 'social whirl'. She suspected that she owed her current invitation to Amy in gratitude for procuring the coveted mink coat.

As she walked she briefly pondered the coat – or not so much that one as its expensive replacement, the sable ordered from Calman Links (and whose cancellation the executors had been quick to order). It was true Marcia's tastes had always been lavish, especially where clothes were concerned, and financially she had been secure. But still, to jettison a perfectly elegant mink in favour of something quite as costly as a premier sable seemed a trifle extravagant even for Marcia... But then hadn't Amy said something about her having received a sudden windfall? Presumably that was the answer – though where it had come from Rosy had no idea. As far as she was aware no relatives remained to supply a sudden legacy (except for the distant Oughterards who were not known for their bounty). Football pools? Hardly! Perhaps she had sold a redundant heirloom... A mystery. But it was one easily dismissed, for by now she was near Oxford Circus and ready to pursue more pressing matters, the taffeta skirt.

Mission accomplished and having elected to carry the purchase herself rather than have it delivered, Rosy took the lift to the ground floor. She was about to make for the exit, but hesitated and then turned towards the jewellery department in search of something blue to match the skirt. The best addition might be a brooch to set off the cream silk blouse intended as its companion. She selected a couple of items from the counter display and, just as she was holding one of them against her shoulder to judge its effect, felt a firm tap on her arm.

'A larger one would be better. Be bold!' someone said. Rosy spun round and was confronted by a grey-haired woman nursing a dachshund. 'Yes,' continued Miss Collinger, 'if you are going to buy cheap jewellery there's no point in being mealy-mouthed. Wear it with pride.'

What? Like your feather? Rosy felt like retorting, but said instead, 'Oh goodness, what a surprise!' She was indeed surprised – and none too pleased either by the term 'cheap jewellery'. A bit much, in fact!

This time the woman was hatless (awaiting a new feather to replace the lost one?) and without the brim her squarish features seemed slightly softened. But the harsh voice was the same, as were the sharp eyes. In comparison the dachshund's were mild and docile. 'I have been following you,' she announced.

Rosy was not sure she liked the idea of being followed by Miss Collinger, especially given the Sapphic persuasion, but said politely, 'Ah – well, so now you've caught up!' She smiled politely.

'Yes,' the woman replied, 'I was going to telephone this very evening – found your number in the book; but just as I was turning out of Berners Street there you were crossing the road. Rather a jolly coincidence, don't you think?'

Couldn't be jollier, Rosy thought acidly.

'You see,' Miss Collinger went on, 'I had to push off rather quickly the other day – pressing matters you know; but there are a couple of things about Marcia I'd like to discuss if you don't mind. I suggest we confer in the tea room, they do an excellent seed cake.' The suggestion was less an invitation than an edict.

Rosy particularly disliked seed cake, and neither was she drawn to 'conferring' with Vera Collinger. However, too surprised to make an effective excuse, she gestured towards the dachshund and said hopefully, 'But I don't think they allow dogs in there, do they?'

'Oh yes,' was the firm reply, 'provided they are carried and kept out of the way. There's never any difficulty. Now, you get on with that brooch business and I'll go ahead and bag a table.' Hitching up the dog she turned briskly and took off towards the tea room.

Rosy stared at the two brooches on the counter and selected the larger. The wretched woman was right, it did look better. She sighed, completed the purchase and reluctantly followed her leader.

In between steady mouthfuls of seed cake Miss Collinger expatiated on this and that and nothing in particular, while Rosy thought, 'Well if this is "conferring" why am I wasting my time?' She sat smiling blandly and getting increasingly irritated.

And then the patter ceased and a direct question was fired: 'Exactly how well did you know your aunt?'

It was not the question as such that annoyed Rosy, but rather its phrasing, i.e. the term 'exactly'. The word carried a hectoring note, a note of command one might hear in a court of law or a military debriefing. It rendered the query officious and she felt reluctant to respond. However, clearly something was required, so giving a slight shrug she said casually, 'Oh, as well as anyone knows a relation, I suppose,' – an answer sufficiently ambiguous as to be meaningless.

A dart of impatience showed in the woman's eyes, but leaning forward she said in a kindlier tone, 'You see, I had the impression that latterly Marcia wasn't quite herself. Seemed to have lost some of the old spark: quieter, more pensive. It

100

was as if she was preoccupied with something but not saying anything. I asked her once but typically she just laughed, filled up the gin and said I was imagining things... But I wasn't, you know. I knew Marcia, and there was definitely something on her mind. I also think she was lonely, or at least felt isolated.'

'Lonely?' exclaimed Rosy. 'I hardly think–'

'Oh, I don't mean in a pathetic sense, crying into her pillow or anything like that – but it was as if she *knew* something that she couldn't divulge, something she was concealing. And it was this that was distancing her from old pals.'

'Such as yourself?' asked Rosy, intrigued as well as sceptical. (The woman hadn't seemed eager to claim close friendship on their first meeting.)

'Well yes, me, but others too... And so I rather wondered, Miss Gilchrist, whether you, being her only close relative, had also been her confidante. Had she, for example, mentioned anything to you ... or even,' she paused, 'entrusted something, perhaps?'

The latter part of the question was put lightly yet the gaze was fixed, and Rosy had the distinct feeling of something important being pursued of which she was unaware. She wondered to what extent the apparent solicitude was genuine. But she was also suddenly caught by the memory of Donald telling her that Marcia had spoken of a vital paper she wanted to send him – a document she wanted out of the country. Could this possibly be the point of Miss Collinger's question? One thing was certain at any rate: she could reply with absolute truth that she knew nothing of

Marcia's affairs and even less of anything tangible that needed to be 'entrusted'. Yet even as she formulated the response she felt a wave of annoyance and a reluctance to cooperate. Why should she reveal anything to this woman about her relationship – or non-relationship – with her aunt? It was a private thing, not for the ears of outsiders. And besides, she didn't like her much.

The other must have noticed the hesitation, for lowering her voice slightly she said, 'Naturally one doesn't wish to intrude, but given the circumstances of poor Marcia's death I think it is one's duty to be as honest as possible. Don't you? We owe it to her – so if you *do* happen to have anything or know of anything I am sure you will let–'

'Of course,' Rosy assured her earnestly, 'I'll tell the police immediately.'

Judging from the stony expression with which this was greeted (and as she had rather predicted), it was not the response being sought. But luckily further enquiry was forestalled by the dachshund. From under the table a cold and questing nose had pressed itself against Rosy's ankle, and she squeaked in surprise. It was a timely diversion and she made the most of it.

'Oh, is that your little dog?' she exclaimed. 'She did give me a surprise!' And lifting the tablecloth and thrusting her head down, she made the appropriate cooing noises. 'She's delightful – what do you call her?'

'His name is Raymond.'

'Oh dear,' Rosy laughed, 'with luck he didn't hear!'

'He hears most things,' the owner said tersely.

Still trying to dodge the subject of Marcia, Rosy pursued the topic. 'Raymond: what a dignified name for a dog! So much better than Bouncer or Billy or that sort of thing.'

'He is named after my brother,' Miss Collinger replied soberly. 'All my dogs have been – or at least, since the war they have.'

'Was your brother a hero?' Rosy asked brightly – and then immediately felt a fool, for she could guess what was coming next.'

'A dead one,' was the cold answer.

'I am so sorry,' Rosy murmured sincerely.

'Yes, he got shot up in Normandy in a sabotage raid. Jaw partially paralysed – nothing too dreadful by many standards. But it left its mark; he was never the same afterwards. Couldn't face Civvy Street, couldn't face women – or anything really. He was given a medal but it didn't do much for him. He started to drink and went, as they say, to the dogs.' She stared at Rosy, looking both at her and through her, before adding, 'And then one day he died. Couldn't cope. He was just thirty ... about your age, I should say, Miss Gilchrist.'

What could one say? Poor woman. Poor young man. And yet even as she thought such things, Rosy was ruffled by the pointed age comparison. After all, damn it, she had been in the war herself and didn't need lessons in personal empathy! However, she made the appropriate responses, but couldn't help feeling a twinge of resentment at having been dragooned into B & H's tea lounge to hear about Vera Collinger's family misfortunes, or indeed to be catechised about her own relations with Marcia. Unfettered she could have been at home by now gloating over the new skirt and telephoning her friend Diana for a long overdue chat.

The waitress appeared offering more tea, but to her relief Miss Collinger shook her head and requested the bill. She scrutinised it closely and announced triumphantly, 'Just as I thought, they have been forced to reduce the price of the seed cake; too many complaints, I shouldn't wonder. It's down to one-and-twopence again.' She looked at Rosy's plate. 'Aren't you going to finish yours?'

'Uhm, well I—'

'Good. In that case Raymond and I will have it.' She appropriated the piece, thrust a morsel at the dog and scoffed the rest. And then with Raymond once more clamped under her arm, she turned and said, 'Nice to have met you again, Miss Gilchrist. I don't suppose it will be the last time... And as said, if anything does occur to you about Marcia and what it was that was on her mind I should be most grateful if you would contact me. I'm not in the book but here's my card. Your aunt and I went back a long time – one is naturally concerned.'

'Naturally,' Rosy echoed taking the card, and added, 'I do hope you found what you were looking for in her house.'

'*What?*'

'In the house – the books you were searching for.'

Miss Collinger hesitated, and then with an uncharacteristic smile said, 'Ah ... yes, indeed I did, thank you. They are all back safely on my bookshelves! Now, I really must rush, got to take Raymond to the vet.' Dog and owner moved quickly towards the swing doors.

CHAPTER FOURTEEN

The decibel level was dire but the drink was good – a fact that doubtless accounted for the former. Lady Fawcett was one of those hostesses who throw parties like other people throw tantrums, i.e. with insatiable relish and single-minded abandon. And as with the tantrum throwers the occasions were frequent and finely orchestrated. For one not known for her tact or intellectual acuity, Lady Fawcett's grip on the finer points of party dynamics was formidable. It was, Rosy concluded, something bred in the bone, some sort of biological gift to obscure from the possessor the tiresome claims of the sensible and humdrum. Yes, the Fawcetts were the sort who, clad warmly in a cloak of myopic self-absorption, sailed through life on a tide of blinkered cheerfulness. Vapid yet resolutely good-natured, entirely confident and largely frivolous, they were both enviable and maddening.

'Well,' said a voice at her elbow, 'he's doing all right, I must say. I doubt if anyone will bother to throw a party for me when I reach seventy!' Clovis Thistlehyde gestured with the remains of a caviar canapé in the direction of a large man smoking a cigar and talking to Harold Gill at the far end of the room.

Rosy wondered whether she was supposed to disabuse him of the assumption but decided not to. Instead she said, 'Ah, but you are not one of the nation's major industrial magnates labouring to revive the country's fortunes after the deluge. Even Churchill paid him a tribute in the *The Times* the other day, and they say he's in line for a K.'

'You're right,' agreed Clovis acidly, scooping up more caviar, 'I'm just a bloody artist. Creative sensibilities rarely get the recognition they deserve. We live in an age of the philistine.' Glancing at his tie, Rosy felt he fitted the age admirably. 'Anyway,' he went on, 'I don't hold with all this title rigmarole; one is so tired of capitalist values.' He tapped a passing waiter smartly on the shoulder and appropriated a glass of vintage Krug. And then before Rosy had time to make an excuse and slip away, he had gripped her by the elbow and said in a low voice, 'You know, my dear, I was frightfully fond of your aunt. You have no idea how shocked I was to hear about it when I got back from Venice. All very disturbing – particularly as I was engaged on a *rather* fascinating portrait of her. I had only done a couple of sketches but it held such promise... and now, and now alas it will be lost for ever!' He gazed earnestly into her eyes, and then said smoothly, 'As a matter of fact I am looking for a replacement sitter and you look so like her, though *heaps* younger of course. I don't suppose you would care to...?'

'Replace Aunt Marcia on the podium? No thank you,' said Rosy, 'I feel the cold.' She turned away and promptly bumped into Amy Fawcett.

The girl screeched a welcome, and then in a mercifully quieter tone said, 'I say, has that old goat been at you as well? He's dead keen to get me into his studio to pose in the buff. Same question every damn time! Mummy says he's as mean as a monkey and that I should ask him what his rates are. Apparently that would shut him up quicker than anything.' She spluttered a laugh and asked Rosy if she had had a chance to talk to 'the birthday boy'. Rosy explained that she barely knew Maynard Latimer, having met him only fleetingly some years ago.

'Oh, we'll soon put that right,' breezed Amy. 'I'll introduce you. He's a great chum of my god-father. I'll see if I can detach him from Harold Gill – such a starchy old buffer. Can't think what they've got in common.'

'Oh, I don't mind Gill,' said Rosy, 'though I know Mrs rather better. They were neighbours of Marcia – rather long-suffering really – and were very helpful with the funeral arrangements and other practicalities.'

'Yes,' replied Amy vaguely, 'Mummy says that type is jolly good at things like that... Oh look! He's moved away at last. I'll try to catch May-nard's eye.' She embarked on a series of windmill gesticulations which fortunately her quarry saw before they became too frenzied. He waved back and made his way to where they were standing.

'Amy, your mother has surpassed herself. I am a lucky boy!' He beamed at them both and intro-duced himself to Rosy who murmured felici-tations.

'Oh well, when you get to my age one tries to

rise above it all. It's not good to be reminded of the onset of decrepitude. Mind you, I was reminded of it only too well the other day by my grandson. He really gave me a broadside!'

'But Dickie's so polite,' exclaimed Amy, 'and besides, no one could accuse you of being decrepit, you're far too handsome!'

Latimer grinned and wagged his finger. 'Now don't try that one, Amy! Oh yes, Dickie's polite all right, that was the trouble. According to his mother, for some reason he had been singing my praises ad nauseam and concluded by declaring to all and sundry: "Oh yes, I should like to be exactly like Grandpa one day – one day when I am a *very* old man too."' He gave a shout of mirth. 'Well that reduced me to size all right! Collapse of stout party you might say. And just when I thought I had been cutting such a fine figure in my cricket whites!'

There was general laughter and Rosy found herself rather liking him. Pleased with himself, of course, but rather fun all the same... He beamed at her and with no difficulty she beamed back.

'I see Rosy Gilchrist's here,' observed Felix to Cedric.

'Looking quite good too, if you like the genre, of course,' replied the professor.

Felix shrugged. 'But then we don't especially, do we?'

'Better than Marcia, that's for certain. And clearly Latimer seems to think so.' Cedric sipped his cocktail thoughtfully and added, 'Sharper too. I wonder if she knows anything.'

'About the murder?'

'I was thinking of the other matter.'

'Unlikely. They weren't particularly close. I can't see Marcia making her niece a confidante.'

'Yes, but one never quite knows with women, they get sudden whims. It's amazing what you can learn about female psychology, even in a short time. I was married to one once, you may remember.'

'Oh I remember,' said Felix dryly. The subject was an irritant he preferred not to dwell upon. Really, sometimes he felt convinced that Cedric introduced the topic just to needle him. It wouldn't have been so bad if the wife had been normal, i.e. easily ignored, but she had been so God-awful intrusive. Putrid in fact!

He scowled into his Martini and tried to think of nicer things, e.g. Clarence House's approval of his latest flower arrangement. He had struggled with it for hours, valiant in the face of footmen and corgis. Yet miraculously it had all ended in fragrant triumph. And of course *she* had been simply charming! A momentary vision of the coveted plaque danced before his eyes: *By Appointment...* He glowed at the possibility, wondering whether he should order a new door in readiness, and felt so much better. That is, until Clovis Thistlehyde appeared at his side and knocked into his glass.

Felix's scowl returned as he watched the liquid soak an immaculate cuff, and he said waspishly, 'A little unsteady, aren't we? Must be the constant smell of the turps bottle. They do say it turns one squiffy.'

'Nothing squiffy about *me*, Smythe,' Clovis retorted angrily. 'Taken rather a lot on board yourself, I should say. In fact, from what I've observed, one more Martini and we'll be stepping over you.' He turned on his heel and stalked as best as he could through the thickening throng.

'That wasn't very clever, was it?' Cedric observed. 'If Rembrandt has a sudden jolt to memory and something comes back to him he'll march straight off to that Sergeant Greenleaf and drop you in it.'

'He's not bright enough and there's no proof,' replied Felix curtly.

'Perhaps. But he has a low cunning and a vindictive spirit. It doesn't do to antagonise those who could do you harm. Do try to be a little more restrained.'

Felix gave a nonchalant shrug and lit a cigarette, but inwardly he was troubled. For he knew his friend was right; and worse still, something hung in his mind which he didn't really want to think about. The hypothetical 'telling detail' they had touched on earlier had been largely dismissed, but now as he thought back on things he knew that there had indeed been such a detail – one not so much telling as screaming to the heavens. And though at the time it may have passed unnoticed, with hindsight who knew what that Clovis cretin might not dredge up!

'How pensive you look, Felix dear,' cried Lady Fawcett as she glided past with yet another offering of foie gras filigrees. 'Have some of these, they'll buck you up no end. Now do tell me, how did things go last week with your *special* client?'

'Wonderful!' he enthused, regaining his spirits,

and proceeded to tell her in every floral detail.

The saga had just finished when there was a commotion by the double doors. 'Oh my God,' the hostess exclaimed, 'it's Auntie, I had completely forgotten she was coming. How awful!' Hastily apologising to Felix, she weaved her way to the far end of the room where she greeted the nonagenarian with dutiful indulgence.

Auntie tottered in on two sticks looking a geriatric million dollars and clearly seeing herself as the Queen of Sheba. With a whirl of an ebony stick she made brief acknowledgement of those present and with hawkish eye surveyed the room. Her gaze fell on the guest of honour, and a swathe was cut as she made solemn progress in the direction of Maynard Latimer. Once there she paused, prodded his ribs with a bejewelled talon, and with a leering grin boomed, 'Who's a naughty boy, then?' Delivered of this and without waiting for a response, she trundled away to one of the drinks trolleys, and ignoring its hovering minder scooped up a Bronx with unerring grip.

The encounter elicited discreet titters from those standing next to the industrialist, and someone was heard to observe, 'Well she's got your number all right, Latimer!' There was more laughter, but rather to Rosy's surprise, the target of the old lady's jest remained stiff-jawed. The earlier bonhomie seemed to have slipped, and just for an instant Rosy thought she saw a flash of anger in his eyes. She was slightly surprised. Why should one as confident as Maynard Latimer be discomfited by the coy banter of some frail ancient not long for this world? Indeed most men

111

would have been flattered to be thus teased and entered jauntily into the spirit of the thing. Why hadn't he? Had the old girl hit a raw nerve, wittingly or unwittingly pinpointed some current indiscretion – an illicit dalliance whose exposure might have embarrassing consequences? But if so, surely he had the social aplomb to affect an indifferent good humour: people like Maynard Latimer had nonchalance down to a fine art...

'Not too keen, was he?' murmured a voice in her ear. It was Professor Dillworthy.

As it happened Rosy wasn't too keen on Dillworthy, but she smiled politely and agreed that the guest of honour had seemed a bit ruffled.

'Ah, but then of course Adelaide Fawcett is good at ruffling people, been at it all her life. A malicious old bitch, actually... Doesn't let go either. Once she's got you in her sights there's no escaping.' His sour look belied the cool tone, and Rosy wondered whether he too was among Auntie's unfortunate elect. But she had no time to consider, for out of the corner of her eye she saw the Gills bearing down on her with faces of fixed solicitude.

'My dear,' Mrs Gill began, 'how brave of you to come, but very wise too. It doesn't do to be reclusive over these things. I always say that grief is like a riding accident – one must leap back upon the steed instantly and pursue the course! Isn't that so, Harold?'

Her husband looked doubtful and muttered something to the effect that Dahlia Drew had done exactly that only the month previously and it had cost her a broken pelvis, not to mention her husband's sanity paying the bills at the King Edward's.

'Oh, you're so literal!' Mrs Gill exclaimed impatiently. 'But Rosy knows what I mean, don't you, my dear? When misfortune strikes, resolution is all. And you are a living example to us!' She took an earnest bite from her canapé, regarding Rosy with kindly sympathy.

Rosy suspected that Mildred Gill had never been near a horse in her life, and was embarrassed at being cast in the role of gallant griever. She felt both fraudulent and guilty, and wished they could turn to lighter topics.

'She was a fascinating person, your aunt,' persisted Harold, 'a little eccentric perhaps, contrary even, and uhm – well, what you might call *forthright*, but...' He hesitated, groping clumsily, 'but wonderful with Temper of course. Yes, very good-tempered with Temper. Ha! Ha!'

'Sorry?' said Rosy, 'I'm not quite sure–'

'Our cat,' explained Mrs Gill. 'Marcia had a knack, you know, and whenever we were away she would take him over. In that respect she could always be relied upon. Well, I mean...' There was a confused pause. 'I mean she was reliable in every way, of course, but especially with cats.'

'Hmm,' thought Rosy wryly, 'is that to be Aunt Marcia's epitaph: *Always reliable with cats?* Still, given the circumstances, at least preferable to *She wore her laurels with style.*

She was about to thank them again about the funeral arrangements but was forestalled by Harold Gill saying darkly, 'Very funny business if you ask me. All very peculiar, keeps one awake at

113

night. At least, it does me – don't know about Mildred, she's made of sterner stuff, but personally I find it very unsettling. Can't help imagining–'

'Yes, well Rosy doesn't want to know what you imagine,' cut in his wife briskly. 'It's enough that the thing happened. It doesn't have to be dwelt upon; that's the province of the police, who I'm sure are doing a splendid job. At least, I suppose they are. That's what we are always told at such times... But what do you think, my dear? Are they making any progress?'

Rosy shrugged. 'I have no idea. And I doubt if they would say much to me even if they were.' She tried to think of a way of detaching herself. Well intentioned though Marcia's neighbours were, she really didn't want to spend further time with the topic, especially in the middle of Lady Fawcett's drawing room. The whole point of the party was enjoyment, and things had taken a turn which she could do without.

'The police, they move in mysterious ways,' observed Harold Gill tritely, 'but my wife is right, you show great fortitude. We admire your spirit.' (What spirit? Rosy wondered, discomfited by their misplaced praise.)

'And do remember,' chimed Mildred Gill, 'if there is anything else we can help you with at this sad time you have only to ask – anything you want to discuss concerning your poor dear aunt, and *we'll* be here.' She squeezed Rosy's arm and Harold gave a sombre nod.

Rosy thanked them gravely, feeling a heel and a charlatan. Mumbling an excuse she melted away in search of strong drink – a relief encountered

114

via the agency of Auntie.

The old lady waylaid her, and grinning through the mask of panstick and rouge proffered a glass of champagne. 'Hellish Harold and Meddling Mildred; you'll need this, I daresay,' she cackled.

Rosy did need it, but despite her earlier embarrassment, couldn't help thinking that Auntie was being a trifle unkind. Dreary, perhaps, but hellish and meddling? Hardly. However, she accepted the glass gratefully, and was about to make some polite remark, when the donor announced, 'I knew your aunt. I didn't like her.'

Rosy was startled and could think of only one thing to say: 'Oh dear.'

'Marcia Beasley,' the other continued, 'was bright in some ways, stupid and dangerous in others. Her end was unsurprising.'

'Really?' said Rosy, recovering herself and feeling indignant. 'And have you mentioned this to the police?'

'The police? Certainly not. I have never spoken to a policeman in my life and have no intention of starting now!' She sounded genuinely surprised.

'But if you think my aunt's death was not unexpected, don't you think they might find your views helpful?'

The old lady gave a careless shrug. 'People rarely find an old woman's views helpful, and besides I have no intention of doing their work for them. Coppers must earn their coppers,' she quipped smugly, adjusting the dazzling rocks at her throat.

'Auntie, your taxi has arrived, and you must be so tired!' Lady Fawcett cajoled. 'Edward will take you home, he's not had a chance to talk to you all evening.'

'So why should he want to begin now?'

There was no real answer to that, but handing Rosy her sticks and clutching the young woman's arm, the old lady permitted herself to be propelled towards the amiable care of her great-nephew. But just as she was going she turned to Rosy, and in a precise but barely audible undertone, said, 'You want to watch that one, Miss Gilchrist, a dubious piece of work if ever there was one.'

Rosy was bewildered. 'Who?' she whispered back. 'Do you mean Edward?'

'*No*, not that buffoon! Latimer, of course.' And she nodded in the direction of the broad shoulders and swirling cigar smoke. 'I remember him in nappies. Beastly then, beastly now.' Then turning to her hostess, she gave an imperious wave and in a louder voice declared, 'One of your better efforts, Angela: guests questionable but drink commendable.'

'Vicious old bat,' muttered Cedric.

CHAPTER FIFTEEN

It was too bad, fumed Clovis, pacing irritably in front of his easel. Not one single guest at the Fawcetts' soirée had shown the slightest interest in his current work; and the gold fountain pen all primed for a coyly requested autograph had proved redundant. As for that cocky little swine Spernal from the *Telegraph*, he had actually had the gall to say, 'How's tricks, Thistlehyde? Still churning 'em out?' The cheek of it! Jumped-up little pipsqueak. To think that at one time when he was being lionised all over Belgravia for his 'robust perceptions and startling technique' Clive bloody Spernal was some provincial cub reporter grubbing away on a local rag with a solitary School Cert. in Arts & Crafts. And now here he was rubbing shoulders with the Fawcetts and Latimers of this world, making fatuous quips on the *Telegraph's* arts page and trying to be clever with yours truly, C. Thistlehyde FAG. It was a bit effing much!

It was also, he brooded, a bit much that his offer to send preliminary sketches of the Marcia portrait to *Lyrical Life* had been summarily declined. Apparently it had to be the finished work or nothing, and since recent events precluded the former they were scrapping the whole project and replacing it with an 'exciting' profile of the 'young, dynamic and amazingly talented' Chico Boulez from Bolivia... Well, he resolved, if ever he had the misfortune to meet said Boulez from Bolivia he would kick his arse!

No, things were not exactly romping along at the moment. The Burley Gallery had been annoyingly vague about his inclusion in their next print exhibition, and even the bedroom zeal of his latest pickup was cooling visibly. She seemed to have developed a sulk and a propensity for yawning ... and was that a stifled titter he had heard the last time he had bounded from the shower, tackle all poised for the fray? Surely not. Doubtless it had been the girl's way of squeaking in ecstasy, though one couldn't be too sure...

Naturally it was all just an unfortunate phase but nevertheless it wouldn't do. The public (but increasingly girls, too, he had noticed) were becoming fickle and undiscerning – probably manipulated by that wasp Spernal. It was time they were re-educated, alerted once more to the special gifts of rapscallion Clovis Thistlehyde! It was largely Marcia's fault, of course. If only he had had the chance to complete it, that picture would have been a veritable star of contemporary portraiture and a timely reminder of his artistic worth. Indeed, it could have heralded what might be termed a Clovisian *risorgimento!* The critics would have gone crazy and even little shit Spernal forced to nod in his direction. But that had been typical of Marcia: always let you down at the last minute. He scowled, recalling bitterly her failure to introduce him to the renowned Sir Gerald Kelly, having promised for weeks that she would. With Kelly as his patron all manner of things might have been secured. As it was...

He jabbed his brush into the canvas making a particularly virulent splodge of vermilion, and ruminated on his last encounter with the victim. She had been all right until that damned parcel business – surprisingly cooperative, in fact. But after that everything had gone to pieces and it was obvious he would get no further. Ironic really: had he remained in the house she might be alive now and he could have finished the thing... But then, he reflected, whoever had come to do the deed might have finished him off too! He shuddered. No, looked at in that light it had definitely been a timely exit.

He continued brooding on those final moments with his sitter. And it occurred to him vaguely that there had been something unexpected in the hall when he had gone through for a pee, something that hadn't been there when he had first entered. Yes, there had definitely been something there. But what was it? Quite an ordinary thing, he thought; unremarkable and yet strangely incongruous. He frowned in concentration, mechanically adding another blob to the vermilion... Of course, that was it: there had been a *mackintosh* dumped on the hall table, thrown carelessly. A yellow mackintosh – well, virtually yellow, a sort of raucous ochre. Unusual really; he had only ever seen one that colour before. Yes, only once before and that had been worn by... He started. Good God! Was it possible? Surely not!

Brush suspended in mid-air, Clovis stood stock-still staring into space, his memory galvanised by excitement. The scene crystallised in his mind's eye, and what he was damn sure of was that the mac had *not* been there when he had returned from the bog... Good Lord, that could be a tale to tell! The previous session with that dreary policeman had been unfruitful, his information about the parcel failing to cause the stir he had hoped, and there had been nothing else he could contribute. But *now* there was indeed something he might report: a matter surely of vital interest!

The Greenleaf chap had telephoned earlier requesting a second interview. At the time it had annoyed him, thinking there was little to add to his previous statement and loath to become embroiled unless it led to his advantage. But things had suddenly changed. Oh yes, indeed they had! And if he played his cards right he might be a star witness. Once again he saw the bright glow of publicity: *Eminent painter's testimony nails the killer.* Yes, conceivably his date with PC Plod might just prove productive! He stood back, making a careful assessment of his handiwork, and then craning forward applied a triumphal flourish to the canvas.

'I say,' a voice said from the doorway, 'may I come in? Been caught up in one or two things, all rather a rush. Hope I'm not late.'

'What? Oh no, of course not,' the artist replied abstractedly. 'Sit down there for the moment, would you? I'm just putting the finishing touches to this. It's nearly done.'

'Artist bludgeoned to death in own studio!' screamed the morning headlines. *'Victim's body found drenched in paint and gore...'*

Disgusting, thought Lady Fawcett, biting firmly into her buttered toast, what extraordinary things happened to people! She poured a second cup of coffee, adjusted her reading glasses and settled herself more comfortably upon her pillows. What a relief there was nothing pressing to do until the visit to Barkers to help Amy choose a new hat. The girl had such execrable taste that if she didn't accompany her she was bound to pick something totally unsuitable. Doubtless there would be strife, so it was just as well she could stay a little longer in bed to muster her strength...

She glanced again at the newspaper, and this time her eyes grew round with disbelief. *'No,'* she gasped, 'it can't possibly be. Ridiculous!' Ridiculous, perhaps, but more than possible, for there it was, confronting her in black and white.

Slowly she reread the article and scrutinised the accompanying photograph of Clovis Thistlehyde. Taken at least ten years ago, she surmised, fifteen probably. She had noted at her party how his features were growing less than juvenile – getting very jowly, in fact. Still, one didn't bludgeon a man for losing his looks – at least, not generally. Presumably there was another reason. Suddenly bed and buttered toast seemed awfully boring, and throwing back the covers she reached for her wrap and then the telephone.

'My dear, have you *heard?*' she breathed.

Her auditor had not heard, and thus with the relish of the news-breaker Lady Fawcett proceeded to inform.

'I must say,' Leo observed, 'your associates do have an unhappy habit of being felled before their time. I shall have to watch out! Did you know this artist chap well?'

'One tried not to,' replied Rosy shortly. And then feeling guilty at her dismissive tone, she added, 'He was a bit tiresome, you see, rather pleased with himself: thought he was the cat's whiskers of the art world and a gift to any female over the age of seventeen. Boring, really. Still, one didn't take him seriously and he hardly deserved that fate.'

'Hmm. No more did your aunt,' said Leo.

Rosy sighed. 'No she didn't, not at all.'

There was a silence as they sipped their coffee and Leo hacked at one of the museum's joyless cakes.

'But you must admit,' he continued, 'it's an extraordinary coincidence that both model and artist should have the same murky end. Pretty damned odd, in fact. I bet the police are after a link, and the newspapers will be in their element. Better watch out, reporters at your door before you can say knife!'

'Well, they'll get short shrift,' Rosy snapped. This was exactly what she feared: pursuit by a posse of press clamouring for insights and 'angles'. So far she had managed to remain in the background of her aunt's death, luckily seeming to be of small account in the police investigation. And apart from the Fawcetts, some of her own circle and a few of Marcia's cronies, no one knew of her kinship with the dead woman – or cared. But the Thistlehyde killing was likely to add a fresh dimension to the whole business; and along with others associated with Marcia (and now indeed with both victims) she could well become a target of wider curiosity. God, what a prospect!

'Look, Leo,' she pleaded, 'do you think you could possibly play this down? I mean, I know it's all very intriguing, but I would rather you didn't say anything to anyone about my involvement.' She paused, and then said defensively, 'Not that I *am* involved, of course – well, not in any material way – but I just don't want idiots asking questions and nosing around making a meal of it all. I couldn't bear it.'

'I understand entirely,' he said solemnly. 'Just like Greta Garbo: methinks the lady wants "to be *alone*".' He turned up the collar of his jacket and with a theatrical flourish shaded his face with his hand.

'What? Oh really, you do talk rubbish!'

'It's working in this place, one absorbs the style. Now, tell me all about poor crummy Clovis and we'll put two and two together...'

'Pipped at the post,' lamented Greenleaf's superior. 'I thought we might be on to a good thing with that Thistlehyde fellow, i.e. either nab him for the murder itself or at least get him to spill a few more beans about what happened that afternoon. Now the geezer's gone and got himself killed as well. Nothing's bloody simple, is it?'

Ignoring the obvious, Greenleaf said, 'Presumably there must be a connection between the two, though it doesn't do to jump the gun – could be entirely unrelated, I suppose, different matter altogether.'

'Oh yes? So what's the motive?'

Greenleaf shrugged. 'Perhaps somebody didn't like his brushwork. Like you've said before, funny lot these artistic types; they get *passions* and take offence easily. Not normal like you and me. They've got what we haven't: *delicate sensibilities*. I remember that case of the Russian ballet dancer who defected here just after the war. There was a hell of a shindig in the chorus line because they didn't like the way he did his pas de whatsit, and one of the swans drew a knife, and then just as he was going to lift–'

'This is not some ruddy ballet!' fumed the inspector. 'It's a serious case of murder – very serious indeed, because if we don't solve it tootie-sweetie we're going to look even bigger charlies than we do already with the Beasley case. The super is starting to give me some very funny looks. There's got to be a link – and you and me, sonny boy, have got to come up with it pretty damn quick!' As if to underline the point he began to knock his pipe out among the biscuit debris on Greenleaf's desk, but stopped abruptly, and frowning asked, 'What do you *mean* the swan drew a knife? Where'd she keep it?'

'Down the front of her tutu.'

'Cor!'

Later over tea in the canteen the inspector asked hopefully, 'I don't suppose your chaps found any bits of coal hanging about in his studio, did they?'

Greenleaf shook his head. 'No such luck: just paint and Durexes, nothing to write home about.'

The inspector sighed. 'Thought not. Only dreaming. What about that flat of his in Islington – find anything useful there?'

'Not so far, but we've still got a fair way to go. It's the size of a shoebox but my God you should see the mess! It'll take some sifting, that will. Mind you, apart from clothes and such, most of the other stuff seems to be piles of old press cuttings and photographs. Took himself very seriously did our Mr Thistlehyde.'

'Presumably somebody else did as well,' observed the other dryly. He stirred his tea thoughtfully. 'There's just got to be a link somewhere... Perhaps he had been having it away with the Beasley woman and someone took exception.'

'On her side or his?'

The inspector shrugged. 'Either way – jealous boyfriend, jealous mistress.'

'But not much point in killing him if she was dead already. End of the affair – waste of time, really. Besides, from what he said to me when he came down to the station that time he hadn't been too keen on the deceased. She may have sat for him in the nude but I didn't get the impression that anything was *going on*. I think she was a bit long in the tooth for him. Liked 'em younger; easier to impress.'

'Perhaps, but somebody didn't like him. So get weaving and find out his enemies. Trawl through his address book – *when* you have found it – and dig out a list of his girlfriends, married or otherwise. Even if it wasn't to do with the Beasley woman it may have involved some other bird.'

'Yes, but one thing's certain – even if it was sexual jealousy it's unlikely to have been a woman who did it. According to the latest pathologist report the assailant used a rabbit punch before bashing the victim with the equivalent of a good-sized truncheon. Doesn't sound like a woman's work to me.'

A slow grin spread over the inspector's face. 'Good Lord, Greenleaf, a *truncheon* you say? If I remember rightly you weren't too fond of Mr Thistlehyde yourself, were you? Not your perishing cup of tea, you said...'

'And when did the news come through?' asked Cedric.

'Half past nine this morning,' Felix replied. 'Angela Fawcett telephoned. Caught me on the hop. I was just arranging the special displays and I was so unnerved I knocked one over. Water everywhere! It took me ages to mop up.'

'Then what did you do? Crack open some champagne?'

Felix gave a rueful smile. 'I think that little indulgence may have to bide its time. It doesn't do to count chickens–'

'But you must admit it does put a safer stamp on matters. One less problem to consider in the scheme of things... Or rather,' Cedric added slyly, 'one less problem for you. And talking of which, one trusts that awful mackintosh no longer survives to dazzle us all. Circumstances may alter cases, but as you've just said yourself, this is no time to be careless.' He knew it was hardly the moment for such needling; it was far from fair but sometimes he just couldn't help himself: Felix was the softest target!

Yet guilt mingled with mild disappointment when his companion ignored the bait, and gazing at the languid Pierrot murmured pensively: 'You know, he really was *such* a vulgarian...'

CHAPTER SIXTEEN

'I'd like you to interview her,' said the inspector to Greenleaf.

'Who?'

'This bint that Harris has traced, Thistlehyde's girlfriend. Apparently she was seeing him regu-

126

larly at the time of the murder.'

'Which one – his or Marcia Beasley's?'

'Both, which is why she could be useful.'

'What's she like?' asked Greenleaf.

The inspector shrugged. 'Young, much younger than him – and French. Works as a waitress at one of the Lyons Corner Houses. Leicester Square, I think.'

'What's her name?'

'Lulu – Lulu Lapin.'

'*Lapin?*' Greenleaf exclaimed. 'But that means rabbit. We had to learn a whole lot of those French words at school and that was one of 'em. Seems a funny sort of name, if you ask me.'

'I am not asking,' said the inspector. 'And since you are so very proficient in the French language you will doubtless pay particular attention to her *rabbiting* on, won't you?' He grinned complacently. 'Go on, quick about it. I've put her in the next room.' He cocked his thumb at the office across the passage.

Greenleaf sighed and unearthed his notebook. He had been hoping to get away early and pick up a fish-and-chip supper and a bottle of stout; instead of which for the next half-hour or so he was to be closeted with the fractured burblings of some foreigner. Just the ticket! He rose wearily...

On the whole, he reflected, Mademoiselle Lulu Lapin was a sizzler and far too good for the dead man. (A view she clearly shared.) But unfortunately her speech proved just as fractured as he had feared and twice as rapid. However, she was easy on the eye if not the ear and he found the interview mildly congenial ... certainly several notches above that of his recent encounter with the fearsome charlady!

From what he could piece together the girl was some sort of art student pursuing a course at the Courtauld Institute and working part-time as a Lyons Nippy to support her six-month sojourn in London. She had met Thistlehyde at a party in Soho (one of those louche Bohemian affairs, he surmised gloomily), and promising to introduce her to the best and biggest names of the London art world the painter had swiftly made her his girlfriend. Evidently it was a transaction she had grown to regret. 'Pouf!' Lulu Lapin had fumed, 'I meet not any nice big name – all *leetle* and big boring! And he, he big boring too – and leetle in *evair-ee* way!' She rolled her *rs* and her eyes on the qualifying term and enquired if Greenleaf understood what she meant.

He felt himself blushing, but with some pride enunciated carefully, *'Oui, Mademoiselle, je tout comprends.'*

This elicited shrieks of mirth and a spate of Gallic gesticulation of the sort he had witnessed only in the films. However, the gaiety ceased abruptly; and leaning forward she intoned darkly, 'You seenk I kill the monsieur?'

'Er, well not really,' began Greenleaf, 'but what I want to know is whether–'

'I did like to, but now 'ees too late. And besides, I 'ave better things to do. I am very busy girl. *Alors,* too busy to be 'ere all alone with Eenglish pol-eece and much fearful!' She took out a hand-kerchief and fluttered doleful eyelashes.

'You misunderstand me, Mademoiselle,' said Greenleaf hastily, 'I just want to know whether Mr Thistlehyde said anything to you about the afternoon he visited Madame Beasley. For example, did he mention seeing anyone there or close by perhaps?'

'But of course he see someone, he see Madame Beasley! She in nude – but she *old*, not like me.' Lulu gave a dismissive laugh and wiggled a shapely ankle before launching into a torrent of impatient French. Clearly the interview was a tiresome interruption to her crowded day.

'But,' persisted Greenleaf stolidly, 'apart from the lady in the nude, did he say if he saw anyone *else?*'

'No, no person else. Nobody.'

'Really? One might have thought that–'

'Except old fart with lawnmower.'

'*What?*' Greenleaf was startled. And then clearing his throat he asked if those had been Thistlehyde's exact words.

'*Comment?*'

'Are you sure that's what he said?' She nodded. 'But who was he talking about? Where was this ... er, person?'

She shrugged majestically. 'I know nothing, that's all he say. I must now go. I have important date with nice man, *verrai* beeg noise in art world. He take me to the Mirabelle. Not like Clovis to some meengy Italian joint!' She tossed her head scornfully.

Lulu's mind was clearly on higher things than lawnmowers, let alone their operators – of whatever ilk. And realising that nothing further

129

could be gained, Greenleaf released her to join the big noise in the Mirabelle.

'She obviously meant the gardener,' said the inspector. 'I'm surprised you hadn't already checked that.'

'Wasn't on your list, *sir*,' Greenleaf replied.

'That's as may be, but there's such a thing as initiative. Young Harris has got it – remember what he was like with those coal scuttles, followed up every single one of them.'

Greenleaf sniffed disparagingly. 'Didn't get us anywhere, though, did it? All in use and all accounted for.'

'Not the point. It's the *spirit* that counts and that's what we've got to show His Eminence up there.' He nodded towards the superintendent's office on the floor above. 'Like I said, Miss Rabbit must have meant the flipping gardener. Look for him.'

'No point. There wasn't a gardener.'

'Oh no? So how do you know that? You told me you hadn't checked.'

'Because according to the neighbours she didn't have one. It's one of the things that annoyed them. Mrs Gill said the place was in an awful state – long grass, unweeded flowerbeds, and fruit trees always hanging over their walls attracting the squirrels. Apparently they had hinted to her a number of times that she should get a chap in but she never did.' He grinned. 'I gather she told them the cat liked it that way, made him think he was a tiger in the jungle.'

The inspector sighed irritably. 'So who was this

old fart, then?'

Greenleaf shrugged. 'One of any number I assume...'

'Probably making it up,' said his wife that evening. 'Girls like that, they like attention. Tell you anything to get noticed.' She sniffed and gave a brisk swirl to the simmering mince.

'Girls like what?'

'Well, you know – foreign and going out with artists and such. From what you said he was old enough to be her father!' She tugged at her apron as if to underline the point.

'That's as may be,' answered Greenleaf eying the mince and wishing it were something else, 'but I don't think she wanted attention particularly. Seemed only too keen to get off on her date. Besides, I shouldn't have thought a French girl would be especially familiar with the word "lawnmower" – not what you'd call part of her normal vocabulary. No, it's more likely she heard it from the bloke.'

'Presumably like the other word,' said his wife tartly.

'Exactly.'

Greenleaf levered off the cap from a bottle of Guinness, and was about to pour himself a glass when his wife said, '*What* did you say the date was?'

'Of her murder? The fourteenth. Why?'

'It was raining.' She put the mince on the table with a clatter and turned to dish up the greens.

'So what's that got to do with it? And anyway, how do you know? It was weeks ago.'

131

'I *know* because that was the day I visited Daisy and it poured every step of the way there and every step back. Never let up for a minute. Soaked to the skin I was. Ruined the perm! It got all frizzy.'

'Which Daisy?'

'Well you don't think I mean the one in John O'Groats, do you? Daisy in Hammersmith, of course. It was her birthday and the rain put a regular dampener on things. We were going to have tea in her back garden. Had to go to the Palais instead.'

Greenleaf grunted. 'All very sad, I'm sure, but I still don't see–'

She gave a pitying sigh. 'If you knew anything about anything, Herbert Greenleaf, you would know that people do not mow their lawns in pouring rain, old farts or not. The wet grass clogs up the blades. So you see I was quite right, it's obvious the girl was lying.'

'Hmm... Or he was,' conceded Greenleaf. Then turning the topic, he said brightly, 'This mince – it's much better than it looks.'

'Well, *really!*'

The matter nagged him. Assuming that his wife was right about wet grass, and since Marcia Beasley was known not to have employed a gardener, the French girl's assertion did seem curious... Perhaps the encounter had been in the street. He wondered vaguely if the denizens of St John's Wood were given to trundling their lawnmowers along the pavements in pouring rain. It seemed unlikely. Yet despite his wife's conviction, it seemed equally unlikely that Lulu had been lying

– or for that matter Thistlehyde. Neither witness had struck him as being particularly sly or humorous. A bit of a mystery, really. But then it wasn't the only one. There was that message attached to the piece of coal in the woman's wardrobe: *To fuel the flames of memory.*

What memory? Obviously of some past event – but how *far* in the past? A few months ago – or years? What exactly had been Marcia Beasley's connection with fires? Perhaps if he turned Harris's muzzle in that direction something would emerge. Meanwhile he must get back to that friend of the victim, Miss Vera Collinger. The two women had known each other in the war. Surely she could come up with something useful, or at any rate more useful than anything the niece had so far offered. The young woman seemed to think she was above it all – a fact that had immediately led his superior to conclude she was bound to be implicated. 'Prime suspect, that's what,' the inspector had confidently pronounced. 'One gets a nose for these things. It's often the hoity-toity; they think themselves immune. You mark my words.' But as Greenleaf had suspected, there was nothing in their subsequent investigations to support such assurance, and he had managed to dislodge that particular bee from his superior's bonnet. The unfortunate thing was that as yet nothing better had taken its place…

CHAPTER SEVENTEEN

Rosy was more perturbed by the news of Thistle-hyde's murder than she had chosen to let on to Leo. She liked her colleague and yet was conscious of the age gap between them, and though he was fun she was hesitant to confide much of her personal life or feelings. True, sitting in the staff café at the museum listening to him speculate about Marcia and the fate of Clovis had been a diverting break in the morning's agenda; but now that she was at home alone and with time to reflect she felt once more a surge of unease.

Why on earth had foolish Clovis met that awful end? Certainly he had always been tiresome but hardly deserving of elimination! But then, of course, the same could be said of her aunt. What *was* it that the two had done to goad such violence? And could the killings really be linked as Leo had insisted? She sighed. Yes, probably.

Propping her elbows on the window sill she stared out at the sallow sky above the chimney pots and watched the leaves of the plane tree as they drifted listlessly down to the pavement. From somewhere there came the pinking of a solitary thrush, and at the street corner she could just discern the lights of the tobacconist switched on early against the gathering dusk. The smell of winter stirred in her imagination, and with a pang she knew she was afraid...

Pathetic! She retreated into the room, switched on the standard lamp, and settled on the sofa with a copy of *Picture Post*. But it was not the distraction she had hoped. Images of naked Marcia absurdly crowned on the drawing room floor swam into her mind and mingled with those of blood-soaked Clovis felled at his easel. With an effort she concentrated her mind on the page in front of her, but the scenes remained.

She cast the magazine aside and tried to rally herself. 'This will not do, Rosemary!' Memory of her mother's brisk voice rang in her ears. 'No time for mopes!' Rosy agreed but could do little. What was happening to her, for goodness' sake? After all, she had faced some pretty grim times operating that searchlight at Dover – terrifying really; yet she didn't recall feeling quite so disturbed then as she did now. Somehow she had always coped, risen above the fears, and facing the death-laden skies simply got on with the job. But this was different – a different sort of fear, and certainly a different situation... In the war the threat had been *known*, obvious, and she had shared it with others; it had been their common plight. But in this she was alone, and what at first had been shocking but manageable had suddenly taken on a macabre taunting insistence.

She tried to rationalise matters. Yes, her aunt had been murdered but there was absolutely no reason to think that the niece would be the next victim – and certainly the police had made no such assumption. And despite having known Clovis she was hardly what one would term a bosom pal. (Had there been any?) Careful to keep her distance she had ensured their association had been tenuous in the extreme. No, clearly she was not in personal danger. But all the same it was unnerving to think that being familiar with both victims, the killer would have an *awareness* of their shared circle and its associates. Indeed, could perhaps be one of that circle!

For the first time Rosy began to wonder if she should volunteer additional information to the police and generally show greater eagerness to assist their enquiries. Initially she had been loath to get more involved than was absolutely necessary; but the new turn of events put an even murkier complexion on things. It was surely her duty to be as useful as possible. When interviewed by Greenleaf about Marcia she had answered his questions and cooperated as best she could, but her contribution had been minimal – precisely because she had known so little. But since then things had moved on: there was, for example, Donald's story of her aunt shouting about the coal scuttle in her sleep, his revelation that she had been in the SOE in the war, and his tale of the document that she wanted to place securely. There was also Miss Collinger's evident search of Marcia's desk – possibly in pursuit of that same document – and the woman's insistent curiosity regarding Marcia's recent activities or preoccupations. And what about that lump of coal she had found in the wardrobe? The more she thought about it the odder it seemed – and it struck her that in some bizarre way it was to do with the coal scuttle.

Were these matters the police needed to know?

Perhaps they were aware of them already. Or perhaps not. Surely it would be sensible to take the initiative and tell them all she knew... Except, of course, she didn't actually *know* anything. Nothing tangible, nothing first hand: mere suspicions and other people's words. She pondered the odds of being seen as an officious crank seeking the limelight, as against those of upright citizen keen to assist the solving of two horrific crimes. Even-stevens, she concluded, and shelving the matter turned back to her perusal of *Picture Post*.

An item caught her eye: a retrospective article on the launching of the Festival of Britain accompanied by a graphic picture of the Skylon and the Battersea funfair on the banks of the Thames. Despite what the writer insisted, she knew that the most awesome ride had not been the Big Dipper, let alone the flying Zeppelins. It had been the giant Rotor, that huge rotating drum in which willing victims would be spun at dizzying speed until the floor dropped away, and by centrifugal force be then pinioned like helpless flies against its whirling walls. Yes, that had been the real excitement: to be stuck to the walls of the Rotor, screaming with delicious terror – and being sick as a cat afterwards. She had tried it out once accompanied by a friend's child. The child had been in seventh heaven; Rosy had not. She shuddered at the memory... And then shuddered again, as with cringing embarrassment she recalled the photograph in the *Evening Standard* of Marcia wedged between two sailors, her skirts up round her suspenders, blonde hair streaming in the slipstream and mouth gaping wide. The caption had read: 'Society gal has the ride of her life!' Yes, the memory was embarrassing all right, and yet it suddenly brought tears to Rosy's eyes. She brushed them aside impatiently and was about to go into the kitchen to forage for supper, when the telephone rang.

It was her boss Dr Stanley. 'I say,' he said cheerfully, 'I don't suppose you want to go to the pantomime, do you?' (The *pantomime!* With him? Was he mad?)

'Well,' she faltered, playing for time. 'It's a long time since I've been to one... But, uhm, isn't it a bit early? I thought they started later in the season.'

'It's at the Palladium. Apparently they were let down by some other production so they are bringing the pantomime forward a couple of weeks. My mother's got a spare ticket and we wondered whether...'

The idea of the pantomime with Dr Stanley had been startling enough – but with his *mother* too?

She started to stammer an excuse, but before she had gone far, he explained, 'There's a small family group organised. A mixture of adults and assorted children, and somebody has dropped out at the last minute and so I thought of you. Leo's going too,' he added. (A hopeful enticement?)

Still not sure of her reply, she gave a faint laugh and said she hadn't realised that such revels were his sort of thing.

'Me? Oh, I'm not going. No fear! This is all mother's doing. It's her annual treat to the family and she gets ratty if her plans are upset... So you *will* take the spare ticket, won't you, Rosy? Other-

138

wise I shall find myself being roped in... Look on it as my early Christmas present to you.' (Oh yes? When had he ever given her a Christmas present, early or late?)

'Well...' she began weakly.

'Excellent,' he boomed, 'I knew you wouldn't let me down. Come to my office first thing tomorrow and the ticket will be placed in your eager hands.' Before she had a chance to say anything he had rung off.

That's all I need, she thought grimly, one pantomime after another! Yet feeling oddly cheered she continued into the kitchen to sort out supper.

CHAPTER EIGHTEEN

The pantomime had been delightful, absurd as only pantomimes can be, and Tommy Trinder's act with the wheelbarrow hilarious. The young had been in their element, entranced with the elves and diminutive prancing ponies, and Leo and the other grown-ups had been transported by their own complicity in the make-believe.

Rosy took out her latchkey, the strains of the ludicrous ditties and shrieks of children's ecstatic laughter still echoing in her ears. Yes, an absurdly magical evening, and a rousing start to the Christmas season. So now all that remained was a quick nightcap and a warm bed before the next day and the rather less magical antics of her benefactor Dr Stanley.

She switched on the hall light and mounted the stairs to the sitting room. The door was closed as when she had left, but even before reaching it she could hear the music: one of her old records of Jack Buchanan and Bea Lillie singing 'Who Stole My Heart Away?'

She stopped, frozen with incredulity as the notes from the gramophone seeped out from within. (Later she would recall how, even in the midst of paralysed shock, the song still exerted its insidious jaunty charm.) She gazed at the door's white panelling, gripped by a fearful sense of unreality. No one could be in her flat at that hour, it was impossible! Besides, only she had access. But the music and the faint gleam of light from the keyhole said otherwise... For an instant she wondered if it might be Leo, somehow intruded to give her a stupid surprise. But even as the thought struck her she knew it was nonsense: he had taken a late train to the country to be dutiful among grandparents. She hesitated, biting her lip. And then in a spasm of boldness closed frightened fingers on the handle and flung open the door... The music swelled, and Buchanan's long held 'Who-oo—' flooded the passage and her ears.

The first thing she saw was indeed the gramophone – on the table with its lid propped up and the empty 78 sleeve and other records lying next to it... And then she saw the listener.

'It's wonderful, isn't it?' the man said. 'But you know, these days you could probably find it on an LP – or even get it transcribed. It's amazing what these boffins can do.' He moved the needle-arm back to its bracket and closed the lid. Then getting up from the chair he limped towards her, hand outstretched: 'My name is Richard Whittington – or, at least, that's as good as any, and given your recent activity one you are bound to recognise.' He smiled faintly. And too stunned to do otherwise, Rosy found herself mechanically reciprocating the proffered hand. Briefly she touched his fingers – four only, the thumb was missing.

'Oh Christ,' she thought, 'no thumb, sallow complexion and a heavy limp – it'll be Fu Manchu at the window next!' She wasn't sure whether she was going to scream with hysterical laughter or faint with fear. The walls of the room suddenly seemed curiously fluid and the overhead lamp unbearably bright. *Faint or flight, flight or faint?* her heart thumped out. He must have seen her indecision, for he asked politely if she would like some whisky.

That did it! Pulling herself together she said squeakily, 'If there is any whisky to be dispensed I think I can do it myself – it *is* mine after all!' She forced her legs towards the cabinet, and with shaky hand took the stopper out of the decanter and poured a small glass, annoyed at the uncustomary spillage. She was about to replace the stopper but hesitated. Was there an etiquette for such occasions?

Old courtesies die hard, and besides, it was a kind of distraction. 'You'd better have one too,' she muttered ungraciously.

'How kind,' he murmured, 'just a very small one.'

'What else had you in mind?' she wished she

was able to say, but somehow the words wouldn't come. She compensated by taking a large gulp of her own, which made her cough.

'I apologise for the intrusion, it's disgracefully late I know–' he began.

'How did you get in?' she snapped, suddenly steadied by the drink. 'And what in hell do you want?'

He shrugged. 'I gained entry in the usual way, with a key, of course. But as to what I want, well that is a trifle more complex – or at least it might be. That rather depends on you, Rosy.'

She gazed at him, taking in the slight frame, the pale skin, heavy brows and shrewd unswerving eyes. Annoyance at the familiar use of her first name was overlaid by something else: memory. She had seen this man before – talking to the Collinger woman at the National Gallery. Her eyes fell on the walking stick at his side. Yes, he had had that in the gallery too. She felt another pang of fear: suppose he tried to use it on her! But even as the thought came she dismissed it. She may not have been any taller but she was the more strongly built, and somehow he didn't look the type to threaten physical violence. All the same she felt deeply apprehensive. He had a quiet sinewy poise which she found unnerving... And how on earth did he have a key? And how did he know she had been to the theatre? Been watching her, obviously. But *why*, for God's sake?

'I don't know what you are talking about,' she replied as coolly as she could. 'Why should any-thing depend on me? Not that it matters because if you are not gone in two minutes I shall ring the

142

police.' But even as she made that last remark she felt how foolish it sounded. Didn't such intruders *always* cut the telephone wires – or so the books said.

He took a reflective sip of whisky and said mildly, 'Yes, I suppose you might, but I rather doubt it – not when you hear what I have to say. You see it might prove a little embarrassing. At least I assume so.'

This was not what she had expected: no snarl of scornful mirth as he taunted her with the usefulness of his trusty penknife, no dangling of severed flex in front of her frightened eyes. Instead the response was of the kind to be had from one manipulating a delicate deal in the boardroom: polite, apologetic but quietly confident.

'Embarrassing?' she queried. 'I hardly think–'

He nodded. 'It's your aunt, you see – your late aunt, Marcia Beasley. She's presented us with a bit of a problem; and I imagine you might find it unsettling if things were to leak out and your name be linked with hers – particularly as I gather you were rather a stalwart in the war.' He regarded her steadily, while Rosy stared back, struggling to grasp, to make sense of the man's words.

'What do you mean?' she asked faintly. 'What sort of problem, and why should it affect me?'

He sighed. 'Look, sit down, have a cigarette and I'll tell you a story.' The four fingers deftly snapped open a silver case. Mechanically she took one while with equal deftness he struck a match for her.

'Did your aunt ever mention to you she was in the SOE?'

'No, but I have been told that she was – by her husband, quite recently as a matter of fact. Well, he was her husband once, but they were divorced and–'

'Ah yes, of course, Donald – nice man. And did he tell you what her role was?'

Rosy hesitated, feeling uncomfortable. 'Not much – I ... er ... gather she was used as – as pillow bait. Isn't that the term for ladies who wheedle out enemy secrets in bed?'

He nodded. 'One of them. And Marcia did a lot of wheedling, very effective she was too. A number of fifth columnists fell for her charms. Indeed, some of her work was invaluable. Mind you, she was never really liked in the outfit – too self-centred perhaps; but she was highly regarded all the same. One of the top operators. Still, all good things come to an end.'

'What do you mean?'

'Blotted her copybook – rather badly. In fact, not to put too fine a point on it, she made a monumental cock-up.' The words were said quietly but Rosy thought she detected a flash of anger in his eyes.

'What sort of cock-up?' she enquired carefully.

For a few moments he was silent, and then said, 'At the time there were some who called Marcia Beasley a traitor, a turncoat. They still do, in fact. I never saw it in that light myself. She was just very, very stupid. Appallingly so. And it cost us dear – a few of us, at any rate.'

Rosy moistened her lips which had suddenly gone bone dry. *Traitor? Turncoat?* The words hung in front of her – leering, jeering, cavorting accusingly before her eyes. It couldn't be! Traitors were other people, not those one knew and certainly not one's aunt. The idea was obscene!

She ground out her cigarette and confronted him furiously. 'What are you *doing* coming here and saying these dreadful things? How dare you!'

'I dare because it has to be said. Because given the situation, it is expedient you should know. And as I have just indicated, I do not myself think there was any deliberate intention or malice in what she did. It was an ignorant blunder that led to, shall we say, unfortunate consequences...'

Rosy gazed at him, absorbing the words, noting the edge in his tone. 'So ... what did she do?' she asked falteringly. 'What happened?'

'What happened was that she fell wildly in love with the man she was sleeping with, i.e. one of her dupes. She got hopelessly tight one night, lowered her guard and in an access of maudlin idiocy, let slip the name of one of our sabotage projects in France. Her bedfellow – who I suspect had already sensed he was being set up – promptly relayed this to his spymasters. They in turn moved smartly and had the saboteurs ambushed before they could reach their target, a big gun emplacement on the Normandy coast.' Richard Whittington paused, and then added dryly, 'Fortunately for us the German defence unit proved almost as witless as your babbling aunt. They intercepted the raiding party all right, but in the melee messed up their hand grenades, and by the time they had sorted things out we had managed to escape with only a few casualties and no one dead or captured – which was just as well for Marcia.'

Rosy stared at him, transfixed. 'My God,' she whispered, 'and – and I take it you were one of these raiders, one of the casualties?'

He stretched out the shortened leg with its metal ankle brace. 'Scars to prove it.'

'I am so sorry,' she whispered helplessly.

He shrugged. 'Not your fault. These things happen – part of the hell of war. And after all, it could have been so much worse.'

There was no answer to that. But she had a question: 'The project, did it have a name?'

He gave a mirthless laugh. '"Operation Coal Scuttle", of course. An apposite title, don't you think?'

She nodded. As she had guessed. 'Yes, that rather fits with something Donald told me, about Marcia shouting the word in her sleep. It must have preyed on her mind.'

'Oh yes, it preyed all right. Preyed for the rest of the war and afterwards. Of course, it was never *proved* that the tip-off came from her, but it doesn't take long to sniff these things out, especially if you're trained in that sort of thing as we were. Eventually she admitted it to me herself, but by then I'd guessed anyway. She merely confirmed what one had thought for some time. Naturally I was angry – furious – to think she could have been so stupid. But I knew it wasn't malevolent or deliberate and so didn't bother to pursue things. No point really. I just made damn sure she was never used again. By that time the war was virtually ended anyway, her job was already surplus to requirements.'

'But,' Rosy said slowly, 'somebody *was* ready to pursue things, weren't they? Ready enough to take their revenge years later by killing her and leaving a calling card in the form of the coal scuttle!'

He shook his head. 'Not exactly.'

'What do you mean "not exactly"? Presumably that's what you've been telling me: that she was shot in revenge for this bloody awful thing she did! The police did say something about the bullet being from a service revolver.'

'Oh no, my dear Rosy, that's not it at all. The headgear was an irrelevance, a sort of additional embroidery it would seem, perhaps the gift of someone with an arcane sense of fun. Who knows? She was killed for something entirely different; something which I fear may have dangerous repercussions. She wasn't killed for anything she had done in the past but for what she might have done in the present – had she been allowed to live.'

'What on earth do you mean?' Rosy exclaimed. 'First you tell me she was responsible for some shameful action in the war, and now you say she was killed not for that but to prevent her doing something dastardly now, in peacetime... Poor Marcia, clearly a walking time bomb. Goodness, one had no idea!' The sarcasm of these last words belied the vortex in her mind. Could it be true what the man was saying? What sort of life had Marcia been leading? And in any case, why was he telling her about it... What the hell did he *want?*'

'What I mean,' he continued quietly, 'is that your aunt held data whose publication would have been more than embarrassing to certain people. She

147

had at her disposal facts that were they to become known to the British authorities would result at best in these people's imprisonment and at worst a walk to the scaffold. Most likely the latter. It was imperative she be silenced.'

'Oh yes?' said Rosy evenly. 'What data would that be? And how did they know she had it?'

He gave a sardonic smile. 'As you may have realised, despite her training in the SOE discretion was not your aunt's forte. Had she kept silent all might have been well, but foolishly she chose to disclose her knowledge – to the gentlemen themselves. She started to blackmail them. Big house in St John's Wood, extravagant evenings at the Ritz, trips to Deauville ... it all had to be paid for. Marcia was no pauper, but hedonism on that level invariably needs the occasional financial boost, and that's what she proposed giving herself via this lucrative little sideline.'

He passed her a cigarette which she declined, lit one for himself and watched the smoke as it spiralled to the ceiling. Rosy also watched it, thinking, 'Stupid idiot woman: first a traitor – or as good as – then a blackmailer. My God, Ma and Pa would turn in their graves!' She felt slightly sick.

'I suppose,' she said coldly, 'it was something sexual – the targets being past conquests, fringe members perhaps of her wartime "clientele" and now fearful of their respectable personas being blown apart.'

He laughed. 'Nothing so jolly. Besides, I told you, their necks are at stake. Even the prudes draw a line at executions for sexual dalliance. She held a more dangerous secret.'

'So what was it?'

'A bomb plot – against Churchill. But like several it was pathetically flawed and never got off the ground. Nevertheless, although clumsy the intention was serious. Those involved were Nazi sympathisers yet British to the core – pathetic hangovers from some of the drawing rooms of the 1930s, and harbouring a collective egotism masquerading as political ideology. As far as we are aware they and their like are now comfortably cushioned within the middle ranks of the British Establishment, fondly assuming that had Germany won the war its unbounded gratitude would have secured them even greater elevation. The very fabric which they were once so ready to destroy is now their cosy eiderdown. Your aunt was unfortunate enough to have learnt their identities and to hold tangible proof of their connection.'

Rosy was silent, not sure what to say – not sure what to believe. But, she reasoned, it had to be true, surely – pointless to invent such a tale; and despite the absurd soubriquet the man was clearly no fool.

'So where did Marcia get this information?' she asked. 'And in any case how do you know about it? What is your concern exactly?'

'My concern, Rosy, is to get their names and enough evidence to make them swing. Members of my family were in the French Resistance. These same reptiles, or at least a couple of them, were responsible for their capture, torture and death – along with several others. I may have overlooked your aunt's blunder of 1944 but I have no intention of letting this particular brand of treachery go by. They have survived so far but I'll find them in the end, whatever the obstacle ... or,' he added softly, 'the cost.' His fingers lightly stroked the cane at his side while the grey eyes fixed her with a hard impersonal stare; and once again she felt a chill of fear.

But she was also perplexed. 'You mentioned "we". Who are the others? MI5 or something? Or are you still linked with the SOE? Though I thought they were disbanded ages ago.'

He shook his head. 'Oh no, my days of office are over. I am now what you might call freelance – a much more convenient and flexible position, and one allowing infinite latitude! Suffice it to say that there are still one or two of us – ex-Intelligence – who are rather keen on flushing out our country's hidden predators, exposing those who have gone to ground and who now thrive under a cloak of national virtue. However, unlike Marcia our aim is not covert blackmail but something much more satisfying: public shame and retribution ... or, if necessary, private dispatch. The means are immaterial but one way or other we will destroy them.' He paused, and then said musingly, 'You could perhaps liken us to a pack of relentless bloodhounds sniffing the air for putrid spore and driven by a moral imperative.'

'Crikey!' thought Rosy; and felt like adding, 'and led by a limping Jack Russell with beetle brows and a snout for vengeance.' However, she kept the observation to herself and instead asked again how her aunt had obtained the information.

'From Flaxman – or Fleichmann, to give him

his proper name. He was the spy she fell in love with and blabbed to about the coal-scuttle operation. He slipped back to Germany shortly afterwards and, as you might expect, she never heard from him again ... that is, until about four months ago when out of the blue she got a letter from Munich. Apparently he was on his death-bed – literally. Legacy of an old war wound. And according to Marcia he felt creased up with remorse for the hurt and "embarrassment" he had caused her in the past! A case of death focusing the mind, I suppose. Anyway, by way of recompense and as a token of expiation, or what-ever you like to call it, he had sent her the German dossier on the Churchill plot con-spirators, plus an original coded message which they had sent to their Nazi masters confirming plans for a coup on the Maquis in Caen – the one that caught my cousins.'

'So what was she supposed to do with the stuff? Take it to the police?'

He gave a wry laugh. 'Oh, nothing so worthy! Dying lover boy suggested that she kept it as a hedge against the exigencies of old age.'

Rosy gasped. 'You mean she was supposed to...?'

'Exactly. He intimated that should she ever feel a pecuniary drought he was sure that those named would be only too ready to accommodate her requests for a little financial bolstering. According to Marcia, his exact words had been, "My dear, screw them for all they're worth. It's the least you deserve." And that, Rosy, is precisely what she did.'

'So how do *you* know this?'

'She told me. Rang me in Paris, gloating about her lucky windfall, the "stick of dynamite" that had fallen into her hands, as she called it. I couldn't quite follow what she was talking about at first. Sounded excited and befuddled at the same time. On the gin, probably. But after a bit of patient probing I suddenly realised what she was saying. I could hardly believe my luck. We had been after this little clique for years but couldn't get hold of their real names, let alone tangible evidence, and here was your dear aunt blithely crowing about it down the telephone!'

'How convenient,' Rosy observed dryly. 'But why did she bother to confide in you? Why not just get on with her own agenda, i.e. "screwing them for all they were worth", as apparently this Fleichmann advised?'

'It was probably her way of trying to make amends for her part in the coal-scuttle fiasco. Despite all that outward insouciance the thing troubled her badly. So once this data fell into her hands she evidently thought she would make double use of it – boost her bank balance and salve her conscience at the same time. The file and names were to be a kind of peace offering, a pro-pitiatory gesture to old comrades, and I think she was simply eager to let me know what she had in store for us... Ironic, really – same pattern of apol-ogy as her lover's, and not notably useful to either.'

'No, I suppose not,' muttered Rosy stonily, eying her glass and wondering how she could give it a discreet refill without replenishing the visitor's. 'Anyway, what did you do?'

'I met her, of course. Came over to London and

took her out to lunch – naively assuming she would produce the goods there and then. Not a bit of it!' He gave a grim laugh. 'Might have guessed she'd be difficult. Always was. "But darling," she said, "of *course* you can have the stuff, but all in good time. A girl's got to look after number one you know, and I am building up a nice little nest egg – in fact a socking great goose's egg. There's just one rather *substantial* transaction to organise and that'll be the last, it really will. And then you can have the whole bang shoot. Frankly, good riddance to it; but for the moment I'm not saying a word. You will just have to be patient." Well naturally I tried to persuade her otherwise but she clammed up entirely. I even tried plying her with some vintage Krug as a kindly inducement, but she waved it aside saying she was off to a matinee and didn't want to sleep through the first half. So I walked her to the theatre and we parted on the understanding that she would deliver the goods the minute she had completed the "transaction".'

'And then she was killed.'

He nodded. 'And then she was killed.'

There was a brief pause, during which Rosy struggled to arrange her thoughts – or rather, grappled to absorb what she had just heard. The whole thing was outlandish, surreal ... and yet, of course, so was Marcia's death, and that was real enough. Clearly the woman must have done something pretty wild to have provoked such an end, to have elicited such hate. Or fear. Yes, on the face of it blackmail seemed as likely a cause as any.

But even as these thoughts flashed through Rosy's mind they were overlaid by a much more pressing concern: why was the man disclosing this at all? He still hadn't said what he wanted of *her!* She looked up to see him regarding her intently. 'And so you see, Rosy,' he said softly, 'one rather needs your cooperation in the matter.'

She returned his gaze impassively and heard herself saying in a tone far more poised than she felt, 'Well, Mr Whittington, assuming that what you say is true, I am hardly in a position to co-operate with your plans – whatever they might be. You see, I knew next to nothing about my aunt – not latterly at any rate. We rarely met, and hadn't much to say to each other when we did. I don't mean that there was an active antagonism but we had so little in common. Our lives were quite separate.'

'Yes, I know,' he said casually.

Rosy was startled. 'What do you mean you *know?*'

He shrugged. 'What I say. She mentioned you when we last met.'

'Mentioned me! Whatever for?'

'She thought you might be useful. That is to say, as a convenient recipient for the bomb plot evidence. "My niece is a frightful prig," she said, "but like her mother, she's stubbornly discreet. And after all, there's nothing like belt and braces. I may keep a copy and send her the original as additional security until I've completed my negotiations. You can be assured it would reside in a rather stuffy safe house."'

Prig, stuffy? Rosy was enraged. But before she

had a chance to protest or produce a cogent re-
tort, the man continued: 'As it happens, I rather
assume she did no such thing; she was always a
procrastinator. But if by chance you do have the
thing somewhere I should be obliged if you
would hand it over.'

Despite the quiet conversational tone, Rosy
knew she was being given an order. But lack of
possession made her both bold and angry. 'Like
hell,' she snapped. 'You're right, I don't have it.
And even if I did it's not the sort of thing I would
give to a total stranger. I mean, you could be
anybody!'

Whittington cleared his throat and with a rueful smile said, 'Ye-es, that's me, I suppose. Anybody and nobody ... an apt description. Your
caution is exemplary. And as said, I don't believe
you have it. But' – and here the tone darkened –
'it is quite likely that others *may*, and I strongly
advise you to be on the qui vive. Watch your step,
change the locks – and get good ones this time, a
child could deal with yours! And above all
contact me if anything should in fact come into
your hands – or if anything unusual occurs that
could lead us to them. Any approach, however
vague or oblique, and I must hear immediately.
It's imperative. Do you understand?'

Rosy shrugged and nodded. 'If you say so. But
how should I contact you?'

He drew out his wallet and scribbled something
on a slip of paper. 'Any information or suspicions
ring this number in Paris. I or a colleague will be
there.' He got up abruptly, gathered hat and stick
and limped briskly to the door, where he turned,

and with a polite smile bade her goodnight.

'Just a moment,' Rosy called, 'being such a frightful prig, what's to stop me telephoning the police to report harassment by an intruder and telling them everything you have just told me?'

'Because, my dear, in your case intelligence precedes priggishness. You are far too bright not to see the implications of such a move.' He raised his hat and slipped from the room shutting the door quietly behind him. For some seconds Rosy stared at the vacated space, listening for the sound of uneven footfalls along the passage; but there was silence.

Like an automaton she tidied the strewn records, wound up the gramophone and revived the elegant swooping tones of Buchanan and Lillie; and for a few merciful moments reality was suspended... Yet even before the needle had moved halfway across the surface she pushed its arm back onto the bracket and slammed the lid. 'Oh Christ almighty!' she breathed.

Sleep of course was impossible, or so it felt. Possibly there had been an hour of snatched oblivion before dawn, but for most of the night she was awake, her mind caught in a whirligig of incredulity and floundering fear. For a while she had wondered if the whole episode had been a ridiculous delusion brought on by too much pantomime drollery. The idea was hardly comforting: of the two – mental muddle or the man's reality – she favoured the latter. But it was a reality she would have preferred not to confront.

The question was, what to do? Something

practical as he had suggested, i.e. change the locks? At least that might be a block to further intrusions of whatever sort. If he had slipped in so casually presumably so could *they*, whoever *they* might be ... always assuming that they really did exist. After all, despite his seeming intellect and decorous air the man might be a raving lunatic inhabiting a world of lurid fantasy in which she had a principal part!

But when she recalled his words the possibility seemed slight. He had shown a close knowledge of Marcia both past and present, and there was also that allusion to the matinee – a fact surely corroborated by Amy Fawcett when, according to her, she had told Greenleaf of Marcia's limping escort outside the theatre. Besides, what about her own glimpse of him talking to Vera Collinger at the National Gallery? The latter might be a little eccentric but she had her marbles all right and did not seem the sort to be found consorting with fools or fantasists... No, on the whole it might be prudent to take Mr Whittington seriously. But other than replacing the locks, what on earth to do?

He had been right. There was one thing she would not do: put the matter in the hands of the police. To make a public revelation of her aunt's wartime madness would be humiliation enough, but there was also this recent activity: concealment and squalid usage of the bomb plot evidence. It was a double ignominy. How *could* the woman have behaved like that? What idiocy, what selfishness ... what *dishonour!*

Suddenly Rosy found herself in floods of tears.

157

Fear for her personal safety might be coped with or suppressed. But the weight of shame, family shame, was intolerable. She thought of her mother and father during the war: patriotic to the core, humorously stoical, unflinching in the Blitz – and destroyed by it. She thought of Johnnie scudding through the clouds on those endless lonely missions, dodging the Luftwaffe, defying the scouring searchlights: wrapped in peril, armed with faith, and laughingly casual to the end. And briefly she thought of herself under fire on the south coast, and the guts and camaraderie of her colleagues, their gaiety and griefs. And she thought of the thousands who had sacrificed themselves in defence of their country at that awful time... And again she thought of her aunt's crass treachery and the later cynical withholding and use of vital facts for personal gain. No, just as Whittington had surmised, she could tell no one. Bloody, bloody Marcia!

CHAPTER NINETEEN

'Well one thing is certain – dead men tell no tales. Whether or not he saw your raincoat doesn't matter now ... unless of course he had just happened to mention it to Greenleaf *before* the event. Have you thought of that?' Cedric looked sternly at his companion. Felix had thought of that, thought of it several times. (Which was why he had got rid of the thing so promptly – a considerable sacrifice,

158

for he had loved its raffish colour.) But he did wish Cedric would stop going on about it! His nerves were bad enough as it was. However, he replied airily, 'I doubt it. If that were the case he would probably have approached me by now, bounded over lickety-split with notebook flapping.'

'Hmm. Could be biding his time, just waiting for the opportune moment...'

'Look, whose side are you on? You seem intent on fearing the worst and spreading alarm and despondency!'

Cedric looked pained. 'The point is, my dear fellow, one must consider every eventuality. It doesn't do to be complacent. Too much is at stake.'

'You can say that again! I wish to God we had never started this charade. It was a mad idea!'

'I don't recall your saying that at the time. At the time you thought it was just the ticket, your exact words being: "That will give her something to think about. Serve the bitch right".'

'Yes and she was better served than one had bargained for!... Oh my God, this is all too dreadful!' Felix covered his eyes with one hand and groped for a violet fondant with the other. He missed and sent the box cascading to the floor.

With a martyred sigh Cedric got down on his knees and gathered up the contents. 'I do think you could be a little more careful, they *are* my favourites you know.' Back on his feet and with the fondants placed firmly out of reach, he moved to a side table and poured two glasses of sherry. 'I think these might revive the spirits – *and* prepare us for the visit of friend Collinger.

What time did you say she was coming?'

'Seven o'clock.'

'Well as long as she's gone by eight. Remember, I did book that corner table at Quaglino's; they won't keep it beyond half past.'

'Oh, she'll be gone,' replied Felix confidently. 'Vera rarely hangs about – unless it's to indulge some female acquaintance or the dachshund. No, she'll keep to the point all right and then take off sharpish.'

'Well, that's a mercy, at least... But I take it she's not bringing the dog with her?' Cedric looked anxiously at his pale pristine carpet and was relieved when Felix shook his head, and then added, 'Tell me, doesn't it bother you rather that she calls the creature Raymond? Personally I would be a trifle piqued if one of my youthful amours were commemorated in that way, especially by a breed not known for its length of leg.'

'One rises above it,' Felix said stiffly. 'And since I am not given to hobnobbing with its owner more than necessary, our paths rarely clash.'

'But don't you think her brother might have minded – having a succession of pet canines named after him? I shouldn't care for it myself.'

'There were few things that Raymond minded except not being the centre of attention. He was one of the vainest men I have ever known – until, courtesy of Marcia, his disfigurement... And as for your own feelings, I very much doubt whether anyone would dub their dog Cedric, so I shouldn't let that worry you too much. Now if you would be so kind as to offer me a smidgen more sherry I should be *most* grateful!' He held out his glass which his host duly replenished. 'Actually,' Felix continued, 'I am not entirely clear why Vera is coming at all. It's hardly an enlivening start to the evening.'

'I told you,' Cedric explained, 'apparently the police are seeking a further interview and she wants to know exactly how much we have divulged of Marcia's past. It's the Raymond connection. She's worried that they will put two and two together and make ten, i.e. put her on the suspect list.'

'Hah! She's not the only one who's worried! But surely you told her that nothing had been said?'

'Oh yes, but she wants "clarification". Never trusts a thing, which is why she was so useful to Grimshaw's outfit in forty-two. Besides, she also intimated that she had made a startling discovery – just recently, I gather. Apparently quite a revelation; something to do with a document belonging to Marcia and she wants to pick our brains. Thinks we may know something about it.'

'What document?'

'I have no idea, but she seemed agitated.'

Felix sighed and cast a wistful glance at the violet fondants. 'How I *wish* things were back to normal: that none of this nightmare had happened and all I had to deal with were the perversities of the Covent Garden delivery men and giving floral pleasure to the Queen Mother. As it is...'

'As it is there is a strong chance of your being one of her daughter's special guests in Parkhurst or Pentonville.'

'Thank you, dear friend. You are such a joy.'

The doorbell rang.

'Ah, that must be the Sapphic invasion,' exclaimed Cedric.

Felix groaned.

Later that evening over coffee and Grappa in Quaglino's Cedric observed, 'Well that certainly puts a fresh complexion on things, I must say.'

'Frankly,' said Felix, 'if Vera is right and there really was a bomb plot against Churchill here in England then I think it's simply disgraceful!'

'The plot or Marcia's blackmail of the plotters?'

'The plot, of course. What Marcia chose to do in her spare time is no concern of mine.' Felix sniffed and looked righteous.

'Hmm. But what she did in her spare time during the *war* has been of some concern, hasn't it?'

'That's different, as you well know. Marcia's stupidity cost me Raymond – more or less anyway. As I told you, we had parted company by then but...'

'In particularly stormy circumstances you said.'

'That's as may be. But it's the principle of the thing. Because of her absurd obsession for that tasteless fifth columnist always propping up the Ritz bar – Flaxman or whatever he called himself – she contributed indirectly to Raymond's death, and the cow deserved to be reminded; she had kept it dark long enough! Still, I don't suppose she acted from malice, just crass pig-idiocy... But *these* people, whoever they are, were cold-blooded conspirators deliberately out to destroy the nation and support a Nazi invasion. Just imagine, by now those of us who were spared would be gabbling Kraut lingo and chewing their beastly sausage! And as for our dear royal family ... well, I can just see *their* replacements besporting themselves on the palace balcony: short-arse Goebbels ranting like a demented puppet and fat Goering waving and goose-stepping right in front of the drawing room windows. Ghastly!' Felix's face had gone quite pink.

'Oh, simply ghastly,' agreed Cedric. 'And I don't suppose any of them would have possessed the Queen Mother's floral sensibilities either. Just think, you might still be flogging faded blooms in the Mile End Road.'

'*Never* have I flogged faded–' Felix exclaimed furiously, and then noting his friend's sly smile took a hasty gulp of Grappa which made him hiccup.

'What you don't seem to have recognised,' Cedric murmured, the smile fading to a frown, 'are the *implications.*'

'Well I grant you, it raises some interesting questions. I mean, just who are these frightful people?'

'These frightful people could put us in even greater danger than we are in already. Hasn't it occurred to you that if the Collinger woman thought that you or I might have that document with the list of names or knew something about it, then presumably so could they. Marcia was fool enough to try blackmail and see what happened to her!'

'Oh my God,' yelped Felix turning white and strangling his napkin, 'I must demand police protection!'

'Are you mad? That really would blow the whole

thing to pieces. The police would be on to things in a trice. And I doubt if your illustrious patron would be prepared to bail you out. "Ex-jailbird" doesn't exactly embellish a Royal Appointment plaque. Besides, I have my own reputation to consider. Academia would never forgive me if they knew I was caught up in this sort of thing – and there would be no more complimentary invitations to lecture aboard the *Queen Mary*, that's for certain!'

'But surely if I *explained* it all to the police and told them why we had–' began Felix.

'I doubt if they would share your sense of humour, they are not noted for their jollity.'

'Actually,' Felix said, 'you may recall that it was not *my* sense of humour that devised the scheme; I was merely the clown who took his cue from the ringmaster and performed the sodding cartwheels.'

'But you enjoyed it, didn't you?' snapped his friend.

'Yes, I did at the time. But I am not enjoying it now. Not one fucking little bit I'm not!'

Cedric was about to form a response, soothing or otherwise, when his attention was caught by a couple who had just been shown to a nearby table.

'Don't look now,' he hissed out of the side of his mouth, 'but I think that's Harold Gill who has just come in – with someone not his wife on his arm.'

'So where does she come from?' asked Felix, who naturally had looked.

'Shepherd Market I should say.'

'Hmm, you're probably right. But why any self-respecting tart should want to align herself with

164

that old prune I cannot imagine. I mean he's not exactly God's most scintillating gift, is he? And where on earth did he find that monstrous waistcoat!'

At that moment the object of his censure glanced in his direction and was greeted with a wave and a smile of lavish sweetness.

'So where's his rightful lady do you think?' Cedric enquired.

'Very likely tucked up at home in St John's Wood, knitting feverishly and counting her blessings that she's free from the racket of Marcia's gramophone!' Felix tittered, suddenly feeling slightly better, and bending towards Cedric added, 'Yes, it's all a question of sitting tight, isn't it? Not allowing oneself to get ruffled, riding out the storm as they say.' He swirled the dregs of his *digestif*. 'In the circumstances I think perhaps I *could* just manage a weenie replenishment...'

CHAPTER TWENTY

By the morning such was Rosy's turmoil after her visitor's revelations that the prospect of resuming work at the museum seemed out of the question. All she wanted was to get away, or at least take to her bed with doors locked and curtains drawn – any means to suspend thought and escape the whole odious business. The last thing she needed was to listen to the irrelevance of Leo's quips or to soothe the querulous grumblings of Dr

Stanley. Indeed, she didn't really want to speak to anybody at all, just pull up the drawbridge and immure herself from the eyes of the world... Yes, that was it: she would call the museum immediately and report sick for at least a week.

But even as she moved towards the telephone she could hear her mother's chiding practical tones: 'Darling, don't be such a goose! Escape achieves nothing. Deal with it, you'll feel *so* much better!' The years rolled away and she saw herself at fourteen, tearful by the compost heap cursing the beastliness of things. She smiled. What on earth had it all been about? She had no idea. But it was not the first time her mother had offered such sage advice, and what held good then surely applied now. Retreat was futile and a waste of energy. Somehow she must confront the thing and cope as best she could.

Thus a little later she walked briskly through the museum's swing doors, settled at her desk, flicked through the engagement diary and with dulcet persuasion prevailed upon Mrs Burkiss to silence the Hoover and produce some coffee. The ensuing quiet was pleasant, the coffee less so. Enveloped in the reassuring world of work Rosy applied herself vigorously to the day's agenda.

For a couple of hours things went well, and visions of death, coal buckets and Wooden Leg Whittington were firmly erased from her mind. But by lunchtime her energy began to flag, and ducking Leo's insistent presence she bought a sandwich from the canteen and took herself off to a bench in Russell Square. Here she sat staring up at the windows of Faber & Faber, wondering how it was that such a staidly waistcoated man could write such stupendous poetry. A line came to mind: *I will show you fear in a handful of dust.* Mechanically she shifted her gaze to the ground with its greying grass and wispy shrivelled leaves, and for a moment caught a whiff of returning panic.

She bit into her sandwich and looked around for distraction. Other than cavorting squirrels and the occasional strolling couple there was none. With an inward shrug she discarded the sandwich in favour of a cigarette and said to herself, 'All right then, *deal* with the bloody thing. Work it out!' But how, for goodness' sake? One was so in the dark!

And yet glancing up at the blue sky, hearing the squabbles of sparrows and watching a crocodile of satchelled infants being marched from pillar to post, she felt the day itself benignly clear. Had the episode of the night really happened? Perhaps her initial reaction had been right: she *was* delusional! Yet if Marcia and wretched Clovis could be murdered just like that why on earth shouldn't the midnight visitor be real?

But was Whittington, or whatever his stupid name was, to be trusted? And what about the Collinger woman – what was her connection with the man? He hadn't mentioned her during his visit, but undoubtedly it had been she he had been with at the National Gallery. And besides, the woman was also clearly after something to do with Marcia. Surely they were in cahoots. Was Miss Collinger too stalking the bomb plotters? Presumably.

But then there was only his word that there *had*

been such a plot, or indeed that Marcia had been blackmailing them... But why go to such lengths to invent it, to break into her flat and spin such a tale if it weren't true? Evidently he hadn't intended to harm her – if anything, to warn her of possible danger. However, disinterested altruism was hardly his prime motive. Pursuit of the quarries had been that.

Yes, she mused, both he and Collinger wanted information and clearly saw herself as a potential source. Well she didn't have any – and even if she did, it was far from likely she would care to share it with them! Thus with that if nothing else resolved she got up from the bench and walked firmly back to the museum to face the task of sorting the chaos in Stanley's office.

The following day was free and Rosy indulged herself with a lie-in and a late breakfast. She was just wondering whether to skip the domestic chores and call a friend re the possibility of a trip to Staines or some other river haunt, when the telephone rang. It was Amy Fawcett. 'Ah,' the girl exclaimed breathlessly, 'so glad to catch you in. I've got something to give you. I've had it for *ages*, but I just didn't *realise* you see, though with luck it's not important. I say, I hope you don't mind?'

'Er, well I'm not really sure what–'

'So extraordinary,' Amy rushed on, 'I simply had no idea it was there. It's terribly well concealed and it's quite by chance that I noticed!'

'Noticed *what?*'

'The pocket!'

'I'm sorry, Amy, you are not making any sense.

What pocket?'

'The *secret* pocket of course, in that fabulous fur coat of your aunt's. Everyone admires it and even Cousin Edward said it makes me look a million bucks – and *he* doesn't dish out compliments easily.' She chortled.

'Well that's nice. But what do you mean you've got something for me?'

'Oh, I have – it's some sort of letter, an envelope addressed to you. It was in the pocket you see, the pocket *inside;* but it has been sewn so beautifully that you really wouldn't know it was there, and I found it quite by chance. I had draped the coat over the back of a chair in Scotts and it fell off, and when Edward was picking it up I suddenly noticed the tiny slit in the lining... Anyway, I know exactly what I'm going to use it for: a folded five-pound note! Mummy always says a girl ought to carry something extra for a taxi or emergencies *just in case*. But my five-pound notes always seem to go so quickly.' She giggled. 'But if I keep one in this concealed pocket I shall forget all about it until the need arises. Don't you think that's a jolly good idea?'

'Excellent,' said Rosy quietly, wondering how soon she could lay hands on the envelope.

'If you like,' suggested Amy brightly, 'I could bring it round to your flat and then perhaps we could go out for a bun at that nice tea shop just near you; although it wouldn't be till this afternoon as I simply must stay in to give Mr Bones a bath. He's getting so smelly and Mummy says she's not prepared to spend another day with him. So what do you think?'

Rosy was about to agree but suddenly had an awful vision of scatterbrain Amy either forgetting to put the thing in her bag or losing it somewhere en route. Anything might go wrong with that girl!

'As a matter of fact,' she lied, 'I have to come down to Knightsbridge this morning and shan't be very far from you, so I could easily drop in and collect it then – though naturally I shouldn't like to trouble Mr Bones and his ablutions.'

There was a squeal of laughter. 'Oh, Mr Bones will love it, he's *such* a show-off. And besides, it means I can treat you to a little fashion parade with the coat!'

Thus with the matter settled Rosy sat on the sofa and brooded. Could this letter just remotely be the document Donald had mentioned, and indeed the thing that 'Dick Whittington' was so eager to obtain – and allegedly others? If so, what was it doing in the pocket of the coat? Put there for safe keeping prior to posting and then forgotten? Or perhaps Marcia had deliberately changed her mind about depositing such vital details with her 'priggish' niece, and having shelved the idea been too busy or preoccupied to remove it. But of course it might be nothing of the kind: more probably something entirely mundane such as a theatre ticket going spare, a circular advertising one of the exhibitions periodically mounted by Marcia's art group, even a rare invitation to lunch or a cocktail at her club – although that was unlikely, and in any case such summonses had usually been delivered by an imperious phone call... No, she had a nagging feeling that it just might be the paper Donald had referred to, the paper Miss Collinger seemed so keen to get her hands on and the one avidly sought by Wooden Leg. Well, she thought grimly, one way or another she would soon find out.

She took a compact from her handbag and started to powder her nose before setting off to catch a bus to Knightsbridge. But as she opened the front door the telephone rang again.

'I say,' said Amy's voice once more, 'do you think you could do me a *tiny* favour, or at least, one for Mummy?'

'Er, yes of course. What is it?'

'You couldn't possibly drop in to Felix Smythe's flower shop on your way here could you? Mummy was there yesterday and she left her lovely new pink brolly behind. I've been instructed to pick it up immediately as she is convinced Felix will start using it himself and probably cause some awful damage to the silk.' She giggled. 'It was a present from an old beau and she treats it like the Crown Jewels! But you see I really must stay in to bath Mr Bones. Would you mind awfully? He's only round the corner from us. There's generally a blue Hillman parked outside.' Rosy laughed and assured Amy she would rescue it straight away.

Smythe's Bountiful Blooms was a discreet single-fronted abode just off Sloane Street, but its interior was sufficiently large to display an eclectically lavish assortment of exotic flora exquisitely arranged. The scent was overpowering.

She had expected to find Felix there, titivating this and that, but except for a dozing cat the place was empty. She looked around for a stray umbrella, examined the flowers and hovered expectantly, her nostrils assailed by blasts from tuberoses and autumn lilies. But then, rather curiously, she thought she could detect something else: the clubby smell of cigar smoke. It mingled with the surrounding sweetness, and for a moment she was a child again in her father's old study... But the moment was shattered by the sudden noise of footsteps and voices from behind the far door.

'Well the last thing we want is to have the niece sniffing out that coal bucket nonsense! I think she suspected something the other week when I was at the house looking for those papers. So for God's sake give her a wide berth!' The door was flung open and Miss Collinger strode into the room cheroot aglow. Behind her stood Felix. They stopped abruptly and gazed nonplussed at the waiting customer.

Rosy was the first to speak. 'What a coincidence!' she said brightly. 'Is little Raymond with you – or does the cat put him off?' She smiled in the direction of the snoring fur.

'Er, no, not really,' Miss Collinger replied vaguely. And then with more animation added, 'It's the cat's owner: Felix is convinced that all dogs are hell-bent on spraying his flowers. Pure paranoia, of course.' She gave a caustic laugh, cleared her throat and moved towards the shop door where she turned and issued a curt goodbye. For an instant Rosy thought she might raise her hat (now freshly feathered) and felt slightly cheated to be denied the gesture.

After she had gone there was an awkward

silence, and then Felix gave a light titter and murmured something to the effect that Vera was such an odd old thing but fearfully nice really, a claim that Rosy found hard to credit.

She explained her mission re the pink umbrella, and with visible relief he seized the matter eagerly: 'I know exactly the one you mean, my dear – *such* an elegant style. I've been guarding it with my very life! Dear Angela would never forgive me if anything happened to it. Won't be a tick.' He dived through the back door and re-emerged bearing it in triumph. 'There you are, you see, all safe and sound!' He beamed.

'Thank you,' said Rosy. 'And now you can tell me what Vera Collinger was talking about.'

'What?' The beam wavered.

Rosy took a deep breath and squaring her shoulders said, 'Why did Vera Collinger say she didn't want me sniffing around the coal bucket?'

'I'm sorry, I don't quite–' began Felix.

'Oh, come off it, you know very well what I mean! I heard her words exactly. She was talking about Marcia's gruesome death and the part you apparently played in it. Kindly explain.'

He regarded her in silence, blank-faced; and then with a resigned shrug muttered, 'You had better come upstairs, it's easier to talk about such things there.' He went to the door, reversed the *Open* sign and then led the way into the back and up the staircase to his private sanctum.

They sat at a small table by the drawing room window. At first he said nothing, staring out into the street fidgeting with his cufflinks, but then he

173

jumped up to adjust a bowl of roses on the mantelpiece.

'Look,' she said firmly, 'I would appreciate it if you sat down and told me whatever it is I need to know. There's not much time, I have to get to the Fawcetts.'

He frowned but resumed his seat. 'That's just it, I don't really see why you do need to know. After all, it's not my fault that you just happened to overhear a private conversation. Frankly, this is all rather awkward...'

'She was my aunt,' Rosy snapped. 'And whatever it is, I should be told. Perhaps you would kindly enlighten me.' She fixed him with a challenging stare.

He sighed, started to light a cigarette, stopped and said wearily, 'Oh well, if you must you must, I suppose.'

'Good,' she said brusquely. And leaning forward she took the lighter, lit the discarded cigarette and passed it back. He took a deep drag and began his tale.

'I met your aunt in nineteen forty-three when I was employed as a rather minor cipher clerk in MI5. In those days she was amusing and what used to be known as a "good-time gal", but via the grapevine one knew she was also engaged in some important war work–'

'On her back?'

'Precisely. You clearly know about that.'

Rosy nodded.

'At the time I was stepping out with one Raymond Collinger – probably the most handsome man I have ever met and certainly the vainest,

174

and if truth be told an absolute bastard. Still, it is amazing how entangled one becomes and for a time I really couldn't keep my hands off him!' Felix gave a little giggle and blew what might have been a commemorative smoke ring. 'But all bad things come to an end and the affair finished in fireworks and fury... Still, that is hardly the point. The point *is* that he was a first-class sapper and a member of an SOE outfit engaged on a sabotage raid in Normandy.'

'You mean Operation Coal Scuttle,' Rosy interjected.

'Yes, the Coalscuttle business. You *are* well informed. So you will probably also be aware that because of Marcia's infatuation with one of the German agents she blew the gaff and the whole thing aborted.'

Rosy could feel herself flushing with discomfort but said nothing, and Felix continued. 'The demolition party was ambushed but miraculously they all escaped including Raymond. But his face was badly scarred by a bullet; I don't mean that it was grotesquely mangled but he could kiss goodbye to those startling looks all right, *and* to his fawning satellites – of which I confess I was originally one. He spent the next few months in a nursing home recovering his face and his nerves and was then given some rather mundane desk job. When the war ended he became increasingly withdrawn – virtually reclusive. It was rumoured he had taken to drink, but nobody saw him for ages and then we suddenly heard that he had topped himself...' Felix paused before adding reflectively, 'I suppose he was what some would call a casualty of boredom and vanity.'

'Yes. But you think something else as well, don't you? I rather imagine you think his death was precipitated by Marcia, that she was ultimately responsible.'

'Don't you? If he had escaped unscathed things might have been very different. As it is...' He shrugged.

'But why on earth did you stay friends with her? Weren't you appalled?'

'I should say "friends" is a slight exaggeration. We were never close, simply rode the same social whirligig. But you see *then* one simply hadn't been *aware!* In fact Vera learnt of it only a year ago through some old SOE colleague and it was she who told me. Naturally I was shocked, as was Vera, and I was also very angry. But there didn't seem anything obvious to do. Police? Newspapers? Home Office? Hardly! The last thing I wanted was to get caught up in some tiresome brouhaha involving allegations for which there was no real proof – or at least none that was accessible. To attempt an exposure would have been tedious and doubtless ineffectual, and in any case considerably more trouble than it was worth, i.e. not good for business. And just think, if Marcia had retaliated with a smart lawyer I might have become a laughing stock!' Felix closed his eyes and shuddered. He opened them and added, 'Besides, it is far from wise to rake up – how shall I put it? – old *affiliations*. The law is sensitive in these matters and takes offence easily. The penalties can be distasteful.' The words were said quietly, but Rosy noticed their underlying bitterness.

'So you said nothing?'

'I discussed the matter with Cedric and we concluded that while it might be injudicious to put things on a public level, privately some sharp penalty might be exacted – something to make her sweat a titsy bit. So we devised a little scheme – or rather Cedric did – and started to make certain arrangements. To be perfectly honest it all seemed a fun idea at the time... Forgive my saying, but your aunt could be such an arrogant bitch. She deserved some grief!'

Ah, thought Rosy, that's what it's really about: not so much moral horror as personal hostility. 'Oh yes? And what form did your "arrangements" take?' she asked dryly.

'Well at first we thought of a series of anonymous letters but that seemed a trifle dull, and Cedric said she should be confronted with her guilt in a tangible *graphic* way – something theatrical to really make her yelp!' Felix gave a faint smile as if savouring the thought. 'So we kicked a few ideas around and it was he who suggested sending her gifts of coal at various intervals – carbon offerings to fit the code name of the mission she had so effectively ruined. These little parcels would be the preliminaries to the ultimate offering: an actual coal scuttle – to be delivered on or near the same date as the original betrayal. We felt the plan held a certain piquancy. Masterly really, wouldn't you say?'

'Masterly,' agreed Rosy. 'I am sure Aunt Marcia was thrilled.'

Felix sniffed and looked pained. 'Take that attitude if you like – but you have to admit it was not exactly undeserved.'

'No,' Rosy agreed soberly, 'not undeserved.' She closed her eyes. 'So then what happened? How did the scuttle get there?'

'I took it of course. The house was supposed to be empty. Marcia generally went to her art group on that afternoon and I had got the house key from Vera. The plan was very simple. I would carry the thing on my arm with my raincoat slung over it and walk into the house bold as brass. I intended leaving it in the middle of the drawing room – brazen on the Aubusson rug. But as it was I didn't get that far.'

'What stopped you?'

'Boorish Thistlehyde. I had just put my mac on the hall table and was about to go towards the drawing room when I heard voices from inside and somebody started to open the door. Not a happy moment, I can tell you! I just had time to slip behind the long window curtain, when out barges Clovis hell-bent for the downstairs gents. It was the last thing I had expected and I was terrified. Doubtless had I been George Sanders or James Mason I would have strolled into the drawing room, kissed Marcia on the cheek and uttered some droll pleasantry. As it was I dropped the bucket by the hall table, and while Thistlehyde was presumably still unbuttoning his flies grabbed my mac and skedaddled down the front steps like a witless rabbit.' Felix ran his fingers through his hair making it stand on end, and for a moment looked not unlike the creature he had described.

Rosy visualised the scene in silence. And then

she asked slowly: 'But the bucket – how precisely did it arrive on my aunt's head?'

'How should I know?' he replied defensively. 'I can assure you it had nothing to do with me!'

'Perhaps not directly but you took it there! Besides, aren't you curious?'

'In principle, yes. In practice my main concern is ensuring that my small part in this nightmare is kept well under wraps. How was I to know that some homicidal lunatic would appropriate my coal scuttle to adorn the head of his victim? It's too ghastly for words. And so humiliating if our little ruse ever became public knowledge. It would mean the end of everything!'

'You mean the Royal Appointment plaque?'

'Well naturally. But more than that – the entire business would collapse: Smythe's Bountiful Blooms would be withered weeds in a matter of days. I'd be lucky to sell a bunch of heather to a Gypsy! Just think, no royal patronage, no more columns in the *Tatler* and one would never be asked *anywhere* again. Oh my God, the shame of it!' There passed into Felix's eyes a look so stricken that Rosy almost felt sorry for him. But not quite.

'Rather a mean trick, if you don't mind my saying,' she observed tartly, 'sending those ridiculous lumps of coal and then sneaking into her house and–'

Felix gaped and then glowered. 'Mean trick? Well that's rich coming from one whose aunt betrayed her country! But yes, you are right, it probably was a mean trick; almost as mean as Marcia allowing her comrades to be ambushed and nearly killed, and of being indirectly

179

responsible for Raymond's subsequent suicide. Have you considered that by any small chance?'

Rosy was mortified and wondered how she could have made so crass a comment. And like Felix, but for far different reasons, she felt herself engulfed in a tidal wave of shame. 'I am so sorry,' she whispered.

There was a brief silence as Felix appeared to reflect; and then nodding graciously he observed, 'Ah well, everyone speaks out of turn occasionally, I daresay. Cedric does it all the time ... in fact, do you know what he had the *gall* to say to me the other day?'

Rosy didn't know and wasn't interested; but repentant of her earlier criticism assumed an expression of rapt curiosity. She needn't have bothered, for at that moment the telephone rang and Felix leapt up like a scalded cat.

'Oh my God, the Queen Mother's housekeeper,' he cried, 'she wants the gardenias replenished, I'd quite forgotten!' Rosy too was quite forgotten, as in a flurry of anguished anticipation he rushed to the phone, and smiling unctuously, crooned 'Of course, of course, dear lady, three dozen immediately – and I can assure you all as fresh as the proverbial daisy! I'll deliver them myself this very instant...' He threw down the receiver and turning to Rosy gasped, 'Must dash, duty calls! Let yourself out, will you? Just pull the door to, it's on a Yale.'

'But just a minute Felix–'

'Sorry, not a moment to lose,' he exclaimed, hastily checking his tie in the mirror.

'But *Felix*, what about the police? Surely they'll

find out about the coal scuttle. They can trace these things you know!'

He gave an impatient sigh. 'Not this one they won't. Cedric and I have dealt with it... Now for goodness' sake Miss Gilchrist, if you don't mind I have important things to attend to. We'll discuss the matter later *should* the need arise. So if you would excuse me...' He scuttled to the door, and a few seconds later frenzied feet could be heard thudding into the shop below. And then as she stood in the empty room feeling slightly dazed and clutching the pink umbrella, a car could be heard revving up in the street. She looked out just in time to see the blue Hillman moving away from the kerb, its back seat smothered in a mountain of white gardenias.

CHAPTER TWENTY-ONE

Ten minutes later, bearing the pink umbrella and her mind in a whirl, Rosy presented herself at the Fawcetts' residence.

'I am so glad you've come!' yelped Amy. 'We've got the awful–' She broke off and lowered her voice to a loud stage whisper. 'We've got the awful Gills here. They want Mummy to distribute the prizes at one of their charity things and won't take no for an answer. She's trying her best to fend them off in the morning room, but you'll see, they'll wear her down in the end – or at least *he* will. Keeps rambling on about the starving Pygmies. Frankly, if they are so small I shouldn't have thought that they would need to eat much... Actually I quite like Mrs, and she's awfully sweet to Mr Bones; but somehow the two of them together do put a bit of a blight on things. Anyway, we'll sneak up to my room and I'll give you a mannequin show. I've bought some super earrings to go with the coat, you'll love them!'

'Wonderful,' said Rosy dutifully as she followed the girl up the swirling staircase, 'and, er, you've got the letter, have you?'

'What? Oh the *letter*. Yes, yes of course... Wasn't it extraordinary my suddenly finding it like that tucked into the little pocket? It was such a surprise, the secret pocket I mean. I was telling Mrs G about it while hubby was twisting Mummy's arm over the Pygmies, and she said she supposed it was always handy to have a hidden pocket somewhere. And I said, "Oh yes, and so much more useful in a fur coat than in one's gym knickers!"' Amy emitted a shrill guffaw and ushered Rosy into the bedroom.

On the bed lay the mink coat, and next to it, on the right and left respectively, were the earrings and an envelope. With a deft movement Rosy appropriated the latter and slipped it quickly into her handbag. And then fixing the girl with a dazzling smile she exclaimed, 'Oh Amy, these are simply enchanting. Do put them on!'

The fashion parade lasted rather longer than she had bargained for. It wasn't simply the fur that was displayed but also numerous other sundry garments, each requiring special appraisal and approval. However, eventually the show was terminated by the appearance of a gleaming Sealyham: Mr Bones in his newly ablutioned glory. Thus the owner's attention was immediately diverted from dresses to dog, and it was with some relief that Rosy accepted the offer of a mid-morning sherry downstairs.

The Gills were on the point of leaving – but whether they had prevailed in the matter of the Pygmies Rosy could not be sure; though judging by Lady Fawcett's unusually harassed expression she rather thought they had.

'We were just talking about your mother's marvellous soirée the other week,' enthused Mrs Gill to Amy. 'It was such a delight, and lovely to meet old friends.'

'Yes,' answered Amy cheerfully, 'but rather a shame about Clovis Thistlehyde. Who would have thought that it was destined to be his final party!'

There was an embarrassed silence. Lady Fawcett smiled at nothing in particular, while Mr Gill cleared his throat and then said, 'Yes, all very unfortunate. Rather a nice fellow, I always thought.' (Goodness! Did he really think that? Rosy wondered.) 'Quite a good artist too, by all accounts.'

'I should have thought moderate,' murmured Mrs Gill.

'Well, my dear, we can't all have your discernment,' her husband replied. The tone was jovial but Rosy thought she detected a flicker of annoyance in his eyes. 'And in any case,' he added, turning to Lady Fawcett, 'it's all a question of *nil nisi bonum*. Wouldn't you agree, Angela?'

The latter hesitated looking perplexed, and then said obligingly, 'Oh, every time!'

'The thing is,' went on Amy, 'I can't imagine who would want to do him in – unless he *knew* something.'

'Knew what, dear?' enquired her mother.

'Oh, I don't know. Something. They generally do.'

'Who do?'

'Murder victims, of course. They are killed to shut them up and–'

'I daresay, but I really don't think we need to go into such matters now. It is hardly a savoury topic just before luncheon.'

The mention of lunch was grasped politely. 'I say, is that the time? We must be off,' exclaimed Harold Gill. 'A busy afternoon!'

'And so must I,' chimed Rosy, wondering why lunch should inhibit talk of murder any more than tea, dinner or any other occasion, but glad to have the chance to get away and investigate the contents of the envelope.

Thus once outside she was about to detach herself from the Gills and set off towards Hyde Park, when Mildred Gill took her lightly by the elbow, and with her husband busily engrossed in eying a well-endowed girl on a bicycle, exclaimed, 'Amy is such a sweet person. And how clever of her to find something of Marcia's for you in that coat. What a surprise! You must be delighted.' And then lowering her voice, she added earnestly, 'Particularly in the circumstances, if you see what I mean.'

Rosy agreed that she was indeed delighted; and

184

before any 'circumstances' could be further pursued she promised to keep in touch, and took off briskly in the direction of the park with the letter burning a hole in her handbag.

In fact she didn't get far, for despite a chilly breeze, curiosity directed her to a bench at the side of the path; and opening her bag she drew out the envelope. She stared down at the familiar scrawl: bold, careless, heavily nibbed. The letter was stamped and bore her address and full name, Miss Rosemary D. Gilchrist MA.

For some reason she was disappointed by the envelope's flimsy thinness. What had she been expecting – a wad of foolscap? She slit it open and drew out the enclosure. It was a single sheet bearing the following words:

and so, my dear Rosy, I trust I can rely on your discretion in this matter. As said, the document is more than explicit and could blow a number of reputations sky-high (no bad thing!) My intention was to send it to Donald for safe keeping but on reflection I think it is probably best left where it is, in the more domestic location. Were I by some remote chance to kick the bucket prematurely (not exactly my intention!) I daresay the Home Office might be interested in it, though I leave that decision up to you.

I don't really wish to speak further about this, and I am sure you will respect my wishes in the matter.
Affectionately,
Aunt M.

Rosy reread the message in baffled frustration. Obviously a sheet was missing, a sheet vital to the whole meaning. Of all the stupid things – how on earth could she have done it? The answer was, quite easily. Rosy could hear her mother's voice of protest: 'Oh Marcia – she's *so* careless! It is too embarrassing – she has just sent our donation for the church spire fund to the bookmaker, and your father's racing dues to the rural dean. We shall never hear the last from either. All she had to do was to read the envelopes!' Yes, Rosy recalled, there had been quite a little rumpus over that, and at ten years old she had thought it very funny. But the present careless oversight was far from funny. It was damned maddening... Where the *hell* had the woman put the thing and what exactly was in it?

Frowning she read the lines for a third time. How literal was the word 'domestic' – within the country or within the house? Either could apply, but if the latter, then getting further access to the place for an extensive and secret search was hardly feasible. She frowned. And then two other details struck her: the unfortunate use of the phrase 'kick the bucket' and the valediction 'affectionately'. She brooded upon the second. Was she a sentimental fool to accord it any significance? Surely it was merely a verbal convention – the sort of thing that aunts were supposed to write to nieces. Or had Marcia in spite of everything harboured some remnant of fondness for her, some vestige of familial sympathy? After all, it would seem she had meant to entrust her niece with some sort of serious confidence... For a brief moment Rosy indulged the thought and then impatiently dismissed it. Why on earth should she

186

want Marcia Beasley to show affection for her? The woman had been a traitor – and according to Lame Leg, latterly a blackmailer. Aunts had no business to behave like that!

She stared angrily at a foraging pigeon and stuffed the letter back in her handbag, and was about to get up, when for no apparent reason she thought of the Fawcetts and Amy's giggling comments on Thistlehyde: *I can't imagine who would want to do him in, unless he knew something... Murder victims, of course. They are killed to shut them up...* So what had Clovis known? Something connected with Marcia's murder? But if so, what and how?

'Well, you do look browned off,' a voice observed cheerfully. 'Lost a quid and found sixpence as they say!' Rosy looked up startled, and was confronted by the tall figure of Maynard Latimer, debonair in tweeds and trilby.

'It's Miss Gilchrist, isn't it?' he continued genially. 'You may remember we met briefly at dear Angela's last week. What a do that girl puts on!'

'Er, yes,' Rosy agreed. And then added, 'But I think it was largely in your honour, wasn't it? Rather a special birthday I seem to recall.'

'Oh well, I suppose so,' he agreed ruefully. 'A bit embarrassing, really – but great fun all the same. People are so kind on such occasions.' Rosy smiled and was about to say something else, when he added, 'Actually I am about to go down for a spot of fishing in Berkshire for the weekend, but when I return may I give you a bell and offer a luncheon date? They tell me you were rather a dab hand in Dover during the war, and of course I was simply nuts about your aunt. I think we might have rather

187

a lot to talk about. Still, must dash now ... will be in touch.' He raised his hat and strode off in the direction of Knightsbridge.

Been nuts about Aunt Marcia had he? Rosy pondered. Well, rather an improvement on Adelaide Fawcett's acerbic 'I knew your aunt and didn't like her'. And then she also recalled what else the old girl had said: 'I remember him in nappies. Beastly then, beastly now!'

'So,' she said to herself, 'should the great man deign to invite me for a date after his fishing trip I must remember to ask him about his infancy.' She stood up, and cursing the cold wind continued her way to the north side of the park.

CHAPTER TWENTY-TWO

Two days later she found herself once more at the Fawcett ménage, Lady Fawcett having telephoned to express gratitude for her daughter's gift of the mink coat and to ask if its donor would care to come for a light lunch unencumbered by 'you know *who*'. By which Rosy assumed she had meant the Gills.

'Auntie wants a facelift,' announced Amy in the course of the preliminary sherries.

'Well, Auntie can go whistle,' snapped Lady Fawcett. 'The experience would be excruciating.'

'For Auntie?'

'For us. Just imagine the drama of the eye-patches and the incessant demands for looking glasses. One would be worn out!'

'She is very determined.'

'I should be surprised if she weren't,' her mother replied grimly.

'But at ninety-two I should think it's a bit late for the old bird, isn't it? I mean horse has bolted and all that sort of thing,' observed Edward.

'It ill behoves you, Edward, to refer to your great-aunt as "old bird",' replied his own aunt. 'And in any case it is never too late for a woman to make the best of herself. It just happens that Auntie has been making more than the best of herself for far too long. It cannot go on!'

'Want a bet?' said Amy.

'What I *need* is rest and liquid sustenance. I've just had Harold Gill on the telephone trying to wheedle another cheque for his wretched Pygmy Fund.'

'Did you stand firm?' Edward asked.

'As a matter of fact I didn't have to because when I asked if the cheque would help supply some stilts he went rather peculiar and rang off...'

Amy's laugh ricocheted around the room. 'Narrow escape!'

Her mother looked puzzled. 'Can't think why you laugh. I should have thought stilts might be rather useful. I mean with all that jungle or what-ever it is they walk about in, probably strengthen their position.'

'What position?'

'*I* don't know! But it can't be very high. Now do stop pestering me and bring another glass of sherry. And you can get Rosy one too. She looks parched.'

As it happened the required sherry was never delivered, for at that moment there was the clanging of the doorbell. 'Now who can that be?' Lady Fawcett exclaimed. 'Nobody calls on a Saturday, everyone's down in the country.'

'Probably a Jehovah's Witness,' said Amy. 'Edward, go and tell them we are the Pope's first cousins. It generally does the trick.'

He got up and meandered into the hall.

They heard the sound of the front door being opened and then Edward's voice calling them. 'I say,' he boomed, 'there's a policeman here. You'll never guess what's happened: it's Auntie, she's fallen down the area steps!'

Lady Fawcett closed her eyes. 'You don't think he is making it up, do you?' she asked hopefully.

Her nephew appeared in the doorway, his alarmed face dispelling such hopes. 'Found at the bottom in a heap. Ankle broken and fuming.'

'Goodness, at least she is conscious!' Rosy exclaimed.

'Oh Lord, yes. In the London Clinic apparently and giving them merry hell. Claims she was pushed.'

'*Pushed?*' Rosy cried.

'Extremely likely,' murmured Lady Fawcett. She turned to Amy. 'You had better get on to Moses Stevens. Tell them to send two dozen lilies.'

'They won't be there on a Saturday, it's the Sabbath. Besides, wouldn't it be better to try Felix Smythe and Bountiful Blooms? He might sulk if he's not asked, and he is bound to find out.'

Her mother closed her eyes again. 'Whatever you think best, but be quick about it. At all costs

190

Auntie must be *quelled!*' She turned to Rosy. 'My dear, do you think you could possibly summon a taxi? We shall have to go and...'

Having done as she was bid Rosy found herself somehow caught up in Auntie's visiting party; and rather diffidently she accompanied the family as they trooped up the hospital stairs to one of the large private suites. Ushered by the nurse they entered hesitantly and stared solemnly down at their relation.

The old lady lay propped on pillows, face pinched but eyes sharp. 'Took your time, didn't you?' she greeted them. 'I might have been dead by now.'

'We came as soon as we heard, Auntie. Taxis are difficult on a Saturday,' protested Lady Fawcett. 'Anyway, how are you?'

'How would you be if you had been pushed down a flight of steps? I am shattered from head to toe.' And then addressing Edward, she said graciously, 'You can put the grapes on that table for the time being, I shan't want any just yet.'

'Er ... well I *would,* only we haven't actually–' began Edward.

'Auntie, I'm sure you can't have been pushed!' broke in Lady Fawcett hastily. 'Who on earth would have done such a thing? I expect you slipped – the pavements are so treacherous after rain and it's really quite misty.'

The patient narrowed her eyes and said frostily, 'I did not slip, I was pushed. And as to who did it, I name no names.' She placed a scrawny finger against the side of her nose and closed one eye.

'Well, at least that's something,' muttered Edward to Rosy. 'No libel damages.'

'I say,' Amy exclaimed, 'how awfully thrilling! Were you being followed?'

The old lady seemed to ruminate. 'Unlikely. I had just left the house to post a letter in the box ten yards away. (One *can* still manage that you know!) So I don't think the question of following arises. I should have thought "being watched" is the better description. Yes, *watched and set upon.*' She articulated the phrase with throaty relish.

There was a silence. And then Lady Fawcett coughed and murmured something about a nice pot of tea. 'I am sure the nurse can bring one – there's bound to be a bell somewhere...' She stood up and looked about with an air of mild desperation.

Auntie waved a dismissive hand. 'Can't abide tea. But a cocktail would be acceptable, though doubtless I shall be told it is too early.' She contrived to look both hopeful and martyred.

'Well, it is rather,' her niece answered doubtfully. 'Besides, they probably won't allow it on account of the pills they've given you. Nurses tend to be stuffy about that kind of thing and–'

'Anyone having suffered the sort of ordeal I have been through deserves indulgence; my shins are black and blue! Do you want to see them?'

'Not really.'

The patient turned to Edward. 'Perhaps you would be so kind as to give your poor suffering great-aunt a nip from your hip flask.' She flashed him what once upon a time might have been a dazzling smile.

The recipient looked nonplussed, while Amy giggled and answered for him: 'But Auntie, Edward doesn't have a hip flask.'

'How disappointing. In my day all bright young men carried hip flasks.'

Amy giggled again. 'But you see Edward isn't terribly–'

'Yes, yes I know,' was the weary reply. 'Never mind, I shall just have to await the flowers of sympathy you will all be sending me. Doubtless they will be exquisite.'

'Oh they will!' Lady Fawcett exclaimed eagerly. 'They are being specially ordered from Felix Smythe.'

'Ye gods,' croaked her aunt, 'bound to be a queer bunch!'

As they prepared to leave with promises to return on the Monday, the patient wafted an imperious hand in the direction of Rosy. 'I appreciate your silence, Miss Gilchrist, far too much noise from my own family. Good of you to visit a helpless old lady, especially in view of your own troubles.'

Rosy smiled awkwardly and made the appropriate responses. And then, just as they were trooping to the door, the helpless one said, 'Oh, and by the way, if anyone is *really* interested – he had a wooden leg.'

'Who did?' Edward asked.

'My attacker, of course.'

Lady Fawcett raised her eyes to the heavens. 'What *is* she talking about? It must be the pills, they've obviously given her too many.' With a sigh she turned into the corridor followed by Rosy suddenly numbed to the bone.

'Had a *wooden* bloody *leg?*' she had asked herself incredulously as she followed the Fawcetts to the hospital exit. 'Surely not!' A coincidence? A figment? An awful truth? Whatever the answer, rather as Lady Fawcett earlier, Rosy needed rest and a stiff drink.

With that in mind she had been about to detach herself from her companions and make off swiftly back to Baker Street, when Amy cried, 'Oh gosh, Mummy, you can't visit on Monday. Don't you remember? You've got to go and open the Gills' bric-a-brac bazaar. You promised you would and they'll be awfully miffed if you don't turn up.'

'So will the Pygmies,' sniggered Edward. 'All proceeds go to the Fund.'

Lady Fawcett regarded them helplessly, evidently weighing up the lesser of two evils and coming to no firm conclusion.

'And what's more,' continued Amy, 'I am afraid Edward and I can't possibly visit as we've *got* to get to Newbury. Big Bertha is running and–'

'Newbury races are on a Saturday,' her mother said firmly.

'But not this year. They've had to change the schedule to fit in with the Queen's...' Her voice trailed off as all three turned to look at Rosy.

'My dear,' murmured Lady Fawcett sweetly, 'I don't suppose by *any* chance you would be free to visit Auntie on our behalf? I mean, I know you are working and all that sort of thing, but perhaps in the afternoon you could just manage to slip in?

194

It would be so helpful, you've no idea!'

Rosy had every idea and normally she would have invented an instant excuse. But prompted by some visceral urge to learn more of Auntie's revelation re the leg, she heard herself saying, 'Yes, of course, no difficulty at all.'

They were visibly relieved. And with that settled Rosy took herself off to the calm of her flat. Here she poured the needed drink but also went to her desk to find the Paris telephone number Whittington had given her. She stared down at it, wondering.

Should she really try to make contact? But if so to what end? To report that she had some news of the document he had been seeking – to confirm that it was still in England and possibly at the St John's Wood house?... Or to check that he was in France and not currently in London pushing old ladies down steps?

In the event, mellowed by the whisky and feeling hungry, she decided against such action. So much pleasanter to just kick off her shoes, fill her glass and contemplate supper. She lit a cigarette and turned on the radio for the six o'clock news; and thus comfortably cocooned decided to shelve such troubling matters till the morning. Or the one after.

CHAPTER TWENTY-THREE

'Well of course I had to tell her!' protested Felix to Cedric when the latter returned from his annual Cambridge visit. 'In the circumstances there wasn't much choice. Vera was banging on in her usual way and the girl heard everything. How was I to know she would be there lurking in the shop? Vera took off smartish and I was left to field the questions. At first I tried to skirt round the matter but when I realised she wasn't going to be fobbed off, I thought: "Oh well, what the hell, why shouldn't Rosy Gilchrist hear the full story? After all, it was her aunt who was the traitor, so see what she makes of this, then!"' He broke off to run his fingers through his hair and scowl at the cat. 'She is hardly likely to go to the police.'

'How can you be sure?' Cedric asked. 'I can't help thinking you may have placed us in a highly precarious position. We have no guarantee of her silence ... in fact, I really feel quite uneasy.' He shot a suspicious glance around the sitting room as if half expecting to see size twelve boots protruding from beneath the curtains or the gleam of handcuffs caught in a shaft of lamplight.

'No,' replied Felix, 'I am not sure, but I would bet ten to one that she won't. Rosy Gilchrist may be strait-laced and not overendowed with high spirits but it is precisely that upright sobriety that will keep the lady quiet.'

'Really? What do you mean?' Cedric cast a speculative eye over the chocolate truffles at his elbow, selected one and as an afterthought slid the box in Felix's direction.

The latter gave it a cursory appraisal but postponed the pleasure. 'Look at it from her point of view,' he continued. 'Highly respected parents admired for their sterling war work and bastion of all that is fine and British, tragically blown to pieces in the Blitz; herself at twenty helping the boys down in Dover to keep the Hun at bay; RAF beau with medals to his name shot down just before Dresden... And now, in these quieter days, here she is leading an unimpeachable life being worthy in the British Museum. Do you imagine for one moment she would want the world to know about the crazy aunt ditching her wartime colleagues and then latterly resorting to a brisk bit of blackmail? No fear! Frankly, if I were Rosy Gilchrist I would keep very quiet indeed. *Very* quiet.' He selected two of the proffered chocolates, put one aside and popped the other into his mouth.

Cedric smiled. 'What empathy you have, my dear Felix – must come from all that aesthetic sensitivity Her Majesty so admires.' He smiled again and then added softly, 'But life teaches one that people do not always run true to type, that sometimes the most predictable patterns of behaviour suddenly abort or become twisted. I learnt that a long time ago in the war. It doesn't do to assume too much. After your somewhat rash revelations to the Gilchrist girl I think it might be politic to invite her here for a friendly drink – get the lie of the land as it were, i.e. assess her discretion and if necessary gently remind her of the discomfort of her *own* position should anything get out about Marcia and "old times". Yes, I think we need a word with the lady. The last thing we want is for her to go marching off to the police in the grip of moral dudgeon and civic duty. Wouldn't do at all.'

Felix heaved a sigh and nodded. 'Perhaps, perhaps; it seems unlikely, but you could be right...' He stared morosely at Cedric's smart new coal scuttle in the grate. 'What on earth possessed us to do it? If only one had realized...'

'More to the point, what possessed her murderer? Had it been Thistlehyde the answer would be obvious: pique and petulance. He never forgave her for being scathing about him in the *Tatler*.'

'Really? When was that?... Oh, of course – yes, I remember. You mean when she said that for one who had learnt to paint by numbers he had a moderately promising future.' Felix tittered. 'That went deep all right, cut him to the quick. Goodness, what was it about Marcia? She had such a knack for riling people!'

'A temptation few of us can resist,' murmured Cedric, 'but it did for her in the end. Vera's right: she went too far, overplayed her hand as usual. Yes, the more I think about it the more I'm certain our original assumption was correct: the murderer was one of her blackmail victims peeved by her importunate demands.'

'Yes but *who?* And in any case, why should he choose to use my coal scuttle to crown his handiwork? Mere chance I had happened to dump the thing in the hall. I mean, if his mission had been to silence the lady and get her off his back I cannot imagine why he would want to footle around with artistic embellishments.'

'Perhaps he was early for a subsequent engagement and was looking for something to fill the time. You know how it is.' Cedric stretched an arm to retrieve the truffles and examined them thoughtfully. 'But as to identity, I take it that is precisely what the police are pondering at this very minute – assuming that they even *know* about the blackmail business; we may be in advance of them there – I am not convinced of that inspector's acumen. But it is certainly what Vera is pondering. She's hunting that confounded paper of Marcia's like a slavering bloodhound. Keeps muttering about the "bastard bombers" and that she'll root them out if it kills her.'

'Hmm. Rather a rash statement in the current climate, I should think! Besides, they didn't actually *do* any bombing. Mercifully the whole plot collapsed.'

'Ah, but it's the thought that counts; and if the authorities ever do get wind of what they were up to they'll probably swing, or at very best be banged up in Pentonville for the rest of their days. Hence dear Marcia's disposal.'

'Vera's a fool,' said Felix. 'Given the situation, playing detective is the last thing she should be doing; courting trouble. It's dangerous enough with the police – if they learn that her brother was a casualty of Marcia's wartime outrage they'll be on to her like a ferret with a rabbit. Unlike us she may not have played silly beggars with a coal bucket, but in their eyes she would still have a strong motive. Speaking as one similarly placed, I should think she has quite enough to worry about without gratuitously inviting the same fate as Marcia!'

'Ah, but then I suspect she is being egged on by Sabatier.'

'*Who?*'

'Sabatier, her wartime boss. The only man she ever really respected. It was quite a pash one gathers, though I can't think why.' Cedric sniffed dismissively. 'From what I remember he looks like a taller version of Goebbels and with the same limp. Not one's type at all! But it's not the physique so much as the mentality. In those days he had the reputation as a brilliant operator, but it's a brilliance that has lost its sparkle and been replaced by obsession. There are certain people who can never get the war out of their system and he is one such. Rumour has it there is some family grudge he's engrossed with, though I don't know what – something to do with the names on this document presumably. Vera would know I suppose...'

'So you think it was from him that she heard this tale of the plot and Marcia's blackmailing?'

'More than likely. According to the grapevine he lives in France these days but periodically comes over here on business, i.e. to trail his enemies, and then slips back to France again. Very discreet, very elusive – a bit like a shuffling Scarlet Pimpernel, you might say.'

'Well, just as long as he doesn't shuffle in our direction I don't care,' Felix said sharply. 'Personally I am finding this whole business more than vexing. If wretched Marcia had behaved herself in the war none of this would have happened and our lives could be cool and unencumbered just as they used to be. As it is, I have a heart attack every time I see a policeman; and now that the press has sniffed out the "mysterious" lump of coal found in the victim's wardrobe with its "tantalising" message I can't even read a newspaper without feeling sick.' He picked up a truffle and discarded it impatiently. 'You might have bought a mixed selection; you know I prefer the white chocolate!'

'I *think*,' said Cedric soothingly, 'it is time for a couple of very dry Martinis. What shall it be – a Gibson or the usual?'

Felix considered and opted for the usual.

'Excellent. And then you can tell me all about your having to deliver flowers to Adelaide Fawcett in the London Clinic.'

Felix brightened. 'Indeed I will. She fell down her steps, you know. So careless. Claims she was pushed.'

Cedric gave a deft swirl of the cocktail wand. 'Hmm. Nice to think so...' He beamed. 'Now, try that for size!'

CHAPTER TWENTY-FOUR

Despite her earlier resolve to shelve making contact with Whittington, Rosy gradually found her reluctance being replaced by a truculent curiosity. Suddenly she was eager to confront the man: to assess and probe, to question, even needle perhaps. In short, to get his measure. Up until that moment images of his fixed gaze, languid calm and silky tone had unsettled her; and the thought of further contact, however slight, had been distasteful. But moods change; and as she swept back the curtains and stared down at the already busy street, fears of the unknown and unwanted evaporated.

She made coffee, and then with the fragment of Marcia's letter at the ready, picked up the telephone and asked the operator to put her through to Paris. She lit a cigarette and waited as casually as if she were summoning the plumber...

'You are through now, caller,' the operator announced.

Rosy braced herself for the response. It was a man's voice: *'Oui?'*

'I am calling from London,' she began in English, 'and I should like to speak to–' She had been about to say 'to Monsieur Whittington' but hesitated, remembering that the name, of course, had been an alias. But just as she paused, the man said curtly, *'Il n'y a personne ici.'*

'But–'

'Il n'y a personne,' the voice repeated, and the line went dead.

'Well, really,' Rosy muttered, 'of all the cheek!' Having grasped the French bull by the horns she now had a distinct sense of anticlimax, and defiantly she tried the number again.

There was an incessant ringing tone eventually interrupted by the operator announcing, 'I am sorry, caller, there is no reply from that number.'

Huh, Rosy thought, so much for all that blague about emergencies and 'vital to contact immediately.' She gazed down at the scrap of paper he had been so insistent in giving her. All hooey! Indignantly she ground out her cigarette, burnt her finger and winced.

But annoyance was swamped by sudden relief, for in a way the failed contact was oddly reassuring: the instruction was shown to be flawed, false even; and without such a bridge the man's reality seemed more blurred, his warnings less urgent. A clear reply – his own or a colleague's – would have renewed the link and confirmed his validity. As it was, her attempt to communicate had yielded nothing. Perhaps they (whoever *they* were) were all out at the Folies-Bèrgere, hatching plots and eating snails. Typical!

Yet relief was overlaid by the nagging voice of Adelaide Fawcett and her extraordinary allegation of a wooden-legged attacker. If Whittington was not available in France, as the taciturn telephone response had seemed to imply, it was indeed just conceivable that he might be back in London; but if so, for what purpose – the annihilation of tiresome old ladies? Ridiculous! Besides, Whittington could hardly be the only man in London with a prosthetic leg... Well, perhaps she would learn something from the *soi-disant* victim later that day.

Meanwhile other matters took precedence. These were her duties at the museum organising Stanley's monthly lecture: collating his papers and sifting the lantern slides, but, above all, mollifying those of his academic colleagues whose toes and egos he had crushed earlier in the week. If she could soft-soap them sufficiently the event would be mildly pleasurable. If not, a session of mayhem and acrimony was in store. She gulped another coffee, and grabbing coat and briefcase set out with misgivings for Great Russell Street.

Her fears were groundless for all went well: Stanley's oratory had been as forceful as ever, his notes impeccably ordered, the acid asides and witticisms received with spontaneous mirth and his peers docile in their observations. (Perhaps, she surmised, they were keeping their powder dry for the Spring Symposium, an event not known for its benevolence.) Yes, remarkably the afternoon had passed without incident – fortunate for the harassed assistant, though possibly a matter of regret for the speaker himself.

However, a further challenge loomed: Auntie languishing in the London Clinic. Encircled by the Fawcett triumvirate Rosy had been powerless to resist the earnest plea to visit their ailing relative, and initially had felt uneasy at the prospect. But with Stanley's lecture safely delivered and still unsettled by the old woman's words, she was eager to face the patient and hear more. Thus, leaving the museum she hurried off to Harley Street, and was just about to enter the clinic's portals when she nearly collided with Felix Smythe.

'My dear,' he exclaimed, 'what a coincidence – though I trust your destination is not from where I've just come. Too wearing for words! Those superb lilies! And she actually had the gall to complain that three were fading – and after all the

204

trouble I had taken to select the very best. Wilful, that's what. If you ask my opinion, except for a few hedgerow weeds she doesn't deserve a thing.' He sniffed angrily, and Rosy rather guessed the name of the recipient.

'Was it Adelaide Fawcett?' she enquired.

'Who else?' was the grim reply. 'Angela rang in an awful state saying the aunt had taken a header and would I deliver a large bouquet of Regale lilies as soon as possible. Naturally one was only too happy to oblige, and you can be sure it certainly was large – and exquisite.' (And expensive, too, no doubt, thought Rosy.) 'But was she grateful? Not a jot; all she could do was cavil. And I had been so ready to be *utterly* charming!' He pouted.

'Ah, but it's the overall effect and the glorious scent that matters,' Rosy said soothingly, 'and I am sure as she gazes at them from fevered pillows delight will flood upon her.'

'You mean you think she might drown in rapture?' Felix asked hopefully. 'Now that would be encouraging.'

Rosy smiled and was about to go, when he suddenly said, 'Oh, by the way, glad to have met you, saves a phone call. Cedric was wondering – well both of us, actually – if you would care to drop in for a drink one evening, Sunday ideally. There are, er, one or two things to discuss. You may remember our little talk the other day...' He looked slightly uncomfortable, and Rosy politely assured him she could manage it.

'Good, good,' he murmured. 'We'll be chez Cedric. I'll give you the address.' He produced a minuscule notebook from his breast pocket and scribbled the details. 'Six o'clock. How nice, it will be lovely!'

Rosy was unconvinced of the loveliness but contrived to look willing; and after mutual farewells she turned towards the clinic and Auntie.

The patient lay staring woodenly at the lilies, and on Rosy's entry observed, 'That man Smythe has just been here with Angela's offerings. One has seen far worse but I wasn't going to let *him* know that. Too pleased with himself that one.'

'Oh, but they are gorgeous,' Rosy exclaimed, genuinely impressed.

'Yes they are, really,' agreed Auntie reluctantly.

They talked of other things: the state of the casualty's shins, the bleakness of the bar facilities, the peculiar youthfulness of doctors, the bossiness of nurses, the outlandish habits of other patients and the barbarity of life in general. Rosy listened dutifully, bored with the content but impressed by the verve of the delivery. Carefully she steered the 'conversation' round to the accident itself.

'It must have been horrifying,' she ventured, 'I mean, plunging headlong like that.'

'You mean like Alice down the rabbit hole? Rather less interesting and certainly more painful.'

'Oh, I'm sure, but it must have been an awful shock as well – so sudden and unexpected. The fog and damp pavement can't have helped. I suppose you must have missed the top step and–'

'I did not miss the top step. I was poised on the brink deciding whether to enter my house by the flight down or the flight up. I had just elected the latter, i.e. to mount the steps to the front door, when I was grabbed from behind and thrown forward. The next thing I knew I was on my back by the kitchen door staring up at those awful black railings. It was exceedingly uncomfortable. Ankle broken and bruises everywhere. Do you want to see my legs?'

Like Lady Fawcett previously, Rosy was able to parry the spectacle and instead expressed indignant concern: 'How appalling! So you really think someone did it deliberately?'

'Without a doubt,' Auntie replied firmly. 'Didn't I say so yesterday?'

Rosy hesitated. 'Well, er, yes, I think it was mentioned but I–'

'Weren't attending, I suppose. Typical of the young these days, they don't concentrate. Still, I daresay it was ever thus. But it is something you should practise, Miss Gilchrist: you will find it exceedingly useful, listening to what people say. It can be a handy skill, most people don't have it.'

Boldly Rosy grasped the cue. She smiled and said gently, 'Perhaps I do have a little of it. For example, when we were leaving yesterday I *thought* you said that your assailant had a wooden leg. Was I right?'

The other looked slightly surprised and then seemed to cogitate, gazing at the lilies. A faraway look came into her eyes. 'Did I say that?' she asked mildly.

'Yes, you did,' Rosy replied.

There was a silence. 'Well in that case perhaps he did. Who knows...?' She continued to contemplate the lilies, before remarking, 'In the old days we used to have whole beds of those, just under the drawing room windows. The scent was utterly overpowering – decadent, really.'

'Delightful,' Rosy said tersely. 'But I still don't see what made you think he had a wooden leg.'

'Perhaps it was the sound of the tap, tap, tapping in the fog, like Long John Silver – or was it Blind Pugh? One gets them so mixed up. Do you know your *Treasure Island*, Miss Gilchrist? Stevenson, such an *inventive* storyteller!' She fixed Rosy with a challenging stare, and somehow the latter knew the subject was closed.

Vague pleasantries were exchanged and a barbed reference to Marcia made: 'Too clever for her own good, I always thought; still, I don't suppose she deserved that fate. No, I'm wrong – not clever, dangerously reckless. Always was. I *think* you have more sense. One should always be wary. Remember that, Miss Gilchrist. Now if you don't mind you could ring for the nurse: a lumpen girl, but like my great-niece Amy, a kindly donkey. One must be grateful for such people.' She sighed and closed her eyes. 'Off you go now; I have much to think about.'

Duty done but curiosity unsatisfied, Rosy walked home in a mood of puzzled frustration. She also had much to think about. Was Auntie just an addled old trout imagining or inventing nonsensical tales to tease and pass the time? Or did she really know or suspect something that she was unwilling to reveal? Certainly she had been insistent about the push itself (though that was not necessarily a guarantee of its truth) but her evasiveness about the alleged assailant had been tantalising. How much had been deliberate, how much confusion? Was the whole thing merely a concoction of one too proud to acknowledge the frailty of old age? But if so, why on earth introduce the detail of the wooden leg? A mischievous sense of theatre? Possibly. But if so, Adelaide Fawcett certainly possessed an uncanny nose for coincidence!

CHAPTER TWENTY-FIVE

She was beginning to regret accepting Felix's invitation to drinks. At the time it had seemed a practical suggestion, and from their point of view she could see how it might be useful. But could the same be said of hers? Surely the more she consorted with Marcia's associates, the more she was being dragged into the whole unsavoury business. Ignorance might be bliss, but more to the point it could also be a kind of protection: distance lent a modicum of safety. On the other hand, she brooded, forewarned was forearmed, and given the circumstances she certainly felt the need for some kind of armour! Thus quelling the impulse to telephone and cancel, she decided to plunge in and see what more could be learnt. In for a penny in for a pound, she told herself tritely.

Hence at the prescribed time she presented herself somewhat nervously at the address Felix had given her. This was a narrow stuccoed town house on the edge of Pimlico, tucked discreetly into a paved cul-de-sac. Beneath its portico there lurked a small cat, sleek and grey – a little like Dillworthy himself – and she assumed it was part of the establishment. This proved the case, for when her host opened the door it streaked inside with a peevish squeak, and eyes tightly closed settled itself Buddha-like in the centre of an oriental rug.

'What a pretty little cat,' she exclaimed. 'What is its name?'

Cedric looked slightly puzzled. 'Name? Er, well it doesn't have one really, it's just the cat.'

Rosy gave a polite laugh. 'Doesn't it mind – not having a name?'

He shook his head. 'I shouldn't think so ... at least, I've never enquired really.'

He took her coat and ushered her up the stairs into a drawing room made spacious by its pale walls and absence of superfluous embellishment. The few pieces of furniture were impeccably chosen and symmetrically placed. There were no flowers, but a warm glow was shed by a briskly burning fire and a tall standard lamp, under which sat Felix plying a piece of tapestry.

On seeing Rosy he laid it aside and rose to greet her with a little bow. 'How delightful to see you again, Miss Gilchrist, and how well you look!'

'Do I?' said Rosy, startled by such effusion but vaguely flattered all the same.

'Radiant!' He fussed about, drawing up a chair by the fire and placing a small table at her elbow while Cedric busied himself with the sherry. He certainly seemed more relaxed than when they

210

had 'discussed' matters in his flat above the flower shop.

She glanced over at the discarded canvas. 'I never had the patience for that sort of thing but I believe one can become quite addicted.'

'Oh, one can,' Felix assured her, 'utterly. It's so soothing; more so than petit point which requires greater concentration. I do that as well, but after a day's work toiling amidst my blooms – not to say toiling with the public – there is nothing so calming as plying one's needle with rhythmic repetition. With Cedric, of course, it's the crossword – you might say that *thought* is his therapy. But for a busy bee like me, what better than a skein of wool and a blank mind to ease the day's travails!' He beamed and proffered a plate of cheese straws.

Cedric glided forward with a glass of sherry. 'I hope this is to your liking. There is a fino should you prefer, but a medium seems to suit most of our guests – unless, of course, you would rather have something more abrasive...' He raised a polite eyebrow.

She assured him that the sherry suited admirably, wondering when and how exactly they would broach the evening's theme, i.e. the subject of Marcia's end.

It didn't take long. After enquiring if she had found the house easily and making some vague remarks about the weather (which happened to be unremarkable), Cedric cleared his throat, and leaning forward said, 'As I am sure you realise, we have asked you here for a specific purpose: to discuss a topic of mutual interest, i.e. the manner of your aunt's demise and the situation it leaves us all in.'

Rosy nodded but said nothing, and he continued. 'As Felix has already explained, it is a matter of some delicacy and indeed general embarrassment. To us, of course, though I rather imagine to you as well...'

He gave a discreet cough, at which point Felix broke in and said affably, 'What Cedric means is that you wouldn't be too keen on the police and press learning of her wartime *services*. The public can be so sniffy about that sort of thing ... and who knows, were they to start delving they might actually suspect *you* of doing the deed itself! It's often a family member, I am told. After all, none of us actually knows that you didn't. And once the police get the bit between their–'

Rosy put down her glass and fixed him with a wintry stare. 'Neither does one *actually* know that it wasn't you either. On your own admission you were there that very afternoon, skulking with the coal scuttle. One has only your word that you didn't also gun her down and ram it on her head.'

'Well, really, that's a bit much!' He looked deeply wounded.

'Be quiet, both of you,' Cedric admonished. 'Despite my friend's blundering tongue we do not believe that you were responsible, Miss Gilchrist, and I am fairly sure that you do not suspect us. What we need to know is exactly who *was* responsible, not only for Marcia's death but also for Thistlehyde's; and in particular we have to decide how best to protect ourselves from the inquisitive probings of the police, or even, indeed, from personal peril.'

Rosy said nothing, wondering whether to tell them about Whittington's midnight visit. But as she cogitated, Cedric said softly, 'One rather gathers you were recently approached by someone, someone seeking information...'

She was startled. 'How do you know?'

Cedric shrugged. 'Obvious. Felix said that you seemed to know all about Operation Coal Scuttle, so you had clearly learnt it from somewhere. But it so happens that Vera has intimated as much. She knows the man. She also said that you had been told about the Churchill bomb plotters and that you were being closely "marked by the Master". Really, that woman has such a histrionic turn of phrase!'

'Marked by the *what?*' Rosy exclaimed. 'What are you talking about?'

'You might well ask. Vera's words, not mine. Sabatier. Odd fellow. He is–'

'Who the hell is Sabatier?'

'Exactly what dear Felix asked. Sabatier is Vera's erstwhile boss and he who approached you; and thanks to your intemperate aunt, one who goes minus an ankle.'

There was no answer to that and Rosy felt slightly sick. She gazed abstractedly at her empty sherry glass. Felix must have noticed, for instantly he had leapt up saying, 'Do let's have something a little more sustaining! How about a whisky for our guest? I rather fancy one myself. I am sure you've got a bottle somewhere, Cedric.'

Whisky was duly produced and lavishly poured. Sips were taken, followed by an awkward silence.

213

And then Felix tittered and said, 'Let's toast Vera and the awful dachshund!'

'Why?' Cedric enquired.

'Because they are not here. Such a relief!'

Rosy was inclined to agree but the mention of the dog jolted her mind, and she heard herself saying coolly to Felix, 'But this Sabatier – or Whittington, as he chose to call himself to me – wasn't the only casualty of the coal-scuttle operation. According to you, Vera's brother Raymond was also an indirect victim of my aunt's blabbing tongue. Mightn't that give *her* a motive for murder? After all, you did say that she had pretty well colluded with you in sending those lumps of coal, so perhaps her desire for revenge went much further than that.'

For a few moments neither answered, and then Cedric said musingly, 'Doubtless that is exactly what the police might assume should they get to hear of it.'

'But their assumption could be right!'

'Unlikely. You see Vera hated her brother.'

Rosy was taken aback. 'But surely... So in that case why on earth name her dogs after him? She seemed to imply it was some sort of homage.'

Cedric shrugged. 'Guilt more likely: a sort of posthumous remorse for loathing his guts. He was very beautiful and she was not, a fact he never allowed her to forget. Played on it constantly.' He turned to Felix. 'Wouldn't you agree?'

The latter nodded, but added, 'I'm not so sure about the guilt part. Knowing Vera I suspect the dog naming may be a form of revenge: Raymond was tall with classical features and graceful deportment. The dogs are invariably short-arsed snuffling little tikes; affectionate and cute, no doubt, but hardly distinguished. It's not as if they're even the long-haired sort. The disparity may appeal to Vera's puerile sense of humour.'

'Doubtless,' agreed Cedric dryly. He turned to Rosy. 'Vera Collinger is a mix of fervid patriotism and gritty integrity on the one hand, and cussed awfulness on the other. Along with the awfulness goes a sly intelligence. It makes relations with her a trifle problematic and on the whole we find flight or circumvention the best tactic. However, despite the lady's shortcomings, murdering an old buddy – as your aunt once was – is not her style.'

'But if she is as fervidly patriotic as you say, that in itself might have prompted her to kill Marcia. She must have been appalled when it emerged that her friend had been responsible for the coal-scuttle failure!'

'Oh, I think she was. But in those days she was close to Marcia, doted on her you might say. Thus she convinced herself that Marcia's treachery was simply a besotted blunder and not a hostile calculation.'

'Which I am sure it wasn't,' Rosy said quickly.

He shrugged. 'That's as may be, but in any event Vera forgave her – up to a point at any rate.'

'But not *quite* enough not to appreciate the justice of our little ruse,' cut in Felix.

Rosy was far from sure of such justice but said nothing, not wishing to ruffle uncertain feathers.

'Poor Vera,' observed Cedric pityingly, 'she's got this document of Marcia's on the brain. Convinced it's the vital key to the identities of the bomb plotters and won't rest till she's sniffed it out and delivered it to Sabatier.' He paused and added reflectively, 'One has to admit she has a talent for that sort of thing – quarrying and pursuit. It's what made her useful in the war and she can't forget it.'

'The war or her usefulness?' Rosy asked.

'Both. She lives in the past: thrives on intrigue and righteous indignation. A bit like Adelaide Fawcett. Not that there's anything righteous about that piece of mischief – should have been put down years ago.'

The reference to Auntie prompted Rosy to ask why the latter should be so hostile to Maynard Latimer; but before she had a chance to speak, Cedric said softly, 'As a matter of fact, Miss Gilchrist, Vera firmly believes the thing is in your possession.' He regarded her speculatively, and from the corner of her eye Rosy saw Felix crane forward.

'Well,' she replied evenly, 'she has certainly been pumping me.' Images of the teatime tête-à-tête in Oxford Street came to mind.

'Ah, but now she is convinced that you have it.'

'Oh really, why?' Rosy affected a cool indifference.

'Edward Fawcett. They–'

'Edward Fawcett! What does he know about anything?'

'Good question,' Felix broke in with a snigger. 'I have been asking myself that for years.'

Cedric ignored the interruption. 'They belong to the same club – the de Vere, one of the few mixed establishments in London – and Fawcett was babbling about a fur coat of Marcia's which

216

you had given Amy, and how she had found a letter addressed to you in a concealed pocket. Apparently he made a joke suggesting it was a missing will or something equally vital. Vera thought the joke feeble but the assumption fair.' He paused. 'Was it?'

Rosy gazed at him not sure of her response. Flat denial? To what end? He probably wouldn't believe her, and more to the point neither would limpet Collinger. The woman was right and doubtless knew it... Still, it was bad enough being interrogated by the police without also being drawn into the dubious sleuthing activities of Collinger and Dick Whittington. She felt a sudden surge of anger at the way the pair had assumed they could insinuate themselves into her life and make covert demands for cooperation and data. If Whittington/Sabatier wanted vengeance then he could damn well get it without involving her – and Vera Collinger could do the same. Presumably the latter was eager to impress her erstwhile boss and stick another feather in her stupid hat. Well, she could do it without Rosy Gilchrist's help!

She smiled ruefully at Cedric. 'Nothing so exciting. It was just a personal note and a couple of spare theatre tickets – wildly out of date now, of course. She obviously forgot to post the thing. Just goes to show, one should never put messages in secret places, they only get lost!' She noted the sceptical lift of Cedric's eyebrow and added earnestly, 'Mind you, *had* it been anything to do with the plot I would naturally have put it in my bank's safe deposit straight away.'

'Most sensible,' exclaimed Felix. 'It would never do to leave something like that lying around. The best place for it in my view.'

'Hmm, but not in Vera's,' said Cedric. 'She would probably try to force entry by blitzing the place with Mills bombs.' He gave a thin laugh.

'So what do you think of that?' Felix asked after Rosy had left.

'Lying, obviously,' replied Cedric. 'The theatre tickets were just a feint; she has found something all right, though whether it's quite the devastating evidence Vera assumes, one can't be certain, and I am far from inclined to ask questions – or mention matters to Vera. Frankly, the less we know the safer we are. Detachment is all.'

'You mean otherwise we might end up smeared with gore like Thistlehyde?'

Cedric winced. 'How baldly you put things! No, I wasn't thinking of anything quite so gross. Simply that in the current scheme of things it would be prudent to be as elusive as possible. We are in enough danger from the authorities as it is. That little sleight of hand with the new coal bucket the other day may have gone smoothly enough but there's no guarantee the police won't come gallumphing back again. Admittedly it seemed to satisfy them at the time but one can never be sure. The last thing we need is to court further problems by allying ourselves to Vera Collinger and her wild pursuits. The next thing we shall have is Sabatier paying us his dubious respects as he did Rosy Gilchrist. No, there is a whole can of worms there and multiple dangers.

We should keep our distance.'

'I agree, but it might be difficult,' said Felix doubtfully. 'After all, Vera was fully aware of our coal venture, thought it quite amusing at the time. I remember her words: "That'll take the cool smile off my lady's face." We are not exactly in a position to ignore her, she knows too much.'

'In that case we must adopt a passive sympathy: interested but non-committal. On no account must we be *drawn*. Far too risky... And yes, you are right, the very worst possibility is that we could end up like Thistlehyde – or Marcia for that matter, though I trust without the additional millinery.'

His companion groaned. 'If only one could just disappear, go away for a long, long holiday: Bermuda perhaps – so much safer now than in Eddie Windsor's time! – or Tangier. They tell me it's very cosy there. *Very* cosy!' He gave a sly titter.

'First place the police would look for you,' Cedric replied scathingly. 'Besides, there's the Hyslop wedding, you wouldn't want to miss that would you?'

'Miss it? Of course not. I am the lynchpin of the whole event! Without Smythe's Bountiful Blooms festooning the place the bride hasn't a hope in hell of getting into the *Tatler*, not the size she is. And as for that mother...' Felix shuddered.

For perhaps ten minutes they were diverted from the problem of Vera. And the tiresome exigencies of Marcia's fate became lost in a plethora of peonies and other nuptial exotica. The vexed question of clematis versus vine leaves was raised and then dropped, anemones brooded upon, lilies extolled. Felix's plans were poetic and costly, and Cedric was amused by his friend's fervour. 'Wonderful,' he murmured encouragingly, 'but will they pay up?'

'Oh yes, they'll pay up all right. With Bunty Hyslop as the blushing bride what else can they do but drape the whole place with flowers? After all, there's got to be *some* aesthetic appeal...'

But inevitably, as a topic of conversation Bunty Hyslop's girth paled in comparison with the fate of Marcia and the enigma of the murdered artist; and once more the spectre of Clovis Thistlehyde intruded itself upon Cedric's drawing room.

'I mean he was so *mere,*' mused Felix, 'hardly important enough to merit murder I shouldn't have thought. And from all accounts there was no robbery.'

'No. The newspapers described his studio as being in a state of "artistic shambles" – a condition they fondly assume to be evidence of bohemian habits – but there was no suggestion of the place being ransacked or disturbed in any way. And certainly that detective sergeant didn't mention it when he interviewed us.'

'Huh!' The memory of the sergeant's questions piqued Felix. 'I cannot think why he should have assumed we were remotely au fait with Thistlehyde's private life,' he complained. 'Greenleaf actually seemed to think that he and I had been some sort of drinking companions. Imagine!'

Cedric smiled in recollection. 'Oh yes ... what was it he said? Something about what with you being "of a flower-arranging bent" he thought you might also have a "penchant for paintings" and so have a bit in common with the victim! There was something else too... Ah, that was it' – he assumed a gravelly tone – '"So perhaps you was both of the same *artistic fraternity*, Mr Smythe?"'

Felix snorted. 'Ridiculous!'

Cedric ceased to smile and stroked the cat meditatively. And then he said slowly: 'But in a way, of course, the pair of you did have something in common. Rather important, really.'

'What on earth do you mean?'

'As the Gilchrist girl so politely reminded you – on the afternoon of the murder you were both at Marcia's house at the same time.'

'Yes but–'

'Doubtless you are right about Clovis not being intrinsically worth murdering, but *I* think he was killed because he happened to be in the wrong place at the wrong time. He saw something there – or somebody.'

'Well it certainly wasn't me,' Felix exclaimed. 'As you know, I was muffled up to my neck behind the hall curtain, and when he was in the bog I ran like a hare!'

Cedric closed his eyes. 'I am not suggesting he saw you, Felix, or your garish mackintosh, but I do think he saw Marcia's murderer. Which is why he was killed.'

'But surely being Clovis he would have shouted it from the rooftops, put an advertisement in the newspaper. Anything for publicity!'

'Not if he was unaware of the significance.'

CHAPTER TWENTY-SIX

Rosy's schedule for the following day threatened to be irksome: a two-hour stint filing catalogues at the museum, a rather dreaded dental appointment, and then in the late afternoon the dubious pleasure of one of Mrs Gill's charity whist drives. Rosy disliked whist, but in an unguarded moment she had succumbed to the urgent plea to substitute for a late cancellation. 'So inconsiderate of him,' Mrs Gill had complained, 'it will mean forfeiting a table unless I can find someone else. Such a waste. I don't suppose you could possibly...?' It was the last thing Rosy wanted, but in view of the generous role Mrs Gill had played in sorting Marcia's affairs it had seemed churlish to refuse.

She was on the point of rushing off to the museum when she was halted by the telephone. 'Terribly short notice, I know,' said the voice, 'but I don't suppose you would be free for lunch by any chance?' It was Maynard Latimer, evidently back from his fishing in Berkshire.

Caught on the hop Rosy hesitated, not sure of her response. 'Well,' she said tentatively, 'it's awfully nice of you but I'm due at the dentist at twelve – not a good prelude for lunch I'm afraid. Perhaps some other–'

There was a laugh. 'You're not being gassed, are you?'

'What? Oh ... no, I don't think so, just a routine check.'

'In that case I am sure the old gnashers will be able to withstand a little caviar at Wiltons, and you can always pass up the grouse in favour of a Dover sole.'

Like hell! Rosy thought. (She was rather partial to grouse.) 'Well, er, yes I suppose I–'

'Excellent. One-thirty at Wiltons. I look forward with eager pleasure.'

Eagerness was not exactly what Rosy felt, but all the same the prospect was not uncongenial. His company promised to be amusing – and would at least cushion the ennui of the whist. Hurriedly she changed her workaday skirt for something more in keeping with Wiltons, replaced her brogues for sky-high heels, and as an afterthought thrust a phial of 'Joy' into her handbag.

'Phew,' exclaimed Leo emitting a loud wolf whistle, 'where's my lady off to? Going to vamp old Stanley?'

'I have a dental appointment,' replied Rosy coldly.

'Lucky dentist,' he said appreciatively, 'probably drill himself in the butt!'

'Don't be coarse,' she admonished, but couldn't help smiling, pleased to think that if young Leo approved, then presumably she would pass muster with Latimer... She frowned. Was that so important? Hmm. *Somewhat,* she admitted.

The dentist wouldn't have been so bad had it not been for the drama of the waiting room: Raymond was there – perched precariously on his owner's lap.

'Ah,' said Miss Collinger, 'I suppose you have come to see Mr Dingle. I always go to Churcher myself, he's so good with Raymond. There's an old sock that he keeps specially, puts him in a good mood for the rest of the day.'

'The dentist?' Rosy asked.

'No, Miss Gilchrist. The dog, of course.'

Rosy smiled apologetically, hoping that the old bat would soon be summoned to the drill. Her hopes were dashed.

'I always come early,' the other announced. 'I prefer to reflect in peace before enduring the probe; it settles one psychologically.'

'Oh don't mind me,' Rosy said hastily, 'I'm happy with a magazine.' She looked for a *London Life* but naturally there was only a stack of *National Geographics*. (Did all dentists have a fetish for that publication?)

'As a matter of fact I've been meaning to get hold of you,' Miss Collinger continued. 'There are certain matters of which I think Felix Smythe may have apprised you – matters concerning your aunt. I am not convinced of his reliability as a narrator; it would be best if I checked his account.' She fixed Rosy with a firm stare, as did the dog.

Rosy did not think she wanted to be got hold of by Vera Collinger but suspected that any attempt to fob her off would be met with stubborn and wearying tenacity. Thus reluctantly she heard herself saying, 'Yes – well, so what do you suggest?'

'What I suggest is a meeting of clarification at

the Pig and Bell off Brewer Street in Soho. I expect you know it. They do decent chips there and the alcoves are useful for private discussion.' She produced a diary, scanned it briskly and proposed a date two days hence. Rosy nodded. She did know the pub, though it was some time since she had been in. From what she recalled it was a gloomy place with draughty corners and uncertain beer.

'Good. That's settled then. I shan't keep you long,' said Miss Collinger, 'but this is a matter of some importance as you doubtless realise.'

There was a sudden yelp from Raymond, and leaping off his keeper's lap he rushed to greet a small man in a white coat standing at the door dangling a sock. Rosy breathed a thankful sigh as the three of them disappeared into a nether region.

After the joint onslaught from dentist and Collinger Rosy felt ravenous; and beckoned by thoughts of Wiltons' grouse she hastily flagged down a taxi and sped to Jermyn Street.

Her host greeted her warmly, and after a few bantering remarks about the perils of dentistry ordered gin and tonics. Rosy sipped hers gratefully, the twin rasp of drill and Miss Collinger's voice rapidly losing potency amidst the convivial drone of contented diners. Then, after the preliminaries of menu and wine list, the promised caviar materialised and she settled to the task of serious consumption and unserious chit-chat.

In fact Latimer's blend of casual wit and easy charm gave such chit-chat an engaging edge, and her initial wariness was soon replaced by genuine interest. But she also noted that alongside the amiability there lurked a shrewd watchfulness, a manipulative energy which had doubtless played a major role in propelling the distinguished career.

Initially their conversation touched on a mix of topics – fishing and golf, an exhibition at the Tate, the phenomenal racing skills of young Lester Piggot (a fine future, Latimer predicted), Rattigan's latest play and the Queen's projected visit to Australia. He gave his views with forthright clarity, often laced with a sly ironic humour which Rosy rather liked. Inevitably, however, the conversation turned – or he turned it – to the subject of Marcia.

'Absolutely appalling,' he murmured, 'grotesque, really. It must be simply frightful for you – and not helped presumably by the attentions of the police. It's always the relatives they give the third degree to!'

She agreed the thing was indeed awful but that on the whole the police had been fairly restrained in their questioning. 'You see, I knew so little of her,' she explained. 'I saw her as a child, of course, but during the war and after we seemed to go our separate ways – like ships in the night, really. As a source of insight or information I suspect the police think I'm rather useless.'

'Best to keep it that way, my dear, whatever you know or don't ... or learn, for that matter. The last thing you want is to be plagued by the heavy squad! I speak as one who has had experience of that – or at least my family did. We had an uncle who committed suicide – years ago when I was a boy. All very sad of course; but even sadder was the palaver made by the police. They got it into their heads that the death was suspicious, smelt a rat where none existed – a bit like mad dogs, really. Fortunately they were proved utterly wrong, but in the meantime my poor father and sister were really put through the mill. Not a jolly time, I can tell you.' He bent forward conspiratorially and with a broad wink said, 'Take my advice, keep well out of it: give 'em half a chance and you won't hear the end of it – the merest thing sets them off. Never underestimate the value of silence, Rosy, it can save a lot of pain.'

Keeping silent was precisely what Rosy had been endeavouring to do. Yet she was slightly surprised at his insistence, jocular though it was. Was her peace of mind really so important to him? And besides, why should he think that she might have 'learnt' anything? She *had* of course, but he wasn't to know that... Obviously the remark had been a mere coincidence, an innocuous generality. She gave a light shrug. 'I like to think they've got a few more trails to follow other than mine, or they really will be at a dead end!' Casually she tossed the ball in his direction: 'But I imagine Marcia's death must have been quite a shock for you as well; I remember your saying some nice things at the Fawcetts' party. Had you known her long?'

'Sort of, though we hadn't met for ages.' He paused fractionally, and then said, 'As a matter of fact we had enjoyed a little walk-out during the war. She and Donald, the husband, weren't hitting it off and she was clearly in need of some mild diversion which I was more than happy to supply. Your aunt was quite a stunner in those days and fun with it.' He smiled in recollection. 'But then it all rather petered out. You know how it was then – bombs, air raids, distractions etcetera. We all tended to lead rather fragile and fluctuating lives: things would change so rapidly. She got caught up elsewhere, principally with a man called Flaxman – rather an amusing chap – and I was sent overseas anyway. Connection severed. Then after the war I was in Berlin administering an engineering project in the British quarter, and when I came back to London we bumped into each other at some party – as a matter of fact I think it was one given by the Fawcetts. Sir Nicholas was alive then and my God didn't the gin flow!' He grinned at the memory, before adding, 'But Angela's still quite a gal, don't you think?'

'Oh yes,' agreed Rosy encouragingly, 'such energy! But ... ah, you were saying about Marcia...'

'So I was... Well naturally by then quite a lot of water had passed under both our bridges. She was divorced and leading a life of colourful but aimless distinction, and I was on my second marriage and starting to be rather successful at what I'm doing now – running half the country's steel industry. Or so they tell me!' He laughed and splashed some more wine into Rosy's glass. 'But we found we still rather liked each other – in a sort of non-committal way – and in both our lives there were what you might call certain lacunae. So to cut a not very exciting tale short, we briefly resumed our earlier acquaintance.' He paused, and then added, 'It was an irregular arrangement in both senses of the word ... yes, an arrangement of mutual convenience to alleviate bouts of boredom. Not one that you would be familiar with, Rosy, I am sure!' He gave her a mocking smile.

She regarded him in silence, and then said quietly: 'Perhaps not. My fiancé was shot down in the war. I loved him with all my heart. I don't think we had an "arrangement" and certainly not one to fill a gap. We just wanted to be together.'

'What it is to be young!' he laughed. 'People are more expendable than one imagines; you will learn that one day, my dear.'

Rosy thought of Adelaide Fawcett and the old woman's words: *I knew him in nappies. Beastly then, beastly now.* Had she a point?

However, the burgundy and prospect of grouse ensured that her host received a polite smile and they steered into less choppy waters.

'Still,' he continued, 'all buried in the deep past now. We rather lost touch, I'm afraid. Strange how one's life goes in phases, and things that seem real enough at the time fade and then suddenly become totally irrelevant. Well, that's certainly what happened between myself and your dear aunt: a brief reckless fling, great fun at the time but without staying power. An age away, I fear!' He laughed easily and hailed the wine waiter to offer his compliments on the Chambertin.

'So what do you do when you are not running half the country's steel industry?' Rosy enquired. 'You have a house in Yorkshire, don't you?'

'Yes, rather a rambling place and damned draughty. I try to escape to Malta whenever possible.'

'Malta?'

'Yes, my wife has a house there. Just outside Valletta with wonderful views over the bay. Weather's warm and with our two islands' wartime links the natives are delightfully friendly. They cook well too. Have you ever been?'

'No, but I–'

'My dear you must come and visit us! Silvia is a good hostess and loves showing off the gardens. I *think* you might love it. Do you the power of good to get away from your sober museum duties, not to mention all this ghastly business over poor Marcia. It must be so draining.' He gave her hand a sympathetic squeeze.

Rosy wasn't quite sure what to say. 'Er, well – no it's not much fun really ... but of course we weren't particularly close. I mean, as I explained–'

'And then of course there was poor old Clovis whatever-his-name. Simply extraordinary the way that happened, and so soon afterwards!' He stopped abruptly, looking embarrassed. 'I say, you two weren't involved or anything, were you? If so I'm terribly sorry if I've–'

'Good Lord, no!' exclaimed Rosy mentally recoiling at the thought, and then felt herself going red: not so much at the idea of herself and Clovis than at the vehemence of her denial. It had been an involuntary response, yet somehow seemed churlish – an unfair betrayal of the dead man.

'No, not your type I shouldn't think. You are too intelligent, too – how shall I put it – discerning?' He regarded her quizzically, and for a moment Rosy feared he was going to ask what her type was. She prepared to deflect the overture but needn't have bothered for he passed smoothly on to something less personal. If Maynard Latimer still practised a seduction technique then it clearly took a more delicate form.

The rest of the meal passed pleasantly, with Rosy's own remarks being met with amusement and appreciative interest. By the coffee stage she felt sufficiently mellow to indulge her curiosity about Adelaide Fawcett's antipathy. 'Dreadful business about Angela's aunt,' she began casually, 'poor old girl fell down the steps recently and is walled up in the London Clinic. But I suppose at that age—'

His normally mobile face assumed a blank expression and the genial eyes hardened. 'So one has heard,' he replied coolly. 'By far the best place for her: at least people will have a respite from those malicious fantasies she weaves.'

Rosy was startled by the sudden change. She had been on the verge of making tactful enquiry about his earlier contact with the old woman, but thought better of it. The censure echoed that of Cedric Dillworthy and Felix; but unlike theirs his held no hint of relish or readiness to be drawn, only an icy disdain. Clearly it was not a subject to be pursued.

Fortunately, at that moment the waiter appeared suggesting brandy and liqueurs, and in a trice Latimer had resumed his earlier bonhomie. 'I insist you have one for the road, Rosy – or at least for the path to the dreaded whist drive. It'll strengthen your hand and make you play like

231

a demon!'

She accepted a cognac, and with ease restored was able to say her goodbyes with genuine warmth. He hailed a taxi, kissed her lightly on the cheek, and as she climbed into the cab said, 'Remember now, I shall expect to see you in Malta. Promise me!'

CHAPTER TWENTY-SEVEN

More than a little mellowed by the luncheon libations, Rosy found Mrs Gill's whist drive less of the ordeal than she had feared. True, she did not play like a demon as Latimer had confidently predicted, but was nevertheless sufficiently insouciant to put up a moderate show and thus earn relieved gratitude from her hostess.

'My dear,' breathed Mildred Gill, 'so good of you to fill a gap, these last-minute cancellations are maddening and disrupt everything. I mean, one goes to such lengths to muster the numbers and organise the tables, and then one is let down! People are so thoughtless. But you've been an absolute brick and saved my bacon!' She emitted a merry laugh and gave Rosy's arm an appreciative squeeze. And then lowering her voice to a confidential whisper, said, 'Tell me, how are *things*? I trust the police are not being too tiresome. You know they've interviewed us again, if you please! But there's simply nothing more we can add. After all one can hardly conjure facts out of thin air – though I think that's what Mr Greenleaf rather expects. Still, I suppose he's only doing his job. Can't be easy, especially with that second horror coming so soon after. Dreadful!

'Anyway, my dear, as I was saying to Harold just the other day, you do seem to be coping awfully well. "Harold," I said, "that Rosy Gilchrist is a model of stoic dignity. A lot of young women would have gone to pieces in those circumstances, but not our Rosy. A chip off Auntie's block if you ask me!"'

Rosy was not entirely easy with the term 'our' but was even more discomfited by what she took to be an allusion to Marcia.

'Er, well, I don't know about that,' she muttered awkwardly.

'Ah but *I* do, and so does Maynard Latimer. Only recently he was saying what a sterling sort you were. And he's not the only–'

'Maynard?' said Rosy in surprise. 'But he hardly knows me, I can't think that–'

'Oh, Maynard Latimer's very shrewd, you can be sure of that. *Such* a sound fellow, and handsome with it! Not many like that these days.' She gave a rueful laugh, before adding dryly, 'Harold could take a leaf out of his book.' There was another laugh but this time the mirth seemed a trifle forced.

Before Rosy could think of a suitable response Mrs Gill was seized by a rabid-looking whist-driver clearly intent on debating some obscure rule beyond Rosy's ken – or interest. And sensing there was little she could contribute she wandered off in search of sherry and sandwiches.

The dining room was filled with a throng of guests making a dedicated raid on their hostess's refreshments. Rosy wondered whether the success of such an event could be judged by the speed at which the participants demolished the prandial offerings, i.e. the greater the speed, the greater the need to replace energies lost in fervid combat. Of course, she reflected, the converse might also be true – greed prompted by crashing boredom. But in this case it seemed it must be the former, for the room resonated with a buzz of muted approval and decorous gaiety.

Mingling politely and hoping she wouldn't be cornered by anyone avid to learn more of Marcia's fate, she edged her way towards the refreshment table where she was handed a glass by a tall man wearing a pallid expression and a clerical collar. She couldn't recall seeing him among the card players yet he looked vaguely familiar; but before she had a chance to speak he had melted away to dispense more sherry. Not counting parsons among her acquaintances Rosy was puzzled as to where she might have seen him.

'Oh, that's Brother Ignatius,' explained the woman standing next to her, 'he's a regular at these sessions, invaluable with the drinks. Always happy to offer his services. Handy, really – takes care of the dregs too. No half-empties left when Ignatius is in charge!' And draining her own glass she roared with laughter.

And then of course Rosy remembered: the man had been one of the trio of clerics presiding at Marcia's funeral – though whether also in charge of the drinks on that occasion she couldn't recall.

Drear and discomfiting, the details of her aunt's obsequies had faded into a darkened blur...

She was just on the point of gathering her things for a quiet getaway, when a finger dug her in the ribs. 'Hope you've had a successful afternoon, Miss Gilchrist,' said the voice of Harold Gill. 'My wife tells me you stepped into the breach at the last minute. Most generous. These charity things are always a little tricky to manage and one never knows what might go wrong before the off – or during the middle for that matter!' He emitted a loud chortle while Rosy looked blank. Seeing her puzzlement, he exclaimed, 'Oh, didn't she tell you? One of our group keeled over in the middle of proceedings last month and had to be carried out. Quite a little drama. Too good a lunch, I shouldn't wonder, plus the novelty of playing well for once. Obviously proved too much. Lady Trumper was most put out and vowed she would never partner her again... Mind you, I was a trifle miffed myself. The Pygmies, you see. I had got her down for at least a fiver and of course she left without contributing a shilling!'

'Oh dear,' Rosy replied vaguely.

'Personally,' he prosed on, 'had I been in that unfortunate position I would have immediately sent a cheque with my apology. The least one could do. As it was, no apology, no cheque. Extraordinary manners people have these days! I put it down to the war: people dropped their standards then and they've never been picked up since.'

Rosy smiled sympathetically, wondering how she could disentangle herself before being touched for a donation. She was blowed if she was going to yield up the crisp ten-shilling note nestling in her handbag. Would half a crown look mean? Probably.

Fortunately the question was academic for he had turned to another topic, though not one entirely reassuring. 'We had another visitation the other day, you know.'

'Visitation?'

'Yes, from Her Majesty's Law Enforcers, i.e. Messrs Greenleaf and – oh, who's the other chap? – the inspector fellow, the one that looks like Boris Karloff on a bad day. They suddenly appeared out of the blue at nine o'clock in the morning. I had barely finished my breakfast. And as they had already checked our alibis I couldn't think what they wanted. It turned out they were interested to know what we knew about Marcia's past. Naturally I told them that being a gentleman I never delve into a lady's past. I mean, there are some questions one simply does not ask!' He emitted a bellow of laughter, while Rosy felt a stab of dismay. The line of enquiry was inevitable, of course, what else had she expected? It had only been a matter of time before the police embarked on their 'historical research', digging down the years, raking up old associations, collating bits of God-knows-what... But knowing something in theory was different from being told it directly. The news was not welcome.

'And what did they say to that?' she asked politely.

'Not much. No humour, the police. I've noticed it before. Anyway, they kept going on about this coal business, i.e. could we throw any light on the matter? As if we could! "Certainly not," I said, "Mrs Beasley was our neighbour, not an intimate; we were not in the habit of discussing the details of her problems and predilections." We hardly–'

'What problems?'

He raised an eyebrow. 'Well, my dear, I should have thought that anyone in the habit of using their wardrobe as a coal cellar was bound to have some sort of problem, wouldn't you?' He gave a faint leer and tapped her playfully on the shoulder.

She recoiled and said coldly, 'I think you rather exaggerate. A single piece of coal was found, that's all. It doesn't do to get things out of proportion.'

He looked slightly abashed. 'Yes, that's what the police said... Oh well, just a little joke. Anyway, far more pressing matters – *how* about a little something for the Pygmies? We've very nearly reached our target!' He beamed encouragingly.

Rosy wanted to say bugger the Pygmies. Instead she replied, 'Ah, in that case I must consult my accountant; he gives such sound advice on that sort of thing.' And with a reciprocal beam she squeezed past a hovering couple and thence to the front door.

CHAPTER TWENTY-EIGHT

The prospect of the evening's appointment with Miss Collinger in a cheerless Soho pub did not lend enchantment to Rosy's day – although when she came to think of it, the pub was immaterial, cheerless or otherwise. The problem was Vera herself. She was not someone Rosy felt readily drawn to. Character might be all right (perhaps) but it was the manner that was daunting – hectoring, humourless, curt. Besides, there was a relentlessness about the woman which she found unnerving. In the course of his Marcia revelations Whittington hadn't mentioned her, but from what had been said by Felix and Cedric it was plain that the two were in cahoots and hell-bent on the same quest: the bomb plot document and wreaking nemesis on the collaborators. Rosy recalled her sighting of the pair huddled in close conference at the National Gallery. Had it been the merits of the Titians that so occupied them? She thought not. Far more likely aspects of strategy! The man's purpose might be overlaid by bitterness at his cousins' treatment by the Nazis – and thus the more obsessive – but Vera's impersonal outrage was nevertheless of a kind to make her a formidable pursuer. Thus Rosy guessed that the evening's meeting had been suggested not simply for 'clarification', as the woman had intimated, but to see whether the Gilchrist girl really was as ignorant of the elusive evidence as she claimed to be.

'Oh well,' Rosy sighed, 'prepare for a grilling... Better start exercising the old brainbox!' She picked up the crossword.

The pub was largely as she remembered – charmless and draughty – and she looked in vain for new radiators. The snooker table by the window had disappeared but the alcoves were still there.

And in one of them, firmly buttoned in tweeds, sipping a pint and nursing the dog, sat Vera. In front of her was a plate of fat and flaccid chips.

She greeted Rosy cordially enough but made no suggestion of buying a drink, and recalling the indifferent quality of the beer, Rosy ordered herself a large whisky; safer, and in the circumstances more fortifying.

Ignoring preliminaries, Miss Collinger got down to brass tacks. 'Thanks to Felix Smythe's rash disclosures I gather you are now fully au fait with the situation, i.e. his abortive pantomime with the coal scuttle at your aunt's house and the more vital issue of nailing those treacherous swine Marcia was blackmailing. One will get them you know. Oh yes!' She spoke with fierce certainty, a glint in her eye not so much of malice as of relish.

'Perhaps,' murmured Rosy, 'unless, of course, they get you first – as they did Marcia and presumably Clovis Thistlehyde.'

Vera shrugged. 'Marcia was a fool and Thistlehyde was doubtless in the way. He generally was.'

'But *they* might think you are. In the way, I mean.'

'Huh!' the other snorted, 'not with my training they won't. We were taught how to take a back seat in SOE, how to melt into a crowd.' Her fingers closed on a particularly bulbous chip. It evidently met with her approval for she immediately grasped another, and as an afterthought pushed the plate in Rosy's direction.

Rosy declined and was not pressed further. She took a sip of whisky, reflecting doubtfully on Miss Collinger's claim to melting anonymity. Her flair for self-effacement was not easily discerned.

'I also gather from Felix that you had already learnt something of Marcia's activities in the war and her crass stupidity over the Flaxman fellow and its consequences. I must say that came as a shock to us all. Personally I have found the whole thing extremely painful – I was very attached to your aunt at one time. Very.' She sounded bitter (as well she might) and scowled at Rosy with a look of belligerent defiance.

Rosy nodded mutely, knowing there was nothing she could say in defence of Marcia and wishing she were somewhere else. But before she could formulate a response, however weak, Miss Collinger continued, 'I suppose you got your information about Marcia from Gilbert Sabatier when he paid you that visit. I didn't know he had done that, only told me about it recently. Plays his cards close to his chest, always has... Anyway, I gather he instructed you to contact him if you discovered anything concerning your aunt's blackmail data – a letter perhaps, a list of names. At the time you apparently denied all know-ledge... I assume that *was* correct?' She stared hard at Rosy, jaw working on another chip but eyes never leaving the girl's face.

'Yes,' Rosy replied coolly, 'perfectly.'

'And is it still?' she persisted.

'Of course,' Rosy lied.

Miss Collinger said nothing but continued to regard her with steady gaze. 'You do realise that it is imperative we get our hands on whatever it is Marcia had. We need that evidence, it's crucial. I trust you realise that.'

240

'Actually, what concerns me,' replied Rosy, 'is not so much *your* need of the evidence but the need of those with most to lose, i.e. Marcia's "victims". Unlike yours, their need isn't for justice, it's to save their skins, and we have already seen what they are capable of. As such, they are highly dangerous and I for one have no intention of getting involved in amateur war games. *Should* anything of relevance come into my hands I would go straight to the police.' She took a gulp of her drink and tried to look assertive.

'Hmm,' said the other thoughtfully, 'you said something to that effect during tea at Bourne and Hollingsworth. At the time it irritated me rather, but with hindsight I realise that the likelihood of your taking that particular step is remote. Revelations too distasteful. After all, it's not everyone who wants it blazoned abroad that their aunt was a traitor to her country. Speaking for myself I shouldn't like to have that slur on my family name. And from what I have observed, Rosy Gilchrist, neither would you. It's the one thing we have in common: a sort of cussed pride.' She gave a wintry smile, shoved her plate aside and fed Raymond the remaining chip.

Rosy sighed. The old bat was right and she knew it. Still, she was damned if she was going to be entirely squashed: Vera herself had something to worry about and it wasn't just hurt pride!

'You are right,' she admitted, 'it would all be most unsavoury. But not as unsavoury as being put on the suspects' list for Marcia's murder... Were the police to learn that your brother had been a casualty of the coal-scuttle operation, had

241

taken his life, perhaps, as a result of Marcia's action, they might well think you had a motive for wanting her dead.' She looked down at the floor, adding quietly, 'And who knows, perhaps you might have been justified...'

'Possibly,' said Miss Collinger tersely. 'But yes, you are perfectly correct. One is indeed only too aware of the delicacy of one's position. Vengeance is a common enough reason for murder, especially in families. Which is why I tread carefully and ensure that I reveal nothing more to the police than they need to know – a feat not too difficult with that inspector in charge. So in that respect you and I are similarly placed. We share an uncomfortable secret and each is dependent on the other's discretion for its safekeeping. An amusing irony, don't you think?' Rosy did not think. But with a reluctant nod conceded the woman had a point re their shared position.

She was just casting about for an excuse to leave, when the other said in a voice that was almost jovial, 'I trust your lunch with Latimer wasn't compromised by a petrified jaw. That man Dingle always pumps in too much stuff!'

Rosy gaped in indignation. How the hell did the old trout know about that?

'How do you–' she began.

'Cedric mentioned it. He was there at the back, lunching with a friend – *not* Felix, you understand, so kindly keep that under your hat.' She gave a wry chuckle.

'*I* didn't see him!' Rosy exclaimed.

'Well, no, you wouldn't. They were discreet. They always are – which is precisely why they

242

were sitting away from the front; Smythe can be very touchy about these things. Anyway, I trust that you were entertained by Latimer. He can be quite amusing when he wants to – and generous.'

'Yes, thank you,' replied Rosy stiffly. She was damned if she was going to discuss her luncheon dates with Vera Collinger.

But the latter seemed disposed to pursue the subject. 'Handsome in a way, if that's what one likes. He knew your aunt, of course.'

'Yes,' Rosy said indifferently, 'so I gather. They were quite close years ago but hadn't been in touch for some time.'

'Is that what he told you?' asked Miss Collinger.

'Well, yes – yes he did.'

'A few edges shaved off the truth there,' the other snorted.

'I am sorry, I'm not quite–'

'Maynard Latimer was conducting an affair with Marcia up to within *days* of her death. He has a small pied-à-terre off Jermyn Street for when he's in London, but just now and again – "under cover of nightfall", as they say – he would visit her at home in St John's Wood.' Miss Collinger gave a dry laugh, adding, 'But every subterfuge has its fraught moments; I gather there was one occasion when he thought he had been seen by a passenger in a passing car – someone he knew, a woman, I believe. But as nothing was ever said, either he had been mistaken or the person took no interest. Still, apparently it quite rattled him.'

Rosy was both astonished and sceptical; but she

was also intrigued. And as antidote to Vera's smouldering cheroot and not wishing to appear startled, she drew out her lighter and lit a cigarette. 'Really?' she said casually. 'He seemed very emphatic in telling me it was over some time ago.'

'Well he would, wouldn't he? Latimer is, or was, a notorious philanderer. It was an open secret – I don't mean with the public but among those within his own tight circle. It is amazing how easily those with style, charm and influence are forgiven their shortcomings. My brother was much the same: he could behave outrageously and no one would care, or if they did they kept their thoughts to themselves... Ask Felix,' she added with a grim smile. 'However, a couple of years ago Latimer's boat was rocked and he had to change tack, or at least conduct himself with rather more discretion. There was an unscheduled sea change.' She broke off, bending down to tickle the dog and disentangle its lead from the table leg.

'So what happened?' asked Rosy, trying to maintain a cool indifference while at the same time curious.

'The sainted Silvia.'

'*Who?*'

'The wife – she lives in Malta, you know.'

Rosy nodded. 'Yes, he did mention her.'

'Only mentioned? Hmm. So I assume you won't know the full story.'

Rosy shook her head, perplexed. 'Why sainted?'

Miss Collinger sighed and lit another cheroot, mercifully a little less acrid than the previous. 'The woman is an invalid ... beautiful in a wheelchair, and latterly taken to wearing a lace

244

mantilla. Rather a showy form of piety I always think. She is rich, exceedingly well connected and not a little boring … always was, even before the accident.' She paused and then said musingly, 'I have known others similarly placed who despite their handicap have been remarkable for their stimulus and gaiety; but such cannot be said of the lovely lady in Malta. Alas, Silvia Beresford was dull from birth.'

'So why did he marry her? And what sort of accident?'

'In answer to your first question, I should say that was obvious: the money, the impressive connections and the undoubted beauty. The first two retained their usefulness, the last I imagine palled quite quickly. Without an accompanying wit it tends to do that. Haven't you noticed?'

'I don't think I've ever thought about it, really.'

'No, I don't suppose you have. Not within your sphere, perhaps.' For a moment Rosy wondered if she had heard an acid note in the voice but couldn't be sure.

'Anyway, regarding the accident,' Miss Collinger continued carelessly, 'she fell out of a tree.'

'Oh…' Rosy felt vaguely surprised.

'Yes, it's not the most distinguished type of accident, is it? Not like being thrown from a horse or mauled by a bear. Wasn't even a very tall tree, and what she was doing there in the first place nobody really knows – most women of my acquaintance tend not to clamber about in trees. But it did for her all right, been stymied ever since.' She stooped down, and blasting its face with a swirl of smoke, fed the dog a biscuit from her pocket. Unperturbed by the fumes the dachshund fell upon the titbit like a marauding lion. Perhaps it thought it was.

'But how very sad,' Rosy said. 'I hadn't realised–'

'Oh yes, it's sad all right. But it's something else too. You see, his friendship with your aunt has put him in a tricky position, which is why he is so keen to keep it concealed, or at least to let it be thought that the whole thing was finished years ago. People are prepared to grant a man of his standing a degree of licence, indeed the image of the "gay dog" can even hold a certain cachet. But they are less tolerant when the betrayed wife is not only beautiful but also crippled: it makes her a martyr and him a heel. Had it become public knowledge the liaison might have done serious damage to his reputation. Still could really. Yes, Silvia falling out of that tree put a different complexion on things: he had to change his ways, or at least be *seen* to do so.'

'But if it was so secret, how did you get to know all about it?'

'In the obvious way: Marcia told me. We were friends – or at any rate I tended to be her confidante.'

Tacitly noting the distinction, Rosy said, 'So Marcia confided in you but not to anyone else?'

'Not as far as I am aware; though of course had she done so then this latest development would jeopardise Latimer's position even further. He's in for a K, you know, possibly even a new creation in the peerage – services to industry etc. Not bad for a man whose father was a fiddle maker ... or was it penny whistles?' She paused musingly.

Ignoring the matter of Latimer's antecedents, Rosy asked, 'What do you mean, "development"?'

Miss Collinger gave her a withering look. 'For someone of your intelligence, Miss Gilchrist, I should have thought that was obvious. The murder, of course! Were it known that Latimer had been conducting an illicit friendship with Marcia the police would be on his tail quicker than you could say knife. I don't suggest that he himself is implicated – no reason to be – but the publicity would be quite enough to sink his hopes of the knighthood, let alone anything further... Yes, that particular event must have given him a very nasty shock. On the whole quite a lot at stake for him, I should say. Could be quite sticky.' She gave a wolfish grin.

Vera Collinger's version of Latimer's story had unsettled Rosy, and she left the pub for the walk home in a state of some dudgeon. If the woman's words were to be believed, then Latimer had been lying to her throughout much of their lunch date, and lying with calculated purpose. Clearly she had been charmingly duped. Idiot!

It wasn't the revelation of a philandering past that upset her (after all, no more than she had expected – and his own business in any case) but the fact that he had used her so cynically to lay a false trail, to spin a smokescreen.

She scowled at a passing cat, reflecting sourly that concern for reputation and the lure of public honours were lethal forces in the human psyche ... but then paused, confronted by her own frail psyche with its fear of her aunt's past activities being exposed to all and sundry. Wasn't it concern for reputation that governed her own reluctance to aid the police? Very largely (just as Vera had discerned). But at least in her case the fear had taken a *negative* form: she had told no lies, volunteered no misleading information, merely said as little as possible and done her best to keep out of it all. In fact precisely as bloody Latimer had counselled. Besides, surely it was not so much her own skin she was trying to save as Marcia's – wasn't it? Not exactly: she would be tainted by association and so in a way was probably as self-preserving as Latimer, if less overtly. Yet the smoothness of his lie rankled and she still felt angry.

And then suddenly anger vanished, eclipsed by a thought as stark as it was shocking. Was it conceivable that Latimer himself had done the murder: felled his mistress to keep her quiet, to scotch the one possible bar to the coveted accolade? Had Marcia become a burden, a potential embarrassment – perhaps cut up rough and threatened to blow the gaff on the affair and so scupper everything?

She stopped abruptly, staring at her reflected face in a shop window. Could he really have done it? No, absurd! The face frowned, even Vera had dismissed the idea: *I don't suggest he is implicated – no reason to be...* Yet, Rosy argued, even a seasoned bloodhound could miss a scent. What Vera had stressed was Latimer's *current* social peril should hints of his recent relations with the murder victim leak out and become a matter of police interest, however temporary. But suppose

248

he had been bedevilled by earlier fears, fears that prompted the deed itself? Vera had said he had much at stake; but perhaps even she had under-rated the value he placed on the winnings – or their loss. Rosy recalled the truism that murders are often committed for the most banal and seemingly trivial motives: it all boiled down to circumstance and personal priority. Presumably fear of lost status or forfeited accolades could be as great a determinant as hate, lust or avarice ... and killings stirred by panic, for whatever cause, were legion. Broad categories there might be, but within those categories motives for murder were as many and varied as its perpetrators.

She walked on, re-living their lunchtime con-versation and the patronising way he had dismissed her feelings for Johnnie: *People are more expendable than one imagines; you will learn that one day, my dear...* Had Marcia become expendable? Indeed, her death imperative? Perhaps so. And if the man had a motive she guessed he also had the nerve to exploit it. As to opportunity, well it was obvious – he could have shot Marcia during an assignation... No, not obvious: Vera had said he visited 'under cover of nightfall', whereas the death had occurred in mid afternoon, the body found at five o'clock. But people didn't always keep to their routines. And besides, if he had been desperate to get the thing done perhaps he had grown bold and risked a daylight entry. Yet what about Clovis painting the portrait? Let alone Felix muffled in the hall curtain. It would have needed pretty neat timing to avoid that pair! Yet obviously someone *had* avoided them and dispatched

Marcia after their exit. So presumably that some-one could have been Latimer as well as any...

She brooded. Plausible? Just about. But if that were so it made mincemeat of Whittington's conviction that Marcia had been killed by one of her blackmail victims haunted by the hangman's noose. Perhaps Latimer's own fears of exposure were as acute as those of the wartime conspirators and he had just happened to do the job first.

The next instant Rosy gasped and nearly tripped over the kerb. As acute *as those of?* Why assume a distinction? Suppose they were one and the same! She recalled Wooden Leg's theory that with the assassination plan no longer relevant, the plotters had swathed themselves in the cloak of the British Establishment, safe in its garb of ser-vice and rectitude. Admittedly Maynard Lati-mer's sexual mores may have raised the odd and envious eyebrow, but his contribution to the country's economic recovery after the ravages of war was indisputable, and (with the exception of Adelaide Fawcett whose judgement was question-able anyway) he was generally regarded as a 'good egg'. Yes, if anyone were wrapped tightly within the folds of the Establishment it was certainly he.

But what about the use of Felix's wretched coal scuttle? Surely an unduly crude gesture for one as poised as Latimer. It suggested either a debased sense of humour or a vindictive impulse. Neither seemed in character. In any case, she mused, could one really suspect a man simply because he happened to fit a social category – or indeed that he was anxious to conceal his relationship with the deceased? No, of course not. She was doubtless barking up the wrong tree, i.e. indulging in outlandish speculation brought on by injured pride and too much drink with the likes of Vera Collinger!

By this time she had reached her front door and was about to insert the key when there was the sound of a cough and a voice from the gloom said, 'Ah, that's lucky, I was just about to give up. Wasn't quite sure if your bell was working.'

Rosy spun round, visions of a murderous Latimer immediately re-forming. 'What the–' she began, but stopped, as out of the shadows glided not Latimer but a man wearing what at first sight appeared to be a dressing gown. She blinked and then realised that the apparel was in fact some sort of cassock and that its owner was the priest she had seen at the Gills' whist drive.

Flustered, she exclaimed, 'Oh I'm sorry, I didn't see you there. It's Brother Ignatius isn't it?'

'It's the habit,' he replied apologetically, 'it doesn't show up in the dark – and by and large most people call me Lola.'

Oh Christ, thought Rosy, that's all I need! She said dryly, 'Do they? Now I wonder why that is.'

'Short for Loyola – Ignatius Loyola, you see.'

'But he was a Jesuit. What were you doing in the Anglican church at my aunt's funeral – you were there, weren't you? Or have the Anglo-Catholics appropriated the names of Roman saints? Newman's notion, I suppose – they always said he was excessive.'

'Oh no, nothing to do with Newman. You see I *am* a Jesuit but the Saint Anselm lot asked me along to help out. Their censer-bearer had broken his wrist and they needed a swift replacement. I am rather a dab hand at swinging the lead – or the censer for that matter!' He gave a bray of mirth, produced a handkerchief and began to trumpet loudly.

Rosy took a step back, and before she could ascertain why exactly he had been ringing her doorbell at that late hour, he said, 'Actually, I am quite a pal of the Reverend Keithley there, and it was he who persuaded me to participate – said there was likely to be some rather fine wine served at the wake, and knowing my partiality for–'

'I don't remember any,' broke in Rosy accusingly, visualising only the British Sherry and rancid fruit cup.

'No,' he said sadly, 'you're right, there wasn't any.' He looked pensive and Rosy grasped the moment to ask what he wanted.

'It's a bit complicated,' he replied slowly, 'and er, well it's getting rather chilly. Do you think we might...?' He gestured hopefully towards the front door. She hesitated, far from sure that such hospitality would be prudent. He must have seen her concern for he smiled and said, 'Oh, have no fear, Miss Gilchrist, my only weapons are my tracts.'

'Tracts? What tracts?' she exclaimed nervously. 'I hope you are not going to bombard me with literature from the Catholic Truth Society!'

'Hah! Don't worry, only my little joke. Actually, I have a message for you.'

If anything the little joke made her even more doubtful; but noting his chattering teeth and intrigued by the mention of a message (from God?) she allowed charity and curiosity to prevail. So crossing fingers that this wasn't to be her last mistake on earth, she unlocked the door and invited him in.

CHAPTER TWENTY-NINE

'So what's this message, then?' she asked warily, once they were seated in the sitting room.

Brother Ignatius cleared his throat and threw a wistful glance at the half-bottle of whisky on the sideboard.

Certainly not, thought Rosy, I'm sick of strangers coming in here at night and guzzling my Scotch uninvited. It was bad enough with the other one! Thus she affected not to notice, and repeated the question.

'Well I don't have the message *as such*, but I think I know of its likely whereabouts,' he replied, crossing his ankles and gazing at her earnestly.

'Really,' said Rosy tersely. 'And who is it from?'

'It's from your aunt. I meant to–'

'Aunt Marcia?' she yelped in astonishment. 'What on earth do you mean?'

'What I say. She gave me to understand that–'

'So where did it come from, this message? Beyond the grave – the *other side*, perhaps?' she enquired acidly.

'Oh no, this side. Entirely this side. She told me about a week before her unfortunate – before her

unhappy accident; said she had left you something important, a packet and—'

'Where?'

'What? Oh under the draining board, well the
sink, actually.'

Rosy regarded him thoughtfully, taking in the
thin primly crossed ankles, sparse eyebrows,
nicotined fingers and slightly stained soutane
(vestiges of 'good wine'?), and reflected ruefully
that it was indeed a great mistake taking this man
in. She resolved to ring the Reverend Keithley
first thing in the morning and advise him to
select his friends more carefully. Meanwhile, how
to get rid of him?

But she had no time to ponder for at the next
moment he said simply, 'Your aunt was always
very kind to me. I think we had a bond. I taught
her to play backgammon, you know.'

'She hated backgammon.'

'Not with me she didn't. We would take it in
turns.'

'Take what in turns?' Rosy asked irritably.

'Well, one week she would supply the gin bottle
and the next week I would. Though I have to say
that I fear my offering was vastly inferior to hers.
In my line of work one can only run to a standard
blend from the off-licence, whereas she always
produced the most exotic stuff. Delicious!' He
crinkled his nose as if scenting vestigial fumes.
'Ah well, nothing lasts does it?'

'No,' Rosy agreed pointedly, glancing at the
clock, 'it doesn't.' And then a thought struck her;
'Tell me – Lola,' she said cautiously, 'this message
– did she tell you about it during one of these jolly

254

sessions, e.g. over the dice and the gin?'

He hesitated. 'Uhm ... yes, yes she did. That's it – we had been engaged in a really good tussle. She was on to a winning streak and had celebrated by opening another bottle. We were well into that when she suddenly announced she had something to confide. And I said I certainly hoped not as I was fed up with listening to people's dreary confessions and the whole point of the game was to escape such penance. She remarked that there was a clear difference between confiding and confessing and she was surprised that I was unaware of it. You know, Miss Gilchrist, your aunt could be quite pernickety where language was concerned. I remember once when–'

'But what did she *say* – or were you both too pickled to notice?'

He smiled thinly. 'Admittedly her words *were* a bit indistinct and I wasn't totally attending – trying to close my ears to any looming confession! – but from what I recall it was something like: "So I've shoved the bloody thing behind the main pipe under the kitchen sink. Safer than the bank any day, snooping busybodies. I did send my niece a letter telling her where it was but damned if I can remember posting it – probably lost the perishing thing. Oh well, doesn't matter much, let's have another drink. Who knows, I might just reveal *all* one day. That would jolt her up a bit!" She seemed to find that very funny and collapsed in gales of laughter. I can't say I entirely saw the joke but thought it polite to join in and we finished the–'

'Finished the bottle?'

'Actually I was going to say the game, but since you mention it, yes – the bottle as well.' He gazed at the ceiling as if in meditation, before adding, 'That was the last time I saw her; a very mellow evening we had. In fact, come to think of it, I am not sure it wasn't the mellowest evening I have ever spent...' The bland face took on a look of wistful regret.

There was a long silence. And then Rosy cleared her throat and asked casually: 'Er, so have you mentioned this to the police?'

'The police? Oh no, on the whole I tend to avoid them. Father Caspian, my superior, says it's best that way – says one should never offer a hostage to fortune. I am not quite sure what he means by that but it is doubtless true. He is very wise, Father Caspian.'

Bully for Father Caspian, thought Rosy. Out loud she said firmly, 'I am sure he is right. Life is complicated enough as it is, don't you find?'

He nodded. 'Indeed, a veritable vale of tears. But if I may say so, Mrs Beasley always contrived to inject a ray of joy into proceedings. I shall miss her.'

'And no doubt the exotic brand of gin too,' Rosy felt like adding, and then flushed, ashamed of so unworthy a thought. To make up for it she heard herself saying briskly: 'Now, Lola, before I hustle you out, how about a small nightcap to speed you back to your – well to wherever you've come from? I'm sure it's cold out there.'

He accepted with alacrity and (as if still in censer mode) dealt with it in one fell swoop. She accompanied him down the stairs. And with a few more pleasantries and murmuring something about lighting her a dozen candles, he glided back into the shadows whence he had come.

Something important under the sink? Was he mad or was she? Or was Aunt Marcia? But Marcia had been cold-bloodedly shot to death – there must have been some sanity there to prompt such an end. So what now, for God's sake?

She went to the window, flung it wide and glared helplessly up at the indifferent moon. Only one answer presented itself: sleep.

Her sleep was long and dreamless; yet she awoke unrefreshed and less than eager to deal with the demands of Stanley and quips from Leo, whose curiosity over Marcia was becoming tiresome. At first his interest in the case had been of little account – if anything the well-meant levity a means of relief from her shock. But at that stage she had been ignorant of the dubious complexities of her aunt's life, and rather like Leo merely a puzzled bystander. But *now*, insidiously drawn into the whole murky web, she had much to hide, and her colleague's amiable probing had grown proportionately onerous.

She made a scratch breakfast and reviewed the priest's revelation. Was the man with his startling tale really to be trusted? Had there been an unperceived menace behind those earnest blue eyes, mischief or malice in the prissy tones? On the whole she thought not. In his own cranky way he had seemed genuine enough, a kindly lush of the sort Marcia might typically have been amused to befriend; one no doubt a trial to his superiors but basically harmless. And picturing the backgammon session she saw the two of them befuddled in matey collusion: he a little maudlin perhaps, Marcia hectoring, giggly, garrulous. So damned garrulous, in fact, and too tight to care, that she had spilt the beans about the cache under the sink! Fortunately Lola's thoughts must have been largely fixed on the board (or occupied with parrying the threat of a confession), for he appeared to know nothing of the packet's contents and had clearly not pursued the matter. Yet if that were the case why had he emerged only now to deliver the 'message'? She stirred her coffee, threw in more sugar and licked the spoon, concluding that perhaps for a mind habitually cast in a haze of gin and incense the finer details of that last rendezvous were only just beginning to surface.

Her own mind gave a sudden lurch. *That last rendezvous?* No wonder 'wise' Father Caspian had warned him off the police! If it got out that the priest had been a regular visitor at the deceased's house, surely he, like Maynard Latimer, would join the ranks of potential suspects. Yes, more than likely – although remembering Lola's words it sounded as if Caspian's counsel had been general rather than specific, a pious hope that his protégé's penchant for drink would not invite undue notice from the law with the attendant embarrassment. She imagined a newspaper item: 'Drunk and disorderly: Jesuit priest found legless in Mayfair, reportedly resting from spiritual labours. Hailing a passing countess, the gentleman asked if she would care to escort him back to his place of sanctuary. Smiling sweetly, said countess declined and passed by on the other side...'

Rosy got up from the table, banished such nonsense and turned instead to the vital question: if the packet was indeed where the man claimed, when could she get it and how?

The question took on additional urgency at the museum where she was accosted by Leo, all beams and bonhomie. 'I say,' he announced, 'I gather there's to be an auction pretty soon, there's a notice in the *Marylebone Gossip*. Interesting to see what the stuff fetches. I wonder if it will be well attended.'

'What? Sorry – I was miles away.'

'Your aunt's house, they've accelerated the sale of the contents. Donkeys must be getting restive!'

She smiled falsely, her mind in a spin. This was a facer all right.

'Mind you,' Leo continued cheerfully, 'it's a moot point whether the fell deed will reduce or enhance the value – all depends whether the punters are squeamish or ghoulish. What do you think? Shall we have a bet on it?'

'I think nothing,' she snapped. 'And I certainly have no intention of betting on the contents of my late aunt's property.' She turned quickly into her office feeling both angry and pompous.

Later, by way of a peace offering, she bought him a cream bun in the canteen, and watched as he scraped out the synthetic filling, replacing it with equally ersatz strawberry jam, and tentatively tried the result.

'Any good?' she asked.

He shook his head. 'Not really, but thanks anyway. My penance for a singularly crass remark. I can quite see that this business must be pretty tough on you, not an easy time at all. But if it's any comfort, there was another item in today's rag which might be of interest – sort of interim statement put out by the police. Something to the effect that after conducting a thorough and sedulous investigation they are confident a breakthrough is imminent and that positive results can be expected in the not-too-distant future.'

Rosy was intrigued but sceptical. 'Do you think that means anything?'

'Your guess is as good as mine. Either they have found a vital clue and are over the moon or it's pure poppycock devised to spread balm and complacency. I rather suspect the latter.' He paused, and added with a slow smile, 'But I wouldn't dare to offer a bet.'

She grinned and just for an instant wished she could tell him all about it. It would be nice to have a friendly ally ... instead of the less than reliable trio of Cedric, Felix and the fearsome Vera. But pride and common sense directed otherwise. It would only need one thoughtless word, one ill-judged confidence, and the domino effect could be appalling. No, on that score her cue must be silence.

Instead she said, 'How's Dr Stanley today? Since you are in the betting vein I'll lay you a bob he's in a huff about Mrs Burkiss. She scrubbed his desk yesterday. I warned her not to.'

'You're on,' Leo laughed, 'five to one?'

CHAPTER THIRTY

Bets were also being offered elsewhere. 'I'll lay you five to one,' grumbled Greenleaf's superior, 'it's a nutcase, some lunatic baying at the moon and having fun at our expense. I know that sort – fruitcakes who take to murder like the rest of us take to billiards or the flicks. A sort of pastime, you might say, a means of spicing up the day and making us all look charlies; and the worst of it is that when it's one of them there's no trail, no logic, nothing to give a lead or make sense. Bastard!' He stared moodily at Greenleaf's biscuits, stretched over and took a couple. There was silence broken only by the pounding of the rain and a remorseless crunching.

Greenleaf cleared his throat. 'That's not what Harris thinks,' he said.

'Harris? What's Harris got to do with anything?'

'He's got a theory. It's about–'

'Then he's no right to have a theory. That little whippersnapper's here to learn, not to teach his elders and betters to suck eggs!'

'Grandmothers.'

'What?'

'It's grandmothers who suck eggs – leastways, who don't need to be taught, if you see what I mean.'

The inspector stared at him. 'Christ Almighty,

Sergeant, no I do not see what you mean. Not one little bit I don't!' And so saying, he got up, filched another biscuit and stalked from the room.

Greenleaf sighed, chewed his pencil and resumed his report on the interview with Vera Collinger.

It was not the easiest of tasks because she had not been the easiest of women: cool, watchful, sardonic; at times seemingly cooperative and forthcoming, but more often than not curt or casually indifferent. She had answered their questions with a gruff assurance. There had been no hesitations, no stumblings or signs of tension – and yet all the time he had had the distinct impression that much could have been said that never was: views suppressed, feelings veiled. He had also sensed an air of calculation, of a mind shrewder than his own subtly directing the whole damn thing as if she had been a seasoned actor slyly controlling the producer's intention: alert (though not necessarily compliant) to cues; finely tuned to audience response; following a script yet at the same time making subtle adjustments to suit her own whim or ego...

Yes, he mused, the woman had yielded up the requested facts all right. (Mental state prior to death? Cheerful. Possible enemies? Only those trounced at cards and the occasional wife upstaged at the races or The Pink Flamingo. Wartime occupation? Useful work: assisting refugees ... etc., etc.) But he sensed that beyond those replies there lay an undisclosed hinterland of intriguing possibility. But it was no use being intrigued if one hadn't got a lever! How to source the unsaid and undivulged, excavate the buried shards – the bits of debris deliberately concealed?

Still, there was one anomaly in her version: the deceased's frame of mind. The artist chap had made a point of saying how disturbed Marcia Beasley had been by the parcel of coal. What was it he had said? That she had cursed, gone dead white and then 'all saggy'. So saggy, in fact, that the painter (rather ungallantly, Greenleaf couldn't help feeling) had called it a day and taken himself off. 'Not another effing one!' had been her cry of dismay. No, it didn't sound much like the reaction of a woman in a state of stable cheerfulness. In fact he had said as much to Miss Collinger, but she had merely shrugged and observed that from what she recalled of Clovis Thistlehyde he would exaggerate anything to command attention. Possibly she had a point. He sighed and turned from Collinger to Harris.

Despite the inspector's scorn, the lad's theory might just hold water; worth pursuing at any rate. Something might turn up – which was more than anything had so far!

Blackmail: that was the boy's theory. 'It is my belief,' he had said solemnly, 'that that Mrs Beasley was an Arch Controller.'

'A *what?*' Greenleaf had exclaimed.

'You know, sir – she'd got someone's number and was giving them merry hell. Probably bleeding them white, that's what!'

'I see,' he had said, 'so in your estimable opinion the deceased was engaging in a spot of blackmail – but what do you mean, "Arch Controller"?'

'Ah well, that's just it, sir, it may not have been

263

only a spot. She may have had a whole string of victims in her sights and was operating a sort of one woman Mafia ... and then – and then one day they had enough, or one of them had, and did her in.'

'Why several and not just one – wouldn't it have been simpler?' Greenleaf had enquired.

'Psychology,' was the sage reply.

'Oh yes?'

'Yes, I've read a lot about it. Blackmailers, they get a sort of *urge*. They like it, it gets a hold; and so one client leads to another. And then sometimes they get blaize–'

'Get what?'

'Blaize – sort of smug and complacent and think they can try it on anywhere. She probably had the whole of St John's Wood on its knees. Yes, I bet that's what she was,' he had repeated darkly, 'an *Arch* Controller!'

Greenleaf had watched with interest as Harris withdrew a couple of toffees from his pocket and started to chew them thoughtfully. 'Hmm. You seem very well informed – where do you get it from?'

'Encyclopaedias ... and then, of course, there's my old gran.'

'Your old gran! What's she got to do with it?'

'Writes detective novels.'

'Does she now,' he had said sardonically, 'so what's her name?'

'Delilah del Rio.'

'*Delilah del–*' Greenleaf had gasped. 'But she's the bodice-ripper writer with all those saucy covers. You're having me on!' But even as he spoke he knew that was unlikely. Harris's flair for comedy was nil.

The blackmailing idea had stuck in his mind, though initially he had been more taken with the image of Harris's granny churning out hot rubbish on an ancient typewriter – or even with a quill. Either way it didn't seem quite nice, not proper... Still, he mused, with a bit of luck and flannel he might persuade the lad to get him a signed copy (not that the wife would approve) and wondered vaguely what brand of toffee Harris favoured.

CHAPTER THIRTY-ONE

For the rest of the day Rosy could think of only one thing: the package under the sink – assuming it was still there or if it existed at all. Still, the priest had seemed sincere enough in his tale, but it would be typical of Marcia's caprice to change the hiding place or destroy the thing altogether. In any case, even if it were there would it amount to anything? After all, there was no guarantee that this *was* the evidence pursued by Vera and Whittington and indeed by the collaborators. It might be something quite other – something personal: a collection of letters and family memorabilia, or even a letter to herself regretting their rift, a belated attempt to retie the knot of kinship...

Rosy sighed. No, that last conjecture was a fantasy and she knew it. Compared to that possibility the 'dynamite' data seemed a far better bet. And in which case she needed to get hold of it pronto. Once the house contents were disposed of and the donkey people took formal possession the thing was anybody's, as sooner or later it was bound to be discovered. And while she had no desire to shield those implicated she certainly didn't want Marcia's name to feature. Questions would naturally be asked as to what it had been doing in the house, why had the former owner possessed such sensational intelligence? Questions which could lead to frightful revelations. Yes, at all costs it had to be retrieved. Besides, she thought with a surge of defiance, wasn't it her right to have the thing, to learn its exact nature and to do with it as she felt fit? Marcia Beasley had been her aunt, for God's sake. And according to Loitering Lola it had been placed there for *her* to read – not for the police or Whittington or any other snooper!

She frowned. The problem was getting the key: she had handed it back to the solicitors and it was doubtful they would like the idea of someone with no formal claim poking around at this stage. And even if they could be persuaded, they would never allow unchaperoned access. The last time had been a fluke.

Desperate cases needed desperate remedies: Vera Collinger. Despite what the woman had said earlier, Rosy was sure she still had her own key – regard for officialdom not being Vera's style. The snag would be her reaction. She was unlikely to produce it without asking the reason and would doubtless guess the truth. But the truth, of course, was the bait, the one thing that would ensure cooperation: cooperation at a price as she was bound to insist that she came as well. In which case, Rosy told herself, so be it. 'Let her, but I'm hanged if I'll let her get her paws on the thing!'

There was a further snag: she was ex-directory and Rosy had lost her card. She went to the telephone and dialled Felix. 'I need Vera's number,' she announced, 'it's urgent!'

'That's a novelty,' he replied. 'Personally I have always found the urgency lay in flight rather than contact.'

'Perhaps. But as it happens I need it rather quickly.'

'Hmm. It's not exactly one of those I hold in my head, but I'll see what I can do.' There were sounds of a drawer being opened and papers shuffled. 'Ah, here it is,' he muttered, 'Langham 4849. But she may not be there. She's off, or about to be.'

'Off? What do you mean?'

'Off to Rome with her new protégée, the adenoidal Deirdre. Wants to show her the delights of the Forum, or what's left of them after Mussolini's capers. They're going tonight on the Golden Arrow. Apparently the girl is fascinated by antiquities, though I should think that sharing a couchette with Vera is a high price to pay for culture. Not my idea of fun!' He gave a snide titter.

'I don't care where she is going or with whom, I just want the key!' Rosy exclaimed.

'What key?' he asked curiously.

'The *key* to Aunt Marcia's house. I'm sure she's got it.'

'But I thought there was going to be an auction there at any minute.'

'*Precisely:* the day after tomorrow, which is why I want it now. There is something there that needs to be rescued and–'

'Rescued? You mean like a stray dog?'

'Of course not,' she said impatiently, 'it's an envelope or a sheaf of papers – oh, I don't know, it's...'

'Ah,' he said slowly, 'daylight dawns. It's the stuff she's been after, I suppose. Not that one wishes to get involved in *that* little mission. I mean when all's said and done I–'

'Look, Felix,' she said hastily, 'thank you so much for your help. Now if you don't mind, I really must try to catch Vera. It's important.'

She rang off and tried the number. After an interminable time the phone was answered. 'Whoever you are you will have to be brief,' the gruff voice announced, 'I am about to depart.'

'Yes, I know,' Rosy said, 'Felix told me. You see it's to do with Aunt Marcia's house...'

When she had finished there was a cough followed by a silence. And then Miss Collinger said, 'This is all very difficult. In normal circumstances I would go there myself instantly, but it really isn't feasible. Therefore, Rosy Gilchrist, I shall entrust the key to you–'

'Oh, thank you so much–' Rosy started to say in relief.

'On *condition* that Felix Smythe goes with you. It is essential that you find whatever it is and bring it to me when I return. A person on their

268

own is not to be relied upon. One cannot risk amateur bungling. Not that I rate Smythe to be the best of accomplices, but in the circumstances he will have to do.'

Amateur bungling! Rosy was indignant. But she knew from the woman's voice that argument was fruitless. However, she did point out that Felix was loath to get involved and would be far from willing.

'Oh, he'll be willing all right, or at least malleable. You'll see.'

'Really?' said Rosy with some scepticism.

'Felix will do most things to further his floral career and I happen to have one or two useful contacts. He can't rely on the patronage of royalty for ever; he needs other strings to his bow and he knows it. For example, there's a certain gentleman I happen to be acquainted with who has a passion for orchids and gardenias. Most of the time he lives on Cap Ferrat writing and, er, other things... But on the few occasions when he's here in London he *has* to be surrounded by sheaves of flowers – only the very best. They remind him of the south I suppose, and his tastes are very fastidious. Yes, I think Felix might supply Mr M's requirements quite well ... *were* one to slip in a good word. And who knows, he might even get an invitation to the villa.' There was an imperceptible chuckle.

For a brief moment Rosy was intrigued by the unlikely synergy of Vera and Mr M and wondered how they had met, but the prospect of the key and access to the papers eclipsed everything. 'Yes, all right then. Give Felix the key and tell him to call me. Enjoy Rome.'

'What I shall enjoy, Miss Gilchrist, is examining those papers when I get back next week. Do not fail me!' The line went dead.

'Well really!' muttered Rosy.

CHAPTER THIRTY-TWO

In fact Felix was not overly impressed by the hints of Mr M's patronage; not because he was indifferent to the prospect but because he had an inbuilt suspicion of Vera.

'One has no guarantee that any such introduction will be made, and without it I really don't care to waste time and effort returning to that awful house. I haven't recovered from the last visit.' He winced, remembering the excruciating time spent behind the hall curtain paralysed in case he should be observed by the oafish Clovis (not to mention his narrow escape from the subsequent horror!).

'But I've heard Cedric say that Vera has a kind of bastard integrity,' Rosy said.

'Very bastard. If Vera gets a bee in her bonnet she can be quite unscrupulous. However, one doesn't wish to be ungracious. She's given me the key so I suppose I had better do as she wants.' He gave a vexed sigh, adding, 'But I just hope it won't take too long, I *had* hoped to listen to dear Johnnie Gielgud on the radio tonight – he is giving a talk on milestones in the theatre. Rather

270

up my street. I would prefer not to miss it.'

Feeling vaguely apologetic Rosy assured him that things could be managed quite quickly. And it was agreed that they would meet at eight-thirty by the telephone box outside Marcia's house, slip into the kitchen via the basement, take the package from under the sink and then scoot like hell.

In principle the agenda sounded fine; in practice things were less straightforward. For a start the weather had turned bitterly cold, and the pavements were glossed with patches of black ice lying in wait for the hurried and unwary. Rosy hated the cold, and although she had come shod for walking her progress towards their rendezvous had been slow and slippery. The second annoyance was the key-bearer: he was late. She felt both perished and foolish loitering by the telephone box hoping she would not be taken for anything other than the lady she was. (In fact the street was deserted, its denizens warmly ensconced behind stout walls and thick blinds.) And then when Felix did eventually arrive it was to announce that his car had a flat battery and that it would be impossible to get a bus or taxi back in time to hear 'dear Johnnie'.

He was clearly put out and the grievance in his voice annoyed her. She looked at him – pinched and disgruntled; hardly the ideal companion to go creeping about within the murk of Marcia's kitchen. 'Look,' she said firmly, 'why don't you give me the key and I'll go down and have a good rootle and you can stand on guard up here. After all, it would be a bit tricky if Brigadier Gill were to suddenly appear walking their cat or whatever he does.' She grinned and held out her hand.

Felix hesitated. 'Well, I'm not sure if Vera...'

'Chop, chop! You'll see, I won't be ten minutes and then we can be off.' Without further urging he handed her the key.

She turned towards the wrought-iron gate with its flight of steps down to the side door, and pausing at the top peered into the depths barely able to see a thing. Rather absurdly she had a vision of Virgil's descent into the gaping jaws of Avernus and just hoped she wouldn't trip and fall flat on her face: the anaemic ray of her pocket torch served little purpose.

She started to edge down the steps, clutching the rail with one hand while pointing the flagging torch with the other. Like Tinkerbell its feeble beam darted ineffectually in the gloom, and then with a wearied flicker finally expired. At first the darkness seemed total and Rosy experienced a pang of vicarious déjà vu: Adelaide Fawcett being grabbed by unknown hands and thrust headlong on to granite flagstones... She flinched and tightened her grip on the handrail before taking a further tentative step downwards.

At the bottom things became a trifle clearer. She had arrived in a narrow passageway poorly lit by the pallid glow from a distant street lamp. She could just discern what was presumably the kitchen door and the shadowy shapes of a pair of dustbins. She moved forward, key at the ready; and then stopped.

There was something else by the door in addition to the dustbins: something on the ground, big and bulky – and not so much by the door as lying across its threshold. Lumber from within? Stuff not wanted in the sale and awaiting collection by the bin men? Tiresome: she would have to step over it to reach the lock.

But irritation turned to fear. For as Rosy approached, the bundle produced a sound, a gurgled moan; and with a flash of revulsion she realised the thing was not lumber but a human form, and a form evidently animate. She recoiled with a gasp and stood rooted. What was it – a tramp, a drunk? An intruder like herself, blundering about on the steps and fallen prey to the ice and darkness? Her immediate instinct was to turn tail and scramble back the way she had come, but shame at such feebleness thrust her forward to investigate.

She edged towards the recumbent shape, and peering down whispered, 'C-can I help? Are you all right?'

There was no response. She hesitated, poised over the figure but reluctant to touch it. And then she registered two things. The first was a flow of liquid seeping from the collar, viscous runnels caught in the street light's sickly beam. The second was the sight of the left trouser cuff – hitched up slightly to expose the rivets and metal fastenings of an artificial foot.

She gazed blankly, stripped of all feeling; and for a few seconds she could have been an icicle, hard and insentient. And then paralysis was broken by a sound, a voice faint yet clear: '*Merde*, the bast...' She stared down at the bloodied face, gashed neck and the four clawing fingers, as with a twitch and a gasp Dick Whittington gave up the ghost.

There was silence. And then as if from a long way off Rosy heard the voice of a little girl – her own voice, whimpering over and over again, 'Oh Christ, oh my Christ, oh Christ Almighty...'

But these words too were interrupted by yet another voice: Felix's, from the top of the steps. 'Oh do hurry up, Miss Gilchrist! It's frightfully cold here and one really can't hang about all night. And besides I really do need to – well I rather need to answer a call of nature.' The information was delivered in tones of querulous reproach, but the words had a galvanising effect, and turning from the awful scene Rosy hauled and stumbled her way back up the icy steps to the street above and the impatient Felix.

'Whatever kept you?' he began testily. 'I thought the thing was supposed to be under the kitchen sink. Couldn't you find–'

'I never went in. There's something dreadful down there,' she wavered, gripping the railing to steady legs and nerves.

'What? I'm sorry I don't get you... Look, I don't want to be rude but I really must go and spend a–' He broke off and scuttled hastily around the corner, leaving Rosy to realise that if the blood was so freshly flowing then the assailant could still be close by. She gripped the railing harder, peering frantically into the lonely dark.

Despite such terrors, on Felix's return she was able to ask in biting tones, 'Tell me, do you normally pee in a crisis?'

Rather to her surprise he seemed to give the

question some thought, before answering, 'On the whole not ... but then this is not a crisis. One simply wants to get in the warmth and–'

'But it *is* a crisis!' she cried.

He sighed. 'In what way, exactly?'

'Sabatier,' she said tightly. 'He's down there at the bottom of the steps with his throat cut. He's dead and it's only just happened.'

Flickering street lamps cast odd shadows, and for an instant it really did seem as if Felix's hair stood on end, though it was probably simply the *en brosse* style cut with more zeal than usual. But the sudden whitening of his features was unmistakable, as was the strangled squeak of *'No!'*

'Yes,' said Rosy firmly. 'Do you want to take a look?'

Clearly this was not his wish, for clutching her arm he whispered hoarsely, 'No time for things like that, we must get away from here at once!' Wild-eyed and desperate, he hustled her along the freezing pavement, and rounding the corner looked vainly for a taxi. They kept going, slipping and sliding along the street, breath rasping against the cold air, and not a cab in sight. Eventually a well-lit pub broke the gloom and she suggested plaintively that perhaps that would do instead.

'Are you mad?' he gasped, and pounded on while Rosy stumbled behind feeling that retreat into madness might well be the answer to everything.

At last a free taxi appeared, and without pausing to consult his companion Felix directed the driver to Cedric's house in Pimlico. But Rosy was in no mood to debate the decision; and in any case, given the circumstances, the option of being dropped off alone at her flat held little appeal. She leant back against the cold leather and closed her eyes. From the silence she assumed Felix had done the same.

But closed lids were powerless to blot out the hideous vision of the murdered man, nor indeed the aural memory of his expiring oath. She suspected she would never again meet that particular French expletive without reliving those dreadful moments... Gruesome images vied with whirling questions: what had he been *doing* there? Trying like herself to get into the house? If so, had he been followed there? Or had there been some prearranged meeting – a sprung trap into which he had confidently limped? (Down those steps? Perhaps there was a less hazardous back entrance!) But if indeed a meeting, why on earth outside Marcia's basement door? It seemed an odd place for a rendezvous.

For some reason she thought again of Adelaide Fawcett and the woman's wild words of being attacked by a man with a wooden leg. She had assumed that part of the old baggage's tale had been pure invention. But perhaps it was true after all, and bent on revenge she had escaped the deluxe bondage of the London Clinic to deliver rough justice beside a kitchen door and on flagstones not dissimilar to her own. A sort of tit-for-tat nemesis; although typically, being Adelaide, she had gone too far... Yes, that was it, of course! Obvious. Another problem for the Fawcett family! Rosy opened her eyes and giggled.

Engrossed in his own imaginings, Felix was startled by the sound and for a delicious second thought that maybe the girl had made the whole thing up. He wasn't sure whether to show relief or fury. However, displaying neither and glancing at the driver's partition, he observed mildly, 'Given the situation, Miss Gilchrist, I fail to see the joke – unless, of course, the joke is on me, i.e. that there was no corpse at the bottom of those steps at all.'

'Oh, I am afraid there was,' Rosy replied contritely. 'I'm sorry. A sort of delayed nervous reaction I suppose.'

Felix sighed heavily. As he had feared. 'So you should be,' he replied tartly. 'Hysteria is neither helpful nor seemly.' It was a mean jibe, but cheated of the clutched straw he didn't care. What about his own nerves, for God's sake!

Stung by the reproach Rosy said that she so agreed – but he would be better fitted to pass judgement had he himself been faced with such a scene and forced to cope with the image of its beastly details.

He made no response, but lighting a cigarette graciously offered her one. They puffed away in shared relief and arrived at Cedric's house in a soothing smog of Turkish Abdullah.

The owner was none too pleased to see them. 'It's late,' he protested, 'I was just going to bed. You could at least have telephoned.'

'Not in the circumstances,' explained Rosy.

'Really? Why not? You've disturbed the cat arriving like this.'

'The cat's disturbance,' said Felix with sudden asperity, 'is of little account. Unlike the cat, your friend Sabatier has had his throat cut and *we* are in pressing need of drink and emotional sustenance.'

For once Cedric had no answer but led them silently up the stairs and into the drawing room. Here he produced a decanter of whisky, and then turning to Felix said quietly, 'Before we proceed further let me correct you: Sabatier was not my friend but Vera's. I merely encountered him a couple of times in the war before his foot was blown off. Afterwards I saw him just once, in the distance – limping. That is the extent of my acquaintance.'

'Well it hardly matters,' Rosy said wearily. 'The man's dead, murdered. I found him an hour ago in a pool of blood outside Aunt Marcia's basement door.'

Cedric raised an eyebrow. 'The amazing thing about your aunt was not only did she generate drama when alive but even now contrives to stage-manage effects from beyond the grave. Remarkable, really.'

'It is not remarkable,' Felix burst out, 'it's bloody hell-awful! What are we going to do?'

There was a brief silence punctuated by petulant sounds from the cat and the clinking of ice cubes in Felix's shaking glass.

'Actually,' Rosy ventured, 'perhaps it really is time we told the police everything. It's getting simply too dreadful. I mean, I don't want to, but don't you think it might be sensible?'

'Certainly not!' they cried in unison.

The swiftness and consensus of their response startled her, and she faltered, 'Well it just seems that with three deaths—'

'Provided they are not ours the number is immaterial,' said Cedric. 'As I have emphasised before, the essential thing is to keep quiet and maintain our distance.'

'Huh!' Rosy snorted. 'Try doing that the next time you encounter a freshly butchered body in a dark alley!'

Cedric winced. 'Yes, doubtless all very grisly and unfortunate; but the fact remains that it would be more than rash to confess knowledge of anything. If the police get the slightest whiff of our connection with events, or indeed of Marcia's unseemly past, we shall be ruined.' He paused, fixing Rosy with a hard look. 'And that includes you, Miss Gilchrist. You may not have been party to our little coal parcel joke, but were your aunt's activities to become public knowledge I very much doubt if the British Museum would see its reputation being enhanced by such an employee, or indeed would any reputable institution.'

'He means you would be booted out,' said Felix helpfully.

'I know exactly what he means,' she retorted, and stared angrily at the cat. She hated the pair of them; she hated the dead Sabatier; she hated bloody Vera; she particularly hated Aunt Marcia, but above all she hated herself for being so craven. Cedric was perfectly right: she would lose her job at the museum and very likely the chance of getting anything similar. She would also lose the pleasure of social invitations – or where she was still accepted would be the butt of pity and curiosity. She could hear the voices– *My dear, that's Rosy Gilchrist, isn't it? Marcia Beasley's niece. I wonder if she minds being related to a traitor – rather ghastly I should think. So good of Daphne to invite her...* How long had the war been over – seven, eight years? Too short a period for it to be forgotten; it ran in the veins of the nation, its welts and casualties insistent reminders of those terrible days... No, this was no time to be linked to a quisling, however thoughtless or gullible: niceties of motive cut little ice with the scarred and bereft.

Bleakly Rosy surveyed her options: stoical indifference, escape to the Antipodes under an assumed name, abject capitulation to her companions' persuasion ... and knew which one she would choose. She turned her gaze away from the cat and back to Cedric. 'You are so right,' she said with gritted sweetness. 'Under the circumstances saying nothing is the best one can do.'

'Excellent,' smiled Cedric, 'an intelligent decision if I may say so. Now, let us freshen our glasses, as the Yanks so quaintly put it.' He unstopped the decanter and proceeded to pour lavish replenishment, while Felix relaxed his hunched pose and with a look of relief settled back in his chair.

Rosy had no illusion that the two might be selflessly concerned for her reputation or loss of job. Cedric's warnings were simply a means of preventing her going to the police and opening up the trail to their coal-scuttle enterprise. Their safety depended on her 'intelligent' reticence ... as did hers on theirs. But meantime what about bloody Vera?

'What about Vera?' Felix asked. 'She's not going to like this. I mean from what you were saying she rather admired him.'

'Yes,' agreed Cedric, 'it will be a nasty shock all right. But I suspect that any sense of personal loss will be largely palliated by her new acquisition – the young woman Deirdre of simpering mien and execrable voice.' He shuddered. 'However, in terms of her professional pursuits, i.e. nailing the plotters, if anything the news may well goad her into more frenzied effort. She will now have the honourable prospect of avenging Sabatier's execution and of furthering the crusade which he had instigated. It will all be very exhausting.'

'Yes, but on the other hand it might even per-suade her to go to the police,' Felix said nervously.

'She won't. Vera has a rooted objection to the boys in blue, goes back to childhood when she was caught sabotaging her neighbours' air-raid shelter in the First World War. The authorities took a dim view and cut up rough.'

'Why was she doing that?' asked Rosy with interest.

Cedric shrugged. 'You know Vera. Something about the hypocrisy of civilians cringing in private shelters while hoarding stocks of white feathers to dole out to the frail and defective. She had a point, I suppose... Also, like her mentor, she is convinced that her own quarrying skills are infinitely superior to anything the law might employ.'

'And,' murmured Rosy, 'there is always the spectre of brother Raymond and Marcia's contribution to his end: a motive which the police might seize. Vera knows that.'

'Precisely.'

There was a snort from Felix. 'Look,' he said, 'doubtless Vera's reaction will bring universal penance, but what I want to know is what was Sabatier doing outside Marcia's side door, and who the hell did him in and why! Frankly, my poor nerves can't stand much more. I mean, what is the swine doing now, *at this very moment?* It only happened this evening!' His glance veered towards the decanter but was deflected by a handily placed box of nut truffles whose contents he proceeded to demolish at spectacular speed.

'I do suggest you leave one, for manners,' remarked Cedric coldly.

'Fuck manners,' was the response.

They chewed it over: the whys, wherefores and what nexts. The general view was that both killer and victim had somehow got wind of the document's hiding place, and like Rosy each had been bent on its swift retrieval before the house fell to the auctioneers and their equine clients. A race for possession and a fight to the death. That the death had been Sabatier's and not his quarry's slightly surprised Rosy. From what she recalled of her midnight visitor he had not seemed the type to be easily wrong-footed (an ill-judged term perhaps?) and presumably his time in Special Ops would have prepared him for sudden ambush. Still, no one was infallible. Perhaps he had grown complacent or his opponent was similarly versed in dealing out death – probably had military training like so many. Return to Civvy Street did not erase old skills.

'Do you think it is just one person or several?' she asked. 'I rather assume it's the same hand at work; though perhaps they are all involved and taking it in turns: one for Marcia, one for Clovis and one for Sabatier.'

'A sort of pass-the-parcel system or a game of forfeits,' Cedric mused. 'Don't suppose it matters, really. The aim is the same: concealment of their role in the Churchill conspiracy and suppression of this specific piece of evidence. As long as that is achieved it doesn't really make much–'

'Of course it bloody matters!' exploded Felix. 'It's bad enough knowing there's one homicidal maniac out there. Now you are suggesting there are three of the buggers. I tell you, we're surrounded by them, all lurking with weapons primed!' He stretched for a now non-existent chocolate, a discovery which visibly increased his woe.

CHAPTER THIRTY-THREE

Rather to her surprise Cedric had asked Rosy if she would care to stay the night. Admittedly it wasn't an invitation issued with the greatest enthusiasm but she appreciated the gesture nevertheless. However, what she really craved was to be by herself at home, doors firmly locked, and mind and limbs cocooned beneath the fug of heavy blankets. She might even indulge in the luxury of a sleeping pill – there could surely be no better excuse. Thus she thanked him but declined.

Unlike Felix's, Cedric's car did work, and he dutifully drove her back to the flat and waited while she let herself in. Little was said during the journey, but as they rounded the corner into Portman Square, he said quietly, 'Nothing to be done now, Miss Gilchrist – er, Rosy – other than to keep quiet and await developments. After this the police will be bound to approach you again, so be *prepared*. Do not for one instant give them cause to think you were in the St John's Wood area last night or they'll never leave you alone.'

'Supposing someone saw me?'

'Do you think they did?'

'No, I shouldn't think so–'

'In that case they probably didn't. Anyway, if necessary brazen it out – say it was your twin or some such. Oh, and do rinse your stockings!'

Thus with such helpful advice in mind she climbed the stairs and went into the kitchen to fill a hot-water bottle. She opened a packet of Craven 'A', inhaled deeply, and to the sound of the spluttering kettle gingerly inspected her legs and skirt for specks of blood. She contemplated the looming future. Awful.

The auction was scheduled for ten o'clock, but the officials would obviously arrive before then to set things up – nine-thirty, nine o'clock? That was when the body would be found; earlier perhaps if a luckless errand boy missed his way and tried the wrong house, or an inquisitive dog on a dawn run with its owner caught the whiff of a cadaverous scent. And after that? All hell let loose! Police, press, public, auction officials – all horrified (delighted) by the corpse at 'the fated house'. And then the questions would begin. Endless, endless. Cedric was right: this time she wouldn't be left to hover in the shadows, anxious but ignorant. This time Greenleaf & Co. would descend with renewed curiosity, convinced now that 'that niece must know something'... Well she did know something, but not half as much as they thought or hoped. Nevertheless she was bound to be roped in for more interrogation, to join the ranks of those pertinent to the enquiry.

Still, better to be an object of police interest than lying dead in an alley! She remembered Felix's anguished question: 'So what is the swine doing *now?*' And with a leap of fear her thoughts echoed his. What *was (were)* the swine doing? By killing their pursuer had they got what they wanted? Was Sabatier silenced the end of their worries? And what of the packet in the kitchen? Still there? Or had Sabatier preempted them and at the point of triumph found it wrested conclusively from his grasp? If so, two birds were felled: the enemy silenced and the evidence suppressed ... in which case, surely, the business was over: they could rest easy and slink back into their salubrious lives and be a threat to no one.

She lifted the kettle and poured a stream of water into the bottle and corked it up. And then suddenly thought – but suppose there was *unfinished* business? Suppose they had failed to find the evidence, and despite eliminating the obvious dangers of Marcia and Sabatier, were now poised to deal with other potential threats, real or imagined. After all, presumably that was what poor Clovis had been – someone in the way, someone who even unknown to himself had had the means to foul things up. Was his disposal a precautionary measure? If so, who else was being eyed – Felix? Vera? Herself?

'I am not going to panic,' she told herself wildly, 'not one little bit!' She thought of Dover in the war and heard the rasping voice of the CO as the enemy planes swarmed overhead: 'Keep the beam steady, Gilchrist. Aim high.'

Yes, well just at the moment her unflinching steady aim was for temporary oblivion: bed and the sleeping draught...

She awoke to a blaze of sunlight, and with dazzled eyes could discern the hands of the bedside clock pointing to eleven-thirty. The auction would be well advanced... No, not advanced, *cancelled* due to 'unforeseen circumstances'. Yet somehow the mix of sun and sleep gave the previous night's episode a spurious unreality, and for a brief moment she indulged the thought that it had been merely a nightmare of epic proportion.

But the fancy could not be sustained. And with a groan she got out of bed, and with the effects of the sleeping pill still upon her, went a little un-steadily into the kitchen to make coffee. This was not so much a physical need as a delaying tactic, a means of putting off whatever the day might yield.

She sipped the coffee but tasted little, being too gripped by the fear of sudden approaches from police and press, or enquiries from startled friends to whom the news had already filtered through... She closed her eyes. How would the silence be broken? A blast from the telephone? The insistent buzz of the doorbell? A thunderous knocking, perhaps. At any minute the noise would start. She drank more coffee and waited.

The phone rang. She let it ring three times, and then resignedly lifted the receiver.

'I say,' a voice said, 'I thought you might have been there.'

'Where?' she replied dully.

'Your aunt's auction, of course,' Amy said, 'we've only just left. It was awfully good. And do you know, I actually made a bid – and got it! What do you think of that?' The question was clearly rhetorical but the next was not. 'Shall I tell you what it was?'

'Do,' she heard herself say.

'It is *the* most lovely plaid rug. A sort of motoring rug, I think, pretty well brand new. I bought it for Mr Bones, actually. He's such a lazy old thing and he does feel the cold so. He'll simply adore it! You probably remember it, I expect; I think she kept it in the small sitting room.'

'Not really, I didn't visit the house much.'

'Ah. Well anyway, it's just the thing for him... And I must say it was a rather jolly sale, quite a number of attractive things, even Maynard said so, and you know how scathing he can be!' There was an eruption of mirth.

287

As if in a trance Rosy murmured, 'Maynard Latimer? What was he doing there?'

Amy giggled. 'Same as the rest of us, I suppose: curious. But he made a successful bid too: for the most *exquisite* Schiaparelli scent bottle. I think it was one of their rare special ones, quite the most–'

'Why did he want it?' Rosy asked absently.

'Don't know – although I *suspect* he may have given it to her himself years ago...' Amy lowered her voice '...you know, before the *second* Mrs Latimer, and he wanted it for old times' sake. Perhaps when it suddenly appeared under the chap's hammer – or is it a gavel? – he simply couldn't resist!' Another snort came down the line.

'How nice,' Rosy muttered. 'And, uhm, it all went smoothly, did it? No hitches?'

'What do you mean? Like a fight between the punters? No, not at all. People were very mannerly – except perhaps for two old girls who were bidding against each other for a set of kitchen plates and utensils. The things weren't actually on show but I gather had been available for scrutiny in the basement beforehand and the women had taken a fancy to them. They got fearfully fierce! Can't think why. It's extraordinary what people will go after.'

The word 'basement' tolled in Rosy's mind like a passing bell, but swallowing hard she said faintly, 'And were Felix and Cedric there?'

'No. But I tell you who was – your boss. Or, at least, I think he's your boss – Stanley or something. *He* wanted the elephant foot umbrella stand but was pipped at the post by... Guess!'

288

Rosy closed her eyes wishing she would get off the line. 'I have no idea.'

'Cousin Edward!' screeched Amy. 'He can be awfully determined when he really wants something.'

'Well, good for him... So, er, all very successful, presumably?'

'Oh *yes* – topping. Must have made a mint, I should think. I'm sure the donkeys will get extra rations!' More merriment. And then lowering her voice again, she added, 'Mind you, I expect a lot of people went just to take a look, to have a good old gawp at where your aunt was murdered. Mummy says people have no shame.'

'Possibly. Was your mother there?'

'Yes, but only for a little while. She scarpered quite quickly – terrified she might bump into the Gills jawing on about their beastly Pygmies!'

Rosy said nothing, wondering how she could get rid of the girl. 'Sweet of you to ring, Amy. I've, uhm, got a tiny bit of a headache, I...'

'Thought you sounded a bit seedy,' was the cheery reply, 'it's probably the strain of it all.' (You bet it is, Rosy thought darkly.) 'What you need is plenty of rest. Mummy's always doing that, she says it's invaluable. Anyway, I'll leave you in peace, so "ciao for now", as the Eyeties say. Oh, I can't *wait* to give that rug to Bones. Cia-o!' She rang off and Rosy slumped into a chair.

What the hell did it mean? Surely the auction could not have gone ahead with the corpse lolling on the pathway outside the basement door! Somebody would have been bound to notice ...

wouldn't they? If not, then the bloody thing must still be there. Impossible!

She glanced at the clock. Half past twelve. Lunch was an irrelevance but a preprandial drink suddenly became more than vital. She poured a medicinal brandy and stared into space.

For the rest of the afternoon she remained in a state of mystified apprehension. According to Amy the auction had taken its normal course, conventional procedures untainted by the presence of a freshly killed corpse. But discovery must surely happen – indeed quite possibly already had and the police were just being secretive. Perhaps an early morning bobby, noting the open iron gate, had taken a casual look down the steps, saw the thing and with exemplary speed whistled up HQ to have it whipped off to the forensic morgue. But it seemed unlikely. Didn't they cordon off half the streets when such discoveries were made, redirect traffic, impede pedestrians and place a stony-faced constable outside the premises? (According to *Pathé News*, anyway.) No, a rumpus must surely be stirring by now!

She was tempted to go out to make a casual reconnaissance of the area or at least hear if the newsboys were exercising their lungs ('Read all abaht it! Another corpse found at the Beasley 'ahse!'), but in spite of her curiosity and the night's pill-induced sleep she suddenly felt overwhelmingly tired and in no state to do anything except drink cocoa and listen to the wireless.

CHAPTER THIRTY-FOUR

It was with practised hands that Felix arranged the hollyhocks. They really were rather special! Absurdly late in the season, of course, and obviously kept under glass, and thus all the more precious – *and* lucrative. He wondered whether Clarence House might just be tempted...

But even as such thoughts swirled through his mind, they were shadowed by something else – something far from fragrant and increasingly puzzling. What news of the *corpse?* None! The time of the auction, which both he and Cedric had most carefully avoided, was long since passed; yet no one had telephoned with news of its cancellation, let alone of the horror discovered outside the house. Surely by now – four o'clock in the afternoon – something would have emerged via the grapevine? If no one else, Angela Fawcett ought certainly to have called, bursting with news and speculation. But nothing. It was all very odd... And what of Rosy Gilchrist? Was she now being catechised by earnest men with notebooks? Or just being typically po-faced, walled up in her flat tersely riding out the storm? For storm there must surely be – *somewhere* at any rate, but it certainly hadn't reached Smythe's Bountiful Blooms.

Frowning, he trimmed the stalks of the hollyhocks and tweaked their foliage. And then a sudden thought struck him. Supposing it really

291

hadn't happened at all: that as he had first hoped, the wretched girl had been lying or at least hallucinating. After all, he had only her word that the thing had been there at all; pure hearsay! He should have gone down the steps and checked for himself, he realised that now. But at the time he had felt so *sick*, devastated by shock. Besides, if what she had said was true then hadn't instant flight been imperative, the only sane thing to do? Absurd to hang around verifying this and that and arguing the toss. Swift tactical retreat had been essential. Yes, either way he had done the right thing... Nevertheless, he reflected, there still remained a fair chance that Rosy Gilchrist was quietly mad. He must phone Cedric immediately!

In fact Felix did not have to telephone his friend for at the next moment the bell on the shop door jangled and Cedric himself appeared. He was carrying the *Evening Standard* which without uttering a word he thrust under Felix's nose. He jabbed his finger at the stop press: *Naked corpse found on seafront at Bexhill. Foul play suspected. No identifying marks except lack of left foot and thumb. Police interviewing local naturists.*

'Oh my God,' Felix breathed, 'that explains everything!'

'Hardly everything but it certainly explains why one has heard nothing. Just think, had we been so minded we could have attended the auction after all.' Cedric gave a caustic laugh.

Felix sighed and closed his eyes. 'I suppose that all the while we were at your house mulling over matters with Rosy, *they* must have been busy sluicing down the passage and then speeding down to the south coast...'

'Hmm,' Cedric mused, 'they didn't waste time, did they? Quite a deft little operation it would seem. I wonder whether they removed the clothes before or after the journey; here or down there?' He shrugged. 'Not that it matters really, one is just curious. And what do you think they did with the fake foot ... chucked it into the Channel? I mean if it had a maker's name or number I imagine the police would find that rather handy. And I wonder–'

But Felix wasn't listening, for something else was in his mind. 'Look,' he said nervously, 'since they were so damned quick off the mark it rather suggests there was no gap between the killing and the removal. From what the Gilchrist girl described, Sabatier had only just been attacked when she found him. It's unlikely that they simply wandered off and then returned an hour or so later to deal with the business at their leisure. They or he must have been–'

'Lurking?'

'Exactly! Watching and waiting till the coast was clear – clear of *us!* And once we had scarpered, they could immediately begin the job of getting him off the premises.' Felix slumped on to the lacquered patio chair reserved for his special clients (i.e. those whose floral commissions merited particular and lucrative attention). He emitted a groan. 'I mean being there at all was ghastly enough, but to think that one was being silently observed, monitored... It doesn't bear thinking about!'

Cedric regarded his friend in silence and with mild sympathy, and judged it tactful not to mention that were that the case then it was very probable the killers would know who the interlopers had been. He also refrained from saying that if they had seen Rosy leaning over the dying man then they might now be wondering if their victim had revealed anything crucial in his last moments – as crucial as a name. The girl, of course, had heard only the muttered words *'merde'* and 'bastard', but it was doubtful if the watchers would be aware of that... The consequent possibilities were unpalatable and on the whole better left unvoiced. It didn't do to spread alarm and despondency, especially when based on mere presumption and least of all to the fragile Felix. It was enough to be faced with the grisly tangibles without venturing into the clammy fog of hypothesis. No, the less said the better.

'Well,' he said lightly, 'at least that's one less cadaver for our police to deal with. What the eye doesn't see etc... Imagine the shindig if it had been left there. Friend Greenleaf and his enchanting boss would have been round to us in a trice, asking more tedious questions about Marcia's associates and doubtless even expecting us to view the body! A narrow escape, really.'

'Escape?' echoed Felix woefully. 'If only one could!' He chewed his thumb, gazing bleakly at a wilting chrysanthemum.

'Perhaps not escape as such, but at least we can start to make plans for a nice little jaunt to the Alps. Zermatt in the spring would be idyllic – smothered in wild flowers and the air so bracing.

Most therapeutic.'

Felix looked sceptical. 'I might like the flowers but I am not sure that I wish to be braced. What I need is to be *soothed* – soothed and smoothed. Anaesthetised, preferably.'

'In that case perhaps the oily languor of the Nile. I rather fancy some of that Egyptian sun... But I tell you one thing, we shall both need to be braced by Thursday.'

'Why?'

'Vera returns.'

Felix said nothing but placed a wearied hand over his eyes. 'And that being the case,' Cedric continued, 'I think we deserve a little respite. I shall book a table at Quaglino's forthwith.'

His friend brightened.

'Berridge rang us this afternoon,' announced Greenleaf's superior.

'Who?'

'You know, *Berridge* – of Bexhill.'

'Oh him... What's he want, then?'

'Nothing much except to moan about his transfer. Says there's too much sea air down there and it gets on his wick. I told him that when he applied. "You won't like it, you know," I said, "it's full of ozone and old ladies." But of course, being Berridge, he thought he knew it all. Well he's made his bed and he's got to stick with it now, I daresay. No more bright lights for that one!... Mind you, he said that a funny thing had happened this afternoon. On the seafront it was, close to the De La Warr Pavilion.'

'Oh yes, what was that?'

'They found a chap.'

'Remarkable!'

'Ah, but this chap was in the buff. Dead in a deckchair.'

'Huh. A bit chilly I should have thought at this time of year, even for a nudist. What did he die of – heart attack from the ozone, or did the old ladies get him?'

'Not unless they carried a clasp knife. His throat had been cut.'

Greenleaf sucked in his breath. 'Hmm, that won't suit Berridge, he has a thing about blood. Do you remember that time when–'

'He said this was old blood, not new. Congealed. Said something about a gammy leg, but I had switched off by then. You know what Berridge is like when he gets going.'

Greenleaf nodded and watched as the inspector deftly probed a back molar with a toothpick. 'Well that's Bexhill's problem,' he said, 'we all have our crosses. And at the moment mine is Mr Clovis blooming Thistlehyde. Why did he tell that French girl he had seen someone with a lawnmower? Doesn't seem to be any trace of such a person and no one's come forward. But you see he might just be a key witness.' He frowned.

'Unless, like I said, the girl was lying.'

'I didn't get that impression – she seemed pretty emphatic.'

'Ah well,' the other replied, pocketing the toothpick, 'can't hang about. I've got an appointment with God. He wasn't in the best of moods when last seen, something to do with shoddy progress reports and fouling up his golf handicap. Wouldn't do to be late, so I'll leave you to your cogitations... Oh, and by the way – ask Harris about the phantom mower, he's bound to have some bright ideas.'

'Thanks,' said Greenleaf bleakly.

CHAPTER THIRTY-FIVE

As predicted, Vera Collinger was none too pleased to learn about the death of her colleague. And since, contrary to expectations, her travelling companion had signally failed to pass muster amidst the Roman ruins, little comfort could be derived from that quarter. Indeed, Felix found it difficult to tell whether the anguished repetitions of 'Ghastly! Ghastly!' applied to the fate of Sabatier or the inadequacy of the girl. Charitably – and possibly correctly – he assumed the first.

'What strikes me as curious,' Cedric mused as the three sipped tea in Felix's flat, 'is why Sabatier should have been at Marcia's house in the first place. What made him go there on a freezing night on the eve of the sale?'

'For the same reason as Rosy Gilchrist, I imagine,' Felix said, 'to get hold of the papers before the auctioneers took over.'

'Yes, but Gilchrist knew it was there because the priest person had told her. How did Sabatier know?'

There was silence. And then with a clatter Vera upset her teacup, the dregs seeping into her host's best damask. He winced. She righted the cup and said quietly, 'He didn't know, he surmised. He must have gone at my suggestion: if I hadn't said anything he would be alive now.' Her face had turned grey, and Felix experienced a rare twinge of sympathy.

'What do you mean?' he asked. 'I thought you had already searched the house the day you bumped into Rosy. What stopped you getting it then or going back later?'

'Because,' Vera replied despondently, 'I had totally forgotten the treasure hunt. It seems years ago now.'

The two men regarded her blankly and exchanged puzzled looks.

Cedric cleared his throat. 'I don't quite follow...' he began.

She sighed. 'You may recall that Marcia was notorious for her parties – rollicking affairs with lethal cocktails and lethal guests. She went through a phase of forcing us to play party games. You know the sort of thing, Sardines, Dumb Crambo – silly children's stuff; but when you're squiffy it all seems frightfully amusing. Anyway, there was one occasion when she had organised a ridiculously elaborate treasure hunt – all over the house, with a couple of fivers as treasure trove. Quite an inducement – imagine the champagne that could buy! She even threw in another quid as a bet that no one would discover the hiding place. I can hear her voice now: "Darlings, you will never find it, not in a month of Sundays. Trust little bright arse to keep things safe!"' Miss Collinger broke off, and the stern features relaxed into a pensive smile. 'Yes, I was fond of Marcia in those days, very fond. She could be good company in a rather awful way...' She regarded the biscuits abstractedly, and then with a dismissive shrug continued: 'Anyway, as you can imagine, with a challenge like that the place was virtually ransacked. But she won her bet all right *and* of course retained the treasure.'

'Ah!' Felix exclaimed. 'I can guess: she had shoved the fivers under the sink, behind the pipe.'

'Exactly. And that's where I suggested Sabatier should look. "It's a long shot," I told him, "but it's worth a try. It's the sort of thing Marcia might do." At the time he didn't say much. Just nodded and muttered "perhaps". But he obviously thought about it later. If only I had remembered earlier things could have been different. Can't think why it never occurred to me... Blighters!' She drummed her fingers angrily on the table and glared at the tea-stained cloth. 'Sorry about that,' she said gruffly.

'Not at all,' replied Felix magnanimously, 'one mustn't do the laundries out of a job. Would you care for another cup?'

The guest declined the offer intimating she had some urgent business to attend to and needed to get home early.

After she had gone Cedric observed that presumably the urgent business involved either feeding the dog or preparing her arsenal for the hounding of Sabatier's killers.

'They had better watch out,' Felix remarked absently.

He got up and began to pace about the room straightening ornaments, tweaking cushions, while Cedric watched in mild annoyance. 'Could you possibly stop fidgeting? It rather disturbs my train of thought.'

Felix returned to his chair. 'Well,' he said testily, 'if having your train of thought disturbed is your only problem then all I can say is you are extremely lucky. Frankly, my whole life is in upheaval because of this business. Can't concentrate on anything – even lost a customer today.'

'Really?' said Cedric with interest. 'That's unusual. Who was it? I trust not the royal personage.'

'Certainly not!' Felix looked askance. 'Actually it was the Barnes-Ripley woman – I've never liked her. She asked if I could get her scarlet begonias for the ornamental urns on her terrace. When I enquired if she wouldn't like something more tasteful, she took umbrage and flounced from the shop.' He sniffed. 'Oh well, no great loss, one does have to maintain standards, after all.'

'Quite right,' agreed Cedric. 'And you do have the Royal Appointment plaque to consider.'

A smile of anxious bliss flashed upon his friend's face. 'Indeed I do! And what's more a little bird has told me that it is virtually in the bag. Just think, I may be hearing from the awards committee any day now...' He became lost in a reverie of royal accolades and kindly corgis. But it was short-lived, disagreeably banished by the vision of Sabatier chilly on the south coast.

'What I don't understand,' said Cedric, his train of thought evidently resumed, 'is why the murderer or murderers should have been there at all. Sabatier may well have been following up Vera's idea, but that doesn't explain the presence of anyone else. Rather odd, I should say...'

'It is also horrible,' exclaimed Felix, 'and I really do not wish to discuss the matter any further!' He picked up his tapestry and started plying the needle with dedicated attention.

Cedric sighed and continued to ruminate.

CHAPTER THIRTY-SIX

Like Cedric, Rosy had also seen an item about the Bexhill 'mystery victim'. Scanning the following day's *Times* she had chanced upon it tucked away on an inside page. The details were sparse, though not as brief as those in the *Evening Standard's* stop press and it did not take an Einstein to draw the inference.

'God Almighty,' she breathed, 'I can't take much more of this! How the hell...?' She closed her eyes feeling rather weak. And then rather unsteadily picked up the phone and dialled Smythe's Bountiful Blooms. There was no answer. Bloody man, she thought, gassing with some countess!

She glanced at the clock and saw she had about ten minutes to reach her office at the museum. She tore out, leapt on a bus to St Giles's Circus, leapt off, and with head still numbed by the morning's revelation hurried the rest of the way to Great Russell Street. At the museum's steps she encountered her boss.

Dr Stanley gave an uncharacteristic beam and greeted her warmly. 'Ah, Rosy, good to see you. A lively sale at your aunt's house the other morning. Thought I might have seen you there ... too busy cataloguing stuff for our Etruscan exhibition next month, I daresay.'

'Yes,' she lied.

'There was some quite decent stuff but nothing of riveting interest – though I have to admit to taking a shine to that umbrella stand, the one made from an elephant's foot. No luck, though; some young chap keen as mustard and hair to match outbid me by a long chalk. Still, I did get one thing. Absurd really, but I like its face.' He scrabbled in his briefcase and produced a particularly disagreeable effigy of a small monkey. 'I gather she bought it in Ceylon before the war. You probably remember it.'

As it happened, Rosy did remember. It had sat on top of the piano in the morning room squinting malevolently at anyone bold enough to approach the keys. She had particularly disliked it.

'Fascinating,' she murmured.

'Thought you would approve. I am going to keep it on my desk, make a handy paperweight – and, of course, a nice little memento for you.'

'Really?' she said taken aback.

'Yes, every time you see it you will be reminded of your poor aunt.' He smiled benignly.

On the whole, Rosy reflected, the day had not begun well.

At her desk sipping a vapid coffee, she applied herself to sorting the post and tried to push the less prosaic matters from her mind. She had almost succeeded in this but was foiled by a familiar voice.

'Ah,' boomed Vera Collinger, 'they told me I might find you here. I came in to cancel my order for the museum's new publication on Roman antiquities, and as I was passing I thought I would–'

'Why? Don't you like it?'

'Oh *I* like it, but Deirdre is clearly not capable of it. Before going to Rome I ordered a copy thinking it would be a nice surprise for her when we returned. Since then I have revised my view of the girl's intelligence. Contrary to her claims, Deirdre would be hard-pressed to distinguish Julius Caesar from a Caesar salad.'

Had there been flowers in the room the note of scorn would have withered them instantly, and Rosy felt sorry for the hapless Deirdre.

'However,' Miss Collinger continued in a more moderate tone, 'that is not my main reason for coming in. I wanted to know if you had heard the news of poor Sabatier.'

'You mean about his being found in Bexhill? Yes, yes I have. It was in this morning's *Times* but his identity isn't known.'

'Except by us,' the other said dryly.

Rosy nodded, and then to her great embarrassment suddenly found her hands shaking violently. She thrust them into her lap but the older woman must have noticed.

'All very unsettling,' she said in a voice bordering on sympathy, 'but the great thing is not to let those fiends defeat us! Bear up, Miss Gilchrist, we're all in this together. Fortify yourself, my dear – go to that tavern opposite at lunchtime and buy yourself a large Scotch, you will feel so much better. Here...' And to Rosy's flustered surprise she drew two half-crowns from her pocket and pushed them across the desk. 'Have it on me,' she said gruffly.

Rosy was just stammering her thanks, when pausing at the door her benefactor said, 'Oh, a word of warning: you may need that drink sooner than later. That Gill woman was hanging around in the entrance. I got the impression she might be looking for you – burbled something about a vase and wanting you to go to tea tomorrow, but I wasn't really listening. Not my type – nearly as stupid as Deirdre!'

After she had gone Rosy regarded the over-generous half-crowns in some awe, and then thought of the visitor in the hall. She did not share Vera's antipathy to Mildred Gill – dull, perhaps, but pleasantly well meaning. One had known worse. She wondered what she wanted. Vera had said something about a tea invitation... Not another whist drive, surely – that would really be too much! But hadn't Vera also mentioned a vase? Perhaps the woman had an urge to have a private view of the Portland! Thus to break the chore of the correspondence and to distract herself further from current anxieties, she went to have a look in the entrance hall.

Vera had been right, Mrs Gill was indeed there, and talking animatedly to Leo. She caught a few of her words: 'What a wonderful place to work in, *so* absorbing, and most inspiring for your own researches. I think Rosy said you were doing something on Gladstone – not, of course, that Gladstone was an *antiquity* exactly, but I am sure the ethos must fuel the muse!'

Looking deeply solemn Leo replied something which Rosy could not catch; but it was clearly well received for Mrs Gill gave a silvery laugh and cried, 'Well I never, who would have thought!'

At that moment the young man glanced up, saw the watcher and hailed her quickly. 'Good morning, Rosy – this lady is dying to get hold of you. I was just wondering where you might be, wasn't sure if you had arrived or not. Anyway, I'll leave you both together, I simply *must* find Professor Burkiss.' He strode off purposefully.

'Is Professor Burkiss his supervisor?' asked Mrs Gill.

'Er, not exactly, just a colleague.' (She thought it best not to explain that the professor was in fact the department's charlady who had yet again lifted the community gin bottle.) 'So what brings you here?' she said hastily, 'I am afraid the lecture catalogue isn't out yet but I'm sure I can find an advance leaflet if you like–'

'Oh no, nothing so cultural I am afraid. But as I was seeing my chiropodist in Gower Street I thought I might drop in here on the off chance to ask if you would be free.'

Rosy smiled. 'Really? Free for what?'

'Free to come to tea tomorrow. You see, when I was at your aunt's sale earlier in the week I couldn't resist bidding for one or two of the items, including that pretty little clock in the hall.'

305

'You mean the one under the donkey painting?'

'Yes. I've always admired it – rather nicer than the donkeys, I always felt!' She gave a little grimace. 'Anyway, I also purchased some other things – those linen sheets were such good quality; one doesn't see many of that kind these days. But I also bought a charming rose bowl – had to fend off a rival bidder, in fact, so I felt quite triumphant! But it has since occurred to me that it might be the sort of thing *you* might like ... a little memento of Marcia, she was so fond of roses.'

Rosy thought of the straggling unpruned rose trees in her aunt's neglected garden and rather doubted the claim. However, she smiled politely but before she could say anything, Mrs Gill went on: 'And – dare I say it – it might be a little souvenir of us too.'

'Of you? Oh...' She was uncertain what to say.

'We are packing up, you see, and thought it would be nice to distribute a few odds and ends among friends.'

'Packing up?'

'Yes. Harold says he finds it too unsettling living next door to where that awful thing happened. And besides, there are rumours that the new owners, the donkey sanctuary people, are going to sell it to an Arab sheik and his entourage. Frankly I think I would rather see donkeys grazing there than a posse of camels!' She shrieked with mirth, something Rosy had never heard her do before. And then recovering herself she said, 'Oh dear, I'm afraid one is being rather naughty! But seriously, camels apart, we are in fact planning on moving to Kenya. We always said we would, and now that Harold's rheumatism is getting worse a warmer climate would suit us so much better. We have friends there in a very nice set and I am sure we shall fit in well.'

'So you are going soon, are you?'

'Yes, we've had it in mind for some time and I am afraid your aunt's tragedy has rather hastened things.' She looked apologetic and added, 'So you will come to tea, won't you, my dear? The next few weeks are going to be so hectic attending to this and that, and I would hate not to be able to squeeze you in before we go.'

Rosy was not entirely sure she wanted to be squeezed into the Gills' busy removal schedule, nor was she especially keen to have the proffered rose bowl. And after the awful events in that vicinity she was even less inclined to go at all. However, caught on the hop and bowing to the diktats of social courtesy she mustered a receptive smile and said she would be delighted.

CHAPTER THIRTY-SEVEN

Arriving home that evening she picked up the afternoon post from the mat and found between the bills and circulars a hand-delivered note. She slit open the envelope and was surprised to see the enclosed sheet bore the engraved London address and bold signature of Maynard Latimer.

What with the startling encounter with the priest 'Lola' and the dreadful Sabatier event, her recent lunch companion had faded from her mind. Now, however, he came hurtling back as she recalled with a jolt what Vera Collinger had told her about his seeing Marcia to within weeks of her death. She also recalled the troubling suspicions which had dogged her walk home from the pub in Soho. These, she was sure, were histrionic and groundless; but his mendacity over Marcia had rankled and she began to scan the note with a dismissive eye.

Its content was disarming. Could she possibly join him for a drink that evening? He was catching a late flight to Malta and would be honoured to have his last cocktail in London shared with one so charming. Unless he heard otherwise he would pick her up just before seven. He had, he added, something special for her...

'One so charming, my foot!' she muttered. 'Does he think I can be flattered?' She could, of course, and went up the stairs two at a time to turn on the bath.

Lying there in bathcap and curlers, she wondered idly what the gift could be. Provided it wasn't another rose bowl she didn't much care ... funny the way people were suddenly so eager to give her things. Even Dr Stanley seemed to think she would be gratified by the sight of that awful monkey!

He arrived driving himself in a Rover and took her to the Connaught. She watched him talking to the barman and had to admit that for one who had recently had his seventieth birthday there was still a lot to be said for Maynard Latimer's looks. Whether she actually liked him she was still not sure: amusing and attractive certainly, but *likeable?* Well, she would have to wait and see...

As before, she found him an easy conversationalist and like many such he sparked lively responses from his listener. She asked him more about his house in Malta and how close it was to Valletta.

'It's my wife's, actually. She loves it there, and being an invalid prefers the sun and peace of the island to the abrasive clatter of London – or the fogs of Yorkshire. She comes over very rarely so I go there on a fairly regular basis, for a couple of weeks usually – as I am doing tonight.' He paused and gave a rueful smile. 'But to tell the truth, one is always glad to get back to London. I'm a restless soul and I like the stimulus of the capital – too much peace can make one turgid.' He gave a wry laugh, and Rosy wondered if the observation had possibly been a veiled reference to the 'sainted Silvia' so disparaged by Vera. It would not, she felt, be quite the right moment to enquire more deeply about his visits to Marcia... In fact she had no intention of broaching the subject: he had lied about it once, and to probe further would possibly jeopardise the offer of a second Martini. Instead she asked him about her present.

'From what I could make out from your note I think you said something about having something for me. I am terribly intrigued!' Her eye must have fallen on the slight bulge spoiling the line of the elegantly cut jacket and he had evidently seen her glance.

'I say, Rosy,' he laughed, 'you're not doing a Mae West on me, are you? I can assure you that is not a gun in my pocket!'

She blushed and mumbled something inaudible as he drew out a small packet wrapped in silver tissue and ribbon. 'There you are, tied with my own fair hands.'

Opening it up she was confronted by an elegant scent bottle – an exquisitely stylish Schiaparelli. She recognised it immediately: one of the collection on Marcia's dressing table, and the same one surely that Amy had seen him bid for at the auction.

She gazed at it with genuine pleasure but was slightly embarrassed that he should give her something so personal. Pleasure and embarrassment mingled further when he said, 'I rather think there is still a drop inside. Try it and see.'

She took out the stopper and sniffed. Yes, it was the old familiar 'Shocking' – sharp, potent, sensual. She knew and loved it; and while she did not especially recall it on Marcia it was a fragrance certainly typical of her aunt – bold and unmistakable. She stammered her thanks while he regarded her with a lazy smile.

'Thought you might like it. And when you come to Malta we could perhaps replenish it...' He rose and went to the bar to order more Martinis.

Huh! When you come to Malta, indeed – the cheek of it! But she couldn't help feeling a little pleased all the same. And then she felt less pleased as she recalled Amy's surmise that it was one he had once bought for Marcia... A gift now repurchased and presented to the niece. Well really! She stared indignantly at the tall broad back at the bar, and then down at the crystal bottle in her lap. Oh well, better than a flower vase or a leering monkey!

Latimer returned to the table and without preamble said, 'I say, did you read about that headless corpse on Bexhill promenade? It was sitting in a deckchair. Amazing what they do on the south coast these days.'

Rosy almost choked on her drink. 'What!' she squeaked. 'But it wasn't headless, just naked!'

'Oh, is *that* all!' he laughed. 'You've obviously got a better memory than I have – or doubtless a less lurid imagination. So you saw the item too, did you? But there was something else the paper said about him, something odd. What was it?' He frowned. 'Oh yes, that was it, he was missing a foot. Of course – *footless* not headless. I knew he was minus something.'

Rosy forced a smile, but it was a subject she cared neither to discuss nor joke about. Latimer, however, was clearly taken with the topic and seemed intent on pursuing it, for his next comment discomfited her even more. 'Didn't the abominable Adelaide claim she had been thrown down the steps by a man with a limp – a wooden leg, in fact? Perhaps it was the same one: limped out of the mist to do her in, foolishly botched the job and then in a fit of pique went down to Bexhill to sunbathe in the buff... What do you think, Rosy? A neat little theory, wouldn't you say?'

The question was asked jovially enough and yet for a reason she could not define she was suddenly unsettled. Perhaps it was her acute sensitivity to the subject or the fact that he seemed

311

to be regarding her closely, but either way she felt a flash of irrational fear. Why on earth had he brought up the incident at all? The item in *The Times* had been tiny. Why should he pick on that when there were other issues of so much more obvious interest?

She returned his gaze and said coolly, 'Since he was also reported as having his throat cut I would prefer not to think about it at all. I am rather squeamish about that sort of thing.'

He raised an eyebrow. 'Sorry, rather a feeble joke. I am obviously becoming clumsy in my old age! One forgets that others have finer sensibilities than oneself.'

Was there an edge of sarcasm to the voice? She couldn't be sure but her instinct was to smile and say nothing. However, instead she heard herself asking bluntly, 'Why do you dislike Adelaide Fawcett so much?' And remembering their earlier meeting and his icy response to the mention of the old lady, feared she might have made a stupid move.

But he seemed unruffled. 'Oh it's reciprocal, I can assure you. She has always hated me since I killed her cat,' and taking a sip of his Martini added, 'a malign creature, as you might expect.'

'Her cat!' Rosy gasped. 'When? How?'

'When I was about twelve and with a catapult – an absolute bullseye. I was rather pleased with that, though the adults cut up rough of course. Especially Adelaide.'

'Ye-es,' Rosy said slowly, 'I suppose she would. I think I might have too. But *why?*'

He shrugged indifferently. 'There's a standard

answer to that. As Mallory said – because it was there.'

'Mallory was a brave hero,' she retorted tartly, 'and he was confronted by a mountain, not a harmless cat.'

'It wasn't harmless, it belonged to Adelaide.'

Despite herself, Rosy burst out laughing. 'You're fixated on that woman!'

He echoed her laugh but there was little mirth in the eyes. 'When I was young we happened to move to a house very close to hers. By our standards it was a large house and our new neighbourhood had seemed very "posh". Adelaide was, and is, an inveterate snob and she made it abundantly clear that we were not the sort of people she approved of. She spread a lot of malicious gossip about my parents which was untrue and unfair. Hence my killing of the cat – a kind of surrogate, I daresay.'

'So you both carry on a vendetta because of the cat business and because she snubbed your family when you were a child? But surely after all these years and you having achieved so much – in line for a peerage it's being whispered – you're not really hurt by an addled old lady are you?'

'Forgive the alliteration, but I can tell you there is nothing addled about Adelaide. She has the sharpest tongue and eye I have ever encountered, and if you get caught in her sights it can be very painful. It happened to me once.' There was a fractional pause, and then he added musingly, 'You know, my dear, there *are* people who deserve to fall upon flagstones ... the righteous and meddlesome. In their way they can be quite ruthless – the sort who foul up life for others.

313

Beware of such people, Rosy.'

A genial smile accompanied the warning, but the preceding words had held a raw resentment, and Rosy was suddenly chilled. Surely he couldn't be alluding to Sabatier *as well* as Adelaide, could he? After all, both might be said to fit the category of the righteous and meddlesome... An image of the former choking to death on the icy flagstones outside Marcia's house slid before her eyes; and as she faced the man's amiable gaze all the earlier fears came plunging back. Yet even as they did she felt a fool. 'Come on, Rosy, for God's sake take a hold on yourself,' she exclaimed inwardly, 'you're getting obsessive like Adelaide!' And thus to Latimer she said, 'This has been such a lovely evening and the scent bottle is beautiful. Thank you so much... I do hope you catch your flight all right – you may have to hurry!'

'Oh, don't worry, I have it down to a fine art. Glad you like the present, a souvenir of your aunt – and perhaps one of me.' He gave a slow wink. (Hmm, she thought, should I want that?)

He drove her home at a speed which suggested a greater urgency than he had admitted. As she eased herself out of the passenger seat he stretched across, and gripping her wrist, said, 'Rosy, I was fonder of your aunt than I may have suggested. I believe she did some stupid things. If you learn anything don't think too badly of her and for Christ's sake don't get involved. It could be unlucky for you.' He engaged the gear, blew her a kiss and drove off.

She stood on the pavement listening to the dwindling whine of the engine. Five seconds ago they had been talking and laughing, and now there was nothing but silence and the dark street. She took the key from her handbag and walked slowly to the front door.

It was a wretched night, rent with dreams of cats and catapults, headless sunbathers and people saying again and again *It could be unlucky for you...*

She woke at five-thirty tense and exhausted and still haunted by those parting words. What were they – genuine expressions of solicitous concern? Or a veiled threat to watch her back and keep her snout out of things? She thought again of Adelaide's comment at the Fawcett party: *a dubious piece of work if ever there was one.* Had the remark been merely an allusion to the unfortunate cat, a memory lodged in the old woman's brain to grow and fester over the years, or had it a deeper significance? Did Adelaide know of darker elements in Latimer's past – elements that might make him run any risk to secure his own interests? A risk, for example, of throwing an old lady down stone steps to ensure her silence ... or to flatter and subtly direct a much younger one to keep her eyes and mouth shut for fear of ending up butchered in a dark alley? Despite the warmth of the bed, Rosy shivered and drew the blanket over her head.

Two hours later she awoke slightly more refreshed and in slightly better spirits. The fears of the night seemed remote and largely ridiculous. She focused half-closed eyes on the scent bottle now gracing her own dressing table... Yes, no doubt about it, it did lend a certain distinction to the surrounding paraphernalia; she really should tidy things up! And then once again she thought of its donor – presumably safely landed in Malta and sharing breakfast with the sainted Silvia on a sunny veranda. All right for some, she supposed.

CHAPTER THIRTY-EIGHT

Walking past her aunt's house en route to the Gills' drive was an uncomfortable experience, and Rosy regretted not having invented a prior engagement. As she drew level with the iron wicket gate at the top of Marcia's area steps she averted her eyes, fixing them firmly instead on the neighbouring laurel hedge.

Gaining the raised portico she surveyed the immaculately cut lawn with its clumps of disciplined rhododendrons, nurtured box and kempt flowerbeds. It was, she noted wryly, a very different domain from next door's wilderness! She turned, pressed the bell and waited.

The door was opened by Mrs Gill all smiles and welcome. 'Harold is out,' she explained, 'so I thought we would have tea in my little sitting room upstairs. It catches the afternoon sun beautifully. Too early for the balcony I am afraid, but you get the illusion of spring all the same.' She led the visitor up the wide staircase and into a smallish room but one light and airy and smelling faintly of potpourri. Through the French windows could be seen the white balustrade of the balcony, and beyond that the tall outline of a weeping beech.

'This is charming,' Rosy murmured, 'and so peaceful.'

'Yes,' her hostess agreed, 'I spend some very agreeable hours here reading quietly or sewing, a restful retreat from the busy world – and, of course, from dear Harold!' She gave a light laugh, before asking, 'Do you sew, my dear? So soothing, I always think.'

Rosy confessed that her own activities in that sphere were confined to tacking fallen hems and securing recalcitrant buttons, neither of which provided much balm to the fevered brow.

'Oh, I am sure you have plenty of other pastimes which keep you busy – masses of picture-going and dancing and all that sort of gaiety, I expect. As a matter of fact, years ago Harold and I used to be rather nifty on the ballroom floor ourselves. Oh yes, before the war we were great fans of Victor Sylvester – at least Harold was, although I have to admit to preferring Carol Gibbons myself. He always struck me as being a little more adventurous, a little more, uhm – how shall I put it...?' She broke off groping for a phrase.

'Upbeat?' Rosy queried.

'Exactly! More *upbeat.*' Mrs Gill beamed. 'Sylvester is very smooth, of course, all very elegant and rhythmic, but just a titchy bit predictable I always feel. It suited Harold, but personally I like an element of surprise just now and again, it spices things up you might say!' She paused and gave a little giggle. 'Goodness, hark at me – I sound quite racy!'

Rosy smiled and enquired politely about their plans for Kenya. 'I imagine that might provide some spice – all those cocktails and big-game hunting. Rather different from St John's Wood I should think.'

'Oh, I don't think we shall get involved in *that* kind of set ... although, you never know, I may encourage Harold to pursue the savage wildebeest. That might cure the rheumatism!' Rosy thought she heard her add something under her breath which sounded suspiciously like 'and other things too', but she couldn't be sure.

She got up and started to rummage in a cabinet. 'Now, Rosy, talking of our decamping to Kenya, I want you to have this. It's the rose bowl I told you about, the one that belonged to your aunt. I am sure you will find a use for it.'

Rosy was less sure. As flower vases go it struck her as singularly unremarkable, a Selfridge staple – bargain basement, in fact – and she certainly didn't recall it in Marcia's house, with or without roses; not that that meant anything, for she had so rarely gone there. However, she expressed grateful thanks, and feeling peckish privately wondered when tea might appear.

Mrs Gill must have read these last thoughts for she said, 'Now, it's high time for the cup that cheers, don't you think? I'll only be a tick. Shan't need to trudge into the kitchen, we have one of those splendid Teasmade machines in the bedroom. *Such* a boon, in fact a veritable nonesuch – saves all that early morning palaver of traipsing up and down stairs. Have you got one, my dear?' Rosy shook her head. 'Oh, you should! Ask your current beau to give you one for your birthday, you will find it invaluable.'

Rosy thought that if she had such a thing as a current beau, then a tea-making machine was the last thing she would request as a birthday present.

While Mrs Gill busied herself in one of the bedrooms with the indispensable nonesuch, Rosy wandered over to the window and watched a couple of pigeons strutting on the balcony. They must have seen her shadow, for with a squawk they took flight, and turning back into the room her glance fell on a small ottoman stacked with books and magazines. Idly she picked up a back number of *Country Life*, and as she did so a thick square envelope slipped to the floor. She stooped to replace it and then stared in astonishment at the inscription – *For my niece Miss Rosy Gilchrist. Personal.* The lettering was in green ink, bold and clear, and underneath in brackets and smaller script was her home address. The flap was unfastened and in startled perplexity she began to withdraw its contents.

'Please don't do that,' Mrs Gill's voice said.

Rosy swung round to see her hostess poised in the doorway bearing a tray of tea things and a plate of sandwiches. Before she could say anything Mrs Gill had placed the tray on a side table and advanced a few steps into the room. 'I am afraid we need that, if you don't mind,' she said pleasantly, extending her hand.

Rosy recoiled and tightened her hold on the envelope. 'Er, well I do actually... I mean it seems to be mine. It's from Marcia.'

'Oh yes, I know that, and frankly you weren't supposed to find it – silly of me to leave it there. But I am afraid that despite what they say, finders can't always be keepers, so I'll have it back please.' The tone was firm.

As was Rosy's. 'I am afraid that is out of the question. It belongs to me.'

'Oh dear,' Mrs Gill sighed, 'that's unfortunate.' She closed the door, locked it and slipped the key into her pocket. It was a swift movement – almost as swift as the following one: the production of a pistol, a small Beretta. She had flipped open the lid of her sewing box and in the next instant had the gun grasped firmly in her hand and pointing at Rosy.

'Sit down, my dear, we have much to talk about.' With stunned mind and uncertain legs, Rosy did exactly as she was told. She gazed in stupefied horror at her hostess.

'I suppose I should apologise,' murmured Mrs Gill, 'I had hoped this wouldn't be required. You see, I had only invited you here to ascertain certain facts, i.e. whether that tiresome man said anything to you the other night. But I'm afraid one has been overtaken by events – your finding that.' She nodded towards the thick envelope still clutched in Rosy's hand, and gave a rueful smile.

'What man?' Rosy asked in dazed incredulity.

'Sabatier of course. Don't tell me you didn't see him, you were only about a foot away. I saw you from our bathroom window – bending over him after Harold had slipped back into Marcia's kitchen. You gave us a nasty turn, I can tell you!'

Rosy closed her eyes and swallowed; opened

them and was dazzled by the afternoon sun pouring in from the French window. Was this real? she wondered, but immediately supplied the answer: 'Of course it *bloody* is, and I'm not going to let the old bitch frighten me!'

She smiled sweetly across the table. 'Ah, Sabatier. Yes, I did discover him; and no, he said nothing.'

Mrs Gill nodded. 'That could have been helpful to you, but alas not any more.' She gestured to the envelope. 'Put it on the table, if you wouldn't mind, it'll be safer there. We haven't finished with it yet – and though you may think this odd, those papers do have a certain nostalgic value.' The tone was casual, the Beretta looked lethal.

Rosy put it aside, and taking a deep breath said, 'So you killed my aunt, did you?'

'Well we had to, you see, she really was becoming quite impossible. I mean, the amount of money she was demanding was ridiculous! And besides, Marcia being Marcia there was no guarantee that even if we did produce the "fee" she wouldn't come back for more – or worse still blab it all to the government anyway!... No, Rosy, I am afraid it has to be said that your aunt was a fearful liability.' Mrs Gill looked indignant. But relaxing her hold on the gun she placed it carefully on the lid of the sewing box and enquired if her guest would like a sandwich. 'I always like a couple at this time of day, keeps one going till supper. I can recommend the lemon and fish paste.'

The guest eyed the sandwiches and felt sick.

'To be perfectly frank,' Mrs Gill continued, 'I have to admit to having found your aunt distinctly wearisome, and I don't just mean her discovery of our political activities. Had I known that she owned the house next door we would never have moved here – nothing but noise and parties and that wretched gramophone! She caused me enough trouble in the war as it was – slept with Harold, you know.'

Rosy must have looked startled for Mrs Gill gave a dry laugh. 'Oh yes, quite smitten with her he was. Naturally it didn't last, she soon threw him over. Still, it was not something I found agreeable – makes one look rather a fool. Frankly it rankled – and not just with me. Harold was *most* resentful when she discarded him, grumbles about it even now... But then he grumbles about a lot of things, particularly the current state of the country. It's all very well having a pretty young queen gracing the pages of the *Tatler* and being kowtowed to by Winston Churchill, but what the nation needs is discipline. There's too much indulgence these days, we've gone flabby; that's always a danger with a great race – as Mr Hitler well knew. If things had been different he might have achieved something here... Oh well, too late now, those days are long gone.' She gave a pensive sigh and took a bite of her sandwich. Rosy wished it were poisoned.

She also wished she had the means of distracting the woman from her immediate purpose, which on the face of things struck her as not being particularly to her own benefit. The obvious thing was to keep the conversation swinging along: while the woman talked she couldn't *act!*

'Was it difficult,' she asked, 'I mean the planning

322

and execution? Must have been quite tricky.'

Mrs Gill reflected. 'No, I wouldn't say difficult really – *exacting* would be a better term. So much depended on the timing. We had put it about to the neighbours that we were going away for a couple of days, me to my sister in Maidstone and Harold to his club in Pall Mall. Nothing unusual in that, he stays there from time to time on business or a late-night dinner; saves me being woken up when he comes stumbling back in the small hours. Thus the house was thought to be empty at the time of Marcia's accident.' (Mrs Gill coughed discreetly.)

'But you were both there, presumably?'

'Oh, not me – at least, not until afterwards. But Harold was, of course. The plan was that he should slip away from his club unobserved, return to our house incognito, wait until that wretched artist man had gone, do the deed and melt back to his club again.' (The idea of the solid Harold Gill melting anywhere struck Rosy as exceedingly unlikely, but she refrained from comment.) *'But,'* Mrs Gill added acidly, 'there was an unforeseen hitch.'

'Ah,' Rosy remarked sagely, 'best laid plans and all that...'

The other sniffed. 'One could say that, but frankly it was Harold's fault. Admittedly he is awfully good at actual *dispatches*. The war helped him in that enormously, and of course there was also his experience with the military police in Palestine – but just now and again he will make what I believe is vulgarly termed a monumental cock-up.' She smiled faintly and added, 'I don't

323

know whether you have noticed, but in my experience, although men are wizards at so many things, they do need to be *steered* – or, at least, Harold does! As said, I was not at home at the time of your aunt's disposal, not immediately, at any rate. Had I been so then I can assure you that his stupid blunder with the lawnmower would never have happened.'

Rosy moistened her lips which were becoming uncomfortably dry. 'What blunder was that?' she enquired politely.

'Well up until then things were going exactly to plan. Having left his club unobserved by the hall porter he returned to St John's Wood in mild disguise, wearing a brown trilby and a navy-blue blazer – normally he wouldn't be seen dead in either. *Always* a dark homburg and a double-breasted. And when he felt the coast was clear he slipped back into our house and–'

'So where did he change his clothes?' Rosy asked. 'At the club?'

'What? Oh no, in a public lavatory. Not a savoury experience... Anyway, as I was saying, he slipped back into the house and hovered discreetly behind the drawn blinds – we always close them when we go away, people can be so nosy – and waited for the appropriate moment to visit Marcia. He knew Clovis was there and would be leaving at some point; as of course he did, though rather earlier than expected. However – and this is what really annoys me – it was raining very heavily, pouring, in fact, and for some reason Harold happened to take a peek out of the hall window ... and what did he see? His *lawnmower*,

324

if you please!' She raised her eyes to the heavens.

Rosy was bemused. 'Oh ... was that important?'

'It certainly was. It's his pride and joy, the latest model and frightfully costly, and it was getting wet! Fred – our weekly gardener – had omitted to put it away and left it on the gravel at the edge of the front lawn, "open to the skies", as Harold put it.' Mrs Gill tapped an impatient finger on the pistol butt, a gesture which made Rosy flinch. 'And do you know what?'

'No,' Rosy replied meekly, eying the drumming finger.

'Well, after all our plans for secrecy, the stupid man felt impelled to rescue the confounded thing, rescue it from the ravages of *rust* ... I ask you!' She shook her head in disbelief as if inviting her listener for fellow sympathy.

Rosy cleared her throat and ventured to say that yes, given the situation, i.e. the prospective shooting of a neighbour, the fate of the lawn-mower did seem a mite irrelevant.

'Exactly. It would to you and me, but not to Harold. Typical. Men can be like that, you know, they compartmentalise things – can't see the wood for the trees, although in this case that was the problem. There *was* no tree, not one sheltering the mower, at any rate!' Mrs Gill broke off and stared at Rosy quizzically, before saying in a solicitous tone, 'You look pale, my dear. I expect you could do with a spot of sherry, I know I could.'

She rose to fetch the decanter from the drinks cabinet, and for a wild instant Rosy thought she might be able to grab the pistol. No chance, of course. The weapon went with its owner.

Back in her chair, Mrs Gill poured the sherry into tiny crystal glasses and offered one to her guest. Rosy regarded it dully, wondering if it was a poisoned chalice, and then decided that on the whole she didn't much care anyway. Besides, her hostess had already taken a sip.

'And so,' Mrs Gill continued, 'you can imagine what happened.'

'Er, not entirely.'

'Well naturally, being Harold, he had to dash out there and then and put it in the shed. I suppose he thought he could sneak it in without anyone observing. What foolishness! Inevitably, of course, he was seen – by of all people Clovis Thistlehyde. Harold said he suddenly emerged at the top of Marcia's steps, clearly about to leave, and clutching his easel and paints which he promptly dropped. Then as he was gathering things up he glanced down over our front lawn – exactly to where Harold was standing fussing with his beastly machine... So you see, obviously he was *seen* and thus known to be at home!'

'But surely it wasn't definite that Clovis had noticed him. I mean he might have been gazing at the sky or at your nice rhododendrons...'

'Rather what I said. But Harold wasn't having it. "He saw me," he said, "the beggar actually waved." And that was that. It preyed on his mind, you see. I did my best to persuade him that Thistlehyde was so absorbed in himself that a casual wave didn't mean a thing and he had doubtless forgotten the whole incident. But Harold can be very stubborn, and when he gets an idea in his head nothing will dislodge it ... a bit like

Mr Hitler in that respect. Anyway, it convinced him that Clovis had to go. "No point in taking chances," he told me. Frankly, I thought that was a bit rich coming from one who had risked all for a wretched lawnmower. However, I said nothing – it doesn't do to question them. I expect you found the same with your young man in the war.' She smiled knowingly, woman to woman.

Rosy gave a lying nod, terrified of causing offence. (Agree with everything, she thought desperately, be her kindly confidante and she may drop her guard.) She mustered a reciprocal smile. 'Hmm – and, ah, I suppose he ... *dealt* with him?'

'Yes. It wasn't difficult. Harold rang the studio and said we had a special wedding anniversary coming up and that I had begged him to have his portrait painted – can't think where he got *that* idea from! – and he would like to go to the studio to discuss matters. So an appointment was made ... and well, the rest is history, as they say.' Mrs Gill sat back in her chair, patted her perm and took a sip of sherry.

As a general rule Rosy was not given to sweating, but it was one of those rare occasions when she felt a clamminess down her back and under her arms. Her throat started to feel tight and she sensed a quickening in her breath. Be calm, she told herself. Do not show fear, show *interest*.

Thus she leant forward and with feigned concern said, 'That must have been quite a blow. I mean, with Marcia out of the way, presumably you felt that was the end of the whole thing – but then came another threat from Clovis. Weren't you worried?'

Mrs Gill gave a dismissive shrug. 'Oh, well one gets used to it. After all, if you have a mission to change the course of your country's future, as Harold and I once did, then one learns resilience. You develop quite a tough skin – as I am sure you did in the war, my dear.' The last words were delivered without apparent sarcasm. 'Mind you,' she added, 'a tough skin is also required living with Harold, but that's another tale...' A flicker of distaste showed in the bland eyes. 'But yes, you are quite right, it *was* somewhat trying – particularly as after the Thistlehyde business there was the problem with Adelaide. I rather slipped up there – or at least she did.' A faint smile crossed Mrs Gill's face.

'Whatever do you mean?' gasped Rosy. 'Surely it wasn't you who–'

'Pushed her down the steps? Oh yes, indeed it was. But as said, I made rather a bish – should have pushed harder. I don't have Harold's dexterity in these matters.' She looked mildly apologetic.

'But *why?*'

'She was really becoming rather tiresome. Always has been, of course – ask Angela Fawcett! I realised the damage she could do. Whether she intended it I have no idea, but she had the *potential* and one simply couldn't take the risk.'

Rosy's shock yielded to curiosity. What was the woman getting at?

Mrs Gill must have seen her puzzlement for she continued quietly: 'You see, it was at that party the Fawcetts gave. I suddenly saw how dangerous she was. It wasn't only Maynard Latimer's

328

feathers she ruffled that night – yes, I rather thought you had noticed that – Harold came in for a few barbs too. At first I didn't take them too seriously, just Adelaide being her waspish self. But afterwards I suddenly saw the implications.'

'Why, what had she been saying?' Despite growing fear, Rosy was fascinated: not just by the narrative but by the narrator's extraordinary sangfroid. It was as if she were exchanging confidences at a vicar's tea party.

'Well, if you remember, she had accused Maynard of being a "naughty boy" – something to do with that invalid wife, I think – but later she sidled up to Harold when no one else was near, and said: "Nice of Angela to give Latimer this party, don't you think? Birthday boy, naughty boy!" She sounded highly amused. And then when Harold made some jocular response, she tugged at those tasteless diamonds she always wears and added: "But of course, he's not nearly as naughty as Brigadier Harold Gill, OBE, is he? Not by a long chalk, he isn't – you and your blonde bombshells!" She actually had the nerve to tweak his tie! Then after one of those grating cackles she hobbled off to plague someone else. It wasn't very pretty.' Mrs Gill looked pained.

And Rosy was perplexed. The old lady's comment to Harold seemed relatively innocuous – vulgar, perhaps, but hardly dangerous.

There was a pause while Mrs Gill took a contemplative sip of sherry. 'Frankly, I was rather annoyed, assuming it to be a crude allusion to Harold's distasteful proclivities.' She sniffed and pursed her lips in a manner which suddenly

329

made Rosy want to giggle, but she stifled the urge and looked suitably sober-faced. 'However,' the other continued, 'when I was thinking about it later that evening I remembered the curious way she had enunciated the word "bombshells": she gave it a slow lingering emphasis as if savouring the term... And do you know, my dear,' Mrs Gill leant forward confidingly, 'I had this sudden stab of sheer horror. Oh my God, I thought, she *knows!*'

So vivid was her re-enactment of the horror, that Rosy felt an involuntary flash of sympathy. One had known such moments... 'But how?' she asked in awe.

The other shrugged. 'People like Adelaide Fawcett make it their business to know everything, and what they don't know they invent. She thrives on human frailty: gossip, innuendo, scandal, whispered confidences. You wouldn't remember, perhaps, but before the war she was a notable political hostess, on a level with Margot Asquith, and a formidable source of all types of social intelligence. She snapped up secrets and tittle-tattle like others collect bric-a-brac. People of any eminence would flock to her soirées: the grand and bland, the great and the good (and the far from good), the old guard and the Johnny-come-latelies – they were all there; but above all the nation's *insiders*, those with power and a tale to tell if they chose. Yes, Adelaide learnt a lot from horses' mouths, and what she wasn't told directly she absorbed or guessed. Such social acuity is a talent and she had it. And now in old age, with that accumulated "wisdom" and her ear still clamped to the ground, she palliates her boredom by making people uncomfortable.'

A note of disapproval had entered Mrs Gill's voice, and again Rosy saw a slight pursing of the mouth. Whether she included her husband's bomb plot in the category of human frailty was not clear (though perhaps she ranked his 'proclivities' a greater affront); but either way, the object of her censure had certainly succeeded in spreading discomfort all right! Diffidently Rosy observed, 'But none of that is actual proof, is it? I mean, you could only surmise that she knew.' And feeling emboldened she added, 'After all, it does seem rather a lot to have inferred from an emphasis.'

Mrs Gill looked at her blankly and then with a slight frown exclaimed, 'But in *our* situation one could hardly afford to take risks. Surely you realise that. That push, ineffectual though it proved, was what Harold likes to call a "belt and braces job". And besides,' she added tartly, 'it just goes to show how carefully people should watch their words, especially Adelaide.'

Dear God, thought Rosy, if ever I get out of this alive I'll never open my mouth again!

The prospect of not getting out alive had begun to trouble her more than a little, and she cast furtive looks around the room seeking means of exit. Other than hurling herself from the balcony there seemed none. The key to the locked door still nestled securely in Mrs Gill's pocket, and the pistol now resting casually on her lap would surely forestall any lunge to grab it.

A random thought struck her, and playing for

time she said, 'But if it was you who pushed Adelaide, what about Sabatier? In the hospital she kept saying she had been attacked by a man with a wooden leg...'

'Typical,' Mrs Gill sniffed. 'Adelaide Fawcett would say anything if she thought it would put her in the limelight or make a good story. She obviously thought such an absurd detail would embellish the tale. I've told you, a very mischievous woman and not to be trusted!'

'No, no, of course not,' Rosy agreed faintly, eying the gun on the pale tweed lap.

And then to distract herself as much as her captor, she asked, 'But regarding Marcia, why on earth did your husband bother with the coal bucket? After all, he had already killed her so why waste time with something like that?'

'Oh that wasn't Harold, that was me. You see, I arrived home from Maidstone about ten minutes after it had happened and found him in the study pacing about and throwing down whisky. It worried me that he may have left things in a mess or overlooked some vital detail – you know how careless men can be. So I packed him off back to his club via our rear entrance, and then slipped next door to check that all was well ... and it was then that I saw it.'

'The coal scuttle?'

'Yes. It was there by the hallstand, which struck me as rather odd as I knew Marcia didn't have any fires – all oil. But I was hardly there to debate her heating arrangements, and it suddenly looked most enticing. So I seized the thing, took it back to the drawing room and rammed it on

332

her head...' A faraway look came into Mrs Gill's eyes, and she said, 'You may not understand, but doing that gave me immense satisfaction. In fact, I am not sure that it wasn't the best thing I have done in my entire life. I can think of only one improvement ... to have rammed it on Harold's.'

A door slammed downstairs and there was a sound of jaunty whistling. 'Ah, that must be him now,' Mrs Gill murmured, rising to unlock the door. 'Late, as usual; been with one of those frightful women, I daresay.' She sniffed disdainfully, before adding, 'Although it's not that he gets carried away – it is simply that it takes him so long these days.'

Rosy was startled by the information, but given the circumstances was less concerned with Harold Gill's problems than with her own. She continued to contemplate the pistol while listening to Harold's heavy (and possibly weary) tread as he mounted the stairs.

He entered the room still clad in overcoat, and bearing a bunch of flowers which clearly afforded little pleasure to his spouse. 'Oh, *do* ring the changes,' she exclaimed irritably. 'Always carnations – *so* predictable!'

He seemed about to protest, but seeing Rosy said, 'Oh, Miss Gilchrist, I didn't realise you might still be here, I–'

'Where did you think I might be,' Rosy retorted, 'six feet under?'

His gaze fell on the gun and he raised a quizzical eyebrow.

'Yes,' said Mrs Gill, 'I fear we were careless –

333

left the documents lying around. Rosy saw the thing and wanted it back. Naturally I had to explain that that was out of the question...' she paused '...and then of course I also had to explain a number of other things. A pity, really.'

He nodded. 'Hmm – we can't have that I'm afraid; not at all.' Together they regarded her with a look of thoughtful regret.

It was a look which seemed to signal Rosy's fate and she was filled with overwhelming dread, earlier truculence shed in an instant. Up till then, though fearful, she had felt she could somehow handle matters: that by keeping calm and her wits about her she could devise a way of dealing with the older woman. But with the return of Harold and seeing the pair gazing at her with such quiet assurance it was clear that escape was impossible. She thought of Marcia, of Clovis, of Sabatier... There wasn't a chance in hell: like the others, she knew too much.

Her thoughts were echoed by Mr Gill. 'You see, my dear, I am afraid you know too much. We really can't take the risk. You are a bright girl – brighter than your aunt, really – so you must understand that.' He paused. 'You do understand, don't you?'

'Of course she does!' exclaimed Mrs Gill impatiently. 'You hardly need to press the point, Harold.' And turning to Rosy she said, 'It is really most unfortunate – we rather liked you; but I fear that's the way of things. It happens too much in life: being in the wrong place at the wrong time – like that interfering Sabatier, for instance. He had been on our trail for some while. We saw him snooping around in Marcia's tradesmen's passage – it's overlooked by our landing windows – but his investigations backfired, led us straight to what we wanted, in fact. He had the thing in his hand when he came out of her kitchen. Harold had sneaked down and was there waiting for him.'

However, by that time her words were irrelevant to Rosy. 'So which way am I going to go?' she asked listlessly.

'Oh, don't worry, my dear,' was the bolstering reply, 'it will be quite quick. Harold can be very deft when he tries. You won't feel a thing.'

'And then what? Plonked in a deckchair at Bexhill – or Brighton, perhaps?'

'Brighton? Oh hardly! There's a nice bench just outside the Grand Hotel at Eastbourne, *much* more suitable.' Mrs Gill began to smile, and then stopped and looked genuinely contrite. 'Oh dear, it's hardly a laughing matter. Unpardonable of me. I am so sorry!'

Rosy closed her eyes. Death was bad enough, but to be killed on a wave of facetiousness was the last straw... She glanced at Gill. He had taken out his pipe and was in the act of lighting it, but the gesture held no homely comfort, for the eyes that met hers were hard and expressionless. It could not be much longer, and she wondered again how it would happen.

CHAPTER THIRTY-NINE

As Rosy spoke with her captors and pondered her last moments much discussion had also been going on in Felix's flat.

'I bumped into Rosy Gilchrist at the museum this morning,' announced Vera. 'She seemed pretty cut up about the Sabatier disappearance – as well she might. To have found a corpse, let alone his, and then to hear it had turned up naked in Bexhill cannot have been particularly jolly. I began to feel somewhat sorry for her.'

'Doubtless you fought down the impulse,' remarked Cedric.

She glared at him. 'Sometimes, Cedric, your observations are so ill timed! I am extremely shaken by his fate myself, as well you know. And if Miss Gilchrist is even mildly disturbed, then I for one can understand her feelings.' She lit a cheroot and expelled the smoke with a violent swirl.

Felix began to cough. 'Huh,' he spluttered, 'she's not the only one that's disturbed. The whole thing is awful! One's great fear is that she will go to the police – nerve bound to crack sooner or later.'

'I'm not so sure. Not my type, of course, far too pleased with herself, but I think she has a certain fibre – not likely to buckle under strain.'

'Unlike your young friend Deirdre,' Cedric

observed softly.

Vera scowled but said nothing.

'Nevertheless,' he continued, 'Felix is right. One cannot take anything for granted and that includes Rosy Gilchrist's nerve. What is she doing now?'

Vera shrugged. 'Probably gassing with the Gills. I bumped into the wife yesterday who said something about wanting her to go to tea this afternoon. They are moving, apparently; said she had some vase or other for Rosy.'

Cedric leant forward in his chair suddenly alert. 'She's there now?'

'Quite possibly, I daresay.'

'I am not entirely sure that is a good thing. Is there anyone else there – cronies or anybody?'

'How should I know? No one else was mentioned. Does it matter?'

Cedric was silent, frowning. And then he said slowly, 'It probably doesn't matter one jot. On the other hand it just might.'

'Why?' they demanded.

'An idea has been in my head for some time, but I didn't mention it as there's no proof, just "a gut feeling", as the Americans would say.' He cleared his throat and looked stern. 'Has it occurred to you that in all this business there has been a common factor?'

'What factor?' Vera asked.

'The Gills. Marcia lived next door to them and had known Harold Gill in the war. Being neighbours they probably had the key. We assume that Clovis may have seen something or someone when he was with Marcia on the afternoon she

337

was killed – her steps and veranda overlook the Gills' garden. You may recall that Marcia's house is on the corner and, other than the Gills' place, has nothing next to it. Very little time elapsed between Clovis's departure and the shooting. Thus somebody must have entered the house between his going and the char's coming. Such entry could be quickly and discreetly managed by an alert close neighbour, but less so by a stranger. I mean, where would one loiter – crouched behind a pillar box?'

'Oh, I don't know,' Felix said doubtfully, 'it all sounds a bit far–'

'Ssh! Just listen and think about Sabatier's murder as well... It happened in the passage that runs between the two houses. Somebody must have seen him enter Marcia's kitchen *and* had the time and opportunity to mop up and dispose of the body after the deed was done – and after you and Rosy had hared off down the road. Which rather suggests the killer had seen Rosy discovering the dying Sabatier. That little alley is on Marcia's property but can be seen from the Gills' upper windows. It cannot be seen from the road unless you go down the private side steps. It is, to quote some poet or other, a fine and private place.' Cedric paused and cleared his throat, before adding, 'You will also note that two of the murders occurred merely yards from the Gills' house and that two of them involved people they knew. Interesting, really.'

'Yes,' Felix said impatiently, 'it is what one calls coincidence. Anyway, what about their alibi? The inspector let drop that they were elsewhere for

Marcia's murder, or, at least, Gill was. In fact I rather gather from the grapevine that neither was at home at the crucial time.'

Vera was less sceptical. 'Hmm. Personally I wouldn't set much store by that inspector's researches! And, in any case, alibis aren't everything; they only need a bit of nous to concoct.'

'Or, indeed, to break,' replied Cedric, 'but from what I've seen of this investigation the nous seems a trifle lacking.'

'Well, I really cannot see the ghastly Gills being the type to engage in treasonable plots, let alone savage murders. Utterly absurd!' Felix exclaimed.

'If people ran true to type life would be considerably simpler,' Cedric retorted. 'Besides, this is not the moment to debate the matter: three killings have already occurred, and of people either in our circle or known to us. Another could happen at any time. It would be unfortunate if the next victim were to be Marcia's niece. We should feel uncomfortable. I think some intervention is called for.'

'Oh really, Cedric,' Felix protested, 'I am sure the two ladies are calmly carding wool and discussing what to wear for the Boat Race or some jolly event. And in any case, what can one possibly *do?* If we go to the police they won't believe a single word, and it will take so long to explain that the deed could be done by the time they've shut their notebooks! Besides, as we've said before, one is hardly in a *position* to voice such suspicions, far too compromising... No, all very fertile, your theories, but hardly convincing. I am sure Rosy Gilchrist is perfectly all right –

that sort generally is.'

'What, like Sabatier?' asked Cedric.

'Easy enough to find out,' Vera remarked casually, 'and we shan't need to get involved at all. The police will act promptly and we can keep our distance.'

'Oh? How?'

'White slavery.'

'*What?*' The two men gaped at her.

'We will make an anonymous call to the police and say we have every reason to believe that the Gills are engaged in buying and selling young women for gross profit and base purpose, and that to our certain knowledge one such unfortunate is being restrained in their house at this very minute.'

There was a heavy silence as her proposal was digested.

'Well I can tell you one thing, Vera Collinger,' Felix cried, 'you are certainly not using *my* telephone. They'll trace the call immediately!'

Cedric sighed. 'I think we can assume that Vera has a public telephone in mind, not yours.'

'Naturally,' she said. 'Now somebody – *not* Felix – must go immediately to the box on the corner and report our suspicions. Of course one won't be believed; they'll assume the caller is a harmless crank, but they will still have to act on the information – daren't do otherwise. *If* by chance our fears are founded and the Gilchrist girl really is in danger, then the sudden appearance of a couple of constables should do the trick. Naturally if all is normal then it will simply place the Gills in an embarrassing position with no harm done – not to us anyway.'

Before either could speak, she rose and strode smartly to the door clearly casting herself as informant. As she grasped the handle, Felix said, 'I say, Vera, I suggest you remove your hat, that awful feather might attract attention.'

When she had gone he turned to Cedric and asked scathingly, 'Did she say a harmless crank?' But slightly to his surprise his friend said nothing, seemingly lost in thought and gazing absently out of the window.

CHAPTER FORTY

Rosy was not religious but a residual impulse awoke the childhood words: 'Our Father which art in heaven,' she inwardly faltered, 'hallowed be thy–'

There was a heavy knocking from below followed by a prolonged shrilling of the doorbell. Gill spun round, scattering sparks and ash. 'What the hell's that?' he snarled.

Beretta in hand, his wife rose and peeped from the window. She looked troubled. 'It's the police,' she declared. 'I can see a helmet on the other side of the privet. One of them must be in the porch.'

'Deal with it,' he snapped. 'I'll hold the girl.' He bounded towards Rosy, applied a half nelson with one arm and clamped her mouth with the other.

Pocketing the pistol and hastily smoothing her hair, Mrs Gill opened the door and went towards

341

the stairs...

Voices wafted up from below: Mrs Gill's plus a deeper burbling one. There was the sound of a laugh: 'Oh *hardly!*' the lighter voice exclaimed. The burbling continued.

Harold tightened his grip on Rosy, and bending his head muttered into her ear, 'Don't get your hopes up, my dear, they'll need a search warrant. Mildred knows that – and besides, she's good at dealing with buffoons.' She felt the hot breath on her neck and could smell his tweed and sweat, and felt physically sick. In spite of the spluttered words, the pipe was still clenched between his teeth. Flinching from the agony of her left arm, Rosy drew back her right elbow and jabbed it as hard as she could into the portly stomach. His hand fell from her mouth. 'Bitch!' he grunted, and fumbled to resume his hold. But it was too late. With a desperate gulp of air, Rosy emitted the loudest scream of her life; indeed one so loud that she startled herself – she never knew she had such lungs!

From the effect it also clearly startled the visitor in the hall, for in the next instant there was a loud hoot from a police whistle and a crashing of hobnailed boots on the stairs. The door was flung wide and a young man with flushed face and tousled hair stood on the threshold.

With a curse Gill released his captive, and lunging forward dropped his pipe, skidded over it and fell heavily on all fours. He remained in that pose gasping in obvious agony. 'Bloody knee,' he whispered to himself, 'bloody fucking knee!'

To her later fury Rosy burst into tears. However, it was a response that must have confirmed the young officer's assumption that all was not well. Surveying the scene of crying girl and cursing man, he looked both stern and relieved – thankful, perhaps, he would be spared an official reprimand for the errors of misplaced zeal. He seemed about to speak, when there was the sound of a shot from below and a splintering crash.

Harris (for it was he) jumped, and swivelling his head cried, 'Jesus, what's that, Henry?'

'It's all right,' a thin voice yelled, 'it's the woman; she's just blasted the Chink vase. I've got the gun off her.'

'Fool!' Harold Gill was heard to mutter as he contemplated the floorboards a foot from his nose.

'Radio for reinforcements,' Harris shouted back imperiously.

In obvious pain Gill started to crawl towards the door. 'Stop that!' the youth said sharply.

Gill stopped, and with a sigh of resignation heaved himself into a sitting position and slumped against the wall. He looked up at the policeman. 'Clever little bugger, aren't you?'

Harris shrugged. 'Dunno, sir.' He gazed at Gill thoughtfully, looking slightly puzzled. 'So are you really up to white slaving?' he enquired.

'Up to what?' rasped the older man.

'White slavery. We've had a tip-off you see and–'

'White *slavery*? What the hell are you talking about, boy?'

Rosy had the impression the young man did not care to be addressed as 'boy' for she noticed a slight pursing of his lips, and the next moment

343

he shouted over his shoulder: 'Bring the lady up here, Henry. I want to interview the pair of them.' He sounded very important.

Mrs Gill appeared, accompanied by a uniformed constable even more youthful than Harris. She glanced down at her husband and gave a helpless twitch of her hands.

'I did try, Harold, but the bullet hit the vase.'

'I know,' he replied wearily, and then added with some asperity: 'You bought it in Singapore; I've been wanting to smash it ever since. Just shows, wait long enough...'

Like the presiding officer, Mrs Gill pursed her lips and regarded him with evident displeasure.

Harris gestured her aside, and squatting down beside her husband said quietly, 'I don't understand this white slavery business, sir ... you see, I had you down for something else – something quite else.' He stared intently at Gill.

'Really?' the other replied indifferently. 'Can't think what that could be.'

The interrogator cleared his throat. 'Does the name Churchill mean anything to you, sir?'

There was a silence, punctuated by the merest intake of breath from Mildred. And then Mr Gill said, 'Naturally. He is the leader of my party – our nation's prime minister. Do you imagine I am an idiot?'

'No, but what I think is–' Harris began, leaning closer.

But at that moment there sounded the clanging bell of a police vehicle, screeching of tyres, slamming of car doors and the nasal gabbling of walkie-talkies. The reinforcements had arrived.

344

Detective Sergeant Greenleaf and the inspector pounded into the room, and nodding briefly to Harris and Henry immediately took charge. Rosy was hustled out, Mildred handcuffed and Gill yanked to his feet and propelled on to the landing. His face had become suddenly ashen – the result of the damaged knee no doubt, but from what little Rosy had seen and heard she guessed there was something else plaguing his mind: Harris's words.

The inspector embarked on the formalities of arrest, enunciating the spiel with toneless gravity. But before he had got far Gill stopped him. 'Excuse me, old man, do you think I could possibly have a gasper? I'm not feeling too good.' He leant heavily against the banister and in a trice drew from his pocket a pack of Kensitas. Rosy later remembered being surprised at this, having always seen him only with the briar pipe. Swiftly he put a cigarette between his lips, while one of the constables mechanically proffered a match.

'He doesn't need one,' Mrs Gill said sharply.

'Oh God,' cried Harris, 'he's bitten the end!'

CHAPTER FORTY-ONE

'Well that was a howdy-do and no mistake,' said the inspector over supper in the canteen. 'What you might call a surprise. Wasn't pretty either, but at least it was quick. Which is just as well, otherwise they'd be saying it was our fault for not being more alert and anticipating things.' He frowned, adding morosely, 'More than likely they will say that anyway, you'll see.'

'Shouldn't worry,' Greenleaf reassured him, 'wasn't our fault. I mean to say, how were we supposed to know his fag was bunged full of cyanide? After all, it's not something you expect from St John's Wood, is it? Not even from a white slaver.' He grinned and added, 'I assume there was some kind of mistake there.'

The other nodded looking puzzled. 'Yes, a mistake. Can't quite make it out – some joker started it off, phoning the duty officer. But the odd thing is that the super hasn't said much about it – almost as if he's concerned with something else. But I can tell you, he's none too pleased all the same. Something fishy going on, I shouldn't wonder. Heard him shouting down the phone to someone saying he was sick and tired of being the lackey of MI5 and why was he never put in the bloody picture. Anyway, what he has said to me is that he wants the whole incident put under wraps for the time being, and that if anyone is heard even mentioning it they'll lose their stripes and rue the day.'

'Do what, sir?'

'Rue the sodding day!'

'Ah, I see... So what about the wife?'

The inspector brightened. 'Well, that's the funny thing. You see, when we took her in for questioning she didn't say a thing, literally didn't open her mouth for two hours. In fact I was beginning to think we had a mute on our hands.

Then all of a sudden she had a sort of fit – went on for quite a long time, had to be sedated.'

'Yes, very funny sir,' said Greenleaf dryly.

'Ah, but it *was* you see, because when she finally surfaced from the sedation she had changed.'

'What do you mean, *changed?*'

'What I say. She had changed from being Mrs Mildred Gill into someone else.' The inspector reached for the sugar and spooned half of it into his cup, while the sergeant digested his words.

'I see. So, er, who is this someone else, if you don't mind my asking?'

'Mata Hari.'

Greenleaf dropped his knife and gaped. 'Mata Hari!'

'Yes. Even uses a few words of Dutch – leastways, I assume that's what it is, sounds like gobbledygook to me.'

'Come on, sir, you're having me on!'

The inspector shrugged. 'If you say so.'

The sergeant coughed and eyed his superior with some suspicion. 'So when she's not talking Dutch what does she say exactly?'

'She is firmly of the opinion that Marcia Beasley was her rival – both in circles of espionage and in matters romantic, that is to say she was enjoying the favours of her husband. Finding the situation disagreeable on both counts she decided to put a stop to her discomfort by felling the rival with a coal scuttle.'

'She was shot,' objected Greenleaf.

'Yes, in 1917.'

'No, not her! The other one, Mrs Beasley.'

'We know that, but apparently it is an aspect of

347

the event Mata Hari does not recall. It's the coal scuttle that has caught her fancy. I did try to suggest otherwise but she got a bit shirty, said I was getting above my station.'

Greenleaf grinned. 'Not so mad after all.'

Ignoring the remark, the inspector went on to say that since the forensics had established that the gun used on Mrs Beasley was the same as that used by Mrs Gill to pulverise the Chinese vase, there was a fair chance that she had indeed been the murderer of her neighbour. 'Somewhere at the bottom of that barminess there's a truth lurking,' he asserted with confidence. 'Still, what with hubby being dead and her too sick to stand trial, I don't suppose we'll ever know, really. A bum case as you might say.'

'But what about the girl – what's she got to say? Looked pretty tearful when we arrived.'

'As well she might, must have been a bit of a shock. When I first started to question her she was fairly vague; but then she seemed to rally and became much clearer – not that it's helped much. I gather she had been invited to tea by Mrs Gill and all was going nice and normal like, when suddenly, for no apparent reason, the woman began getting aggressive, and then out of the blue pulled a gun. Not used to being threatened across the tea table, Miss Gilchrist was taken aback and tried calming her down. But before she got very far Gill appeared and grabbed her.'

'What for? Sex?'

'I did ask that, but the girl said there hadn't been time to find out as at that juncture Harris and Henry turned up, followed by us, of course.'

He flicked ash into his saucer. 'Funny, really, the scrapes people get themselves into...'

'I wonder why Mata Hari,' pondered Greenleaf.

'Oh, ask Harris, *he'll* tell you. Reckons it's Freudian. Says it's very common in ladies of a certain ilk and age – sublimation or some such.'

'How does Harris know that?'

'Like he knows everything: it's that set of encyclopaedias his gran gave him for Christmas.'

'Well if he knows so much, what does he make of Gill and his suicide?'

'As a matter of fact he hasn't said a word about it – which given the super's embargo is just as well. In fact he's been very silent all day, keeps frowning.'

'Perhaps he's not had time to consult his oracles!'

They laughed and turned to other things, namely Clovis Thistlehyde.

'So,' Greenleaf said, 'if Mrs Gill *did* murder the Beasley woman as she alleges, do we assume that being barking mad, i.e. in her Mata Hari mode, that she also went to the studio and dealt with the painter?'

'Oh *no*. I think that's something quite separate: a coincidence, certainly, but no connection. If you recall, Sergeant, it was you that kept going on about him being a witness to something at the victim's house and seeing that mythical geezer with a lawnmower ... a bit of a red herring, if you ask me.' The voice held a note of reproach.

'I seem to recall, *sir*,' said Greenleaf stoutly, 'that you gave me firm instructions to follow it

349

up. You seemed quite interested at the time.'

'Well I am not now,' snapped the other. 'Look, we've got a confession, haven't we? That'll do. Don't let's muddy the waters!'

Greenleaf was not entirely convinced, but on the whole thought it best to say nothing. Instead he suggested that Harold Gill's suicide was doubtless prompted by the strain of living with one fixated on the idea that she was an exotic spy and insatiable siren.

The inspector agreed that it was more than likely.

CHAPTER FORTY-TWO

'Do you think we should send flowers?' asked Felix eagerly. 'I've just had the most ravishing consignment of early azaleas, just the thing for an invalid.'

'She is not an invalid,' replied Vera.

'But might have become a corpse,' said Cedric.

Felix nodded. 'Exactly! And we've had far too many of those as it is. From what she said on the phone it sounds as if it was quite a close-run thing. It was really very shrewd of you, Cedric, to suspect the Gills. I trust she is suitably grateful... Now, what about the flowers?'

'Forget the flowers,' snapped Vera. 'There are more pressing matters. We are not in possession of the *details* – and the details could be very disagreeable for us. Very disagreeable. The only information we have so far is what Rosy Gilchrist gabbled down the telephone, i.e. that there had been a ghastly fracas at the house, that Gill had committed suicide and she was safe. Yesterday's paper merely says that the house owner had died in unusual circumstances and that two women were escorted from the premises. Obviously the press have been kept at a distance, or even muzzled – they are not normally so reticent. What isn't clear is whether Gill divulged anything to the police before his death, or indeed whether the girl herself has said anything. For all we know she could have blown the whole gaff – about Sabatier and everything else. It is not unknown for people to go to pieces in such situations.'

'Well I doubt whether Miss Gilchrist–' began Felix.

Vera glared. 'Don't you see? We can rely on nothing! We only have the vaguest notion of what went on in that house and have no idea what was said in the police station afterwards. Anything might have emerged! Gill's death may be a blessing but equally it may open up a whole can of embarrassing worms. If the authorities get even a sniff of the Sabatier murder and our part in the coal business we could be accused of all manner of things such as misleading the police, hindering their enquiries and concealing crucial evidence. The law takes a dim view of that sort of thing. And as for myself, I could be facing a murder charge.'

'But Vera,' Felix exclaimed, 'that's not very likely; I mean presumably Gill did it and–'

'Huh! Simply because Gill committed suicide

351

and was found attacking the girl does not necessarily mean that he murdered Marcia... I daresay he did, but the *police* may not be sure; and until they are they will be examining other possibilities, one of which is myself. As said previously, I'm not too keen on my brother's role being rooted up: there's a potential motive there which, failing anything better, they'll be sure to seize on... I tell you, we are *totally* in the dark as to how much they know, and that means being in a position of extreme delicacy. I don't like it.' She paused, adjusted the pork-pie hat and scowled.

'In that case,' said Cedric briskly, 'we must get out of the dark and into the light.' He rose from his chair. 'Gather your flowers, Felix. We shall visit Miss Gilchrist's flat and hear things from the horse's mouth!'

The horse meanwhile was sitting on her sofa thanking her lucky stars she was all right and brooding on what she had recently learnt. After the interview with the inspector following the dreadful event, she had been driven home and left to her own devices. But that morning the inspector, plus a tall officer she had never seen before, appeared on her doorstep and enquired if it was convenient to speak to her. Since their demeanour suggested that her convenience was of little interest, she resigned herself to a further interview. In fact, this turned out to be less onerous than expected.

The questions were mild and easily parried, but she was given information of a startling nature and also issued with a stern warning. This latter was that if she were not to fall foul of the Official Secrets Act it was imperative that she revealed nothing about the recent incident. When she expressed quizzical surprise the inspector had said woodenly that 'them that ask no questions are told no lies'.

Fortunately his commanding officer, i.e. the superintendent, was more civil and forthcoming. 'You see, Miss Gilchrist,' he had said in a confiding tone, 'some rather interesting facts have recently come to light regarding our friend's activities during the war... Gill was not entirely what you might think and I gather has been the subject of some rather close scrutiny from MI5. In fact, there is currently a very intensive enquiry being conducted which is *absolutely* top secret. The Cabinet – our prime minister and his advisors – are determined that nothing should be said that would compromise its proceedings. Thus I must advise you that any breach of this directive will be met with the severest sanctions.' The tone had been pleasant, the point unmistakable.

Rosy had nodded meekly and indicated she would of course be suitably discreet. But curiosity prevailed and she had asked cautiously, 'But what about Mrs Gill? She was certainly acting very strangely when I last saw her.'

'Ye-es,' he had replied slowly, 'the lady seems to have had a breakdown of sorts – permanent probably – and is talking very wildly. *Very* wildly. She is under the impression that she is the spy Mata Hari.' He gave a wintry smile. 'But she has also indicated that it was she who had been responsible for the murder of your poor aunt;

353

seems most emphatic about it ... some sort of domestic jealousy, one gathers. Despite her patent confusion we are inclined to believe what she says. Among other things the gun in her possession was the same as that used on Mrs Beasley, but she has also been most explicit about how – as Mata Hari, you understand – she had been biding her time for months to get revenge on her "arch rival". Apparently it began with the beribboned bits of coal and went on from there ... all calculated to a nicety it seems, as is the style with your better class of assassin.' He allowed himself another chilly smile.

'Totally bonkers, you see!' interrupted the inspector with some satisfaction.

The superintendent winced but disregarded him. 'Thus, until she recovers – *if* she recovers – she has been sent to a place of seclusion and supervised rest. And so I must tell you that, in principle, the case involving your aunt is closed – or to be more accurate, *relegated* for the foreseeable future.'

He looked vaguely apologetic as if assuming the grieving niece might feel short-changed or demand further explanation. Thus Rosy's instant response of compliant understanding was clearly approved, and perhaps as a gesture of gratitude he nodded towards the bookshelf displaying the old photographs of her parents and Marcia. Pointing to the latter he observed, 'Must have been quite a stunner as a girl, a real beauty, in fact...' He shook his head sadly. 'Just shows, you never know what life's going to throw at you, do you?'

Rosy agreed that you did not. And then promis-

354

ing again that she would say nothing that might encourage the press in their speculation over the mode or cause of Mr Gill's suicide, she showed them to the door and returned to the sitting room in a state of dazed relief. Clearly the Churchill conspiracy had far outstripped the importance of the Beasley case! She opened the window and sniffed the scent of the approaching spring, sombrely triumphant that Marcia's past could remain a secret and family honour be upheld.

She was just basking in that realisation when her thoughts were shattered by the telephone. 'We are coming to see you,' announced the unmistakable voice of Vera Collinger.

And come they did, worried and avid for news. Cedric murmured a few words of polite enquiry re her welfare and Felix flourished his flowers; but it was obvious that their main objective was to learn just how much Rosy Gilchrist or Harold Gill had let drop to the police.

'Nothing,' she told them coolly. 'Gill topped himself without saying a word – well nothing that was relevant – and I omitted everything.'

'Really?' said Cedric. 'You mean all references to Sabatier and to our nonsense with the coal?'

She nodded.

'Hmm. Very commendable.'

'Are you sure?' demanded Vera sceptically. 'I don't imagine you were in the sharpest frame of mind to cope with their questions.'

'Don't you?' Rosy asked mildly.

'But what about the *wife?*' cried Felix. 'We rather assumed they were operating together.

355

Surely they could have obtained a lot from her!'
He gazed anxiously at Rosy.

She gave a slow grin. 'Oh they *did* – and so did
I.' And she proceeded to tell them all that Mrs
Gill had told her, and what apparently the lady –
or her alter ego – had later confessed when
interviewed in the police station.

The account took rather a long time and when
she had finished there was a heavy silence. And
then Felix began to titter. 'Who would have
thought that po-faced woman could harbour such
fantasies? Just goes to show, still waters run in *very*
subterranean depths! Do you think they have to
restrain her from doing a striptease in the cell or
wherever she is?' He continued to giggle loudly.

'Be quiet, Felix,' Vera barked. 'I doubt if she's
quite the lunatic you imagine. Personally I am not
entirely convinced by this business of her
suffering a breakdown and all the rest of it. You
will note that the version of events she gave to
Miss Gilchrist diverged considerably from what
she claimed to the police. She had been perfectly
confident in admitting so much detail to her
captive because she knew, or thought she knew,
that Rosy was going to be silenced. However,
events took a different turn... And having been
caught attempting to blow the young policeman's
head off with the Beretta she was naturally in a
dangerous position – a position that would become even more dangerous when she was taken
into custody and in all likelihood confronted with
her account as told to Miss Gilchrist.

'But Rosy didn't reveal any of that,' objected
Felix.

'Of course she didn't,' Cedric said. 'We now know that but at the time Mrs Gill did not. Do let Vera get on, dear chap!'

The expositor gave him a gracious nod and continued. 'In that account she revealed a whole spate of damning things: she had colluded with her husband to kill her visitor, had been closely involved in Marcia's murder and an accessory to Clovis's, had personally tried to kill Adelaide Fawcett – and most vital of all, had been engaged in a wartime plot to annihilate Churchill and ease the pathway to a Nazi invasion. Frankly, placed in similar circumstances I would not hesitate to fabricate a breakdown – though whether I would choose to inhabit the persona of such a one as Mata Hari I rather doubt.' Miss Collinger frowned as if pondering the possibility.

'Yes, it does stretch the imagination,' Felix murmured, gazing with apparent absorption at Rosy's standard lamp.

'Vera could be right,' mused Cedric. 'Sharp of the woman to take the blame for Marcia's murder. By freely admitting to that she probably hoped to obscure the real motive. The killing would be seen as an isolated *crime passionnel*, not a carefully planned response to political blackmail and all that it entailed; simply the act of a jealous crank deserving of medication instead of the gallows. The breakdown and gibberish about Mata Hari would help confirm that view ... as, judging from what Miss Gilchrist's visitors were saying, seems to have been the case. What do you think?'

There was a short silence, followed by a lively debate as to whether Mrs Gill was indeed a raving lunatic or, as Vera had suggested, a lady of consummate guile and enterprise. No firm conclusion was reached.

'It is of little consequence,' Felix opined, 'the essential thing is that they have *closed* the case! Do you realise what that means? We are now all free. Free as the veritable birds of paradise!' he cried gaily, executing a little jig on the hearthrug.

'Just watch your plumage,' Miss Collinger growled, 'you could come a nasty cropper doing that.'

Cedric cleared his throat. 'I propose,' he announced, 'that in view of the fortuitous outcome we might go a burst and avail ourselves of luncheon at the Berkeley. What do you think, Miss Gilchrist – Rosy? Perhaps you will be our guest?' He flashed a rare smile.

Rosy replied that she thought it a lovely idea and she so appreciated his kind invitation, but in view of the recent shocks and theatricals she wasn't quite up to such festive ventures. 'If you don't mind,' she said, 'I think I will just stay here quietly for the time being – still rather a lot to think about.'

'You do look pretty haggard,' Felix agreed. 'Another time perhaps...' He turned to Vera. 'I hope you are not going to wear that hat!'

They trooped out leaving Rosy alone and in peace. For a few moments she contemplated the empty air, her mind still a bemused jumble. And then she smiled as a thought struck her. One good thing had emerged at any rate: at least Lady Fawcett would be spared any further donations to the Pygmy fund!

The thought vanished as her eye was caught by the photograph of Marcia on the bookcase. She picked it up and studied the firm features and wide challenging eyes. What was it the police superintendent had said? *Must have been quite a stunner as a girl – a real beauty...* Yes, he was right, she had been beautiful once – attractive too, as even Vera had acknowledged: *I was frightfully fond of your aunt.* And so it seemed had others. The words of Brother Ignatius echoed in her mind: *Your aunt was always very kind to me. I think we had a bond.* But she had been a lot of other things too, less endearing, less amusing...

Rosy continued to gaze down at the face, perplexed and ambivalent. What the *hell* had the girl been up to? What had she been pursuing all those years? What had she been seeking or feeling? Impossible to tell. But one thing was certain: whatever her faults, vices even, she hadn't deserved that bloody bucket!

She stretched out on the sofa, and for the umpteenth time scrutinised and tried to decipher the contents of the packet she had slipped into her handbag during the police shindig at the Gills' house. The difficulty was the language. It was German – of which she knew four terms: *ja, nein, schweinhund* and *hände hoch.* None of these seemed to feature in the text and she was hanged if she would go to the expense of buying a Kraut dictionary!

That the documents were important she had no doubt. Yes, they were patently Marcia's black-mailing 'dynamite', for apart from the name of

Churchill appearing on virtually every page there was a small plan of central London with Downing Street and the War Office heavily marked, plus a short list of names including those of a Brig. H.M. Gill, an F.D. Pitlake and a K.D.A. Clerk-Herbert – all of whom she recognised.

Kerridge Clerk-Herbert had been a minor politician and poet of large ego and small talent, whose verses might have been dubbed tub-thumpingly jingoistic had they been less turgid. Two weeks previously he had attracted some mild attention by expiring from a heart attack in his bath at the Savoy. (Another of Marcia's indirect casualties?) Lord Pitlake, on the other hand, she knew to be alive. Only that morning *The Times* had featured a large photograph of him on the tarmac at London Airport bidding a fond farewell to 'dear old England' as he flew off to spin out the rest of his days in Kenya (a part of Africa evidently popular with a certain brand of quisling). Asked by a reporter what he intended to do in his adopted homeland, the noble lord had replied that he would write his memoirs, keep the British flag flying and pursue his favourite sports of stalking, trapping and shooting.

Rather guiltily Rosy had also scanned the text for any mention of the name Maynard Latimer. To her relief she saw none ... and then for no apparent reason an image of Adelaide's ill-served cat flashed upon her mind, followed randomly by a picture of the rich and saintly Silvia. She mused not for the first time how it was the woman had managed to fall out of that 'not very tall' tree.

Then sniffing the last residue of the Schiaparelli on her wrist, she returned her attention to the document in hand and slowly and precisely tore it into shreds. These she placed in an empty fruit bowl, and clicking open her cigarette lighter set fire to the lot. Suppressing evidence? The thing was her own to treat as she chose. It had been given to her by her aunt.

CHAPTER FORTY-THREE

POSTSCRIPT

A short while after Mata Hari's confinement the following exchanges took place – in police station, flower shop and drawing room.

'So what did Berridge have to say this time?' asked Greenleaf of his boss.

'Complaints as usual. Says it's freezing on the south coast, that he's already caught a cold and they have left him to deal with that stiff-in-the-deckchair case. You would think that having to interview all those nudists would have perked him up a bit. But not Berridge, oh no! Nothing but grumble, grumble...'

There was silence as they considered Berridge and his woes.

And then Greenleaf said, 'But what I don't understand about our case is why God suddenly turned all brisk and galvanised. Last time I saw him he was rambling on about dining with the chief constable. But then all of a sudden you would think he had been fired by a Bofors... So somebody must have been getting at him.'

'Harris,' said the inspector. 'It was Harris. Little bugger had been doing some snooping of his own. Quite unsanctioned. The super got wind, and feeling like a spare coat hanger made enquiries of the powers that be who then gave him a briefing about their Gill surveillance. But apparently Harris had been harbouring suspicions for some time. Not a word to me, of course!'

'Nor me,' Greenleaf said huffily. 'Bit of a brass neck really.'

There was silence as they cogitated upon Harris and his brass neck.

'Mind you,' said the inspector, 'he had obviously picked up some gen from that uncle of his.'

'What uncle?'

'The one in MI5. Been giving him a nod and a wink, if you ask me. Still, you have to give him his due.'

'Why?'

'Single-minded, that's what.'

'You mean his single-minded pursuit of Gill?'

His colleague sighed. 'Including him, but it goes further than that.'

'What do you mean further? He nailed him didn't he ... well sort of. I wondered why he was so keen to go on that routine reconnaissance when we had the crank call. No one else volunteered! Must have been smelling a rat for some time.'

'Yes, but what he really wants to nail – and will – is the top job: "Harris of the Yard", that's what he has in mind. You'll see, a decade from now and the name will be on everyone's lips: *Harris of the Yard.*' The inspector repeated it dolefully.

There was another silence. And then Greenleaf said, 'What I want on my lips just now is a nice head of Guinness.'

'You've got something there, Herbert,' said his superior, matey all of a sudden, 'and then we can raise a jar to the next case – that darts player with his head bashed in at Wapping. Now that's what I call a decent assignment – none of this poncey West End nonsense!'

Greenleaf nodded, and with squared shoulders they set off briskly for the Nag's Rump.

'Oh, by the way,' Felix said casually, 'it's come through.'

'What has?'

'My plaque, of course.'

Cedric put down *The Times*. 'You mean the Royal...?'

'What else?'

Felix bent his head to the tapestry, but not before Cedric had glimpsed the smirk of pleasure suffusing his friend's features. 'Cap Ferrat, here we come!' the professor cried.

'It's really been rather a trying period, don't you think?' enquired Lady Fawcett. 'I don't know about you, Rosy, but personally I feel quite *wrung out!*' (She looked remarkably hale.) 'In fact, so much so, that I have a booked a voyage to New York on one of the Cunards. We have cousins there who keep pestering me to pay them a visit. I gather they live somewhere on Park Avenue –

not sure where that is, but Edward assures me it is very *safe*. In any case, I thought that a few days cruising on board the *Queen Mary* – or is it the *Queen Elizabeth?* One gets them so mixed up – would be most helpful.' She paused, frowning slightly. 'The only problem is that dear Amy is accompanying me, which will be lovely, of course, but she is not the most *restful* of girls... So I was wondering, Rosy dear, whether by any chance you might care to join us – as our guest, naturally. Edward is taking a Pan Am flight, and the moment we have docked he will be there waiting on the quayside to steer us through the gaieties and guiles of Manhattan. Quite an adventure!' She beamed encouragingly.

It wasn't simply the prospect of Edward's tutelage in New York, nor the staggering volume of Amy's guffaws that made Rosy decline Lady Fawcett's most kindly meant offer, but rather her own need to recuperate. She was not 'wrung out' exactly, but the last few months had taken their toll and she needed to reflect and take stock; and suddenly the sodden lonely marshlands of Norfolk or Kentish Romney presented an image of tranquillity which New York and the Fawcetts could never yield.

Thus with gratitude and genuine regret she heard herself pleading a prior arrangement. Yet even as she made the excuses a thought struck her: 'How about asking Felix Smythe? They have had to postpone their jaunt to the Riviera, their host is indisposed, and meanwhile the professor is off to examine Carpathian rock monasteries, but Felix won't go. Says he can't stand monks ...

364

or was it heights? One of them. Anyway he's not going. But I am sure he would love New York.'

There was a silence as Lady Fawcett considered the suggestion. 'Well he *is* emollient,' she murmured, 'and he would be frightfully handy with the cocktails – Amy gets so muddled at sea!' She hesitated, before adding, 'But if he were away what would the Queen Mother do?'

'Oh, I am sure she would manage somehow,' replied Rosy smiling.

The publishers hope that this book has given you enjoyable reading. Large Print Books are especially designed to be as easy to see and hold as possible. If you wish a complete list of our books please ask at your local library or write directly to:

Magna Large Print Books
Magna House, Long Preston,
Skipton, North Yorkshire.
BD23 4ND

This Large Print Book for the partially sighted, who cannot read normal print, is published under the auspices of

THE ULVERSCROFT FOUNDATION